Massacre at Santa Rita

A loud blast from a musician's horn pierced the air, and Brant-son stood, holding his arms wide and shouting in Spanish, "It's time for your gifts, my friends! Come for your rewards!" And the Chihenne began to stir, heading for the piles of bounty.

Suddenly Lazaro jerked to full alertness. The premonition, the sadness, the strangeness of the morning—it was all a warning! He felt the same tension he always sensed just before a battle. There—at the top of the bowl—Brant-son's men and the Nakai-ye commandante of the presidio . . . kneeling over their muskets!

His people were converging on the socorro, women in front, carrying empty bags for their gifts. *No!* His hands went to his knife, but his feet refused to budge. No! he screamed. *"Get back!"*

But his words were drowned out by a rocking explosion from the center of the socorro. Horrified, Lazaro saw fire and smoke belch from the pile. Chihenne who were closest to the blast were tossed into the air or smashed into the ground, already bleeding from the jagged pieces of metal that had ripped into their bodies. . . .

"A wonderful mix of history and fiction, woven cleverly by an author who obviously loves his craft. This fast-paced novel is to be savored."

—*Rave Reviews*

*St. Martin's Paperbacks Titles
by Robert Skimin*

GRAY VICTORY
APACHE AUTUMN

APACHE AUTUMN

Robert Skimin

ST. MARTIN'S PAPERBACKS

APACHE AUTUMN

Copyright © 1993 by Robert Skimin.

Library of Congress Catalog Card Number: 92-34387

ISBN: 0-312-95195-7

Printed in the United States of America

St. Martin's Press hardcover edition / January 1993
St. Martin's Paperbacks edition / May 1994

10 9 8 7 6 5 4 3 2 1

ACKNOWLEDGMENTS

My heartfelt thanks to the many scholars whose books served as sources, and to the many librarians, both here in El Paso and in New Mexico, who gave me enthusiastic assistance. Thanks specifically to Edgar Perry, the Apache curator of the Fort Apache museum, who also compiled the Western Apache Dictionary. To Susan and David Berry of Silver City, she as curator of that museum and he as one of the last real mountain men who took me out in those hills to places where few strangers have trod. To the remarkable historian Eve Ball, who was still alive and writing in her nineties when I began this research in 1983. To Tu Moonwalker, an Apache medicine woman and noted healer. And to those of you who aided me in other ways. *Ashoog/d ahíyi'ee!*

CAST OF MAJOR CHARACTERS

Silsoose	Ancestral chief
Gagi-tash	Silsoose's shaman
Carlota	Mexican lady/protagonist
Lazaro	Apache chief/protagonist
Nadzeela	Lazaro's wife
Roberto	Chief/Lazaro's stepfather
Benita	Captive/wife
Tze-go-juni	Medicine woman
Andres de Cardenas	Carlota's father/army officer
Old Man	Lazaro's mentor
Agustin de Gante	Wealthy Mexican whom Carlota loves
Bacho	Lazaro's nemesis
Rafael Murphy	American army officer
Andres	Carlota's son
Taza	Lazaro's son
Taza Murphy	Carlota's grandson
Lizah	Woman warrior
Victorio	Warm Springs chief
Cochise	Chiricahua chief
Richard Hartman	Politician
Old Woman	Old Woman's escort on train
Reporter	Narrator on train

PROLOGUE

The white-haired woman watched through the lace curtains of her front parlor as a hackney pulled up before her house. Nice team of roans, she thought, watching the tall reporter climb down and start up the walkway. Glancing into an oval mirror, she adjusted her wide-brimmed hat for the twentieth time to make sure it was pinned properly. She made a face, still not sure she should have bought the one with the huge blue feathers. Might be way too dressy. Reaching the vestibule, she looked down at the old cloth valise—should have bought a new grip also. After all, nothing was too good for this trip!

The younger man, tall and dark with a bright smile, spoke cheerily as he helped her down the steps of the front porch. "Pretty day for a train ride, isn't it?"

She replied with her characteristic quick smile. This would be her first trip in nearly two years and she had been dressed and ready for over an hour. A person her age didn't go traipsing around the country much anymore. She greeted the driver as she was helped into the hackney; she had used this very same carriage during the previous winter's icy period. Glancing about with curiosity as they headed for the train depot, she thought it *was* a nice day for a train ride—it was a nice day for anything.

The retired cavalry sergeant was sitting on his favorite bench in front of the courthouse; he'd been perched there for years whenever the weather permitted. He recrossed his arthritic legs and touched a finger to his faded army hat in a respectful salute. The sight brought back memories of a thousand uniforms, of parades and sweating horses, of the sun glinting off a tuba, of jangling spurs and yellow ribbons, of a cannon going off at retreat while a red-white-and-blue flag came down the pole . . . of the merriment of a post dance, of blood and the sharp reports of rifles being fired over an open grave, and the echoing of endless bugle calls.

"Have you thought about where we should begin?" the reporter asked.

She shook her head, the quick smile darting over her face. "How about at the 'tarnished woman' part?"

"No, I think it would better at the origins—of both you and the chief. The whole history. Yes, go back as far as possible."

She started to speak but was startled by the sudden explosion of an open Ford touring car backfiring fifty yards away. The horses started, one of them trying to rear as the noisy vehicle rounded a corner. "Certainly you know most of it," she replied softly.

"Yes, but I want it in your words."

She nodded. "Let me think about it until we get on the train. Then we can begin. Do you have plenty of paper?"

The young reporter grinned broadly as he patted his briefcase. "Enough to make smoke signals for a week."

The train was sitting beside the little gray depot, a trickle of white steam drifting softly into the windless blue sky. They took seats facing each other in the nearly empty third car and settled back for the long ride to El Paso. Shortly, a sudden lurch announced their departure and the reporter, pencil in hand, asked if she would begin. She looked off into the distance to the Antelope Plains, then to the other side where the hills to the east held a remarkable rock formation known as the Kneeling Nun. She nodded imperceptively. It was such an incredible story. . . .

"Sometime in the eleventh millennium before Christ," she began in her cultured Spanish accent, "the ancestors of many tribes came to North America over a land bridge between what is now Siberia and Alaska. Though the great glaciers were diminishing, the water level of the northern seas was still low enough that such passage was possible. From these Asiatic clans that crossed in small groups, a number of immigrants speaking roughly the same language worked its way south through Canada to various parts of North and Central America."

Her blue eyes were bright as she capsulized knowledge that had taken hundreds of hours of research to acquire over the years of her enlightenment. "That's the scientific theory of how the chief's tribe— also know as the People or the Chihenne Apache—arrived on the Great Plains as nomadic hunters of the bison. But there is another story, the religious one."

She stopped to check her hatpin and rest for a moment, thinking back to her own religious denial. "It's unbelievably close to Christian beliefs. In the beginning there was Ussen, Creator of Life, Who was similar to the Hebrew Jehovah. After creating Mother Earth, He produced White Painted Woman. There also existed a terrible *Yehyeh*, who was of massive human form and who was called Giant. This

Yehyeh did not permit people to live, and had devoured White Painted Woman's children. A beautiful young woman, she went about weeping and asking, 'How can people be created?'

"There was a bad drought and White Painted Woman prayed constantly. She decided to sacrifice herself, lying face upward on a rock while the rain came down in torrents. And during the long night a child was conceived. He was called Child of the Water and He was the Son of Ussen. To protect Him from Giant, she dug a secret hole and built a fire over it. She took Him out only for feeding and washing, and each time the Yehyeh came looking for the Child, she told him a different story.

"The Child grew and White Painted Woman made arrows for Him to hunt. Often He brought her meat. One day He shot a deer and while He was roasting it, Giant came to Him and demanded the venison. The Child refused. Four times Giant took the meat and four times Child of the Water took it back. They decided to fight—Giant in his four coats of flint, Child in His flimsy breechclout. The Yehyeh had huge arrows of pine logs, while Child had nothing but shafts of grama grass for His arrows.

"Giant shot his four arrows first, but each was shattered in midair by the Power of Child of the Water. And then it was Child's turn. He fired one of His shafts of grama grass into Giant's chest and a coat of flint fell away. Two more arrows chipped away at Giant's hard stone armor and finally Child of the Water took careful aim and drove His last shaft through the remaining coat of flint and into the heart of the terrible ogre."

The lady sighed, flashing her quick smile. "And that's how the People were finally allowed to be born without being eaten. Child of the Water then grew to manhood so He could serve and guide His People forever in the ways of goodness."

The reporter stopped his furious scribbling to ask, "And what happened to White Painted Woman?"

She patted his arm. "You know very well—she watches over the People from her mountaintop."

The reporter's dark eyes were shining. "You know," he said softly, "I think *you* are White Painted Woman."

"No," she replied with a firm shake of her huge hat. "I'm merely the *tainted* woman." She chuckled at her pun and stared out the window at the Burro Mountains for several moments before continuing. "As far as the Spanish and Mexican side goes, everyone knows about the conquest of Mexico in the early sixteenth century. The conquistadors, whether in shiny armor or the gray robes of Rome, were nothing but greedy acquisitors of riches and souls. A decade after Cortez robbed the Aztecs at Tenochtitlan, a new find was reported far to the north: the Seven Cities of Gold—*Cibola!*

"The Spanish columns rode all the way to what is now our fine state of New Mexico only to find that they had been hoodwinked. Cibola's fabulous cities of gold were merely mud pueblos with but a few small turquoises! Oh, there were heathen souls aplenty to be saved by the priests, but the noble Coronado returned empty-handed to the Viceroy. Now as you well know, a hard-headed Spaniard doesn't give up easily, no sir! New expeditions returned bearing the cross and firearms, riding the most amazing animal the primitive Chihenne had ever seen—the horse! Young man, you have no idea what that beast meant to the People!

"But back to the invaders. My noble forebears ruthlessly took whatever they could find of value, including women and children as slaves. And they killed many natives. In a place called Ácoma, the Sky City, they punished an uprising by killing hundreds, then lopping off one foot of many more before making slaves of them. These noble conquerors, mostly the governors and the clergy, also fought among themselves as they struggled for power. At times, excommunication was common. But even though one rebellion—the heroic Pueblo Uprising of 1680—forced them out of New Mexico, they returned. Regardless of the stated motives of the Spaniards, it was always *greed* in one form or another."

She chuckled, patting an imagined loose strand of white hair. "All the time they wanted that gold that's right up there in our hills."

She removed a hanky from her purse and dabbed lightly at her brow. It was getting warm in the car. She sighed, thinking of old Santa Fe, and of a bright-eyed little boy. Abruptly, her thoughts shifted to what was in store at the end of this journey. Exciting, but also threatening . . . surely the most important day of her long life—its redemption.

The reporter's words brought her back. "Can you tell me the story of the People coming to the Willows Country?"

She nodded. "Yes, I was getting ahead of myself. Old people have trouble staying on track, you know. Too many rich memories to lure us off the path. As you know, there is no written Apache history and the oral accounts tend to get distorted as they are passed around the campfire. But it is said that a great chief named Silsoose brought the Chihenne to this country. It was about the time of Coronado's expedition to find Cibola. . . ."

The willows
So thin, so straight,
By the silvery stream,
the eagles.

In early September of the year 1539 A.D. a clan of the People was making its final bison hunt of the summer on the plains east of the Rocky Mountains in what would later be called Colorado. The clan—called the Chihenne, or Red People, because of the band of red clay drawn across their faces—had been on the high plains for nearly a hundred generations and were ably led by Silsoose, son of Itsan.

The summer of 1539, like the preceding two, had been extremely dry—in fact, only a single black and blowing rainstorm had hurtled down from the high western mountains to soak the parched earth. And all through the hot season the winds had seemed even more capricious than usual, at times taking the form of withering blasts as from a storming volcano, at other times withdrawing completely and creating a massive vacuum, in which the glaring sun further withered the precious tall grass that made the high plains habitable. For without the grass the bison could not survive. And the bison had been placed on earth to be all things to the People: food, clothing, and tools.

The meat, with its rich, gamy taste, was both delicious and nourishing. Dressed cowskins, sewn together with bison sinew, served as tipi covers. The heavy winter hides, thick and shaggy, were wrapped around the body—hair side in—to provide warm overcoats for the deep snow season. They also served as bedding and provided material for moccasins, caps, and mittens; green rawhide was used for securely binding utensils to wooden handles. The sinew further supplied bowstrings and cord for binding feathers to arrow shafts, while good spoons and drinking cups were made from the horns. The animal's tough paunch provided an airtight water bucket.

It wasn't just the drought that had finally convinced Silsoose to move his clan south, it was his never-ending curiosity and sense of adventure. In fact, he was known as the Inquisitive One among the People. The previous year he had gone on a long trip south to the land of the traders in the tall houses, and there he heard about a great country of big hills where a good hunter would never have to worry about game. High and clear it was, with sweet fresh air, and no other clans or enemies for several days' journey. He had gone down the Great River for six leisurely days before crossing a huge range of dark mountains to a place in the foothills where a silvery stream that would never go dry provided running water as clear as the sky! It was surrounded by abundant willows and its waters were tasted by every game animal he knew.

No bison, of course. It would mean a complete change in the way his people lived, but the new path would not be difficult. When one had great privacy and all of the rich meat in the world, change could come easily. And in the hot time, his people could simply pack up and move into the high hills where it was cool. When the cold time returned, they would go back down to the silver river.

He had already named the place *Kai*, short for willow tree.

It was a very long journey, but he had no doubt that his people could make it if they could just have one final bison hunt to provide enough food for the trip.

Silsoose was tall and erect, a strong and caring leader of thirty-four summers—a chief for four, since the death of his father. To be the son of a chief did not ensure the mantle of leadership; it had to be earned and entrusted in the way of the People. But no one in his clan could remember when Silsoose wasn't a certainty to be his father's successor. Even since childhood, the aura of primacy seemed to glow about everything he did.

"*Nantan*, the herd is large!" the chief scout said, beaming with pleasure.

Silsoose dropped the arrow shaft he had been shaping, throwing a meaningful glance at his wife as he drew himself to his feet. "How far away?"

"Just over two hours, but grazing quietly."

Silsoose nodded. "*Enjuh*—good! Pass the word to move at once."

His wife, Linot, went swiftly to get the loading started. Tall and sturdy at twenty-eight summers, she was the mother of his two sons and his first wife. He had inherited another when his younger brother was killed in a raid on the hated Siks, a warlike tribe that had arrived on their part of the High Plains a few years earlier. The younger wife, Biza, a slender woman with a tiny daughter, would take care of most of the loading of their personal belongings while Linot assumed her own role of baggage master for the column.

The camp was quickly abuzz with activity in the bright midmorning sun. The women, and children large enough to help, began striking the tipis, expertly folding their skin coverings and piling the poles to be loaded on what the hairy-faced strangers who spoke a musical language would one day call *travois*. Dust and noise were everywhere as the People scurried to get on the trail. The large dogs, being held by some children, barked loudly and excitedly as they wiggled in their harnesses. Fires were put out and possessions that couldn't be carried in backpacks were jammed into skin sacks and loaded on the travois or on the dogs' hide straps.

Within half an hour the clan was ready to move—forty-one able-bodied men, sixty-two women, seventy-nine children, and nineteen old people who did little of value but would resolutely push themselves to keep up with the march, for to fall back meant abandonment. The men traveled light, with only their weapons.

When the entourage started moving southeast under the hot sun, it was shaped like a large porpoise. The scouts were well out in front, the able-bodied men on the flanks and in the rear to provide security, and the large body of others in the middle with the dogs and baggage. In the center of the rounded snout, Silsoose walked erectly carrying his best hunting spear from which hung a crimson strip of thin doeskin. Only the tall, dry grass impeded their resolute movement.

The small defile where the corral would be set up was downwind from the herd about five hundred paces. There the women unloaded the travois and set them up abutting each other with their wide ends lashed together on the ground in a semicircle. Linot was everywhere, encouraging the women, helping with the tying of thong ropes and reminding the children that the dogs had to be kept quiet. She nodded to the timid Biza, whose baby was in the basket on her back. "Remember, shout only when I give the signal," she said with a slight edge in her voice. The girl never seemed to get anything right.

Running out in front of the arc, she stopped to survey her handiwork. The wall of travois didn't look too imposing, but she knew from many hunts how well it worked in stopping the bison if they got close enough to it. She frowned as her elder son, the six-year-old Gidin, ran out to join her. He knew better. She spoke to him sharply, sending him back behind the barrier.

Striding toward the hide wall, she failed to see a motionless Sik warrior hiding behind a scrub bush a hundred paces away. A slash of yellow-colored paint accented each of his cheeks and a quick grin creased his face as he watched the proud Linot. He licked his lips in anticipation, then slipped away, breaking into a crouching run as soon as he was out of earshot.

Hurrying into the center of the upwind driving position with his lead scout, Silsoose gave the signal to get the bison moving. *"Aiheeee!"* he shouted as loudly as possible, rising and waving his spear with its crimson banner. Off to his right and left at intervals of thirty paces, his hunters began to move forward in a wide arc that closed as it proceeded. The swiftest runners were on the points in case the herd was frightened into running.

The group of bison stopped eating and looked up at the sudden intrusion, startled but not overly alarmed. Their summer coats looked dull, dusty from the dry grass, and they appeared thin, less active than usual. There were about forty of them, including several partially grown calves.

Silsoose's eyes narrowed as he strode forward. They were fortunate to even find this herd, so he shouldn't be critical. Still—he couldn't remember ever seeing poorer looking bison. When he was about ninety paces away, they began to move, at first slowly, then more swiftly as they spotted the hunters on each side. As the pace increased, the hunters on the point of the horseshoe stayed even with the leaders, keeping them headed directly for the hidden corral of travois. Suddenly the bison looked up to see a strange apparition that barred their progress and made odd shouting and barking sounds. They stopped, confused and frightened.

At that moment the hunters struck with *whirring* arrows from three sides. In some cases the sharp flint tips went nearly through the sides of the gaunt beasts. The bison dropped suddenly, some taking a few steps, others felled in their tracks. And then, with sharp cries of victory, the hunters were in their midst with lances and stone knives flashing. It was over in minutes, with no more than a third of the animals escaping in a wild burst of fear.

Silsoose grinned as he tasted the warm blood from the throat of a cow he had just slashed. His people would have full bellies on which to march south to the high country. And this night there would be a feast of sweet bison meat cooked over one of the last fires he would ever see in this country. It would also be a night of dancing and the telling of old stories, and singing and lovemaking, for the People had something to celebrate.

* * *

Silsoose was not sure what brought him so fully awake an hour before dawn, but after relieving himself outside of the camp in the shallow defile, he felt the restlessness and decided to walk off a distance and clear the traces of worry from his head. It was only a meaningless dream, he told himself; nothing terrible could happen to his people now. In just a few hours the clan would be headed directly south, loaded to its limit with bison meat and water. Yet the feeling of foreboding from the dream continued to plague him and he knew better than to push it completely aside.

To feel danger and foreboding was his particular Power. His father had had the Power to find water; the shaman's Power told him when a big storm was coming. His grandmother had had the Power over snakes.

He reached a low ridge topped by a small formation of rocks and sat down among them to isolate his sense of impending trouble. It was then that he heard the low tones of a man talking to others—in the language of the hated Sik! He had learned some of their language from a captive woman kept by his chief scout, enough to tell that this was a war leader, and that he was only part of a larger war party that was about to strike the People's camp!

He lay still for several minutes, then softly slipped back down the other side of his hiding place and away into the tall grass. Picking his way swiftly in the meager light, he reached his camp shortly and awakened his chief scout, Kigowo.

The chief of the Sik band absently touched the yellow ocher streaks that crossed the bridge of his nose and nodded his head. The enemy camp lay still and unsuspecting as he stared down at it from the edge of the low ridge. Their tipis stood inviting and shadowy in the first softening of light from a gray horizon to the east. And apparently they had even let their fires go out. He grunted with satisfaction—they must have gorged themselves the night before if everyone was sleeping so late. A smile touched his lips—tonight the Sik would stuff themselves full on the rich bison meat, meat that had been all dressed out by these stupid trespassers.

It would be easy, he thought to himself with another satisfied nod, the dogs hadn't picked up their scent yet. He raised his hand and gave the attack signal to his war leaders.

The Sik warriors moved swiftly into the shallow defile, challenged at the last moment by only one dog—a large brown animal that barked furiously and charged into the first running warrior he saw. A war axe caught the dog alongside the head, ending his opposition. Instantly the dark figures hurried inside the tipis, knives and axes at the ready.

But something was wrong. The forms in the bedskins weren't the enemy, they were merely more skins! One by one, they backed out of the tipis on their knees, staring around in confusion and alarm. The word quickly spread to the chief, but before he could order his warriors out of the camp proper, a wild scream split the early morning light. *Aiheeeee!* It was joined by other war cries and the furious barking of dogs as the People's arrows thudded into the raiding warriors with deadly accuracy. Over half the Siks in the camp were slain in that first volley, half of the remainder went down in the next.

With another chorus of war screams, the People rushed into the camp to finish off the battle in close combat. Axes and knives bit into human flesh as screams of pain, fury, and fear continued to shatter the stillness. The blood of the Siks flowed as freely as that of the bison had the day before. The light to the east seemed to join in, turning a dark pink as the sun readied itself to climb up for an early morning look.

Silsoose's axe, covered with yellow war paint and Sik blood, crashed into the neck of the last remaining raider. Instantly he was on the warrior, jerking his head backward, ready to smash the intruder's life away—

The arrow struck him in the upper right thigh with a jolt of pain sharper than he had ever known. A sudden wave of dull, aching immobility followed, rendering his whole right leg useless. As his eyes widened in disbelief, he crashed to the ground clutching at the shaft.

It was impossible!

The shaman's name was Gagi-tash and though his primary Power was predicting when a big storm was on the way, he also had a strong healing Power that had been detected when he was in his fifteenth summer. It was then that he first applied a salve he had made from some strange-colored moss to a raven's broken wing and the bird had quickly recovered and was able to fly again. It was from that incident that he got his name and the beginning of his path to becoming the main shaman for Silsoose's clan. Now his Power was being put to one of its most trying tests.

It had been four days since the Sik attack and wounding of Silsoose, and instead of his nantan recovering from the injury, he was poisoned by it. He had tried the special poultice of doeskin soaked with dead fox urine, and also the one of black spider hair and two-day-old buffalo semen, but neither had affected the deep wound the sharp flint arrowhead had created. And he had chanted to his special gods, the raven and hyena, nonstop for the entire day and night of the Sik attack. He had returned to his station with merely two hours' sleep the next morning to try other charms and supplications to different gods.

But his nantan's thigh and leg continued to resist his entire range of cures. Not only was it highly frustrating to himself, but Silsoose's leg was badly swollen and a deep red in color. And he knew it would be merely a few hours until the poison reached his nantan's head and killed him. Such was the Way.

His nantan had to be saved! It was not only a matter of his own standing as a shaman that was at stake, but the future of the clan. After Silsoose, the most powerful man in the clan was the chief scout, Kigowo. And Gagi-tash knew him to be a vain and sometimes foolish man—not one to be trusted with the future of the People. And even now it was nearly too late; Kigowo had already reported that the Siks were gathering other bands and would soon strike again if they remained in the place of the buffalo kill. But there was a way—a vision had come to him showing him a new Power that would overshadow all before. It might kill him in the making of this new Power, but his nantan would be cured, and it would be the most powerful medicine ever known to the People. Yes, even exceeding that of Lightning, the arrow of the Thunder People!

"The tipi must be moved beyond that ridge," he told Linot. "All of the nantan's belongings must be placed in it at his side on a bed of fresh buffalo hide. By then, the sun will have fled. Listen carefully, woman—all of the People are to gather around a large fire fed by buffalo bones and pray to *sho-lekay*, the great white bear, until I return from the nantan." Gagi-tash's large black eyes, now exaggerated by wide circles of shiny black paint, bore into Linot with more intensity than she had ever seen.

But the first wife had had an uncle who was a shaman and she was not easily intimidated. However, if Gagi-tash were to tell her to throw herself on the fire to save Silsoose, she would do so in a moment. Her husband had never been sick, even when he fought the mountain lion and was badly torn. And now Kigowo was spreading talk that they should move on, leaving Silsoose's poisoned body to appease the

Thunder People. She nodded, turned on her heel, and called out urgently to Biza to start pulling down the tipi.

Gagi-tash stood in the last light, holding the pouch of *hoddentin* high with both hands as he stared into the darkening sky and chanted to his raven god. He had never tried the tule's magical powder for such an important need before, having only heard of it recently from a passing shaman. *"Izigo-at-ee agaage,"* he intoned over and over in a high singsong voice. He stood on the balls of his feet, reaching with all his strength toward his gods, unblinking, forcing away even the gnats that were attracted to the strong odor of the hyena grease he had smeared over his body.

"Izigo-at-ee agaage! Izigo-at-ee agaage!"

Twenty minutes passed and as the tip of the large early moon crested the horizon, he slowly turned and entered the tipi. Breathing jerkily on his bed of fresh bison hide, the chief lay naked in the center of the conical structure. His clothes, moccasins, and weapons were laid out on both sides of the bed. His brow was feverish and his wounded thigh looked like it would explode. Now and then a meaningless word escaped from his parched lips.

Gagi-tash quickly stripped, leaving himself naked except for the riven wood amulet at his throat and bear claws circling his ankles. Slowly, he applied a thick coat of white paint to his forehead and cheeks outside of the black eye circles. Slicing the skin of his right cheek, he quickly smeared the spurting blood over Silsoose's lips and his festering wound. He nodded solemnly—the scar on his cheek would forever remind the People of what great Power he had created on this night.

He reached into his brightly decorated medicine bag and took out a necklace of dead and dried baby mice that had been killed in their nest during a vicious storm from the Thunder People. Placing it around his neck, he touched the trickle of blood that ran down his cheek and neck, and put a dab on each of his eyeballs.

It was time.

Climbing with his legs astraddle Silsoose's chest, Gagi-tash sprinkled a liberal amount of hoddentin over the nantan's face and began a new chant of unintelligible words that tumbled from his lips with neither thought nor meaning. He stiffened, throwing back his head and closing his eyes as he felt the Power coursing through his body. As the intensity of his chant increased, so did his feeling of strength. Bright light streamed through the opening in the top of the tipi, and the sound of drums from the camp came crashing into his ears.

Suddenly he bent forward, placing his lips on Silsoose's dry mouth. Sucking hard, forcing the poisoned breath from his nantan's dying body, he continued murmuring the strange words to himself. All at once the tipi began to tremble ever so slightly, then increasingly. Even the ground seemed to shake as if stricken by an earth tremor.

He could hear the scream of the raven and the wild howl of the hyena as a massive bolt of lightning crashed into a lone tall tree on the prairie. A deafening roar of thunder followed. When it diminished, the tree stood rigidly against the flickering sky.

"Even if the shaman keeps him alive, he won't be able to walk," Kigowo argued as he stood by the fire in the middle of the camp. The war leaders and the one elder who had a say in the clan's council listened quietly, as was the custom. "We must leave early in the morning or be prepared to fight the Siks before another day passes. Silsoose has been a great leader, but we must think of the People. He would *want* to be left behind to join the gods. I will personally end it for him and place him in his stones tonight. And then I will lead you south to safety at first light, on to the land of the tall water that our brave nantan has told you about."

The chief scout went on, telling of how he had been Silsoose's strength in both the hunt and battle during the years since he had become nantan, and that he had the Power to keep the People safe and free from want in the years to come. His application for the clan's leadership over, Kigowo nodded solemnly and sat down beside the fire.

Linot interrupted before another man started to speak. Moving quickly to the fire with an armful of bison bones, she threw them into the flames and spoke sharply. "No! Your nantan lives, and until he is taken by the gods, I will stay with him. And if he smiles again, our lodge will bring him after you, on my back if necessary, all the way to the new place. Go at first light, but say no more about Silsoose!"

The men looked sharply at her stern expression. Not one of them failed to respect her, but women didn't speak in such a manner. Still, as she left the circle of firelight, they agreed that more discussion would be necessary. Shortly, she was past the ridge, stopping near the tipi that held her dying husband. Facing east, she held up her arms and prayed for several minutes to Ussen, the Creator of All. Then she asked White Painted Woman to intercede.

An hour passed, and another, but Linot didn't move. She had decided she would wait until dawn before going to Silsoose—she owed that much to the shaman. When the moon was at its brightest, nearly overhead, a strange sensation swept over her. The tipi seemed to be *shaking!* She rubbed her eyes, sure that she was dreaming, but the movement merely increased. The eerie, high-pitched chant of Gagi-tash came to her, clear and ringing in its intensity.

Suddenly all movement and sound ceased.

She reached out involuntarily. "Husband," she cried out softly, afraid to move.

A form emerged from the tipi's open entry. Its face was white with black circles for eyes and it said, "The nantan is cured." And Gagi-tash fell to the ground in a stupor, his eyes rolling and his breath coming in deep sighs.

Linot rushed past him, bending and pushing into the tipi. There, on his new bed, Silsoose sat, his dark eyes aglow in the firelight. She dropped to her knees by his side, taking his hand as she tried to hold back the tears a nantan's wife was never supposed to shed. His voice was low and barely above a whisper as he said, "I'm hungry, woman. Why do I sleep alone like this? Where are my children, my second—"

"You have been sick, husband." Her hand went gently to the wound in his thigh. The skin felt normal with no apparent swelling. She thanked Ussen and White Painted Woman in the same breath.

Silsoose tried to get up, but a sharp pain in his thigh stopped him. Linot told him about the arrow wound and all that followed, including the tremors of the tipi. When she finished, Silsoose nodded. Glimpses of a black-and-white face came back to him, and chanting, flashes of brilliance from the Thunder People. He spoke softly. "Gagi-tash has more Power than any shaman the People have ever known. Every child is to be told of this night, and their children after them."

The following morning the porpoise-shaped caravan of the People departed the buffalo-killing site at just after dawn. Its dogs were further weighted down by several hundred pounds of buffalo meat and hides, and in its center on a large new triangular frame, their wounded nantan rode in discomfort. In a few days he would limp at the head of his column as it continued toward the land of the high hills and clear water.

And at the rear of the column, a proud shaman, ready to tell all of the People on Mother Earth about his prized hoddentin, strode along wondering what rewards he could extract from his nantan.

* * *

The long journey to the new homeland of Kai took nearly three moons because of the slow pace necessary for Silsoose's big porpoise. One old woman died on the way; two younger ones gave birth to boys. Sik scouts followed them for a distance, then disappeared—a clan on the march in open country was too compact to attack, and it tended to be well guarded at night. After three weeks on the trail, Silsoose was completely healed. Only a trace of a limp, a slight dip in his gait when his right foot landed, remained—an oddity he would never lose. In fact, some of the smaller boys in his clan would refer to him in private over the years as "He-who-drops." But only in private, for the Inquisitive One was highly regarded everywhere.

Silsoose now recalled parts of his ordeal with Gagi-tash, and each time a flash of memory came to him, he would feel his thigh and sense some new and mystical Power. He questioned the shaman about it, but received only a knowing smile in reply. It didn't matter; he was so full of himself and the promise of his destination that he remained in a high state of anticipation and good humor. Linot even marveled to a close friend about his lovemaking. "He is never tired, and more lustful than when he was a young brave!" And when this report spread through the women of the clan, more than one of them looked at Silsoose with a special brightness in her eyes.

But though he detected the new interest and would gladly have responded, adultery was one of the most serious offenses a Chihenne could commit. A man could be killed or banished for adultery, a woman could have her nose cut off as punishment. And he was the leader, the one who must oversee the rigid moral code of his clan like a castrated judge. Other tribes looked at the matter differently.

One such place where the women were looser and the men more liberal was the city of tall houses where so many goods were traded. There, the people made fine clothing from white balls that grew on bushes, and tribal traders came from the four directions. He had wandered around that famous place agape on his other visit, and had told Linot so much about it that she had sewed each night by firelight to make a new doeskin dress for their visit.

But just as they reached the hole in the mountains where he could turn toward the setting sun and take his clan there, a trader told him the people in the tall houses were at war with a bad tribe from the north. Much to the disappointment of all, he decided not to expose them to any further risk.

There was a light snowfall just a few days before they reached their new home of Kai, but the bright sun that seemed to be a part of nearly

every day burned it off almost immediately. Then, one afternoo
before the sun dipped behind the distant hills, they topped a rise tha
overlooked a broad valley running off as far as one could see to th
south. Other small hills could also be seen in that direction, but the
were nothing compared to those the clan had just crossed.

Directly above where they halted stood a strange rock formatior
Below a sheer cliff of reddish stone, a form like a huge kneeling figur
appeared, almost lifelike. Everyone in the clan stared up at it, wonde
ing if it represented some kind of Power. Gagi-tash announced, "It
our new protector praying to Ussen!" And he tossed several clutche
of hoddentin into the light breeze.

The clan's council of headmen gathered around Silsoose as h
proudly spread his arms high and proclaimed, "This is the homeland «
the Chihenne now and forever!" And, as was the custom, he talked o
about the new land, its animals, and the spirits of the mountain goc
that were ready to welcome them.

Linot listened proudly from a few paces away, and drew her tw
children to her side. It was a great moment; a rare tear slipped dow
her cheek as she freed her seldom-seen emotion. Tightening her hol
on the older boy's arm, she said softly, "This is your new land, m
son. Here you will grow to greatness like your father." But your
Gidin was more interested in the kneeling rock figure above. H
thought it looked like a giant warrior bending over a defeated enem
and the thought excited him.

The valley that held the river of willows stretched northward betwee
two mountainous ridge lines. Here, in the brisk, clear air of la
November, the People found everything Silsoose had promised:
broad sloping campground near the spring-fed stream, bushes of wi
berries and other foods such as the muguey plant, and fat gan
animals that roamed nearly to the edge of their new village. The
faced a whole new way of life, primarily a transference from depe
dence on the bison to that of the fur-bearing beasts of the mountair
It was the first time any of them had ever known the meaning
"home."

Linot supervised the layout of the new camp, recommending loc
tions for the bison skin tipis that would place them comfortab
distances apart, facing east in the traditional manner that permitte
every person a chance for prayer to Ussen first thing each mornin
She and the younger wife, Biza, erected their tipis some fifteen pac
apart and slightly separated from the rest; such was befitting t

family of the chief. It was the custom for the women to manage everything and perform most of the labor, just as it was their wont to set up the caches—the hidden stores of food and weapons that could be used in an emergency. Wherever the clan might move from this time forward, they would perform this vital task.

Like a squirrel hiding nuts for the winter, Linot planned to have caches set up in many locations throughout these hills that were her new home. She couldn't explain the strong feeling she had about Kai and its parts—a feeling of possession, of leaning back in the morning and inhaling deeply, of wanting to reach out and draw everything into her arms and clasp it to her breast in an overwhelming gesture of love. The sky, the hills, the sun, the trees—everything! *This was hers!*

Commencing the day after arrival, Silsoose and his men began a systematic series of exploratory scouting tours. His orders were clear: travel in all directions like the rays of the sun, in pairs, noting all landmarks, vegetation, and animals they might encounter. They were to go a distance of five days before returning from each trip and diligently report all findings upon their arrival. And then they would go out again and again, finally retracing the routes of the others until every brave and older boy would know this great wilderness like the lines in his hand.

This, Silsoose knew, was the key to their survival.

And survival was a part of that new Power he didn't understand. He sensed that someday his people would have to fight to keep this vastness that he sometimes called Willow Country.

But he had no idea it might be so soon.

Eight weeks following the clan's arrival at Kai, two braves had gone on an exploration trip to the northwest in the area of two tall peaks Silsoose had named the Twin Sisters, and they had failed to return. Since the chief insisted on close timing in these ventures, he became concerned when the men were more than a day overdue. When they failed to appear by the following noon, he departed with his head scout, Kigowo, and six others who had completed an exploration on the same route. Moving in a spread formation that permitted vocal contact, they worked their way well up into the high mountains by nightfall, finding no signs of their missing brothers.

It was bitterly cold at that elevation in late January, but fortunately there was no heavy snow to contend with as they continued on the next morning. Silsoose knew his chances of success were slim—in this type of rough country with so many twists and turns, so many abrupt hills, so many different ways to go around or through, he would have to be highly fortunate to find anyone. But he had no doubts about continuing; these were his men who were missing, and possibly injured. He had sent them out and he would bring them back. His new Power told him so.

Late that afternoon Kigowo found their trail, a moccasin track in a patch of shallow snow. And at midmorning the next day one of the braves sounded the sharp bark of the hyena that alerted everyone to come to him. Again he made the hyena sound, and this time Silsoose noted a sense of alarm in it.

The two missing braves were hanging impaled on sharpened tree limbs of side-by-side ponderosa pines. The blood that had poured down their fronts had long since dried and the smell of death was just beginning to assert itself. Silsoose nodded grimly as the bodies were taken down, unable to shake a terrible sense of anger and violation *Who was in his hills? Who had given him this violent sign telling him to stay away?* His face burned as if in shame—had he found the great homeland only to learn that it belonged to others?

He told them to bury the bodies in the nearby creek bed where there were plenty of stones to mark the graves.

That night as they huddled around the small fire, he gave them his decision. "The ones who did this terrible thing are afraid of us, or they would not have made such a spectacle of it. But they have killed your brothers and I will not be frightened away. Tomorrow we'll begin to look for them."

Kigowo had once bragged that he could track a hummingbird on a rock shelf, but he found no trace whatsoever of the people who had killed the two Chihenne. They had apparently removed any possible trace, or had simply touched nothing in their approach to the death site. The braves in the search party were further disquieted by this fact, but said nothing within earshot of Silsoose as the broad search began.

The tall chief was also uneasy in his anger, but he couldn't show it. What kind of an enemy lay waiting in these hills? Some kind of witch that could fly? Whose homeland had he violated, if any? And where were they? The land was so rugged with abrupt hills and sharp canyons that a trap could lie anywhere. His men could be picked off one by one.

And it had gotten even colder.

Finally, Silsoose had to overcome his growing frustration. When the fruitless search reached the second night, he told the others they must return to Kai to wait for warmer weather. They would renew the quest later with more men. All of them agreed wholeheartedly. They began the return trip early the next day.

Thus, for two months, the Inquisitive One was burdened by an enigma and the dark cloud of an unseen enemy. More than once he had wanted to go off past the distant Twin Sisters by himself—to just go and probe, climb and seek, draw his enemy out without having any responsibility other than for himself. And then deal with it. But he couldn't—he was the leader of his clan, and his responsibility lay to all of them in their new home.

Following the first full warming and early spring rain, Silsoose led the search party to the place where he had found his dead braves impaled in January. With him were nineteen of his best scouts and fighting men, all equipped to stay in the high hills for an extended period. Even Gagi-tash had come along with a huge supply of the magic powder—hoddentin—and a bag of other charms and fetishes.

The chief's plan was simple: Five groups would move within shouting distance of each other for a period of four hours in a northerly direction, then turn west for one thousand paces and go back to the south; on the following day the same plan would be performed to the south. By moving as rapidly as the terrain would permit, a large area could be covered and nothing of importance would be missed. A fine plan indeed—but again, the sheer ruggedness of the country made the search extremely difficult. As the days went by with no sign of other humans, Silsoose grew more impatient. He could *feel* enemy eyes watching him and his futility made him angry.

More days passed as the searchers worked westward. And then Kigowo picked up a sign. A steep cliff rising from a stream bed blocked their way to the next ridge, but a short distance downstream a narrow ledge led up the side of the wall. And on that ledge in two places Kigowo found human sign—a piece of tanned deerskin and feathers that were unmistakably from the shaft of an arrow.

Silsoose nodded excitedly at the second sign—now he had a *piece* of the enemy. No more of the witchcraft, no more elusive shadows; whatever was up there was his nemesis. He felt a surge of the same Power that had urged him on after his lost braves. Sending word to the other groups, he started up the trail with Kigowo and Gagi-tash. As they climbed higher, the force that drew him forward became more powerful. Something vital for him or the People awaited at the top.

After climbing up the well-hidden trail for another six hundred paces, they suddenly broke over the rim of a huge oval bowl. Ragged rock walls of rich earth tones that graduated from soft creams to dark rust lined its sides, but most striking were the dozens of massive rock formations that rose like huge spires from bases as large as a dozen bison—as tall as perhaps forty men. In places, huge boulders teamed with small rocks that looked like beads from a necklace to create what might be playthings of some colossal being. Silsoose thought immediately of Giant, the terrible god of their religion who had been slain after the Creation, and he wondered fleetingly if the Yehyeh could have resided in this awesome place.

Kigowo and Gagi-tash were also speechless as they stared around the huge basin of supernatural forms. Finally the head scout asked "Should I get the others, Nantan?"

But before Silsoose could answer, a man stepped from behind a boulder just six paces away. He was tall, wearing a robe of mountain lion skins, and in his headband was stuck a huge eagle feather. He held his hand high in the universal sign of peaceful greeting that all the tribes of the plains knew. His words were foreign, of a language Silsoose had never heard. He spoke a phrase in another language, then another, and finally in that of the Dineh—the Chihenne's brother who spoke almost the same words as the People.

Silsoose nodded. "I understand the words of the Dineh," he said guardedly, and told the stranger who he was.

"My chief awaits you," the man said. "He has been watching you arrival for these many days. I am Kiasi the interpreter."

"Where is your chief?"

"He waits in his big house nearby."

"How do I know he will not kill me as he did my two braves?" Silsoose asked tightly.

"My chief wants to speak to you in peace," the man replied. He made a sharp short whistle and a young brave stepped out from behind another boulder. "This is the son of the chief. He will stay with your people as a hostage until your safe return."

"I think you should wait for several others, Nantan," Kigowo growled. "They may be sacrificing this young one."

Silsoose looked steadily into the eyes of the man wearing the eagle feather. It could be a trick. But then it would have been a simple matter for these people to have already killed them from above while they climbed the narrow trail. He nodded. "I will speak to your chief and I will bring my shaman. He has great Power in my house."

The man nodded, speaking softly to the young brave, who hurried forward.

They were led across the center of the grassy bowl, past several of the huge rock spires to a line of trees. On the other side, protruding from the rock cliff, stood the mud and stone buildings of an imposing town. It was similar to the tall houses he had seen in the city of the trading people to the north, but something about it seemed brighter, special. The color of the walls was lighter, but it was more than that—they seemed to reflect the sunlight in tiny bits of something luminous.

The first level was the height of three men and held an opening tall enough for a man to enter. Atop that and farther back was another level that held deep openings for light. And above that was yet another level that extended out from the cliff. He guessed that if it were like the ones to the north, the big house might hold hundreds of rooms; he knew it probably had the warm bathing rooms in the ground, the *kivas*. Along the first roof level, he saw many people watching quietly as he proceeded to the entrance.

On the first upper level, they were led into a large heated room. There, on a chair with a high back that was the color of *oodo*—the sacred yellow metal of Ussen—sat a tall man with many wrinkles in his face, and hair the color of fresh snow. The interpreter introduced him as Chief Ramah. Beside the chief stood two advisors or subchiefs. Each of them had vertical stripes of paint the color of oodo on their faces. Other headmen also adorned with the oodo paint eyed them guardedly from around the room. A young brave hurried forward with a bright blanket of yellow and black, and spread it before the high chair. The words of Chief Ramah were interpreted by Kiasi. "We are the Anasazi," he said. "Why do you invade our country?"

Ignoring the blanket, Silsoose continued to stand a few paces in front of Chief Ramah. "Why did you kill my braves?" he asked with a stern expression.

"As a warning."

"Why did you not kill me?"

"I do not want war." The old chief's eyes glittered blackly inside the wrinkles. He fingered a necklace of shiny oodo. "Why do you invade my country?"

Silsoose's gaze didn't waver. His voice was deep, controlled. "I have chosen the Land of the Willows to be the land of my people. We have come a long way from bison country, and we, too, wish to live in peace. Why do you fear me?"

Ramah started, showing quick anger, but controlled himself. "Why should I fear a people who do not even own a house? How many warriors do you have?"

"Five hundred," Silsoose lied.

Ramah snorted. "Ha! I have a thousand!" he lied.

"Then there is no need for fear. What do you wish of me?"

The old chief avoided his question; instead he spoke about his people. The Anasazi had come to the high place which they called Eaglestone over two hundred summers before. Part of a large tribe of big house people in the north, they had been involved in a fight with another large clan, and their ancestral chief had departed in great rage. After a year of wandering, his Power had brought them to this land of ample game, pure water, and true safety. Inhabited by a hundred great eagles when they arrived, the sanctuary was easily named. Only one trader, who came from the sun side of the Great River, had known of Eaglestone, and he and his decendents had long been sworn to secrecy.

As the talk progressed, Silsoose studied the Anasazi. The men wore woven clothing, their hair was shorter, and eagle feathers seemed to be a part of everything. Even the wall behind the chief held a huge drawing in charcoal of the large bird. There seemed to be more of the sun-colored oodo at this place than he had ever seen. He considered asking if the Anasazi had brought it from their homeland. It made him uneasy that these people could be so casual about the sacred stone that Ussen had placed in the bowels of Mother Earth, stones that were never meant to be disturbed.

Finally he told Chief Ramah, "I have come to the Land of the Willows to stay, Great Nantan. There is room for both peoples to live in peace, but first I must know how you intend to pay for the warrior whom you have killed so cruelly. I'll go back to my people tonight and think, taking your interpreter with me and leaving my shaman here with you. I'll return for your answer tomorrow when the sun is high."

Chief Ramah nodded in reply; the meeting was over. As the interpreter, Kiasi, led him back to the entrance, Silsoose noticed that the people of Eaglestone had come out of their houses and were watching him with open interest. He looked directly at one tall and handsome young woman who gave him "the bright eyes" and wondered if these people were loose with their women. The thought excited him momentarily, but he pushed it aside and painted a memory picture of Eaglestone in case he should ever have to attack it.

In camp later, he sat huddled in his robe in the firelight. "There should be no more bloodshed," he said to Kiasi after a long silence. "You must help me understand your chief."

The interpreter frowned, but at length he replied, "My nantan is afraid of the prophecy . . . his father's father passed it down . . . a payment from the gods for our bad ways will visit us in the time of this summer. First, a violent leader will come from afar and make war, and though he may be defeated, many of our people will die. And then the stars will fall upon the earth, or hot rain will fall. Or our Father, the sun, will not rise to start the day . . . or with a great shudder, the land will turn under and Eaglestone will be no more. It is foretold."

Silsoose knew about prophecies and respected them. He nodded. "Are you sure this is the time?"

"Three moons ago, a bright star burned across the sky and fell to the earth."

Silsoose nodded again. A certain sign—it was from disturbing the oodo. "I am not a violent leader," he said quietly. "So the prophecy does not involve me. Tomorrow you can tell your nantan that I want two unmarried and healthy braves from your people for the families of my dead ones. And your women make fine blankets—I want two for each family. Then we will be friends forever."

The following day at midmorning, Silsoose was again led into the chamber of Chief Ramah in the big house at Eaglestone. After some roundabout talk, the Anasazi leader asked for the Chihenne's decision and Kiasi gave him the reply. Ramah, seated on his tall chair of oodo, frowned and spoke to the headman closest to him. As Silsoose and Gagi-tash stood erect and silent before the chief, the Anasazi argued among themselves. But after a short time, Ramah nodded and went into a long discourse that the interpreter translated. The terms were acceptable and Ramah hoped he could long be at peace with his new brother.

Relieved that his bluff had worked—he could never have taken Eaglestone with his limited number of warriors—Silsoose presented his best stone knife to the Anasazi chief. As the interpreter again escorted him and his shaman to the exit trail at the top of the ridge, he felt a strange movement under his feet. Thinking it was his imagination, he said to Kiasi, "The hostage son will be—"

The ground was moving! Up and down, shaking, shuddering!

A rock crashed down from its perch a few paces away. With a

wrenching shudder, a massive crack ripped open the gravel surface beside the nearest rock spire. *Craaaaack!* Another new crevice ran toward the wall houses, toppling two of the huge rock pillars with deafening crashes.

Silsoose was thrown to the ground, but managed to hang onto a nearby shrub. He watched wide-eyed as massive boulders rolled like tiny pebbles in a rushing torrent. The roar was deafening, and dust was everywhere. On the other side of the bowl the tall, magnificent houses crumbled as if their foundations had been ripped away by a giant hand. They actually *disappeared*, leaving a jagged scar on the cliff. Even the shrill human screams were drowned out in the smashing, grinding explosions that continued to overlap each other.

And as suddenly as it had come, the massive earth tremor was gone. A high cloud of dust, roiling overhead, slowly began to settle on the flames that licked up from where a proud city had once stood. A woman with a baby in her arms, black in the face and streaming blood, rushed by Silsoose screaming, then plunged down the hill. As Silsoose got shakily to his feet, he saw that Gagi-tash and Kiasi had survived. Without a word, they slowly followed the cries of trapped and injured survivors and went to the place where the tall houses had stood. All that remained was a massive pile of dirt and shattered rocks. Now and then a moaning body would climb out and shake off the dirt, or just stare in bloody shock at a mangled limb or at the rubble that had once been his home.

Gathering his senses, Silsoose barked, "Hurry! Many are alive. Dig!"

The dazed Kiasi stood motionless at his side mumbling, "The land will turn under, the land will turn under."

A total of forty-one survivors in various stages of injury and shock were treated by Gagi-tash and an Anasazi shaman with a broken arm. By the next morning, twenty-nine were alive. There were no headmen—they had all expired with Ramah in the buried city. Silsoose made his offer at midday: Those who wished to do so were welcome to join his clan in the Willow Country of Kai. There, if they so desired, they would be accepted as full members of the Chihenne—or they could leave and find their own culture.

Kiasi spoke of a distant place called Cibola where their brothers lived. A small group, including his family, elected to go there. The remainder decided to go to Willow Country. Gagi-tash was pleased—he would do a big business in fetishes and the making of medicine for strangers who did not know the ways. But Silsoose was wary: though the People would now have craftsmen who could weave and make round things from which to eat, it would mean many new tipis on the grassy banks of his village and many new mouths to feed.

Before departing, Silsoose stood by a freshly created crevice. A reflection caught his eye. It was a square ornament of oodo with the head of an eagle inscribed on its face. "This," he said quietly to Kiasi, "is the reason your city has been turned under. Our Ussen, the Creator, punishes those who disturb His possessions. Caution your people to forget the old ways of using it, and tell them not to speak of it in their new home."

The interpreter nodded gravely.

When everyone had departed, Silsoose stood alone on an outcropping of rock. He looked around the huge bowl with its massive rock spires and was again struck by the impression that some supernatural being had once existed here. It was utterly silent; there was no breeze, not a whisper of movement. Suddenly he experienced a flash of memory—lightning and thunder and the hideous black-and-white face of Gagi-tash. He felt a tightening of his thigh and a surge of strength flowed through his body. Inhaling deeply and drawing himself rigidly to his full height, he clenched his fists and sustained the greatest sense of Power he had ever known.

It was a sign!

This wild and rugged place had some special, mighty meaning to him. Was it Giant? He spread his arms wide and looked at the sky. Was the Yehyeh's spirit here? Certainly the terrible eruption that had turned the earth under had a special meaning. Could it be Giant fighting back?

His clenched fists still felt as if he could crush any threat.

And then he knew. This brawny place of death and beauty was *his.* It was his personal, private place to do with as he pleased. A sanctuary? Yes, for whatever use he had for it. Eaglestone—no. This place was Giant's mighty hand, and it had been cut off. It was his cupped palm and the massive stone spires were his severed fingers. It was . . . Giant's Claw—yes, that was what he would call it.

Giant's Claw.

>> THE OLD WOMAN'S JOURNEY <<

The white-haired lady sipped gratefully from a cup of water the young reporter had provided. The gentle swaying of the train as it swept along the open track had caused her mind to wander, but now it was refreshed. "The legends about Silsoose were many," she said. "It is believed he lived to a very old age and created a rich life for his people, and that the Chihenne in the Willows Country grew in number during his time.

"About the beginning of the seventeenth century when the Oñate expedition settled in the Pueblo Country around what is now Santa Fe, a Hopi Indian word for 'enemy' was applied to the People—which included their brothers, the Navajo. It was *apachu*, but was soon corrupted to *Apache*.

"Soon the Apache consisted of various tribes—the Lipan, the Jicarilla, the Mescaleros, the Western Apache, and the Chiricahua, of which the Chihenne were the eastern branch. The Chihenne were further referred to as the Willows, the Warm Springs, the Copper Mine Apaches. There were, of course, smaller tribes and branches that went by other names.

"Except for the mention of raids in Spanish chronicles, little is known of the Chihenne during those two centuries. They went through wars and alliances with the Navajo and other neighboring tribes, and we know they fought the fierce Comanche from the plains at times. No leaders of any note have been mentioned. The Apache existed only in loosely related clans or bands until the chief came into power in the mid-nineteenth century.

"The blood of Silsoose never stopped flowing down through the generations. In the year 1813, a female descendant of that great chief gave birth to a boy. This woman had the Power of seeing ahead and throughout her pregnancy she had visions of a tall warrior leading his people into battle and standing before them in an eagle feather headdress that trailed far behind him. His arms were spread wide and there was a special brightness about his head.

"But we will get back to that. First let me tell you more about the people of Mexico. In the two centuries, the Spanish fumbled through various settlement attempts, mostly involving the Great River—the Rio Grande—which ran from the highlands of north central New Mexico to later form the border of Texas. The Spanish continued to seek the elusive riches that had first attracted them to New Mexico, and their high-handed cruelties made them the permanent enemy of the People.

"But the day of the Spaniard was about to end. It is vital for your readers to understand the rigid caste system in colonial Mexico. At the top were the Spaniards born in Spain—the *gachupins*—who controlled the political and spiritual life of the populace. Next came the *Creoles*, the children of Spaniards born in Mexico of pure Spanish blood. Normally they were the idle wealthy who were denied the right to hold high government office or top stations in the Church. The third layer consisted of the *mestizos*, those of mixed Spanish and Indian blood, who grew to make up the majority of the population as the Indians—the bottom rung—continued to diminish in number. The Negro slaves who were brought into New Spain were not a factor because they were absorbed into the mestizo element.

"By the turn of the nineteenth century, most of the settlers in New Mexico were mestizo Mexicans. The province of New Mexico lay, of course, above the northern frontier, a vastness that reached far to the north and all the way to the Pacific Ocean. It was a staggeringly beautiful land and also one of unyielding demands. In it, the Apache was difficult to find and impossible to conquer. And he struck deep into northern Mexico to avenge his wrongs or to raid for cattle and horses—which was his way of life.

"In the origins of our story, 1821 is a pivotal year. It is the year of Mexican independence, acquired after over a decade of sporadic revolution. And it is the year in which a small Chihenne boy with a fateful future lost one father and gained another. . . .

September 27, 1821

Normally children did not attend a burial because of the proximity of ghosts, but since the eight-year-old boy was an only child, and because there were no brothers or sisters to either of his parents, he joined the small procession that took the body of his father into the hills. He walked stiffly beside his mother, who tightly held the right leg of his father's corpse in the stirrup. Her cousin, a short brave who had been his father's closest friend, led the pony, while other relatives helped steady the body in the saddle.

It was a low, darkly overcast day with no rain, and only the sounds of the horse's hooves striking stones on the riverbed broke the tight, eerie stillness.

The pony, like the saddle in which the body rode, was the dead man's favorite. A brown and white paint, the animal had faithfully carried his master on hunts and to war for over six summers. Now the beast had but one final journey to make in this world. The boy had been the pony's friend since it was a young colt and his father had first begun to train the frisky animal. Every memory of his tall father was connected to this brown and white pony.

His father, Giantah, had died early that morning of a Mexican bullet wound sustained while on a raid three days earlier. A powerful war leader, his father might have some day become a chief had he lived. Now his name would cease to be used only if unavoidable and then with an added, "who used to be called." Even this reference would not be used after dark.

Still unable to believe that his father was anything but asleep, the boy looked up at the slumping body in the saddle. He felt a numbing sadness, a confusion. His father was a great warrior who would live forever, so this was all a bad dream conjured up by some witch—he was certain of it! He had just recently heard his father speak to his mother of a witch who was jealous of him. He dropped behind his mother and touched the long single arc bow that protruded from the saddle.

Tied to his father's belt and to the saddle were the dead man's favorite possessions. They would accompany him so that he would be well equipped for his new life in the Happy Place in the Underground. He was dressed in his best clothes, adorned by his amulets and other charms, his bag of hoddentin, his bullet pouch; his head was covered by an ornately beaded ceremonial skull cap that he had worn on various occasions when he made war. His face was painted with the red clay of the Chihenne tradition.

The clip-clop of the pony's hooves continued to make the only sounds, for the People had no songs of death.

The boy thought of the Underground. He had been told it was a beautiful place beneath the ground where the sun always shines and a clean stream of water flows between stately cottonwoods standing in a long line—where everything is green except the ground that is streaked in warm red, and the People are always smiling and happy, and there is always plenty of food and good fast horses.

He went back to his mother's side and touched her hand. Called Adala, the woman who was always so tall and beautiful to him was the granddaughter of a wise chief and a descendant of Silsoose, the great nantan who had—the storytellers said—one day brought the Chihenne people to their homeland.

At the head of the tiny procession marched Tze-go-juni, the repulsive-looking medicine woman whose face had once been badly torn by a mountain lion. Though there were whispers that the shaman was a witch, no one had ever confronted her with such an accusation, for she boldly claimed a direct bloodline from the legendary shaman who the myth said placed the Power in the cattail—hoddentin powder— the same one who had given the great Silsoose his life and powers. She always watched over the boy's mother, Adala, and was now providing her services for the burial free of charge.

And in the rear, carrying the dead man's heavy musket, Roberto walked solemnly. Though powerfully built on a stocky frame, the chief of the Chihenne had a sensitive face and a gentle manner that belied his inner strengths. Taken as a captive when he was five years of age, Roberto had been sold into the household of a caring, middle-class Mexican family in Chihuahua. When he was old enough, the bright young Apache had been placed in a seminary to study for the priesthood. But in his twentieth year the curiosity about his origins began to override his religious zeal. When he heard that his father had been killed by a Mexican army patrol, he threw aside the cloth and returned to the Willows Country to earn the leadership of his people.

Suddenly Tze-go-juni began a low, unintelligible chant, and moments later led the processions into a narrow *arroyo*. The boy heard a short sob from his mother and looked up to see tears running down her cheeks. He had never seen her cry before. She squeezed his hand as the shaman pointed to a narrow crevice fifty paces ahead. At that point, his father's body was lifted down from the horse and placed well inside the crevice in a shallow depression in the rocky ground. As was the custom, his head was in the direction of the sunrise.

Now totally devoid of expression, Adala stared with unfocused eyes as the others quickly placed her husband's possessions about him and piled stones around the grave. Tze-go-juni resumed her chant as she sprinkled hoddentin over and around the body. Suddenly she stopped and drew out a long sharp knife. Nodding meaningfully to Adala, she came around the grave to where the young widow had dropped to her knees. With several quick strokes, the shaman cut Adala's long shiny hair off at her ears. The boy was next. He was proud of the thick hair that reached to his waist and saw no purpose in having it cut so short. But it was the custom of showing grief, and there was nothing he could do about it.

Roberto silently placed the dead man's musket in the cradle of his left arm, then stepped back from the grave. Only one element of the ritual remained. The brown and white pony on which the dead man would ride to the Happy Place, and would continue to ride ever after, must now accompany him. The short cousin who had led the animal to the burial site now drew him inside the crevice, where the medicine woman took his halter. Again the long knife flashed as she deftly slashed the horse's throat in a single motion. Blood spurted from the gaping wound as the wild-eyed pony tried to rear back. His scream shattered the mountain stillness, and then he slid to his front knees, already dying.

The boy wanted to rush to the poor animal and hold its bleeding head to his breast, but it was not the Way. He had to remember—the faithful pony was taking his father to the Underground. He fought back the tears as a strong hand found his shoulder. In a quiet voice, Roberto said, "Come, my son, your brave father has gone."

Back at the village close to the river, they went directly to their *wickiup*. Other women had removed the mother's and son's belongings and placed them in the new wickiup they had constructed not far from that of Roberto. All that remained of the dead man's possessions were now piled in the middle of the hut and the whole was ignited by a blazing fagot. Within minutes all that remained was a smoking pile of memory for the wide-eyed boy.

The next stop for the burial party was the river, where the women went in one direction and the men in another. In a pool where willow bushes provided privacy, the boy stripped off his clothes and threw them into a pile that would be burned by one of the men. After a thorough scrubbing in the clear water, everyone dressed in fresh clothes and returned to a large dying fire in the middle of the village. There, Tze-go-juni, her face now painted in circles of black and vermillion, handed each person a large pinch of what was called "ghost medicine."

Shortly, each person threw the powder on the fire and at once dense smoke began to rise from the embers. Everyone from the burial party leaned over the fire and into the smoke, letting it envelop their bodies. Finally, when they could no longer hold their breath, they stepped back, opened their eyes and inhaled deeply before another dose. After four times in the smoke, the ceremony was over. The boy blinked his burning eyes and was surprised to see that the whole village was gathering in a circle around them.

It was late in the day and the sun was a mammoth red ball dropping behind the western hills. Quietly, Roberto stood near the fire and announced that he had taken the new widow, Adala, to be his wife, and that her son had become his son. The words seemed hollow to the confused and grieving boy, but he held himself in tight control as the chief motioned for him to come close.

"As is the custom," he declared in a clear voice, "this boy will no longer be called by that name which was given to him by his father. Instead, he shall be *La*-za-ro of the Spanish tongue. Many summers ago in a faraway land, a wise man named Lazaro was a friend of the Spanish Son of Ussen. And when Lazaro had ridden the pony of death for four days, this Son of Ussen gave the breath of life back to him. And later, this Lazaro became a great nantan who is honored to this day."

Placing his hand on the boy's shoulder, Roberto added, "This is my son, Lazaro."

Lazaro, the boy thought to himself, over and over. What a strange sounding name! He couldn't look up from his feet, so strong was his shyness. When he soon withdrew from the gathering of adults, his mother held him close for a moment before saying soberly, "You are fortunate, my son. Now you have two fathers to make you proud."

Lazaro nodded, unable to say anything in reply. As his mother went to her new wickiup, the boy started to walk away but glanced up into the intense expression of Tze-go-juni. Her eyes were glowing beneath the bright black and red face paint. Suddenly she grinned with her lopsided, gaping mouth, and he felt a chill. She drew her hand up in the position of respect and nodded. "You are also *my* son now," she said, then nodded again and darted away.

As new logs were placed on the council fire in the middle of the village, Roberto drew on his cigar of native tobacco and thought about what an important day it was. He had acquired a healthy young wife and a son with the blood of Silsoose. Perhaps when the sadness left this strong young Adala, she might give him more sons of that powerful strain. He thought of how good that would be—a house of leaders that would be spoken of at council fires for centuries to come. . . .

And then he thought about the other reason for the day's importance. In the councils of the *Nakai-ye*, the hated Mexicans, there would be great celebration on this day. A dispatch one of his raiding parties had captured a week earlier contained an official proclamation announcing the independence of Mexico from the Spanish throne on this date—September 27. And he kept the Spanish calendar, so he knew this was the day.

He drifted back to his youth in Chihuahua and recalled fiesta days and how the Nakai-ye danced and drank in wild merriment on such occasions. How mad it must be for an occasion such as this! And then he thought about what changes might be brought about with the influence of the Spanish throne no longer a factor over the City of Mexico. He thought about this at length, then drank the remainder of his *tiswin* and decided it would make no difference to the Chihenne. They were enemies and they would always be at some sort of war—maybe not overall, and maybe not at all times, but it would never completely end.

It was the Way.

* * *

¡La Religion, la Union, la Independencia!

Whatever one's political inclination, there was overwhelming cause for excitement on this momentous day. Republican, Bourbonist, conservative, liberal, royalist, revolutionary—every man, woman, and child old enough to walk was emotionally involved. Independence!

No more New Spain, only *Mexico!* After eleven years of fruitless strife, the independence of Mexico was the most dynamic event since Captain Hernan Cortes first rode into Tenochtitlan three hundred and two years earlier. And the greatest city in the New World was decked out in her most robust finery to greet its heralds.

The Liberator, General Agustin de Iturbide, and his jubilant Army of Three Guarantees had entered the outskirts of the city just before ten, proceeding through rejoicing throngs of people toward the heart of the city—the famed Plaza de Aramas. The soldiers of the liberation army, mostly without uniforms and in worn sandals, were led by the handsome generalissimo who waved his brightly plumed hat and grinned appealingly from astride a prancing black stallion. It was the Liberator's thirty-eighth birthday and the City of Mexico was throwing him a grand party!

Bells pealed constantly from every church within earshot, salvos of artillery roared steadily, and overhead flashing rockets burst in the bright sunshine. Red, white, and green—the colors of the new flag—bedecked everything from the flowers thrown from balconies to the bright ribbons in the hair of smiling señoritas. Continuous applause and thundering *vivas!* rained down from rooftops on the largest army ever to march in the former capital of the Aztecs.

Captain Andres de Cardenas, standing on a resplendent balcony across from the great Cathedral of Mexico, nodded and watched the young generalissimo lead his staff and the first elements of his victorious army into the Plaza de Aramas. It was certainly a spectacle, he told himself, but his mood was troubled rather than exuberant. For the twenty-eight-year-old officer was both a strong loyalist to the throne of Spain and an ardent patriot of Mexico. And this whole business of emotional liberty with no solid plan of rule or financial base worried him—so much so that he couldn't resolve his personal conflict.

At his side, Rosa, the Spanish bride he had married four months earlier in Madrid, touched his hand and smiled softly.

"Viva Mexico!" Fidel de Gante shouted, firing his big pistol from the other side of the small balcony. Two years older than Andres, the wealthy Creole had been his friend since childhood. Though he was a conservative who strongly supported the Church and desired a monarchy, he was an avid enthusiast of the independence and severance from Spain.

They watched as the generalissimo dismounted and amidst loud cheering disappeared inside what had been redesignated the National Palace. Moments later, he reappeared on a balcony with the outgoing

Spanish Captain General to review the long line of troops. Fidel de Gante held a bottle of red wine to his lips and drank heartily, spilling some down his chin. "Here, long face," he said, handing the bottle to Andres. "Drink up and rejoice! Long live the Mexican king!"

Andres took a small swig from the bottle, but it didn't help.

"I've already heard talk that he will be made emperor," Rosa said quietly, "after the monarchy is turned down by all of the royal blood." She was the fair and very lovely daughter of a lesser noble in Madrid.

"He has earned it," de Gante said with an emphatic nod as he tipped the bottle back again. His wife was eight months pregnant and, quite naturally, unable to attend the great event with them. One of his servants stood behind them with a basket that contained food and more bottles of fine wine. "But I'm not so sure everyone in Ferdinand's family will reject the chance for a crown."

"What would we do if the Church assumed the government?"

Fidel de Gante looked at Andres as if he had made a joke. He laughed. "Might as well. They already own half the land and wealth in the country anyway."

"Yes, and they don't pay a *real* of tax on it."

Rosa turned her attention back to the parade. It was fascinating, and besides, she was always uncomfortable when someone criticized the Church. Her husband had mentioned resigning his commission and returning to Spain permanently, which would suit her just fine. But all of his possessions were here in Mexico, and they certainly couldn't live on a military salary if he served in the Spanish army. Her own father would provide her with a small annuity, but that still wouldn't be enough. She sighed inwardly. These Creoles!

Meanwhile, a small drum and bugle corps drowned out the men's ongoing argument.

Shortly, Fidel de Gante went on, "The day of the gachupin is finished, my friend. Forever. No longer will our own hidalgos be denied the leadership and their rightful due in this country. It has always been ours, but never have we had it!"

Andres agreed that the gachupins—the Spanish born—had ruled far too long. He wanted to remind his friend that all Mexicans—from don to peon—were supposed to be equal following the independence, but he didn't want to get into that age-old argument. He stared at the large flag of red, white, and green, and felt a slight stirring deep within himself. Mexico's first real flag—not New Spain's flag, but *Mexico's!* And in that moment he knew. All those agonizing hours of indecision, the days of torment that had torn at him like a disease;

they were finished. He watched the colors being presented to the commander in chief below his reviewing balcony and felt a stronger burst of, of whatever it was. . . .

"Where would you like to be posted?" de Gante asked suddenly.

Andres shrugged. He hadn't made a definite decision yet. He took Rosa's hand, smiling gently into her deep blue eyes. She had once told him whatever he decided would suit her. God, how he loved her! He barely heard the rousing ¡viva! as he looked back at the Liberator, arms spread wide on his balcony. "If I stay," he finally replied, "I don't want any part of this new government, not directly. I don't think it'll be healthy for a long career."

De Gante grabbed his arms. "Where, man? Just tell me where you wish to go. North, south? Spain—that's it, another attaché assignment! How about Paris? The great Liberator owes me a few favors for services and money rendered. Tell me, Andres! Tell me, *Colonel* Cardenas—for your promotion is most certainly the first payment I'll demand!"

Andres laughed. "What—no field marshal's baton?"

Fidel de Gante tipped the bottle back again. Wiping his mouth with the back of his hand, he replied, "Not before you're thirty-eight. The Liberator would never allow it."

Andres nodded, sobering. "Let me think about all of this, and tomorrow when we're sober, I'll tell you of my decisions. In the meantime"—he squeezed Rosa—"I'll consult with my staff tonight."

≫ **3** ≪

"Four is the sacred number of the Apache. It takes four days to ride the pony of death to the Happy Place. There are four sacred directions, four colors, four clans. There are four masked dancers. Everything is four. To be Apache is to be four. To be Chihenne is to be four."

Lazaro joined the other youngsters in the singsong recitation for Old Man. Even if he was eleven years old and about to perform his first duty as a man in a few hours, he had to conform. Old Man did not permit one single omission or deviation from his ritual, regardless of how many times a child had been to his storytelling campfire, or how old that youngster might be.

"Never mock or harm an owl—they are ghosts.

"Never eat or wear red when the lightning flashes. Always make a spitting sound when the lightning flashes in a storm.

"Never kill a bear except in self-defense. Sometimes the dead return in the form of a bear. One of your own relatives could be in a bear. Sometimes bears help you. Never eat a bear.

"Never eat fish—they are the spirits of wicked women.

"Never fight at night—the snakes are out at night.

"A witch can be a man or a woman. Never go near them or anger them. Never say anything bad about witches. Never say anything bad about anyone—he may be a witch. And it is bad luck.

"Never call a person's name to that person.

"Never wet on an ant hill.

"To be Chihenne is to be four."

Old Man was also more apt to scold him because he was the son of Roberto, and he continually reminded him that the son of a chief had to be better than any other. Old Man had punished him each time the occasion demanded during these last three years. The first time, Old Man had put him in a sack and told him he would leave him for the owls. And the other time, Old Man had made him fight with Bacho—who had stolen from his cousin—until they were both skinned and bloody. He watched over his training in the absence of his busy father, Roberto. Old Man had been a successful war leader until he lost his leg, and now he earned his livelihood by being a storyteller and making weapons—bows, lances, and arrows—that had his special Power in them.

Lazaro was the only son of Roberto, in fact his only child. The chief's first wife had given him no children, nor had Adala. Lazaro enjoyed a rich relationship with his interesting father, particularly in learning the Spanish ways and the language—which he not only learned to speak, but also to read and write to a limited degree. With his nimble mind, he learned easily. Most intriguing were Roberto's stories of the Mexican House of Ussen that he called a *church*, with its mystery, symbolism, and chants, and the picture he had of bright robes. Someday, when he was old enough to go on his first Nakai-ye raid, he would hear the bells!

Often he tried to relate his father's stories with all that Tze-go-juni was teaching him. She sometimes scared him, being so possessive and mystical about everything. And he didn't like her touching him so much. She had made him several amulets to wear around his neck before deciding the one with the ashes of an eagle's beak might have the Power to complement his own Power at this stage of his development.

The strangeness that the shaman called his Power was gradually manifesting itself since He-who-was-his-first-father went to the Happy Place. The first time he felt anything, it was like a twitch in his right thigh, followed by a rush of good feeling. Another time, it seemed he could see very clearly. And in subsequent experiences, it was a feeling of strength. Once, when he stumbled and fell while on a long, exhausting run, he remembered Tze-go-juni's words, "Try your Power for emergency strength." And when he regained his feet, he felt stronger than when he began the run!

He had tried it once in the morning when he had to break the ice and jump into the cold water as part of his training. He was numb and suffered a cramp. Imagining the twitch in his thigh, he felt instant relief. But on other occasions there was no response. The medicine woman explained, "Your Power is growing like you and trying to find itself. When it's ready, you'll know."

The last time he had tried to summon his Power was the night two weeks earlier when he was given the wakefulness test. The ordeal was for him to stay awake for a full day—sunrise to sunrise—with two older boys alternating as watchers. At about two hours before dawn it had been absolutely impossible for him to keep his eyes open any longer. The lids were like stones. Suddenly he shook his head and thought about the twitch. A sense of jumping in the icy stream jolted him and he was immediately alert!

This time Tze-go-juni told him the Power was saying, "I am here only for problems. Do not abuse me."

Lazaro's daydreaming was interrupted by a sharp thump on the head and the snickers of the other boys. Old Man was ready to begin his first story and he demanded everyone's undivided attention. He began the short favorite about the Quarrel Between Thunder and Wind. He spoke in a range of low-and-high-pitched tones, always mimicking the voices of his characters or dropping the narrative to a whisper. Old Man was the best storyteller in the village. His eyes danced in the firelight as he began:

"Now this is another of the things that happened long ago when Ussen was creating Mother Earth. The Wind and the Thunder were to work together, but suddenly they got angry at each other—and they separated.

"The reason that they got angry at each other and separated was that the Thunder spoke thus to the Wind: 'I alone do good even if you do not help.'

"Then the Wind spoke thus to him: 'Because you say that you alone do good, I'll go far away from you.'

"Then the Thunder caused much rain but it was always very hot. There were no grasses or foods grown. It was not good. The Wind was nowhere and the Thunder didn't like it. Then he set up feathers to see if he could lure the Wind into blowing on them, but they stood still in the hot sun. He looked in vain for the Wind.

"Then he did not feel right about it. He sent for the Wind. 'My brother, you are nowhere and it isn't good. There is nothing growing. It's very, very hot. Because of that, I beg you to come back to me. From now on, both of us will do good on the surface of Mother Earth for the People. We will work together. We will travel together. Because of us, there will be good food growing,' the Thunder said to him, pleading with him.

"Then the stubborn Wind smiled and came back to him. He became his friend again. That is why, when it rains, there is thunder with the wind. They go along together in friendship always."

Lazaro smiled along with the rest of Old Man's young listeners. It was always a good story. Now he hoped Old Man would tell a Coyote story. He liked the Coyote stories. A good long one would last until it was time for him to go. He felt a surge of excitement at the thought. He'd almost forgotten—tonight was his first guard time! Usually boys had to be older before being trusted with this vital duty, but he had been through all the tests, and he was taller than other boys his age, and he'd asked for it. He looked up at the bright full moon. It wouldn't be long before it would be time. He felt the familiar sling on his belt. With it, he could hit a bird sitting in a tree from a hundred paces. Taking a deep breath, he told himself no enemy had better try to steal their horses tonight—or get into their village. Because he'd—

No, he'd better not boast.

The excitement made his stomach feel strange. What if they did come in tonight? Would he stand his ground and kill them with his sling—like that Spaniard, David, his father had told him about? But he was only supposed to awaken the village, that was the Way. Still—they'd better not come in while he was out there!

The radiant moon washed over the landscape, creating an enchanting brightness that was like an eerie daylight. But for an eleven-year-old, the dark shadows and gray-blues merely created illusions of enemy hiding places. Lazaro walked on the turned-up toes of his knee-high moccasins, barely breathing as he made his first circuit from the horse corral to the village proper and back. Twice he had jumped when a small animal had made a noise, and each time he had chastised himself for his alarm. His primary post was the corral. That was where most of the ponies were kept, though some were fastened together in the woods on the other side of the village. That was where Tzoe, the older boy, was standing guard.

Time passed rapidly as the moon moved toward its zenith—Apache midnight. And with each trip from the wickiups to the corral, he grew more confident—this was the way of the warrior. No enemies would sneak in while he was on guard! Even the horses knew he was taking care of them, for his father's favorite pony, a handsome black, had whinnied at him once. He smiled to himself; he had ridden that pony early on several mornings when no one was up to see him. His father had promised him a pony of his own soon. Maybe after this guard time proved he was a man.

He felt so full of himself. It was so important to be a man.

He had just returned to the corral on what must have been his twelfth circle from the horses to the tipis when he heard the low cry of an owl. It was soft, barely perceptible. He stopped still, holding his breath. *Hoot*, it was louder, on the other side of the horses. He quickly placed a smooth stone in his sling and held it at the ready. He tried to shake off the tremor in his hands. A ghost!

He edged slowly to a tree trunk that was a corner of the corral and stood on its dark side. *Hoot!* It was louder and closer. He thought he saw a figure move on the other side of the horses! Sucking in his breath, he gripped the sling tightly. Should he call out to the other guard?

Hoot!

He had to do something! He edged around the tree trunk, staring wide-eyed across the corral, seeing nothing. Slowly, in a low crouch, he began to work his way around the enclosure of stakes toward a tall tree on the other side. But he had no more than reached its shadow when another loud *hoot!* made him jump. *It came from above him in the branches!*

Stuck to the ground, his mouth was agape as he tried to see into the darkness of the foliage. Something moved! *Wrrrrr!* It was a massive ghost-owl coming down after him!

"*Ha!*" The huge owl stood up and spread its wings and laughed again, then broke into a peal of laughter. It was Bacho slapping his sides in wild mirth! "You are dead, little coward," he jeered. "If I had been a real owl or a Nakai-ye, I would have killed you already!" He laughed again.

All Lazaro could do was stand there and try to control his white-hot anger. The humiliation kept him in check. Bacho would tell everyone. Bacho would go to every Chihenne village and tell them the son of the chief had frozen in fear on his first guard. Bacho was his nemesis, his rival in everything. A year older, the boy named Wolf had plagued him with ridicule since the day Lazaro moved into Roberto's wickiup. Thickset and strong, while Lazaro was tall and wiry, he usually won any wrestling matches or fights they had. And Bacho was good with the bow, better than any of the boys their age. He usually won Lazaro's arrows in the target game.

Bacho waved his arms again, making the deerskin flap. "Go, coward, run back to your mother's arms and cry on her breast!" He laughed harshly. "Go, suck on her tit while you are there, little baby."

It took all of his will, but Lazaro turned away. He was on guard and had responsibility—he could not fight this terrible one and roll in the dirt with him, he just could not! Ignoring his burning cheeks, he reminded himself that he was in charge of protecting the village. He was being trusted. And he was Lazaro, son of Roberto.

All he had to do was finish his time as guard, because the next day his father was finally going to take him to the wondrous place known as Giant's Claw.

At the same time, Rosa de Cardenas was giving birth to a protesting baby girl in the province capital of Santa Fe, some six days' ride to the northeast. The birth was difficult, and since the small city had no doctor, the midwife did all she could to save the mother and child. Rosa would have no other children.

The baby was named Carlota Evangelina.

Andres de Cardenas had been promoted to lieutenant colonel in the army of the Empire of Mexico three weeks after the triumphal arrival of the Liberator and his army in the capital. Four months later, and three months before the Liberator was crowned emperor, Andres and Rosa had arrived in the crude but fascinating city of Santa Fe. Aside from the usual disagreement between the Church and the civil government, the independence of Mexico had brought about additional conflict in the province—of loyalties and disagreements between Spaniard and New Mexican. Added to this was the discord between the governor and the military commander for the province—an officer who happened to be far south in the city of Chihuahua.

Andres had a dual assignment: commandant of the *presidio*—the garrison of soldiers—and military advisor to the governor. Regardless of the remoteness of Santa Fe, he had grabbed at the opportunity for an important command far from the intrigues of the City of Mexico. His choice had proven wise from a standpoint of avoiding a political dilemma, because the Liberator had lasted a mere ten months on the throne, and governmental chaos had settled over the capital.

Andres was away inspecting the small presidio at Taos and had missed the agony and near terror of Rosa's ordeal. He hurried anxiously into the bedroom of their adobe house nearly nine hours after the birth of their daughter to find his wan wife resting but still in pain. "I should never have left," he said with deep concern, taking her in his arms and holding her tightly. "It must have been terrible."

She nodded, not wishing to waste the effort to sound brave. It *had* been terrible—just as their assignment in this wilderness had been terrible for a young woman used to the flattery and excitement of Madrid society. She had not tried to dissuade him from his decision to come to New Mexico, and she had complained only minimally since arriving in Santa Fe—and most of her complaints had occurred in the last stages of her pregnancy—but she certainly hadn't intended to give birth in this barren place. What kind of birthright was *that?* "Have you seen your daughter yet, Andres?" she asked softly.

"Yes, she has the bluest eyes I've ever seen. She's truly beautiful!"

Rosa found a smile. "The midwife says she will be a tall queen with the fairest skin in the republic."

Andres stroked her hand. "Remember our farewell dinner at the de Gante house the night before we left the City of Mexico? I guess that takes care of my promise to Fidel," he said with a smile.

"Yes, we have a beautiful daughter for their son. But don't you think the marriage can wait until she learns how to say, 'Mama'?"

Andres shook his head in mock concern. His old friend's son, born shortly after Mexico's independence, was named Agustin after the Liberator. "Agustin and Carlota—those are certainly romantic names! No, that poor boy and his worried parents shall not be kept waiting another day. I'll write to them at once."

Rosa found another smile before closing her eyes. She had survived a dreadful ordeal in bringing a lovely little Creole of noble Spanish blood into this godforsaken place, and she had made her husband happy. What more could a women want in one day? She drifted back to sleep.

Late that afternoon, Captain Padilla, the commandant of the Socorro presidio far down the Rio Grande below Albuquerque, arrived. He was two years older than Andres and somewhat surly about being subordinate to him. A swarthy man who seldom bathed, he had the most remote presidio in the Santa Fe command. It was situated at the top of the *Jornado de Meurte*—the Journey of Death—that ran along the river south to Doña Ana. Andres quickly got down to business. "Within sixty days you will receive twenty-two new men, including an officer. They will come from Chihuahua and when they arrive in Doña Ana, you will augment the force with five privates from Socorro. They will then proceed directly to the copper mines at Santa Rita near the Mimbres River."

Captain Padilla scowled darkly as he shook his head. "I can't spare even *two* men."

Ignoring the response, Andres went on. "As you know, there is a major mining operation there. Also, the Santa Rita area is the homeland of the Chihenne Apache. I don't like it because we haven't enough men for our primary needs, but political pressure has been brought to bear and a presidio must be built there."

Padilla shook his head again. "I can't do it."

Andres's face hardened. "Have those men in Doña Ana in fifty-five days, *Captain!*" he said coldly. Leafing through some papers, he withdrew a sheet and pushed it toward the officer. "Here is a sworn statement that you are conducting a slaving operation with the Apaches you capture—the women and children. In short, it states that the good padre baptizes them one minute and your slavery party rushes them down the river the next."

"It's a damned lie!" Padilla spat out, tossing the paper back toward Andres. "The man who made this accusation was nothing but a troublemaker, which is why I court-martialed him."

Andres shrugged. With such a shortage of officers, there was so little he could do. The Indian slave trade had been going on for over two centuries and would probably flourish well after he was gone. "I want it *stopped*, Padilla! Or I'll come down there and put *you* in irons!"

"The reason we can let the Nakai-ye come into Willows Country for the red dirt is because we benefit without danger, my son. Remember, our survival as a fighting force is necessary if the Chihenne are to live."

Lazaro listened attentively to his father's answer. He always enjoyed these opportunities to hear Roberto speak of leadership and wisdom.

"The Nakai-ye have a thousand men to our one," the chief continued. "We cannot ever have a pitched battle, which is why we show our bravery by never fighting a larger force, or even one of equal strength. We just cannot afford to lose our warriors—any of them. Raiding for horses and other livestock is our Way, but it is also risky. Here, because Ussen has provided the red dirt and the enemy comes in peace, we can be given animals, food, and ammunition for our muskets. Therefore, *these* Nakai-ye at this time are not our enemy."

Lazaro frowned. "But how can we stop hating, stop remembering all of the bad things they've done to us?"

Roberto smiled patiently. "A wise chief learns when to bend like the willows when it will be good for his people."

Lazaro nodded in agreement, but he was still confused. As a twelve-year-old boy imbued with the deeds of great warriors who dreamed of heroic feats, he just could not accept such allowances at the wave of a hand. But for the moment, he had to accede to his father's explanation. He just didn't like the idea of the Nakai-ye building houses and a place for soldiers. That meant they were going to stay. They called it Santa Rita. The town also had a church, a house where his father sometimes went to smoke the good tobacco with the Nakai-ye medicine man who wore the long gray robes of a woman.

It was the White Eyes—*Los Godammies*—who intrigued Lazaro. The first group of them came through in his tenth summer, the next a year later. One party stayed on for a time with the Nakai-ye at the mines. It seemed to him that they were all immensely tall, with bushy dark beards that reached to their thick belts. They laughed loudly a lot, and never bathed in the river. They could shoot their long guns with unbelievable accuracy at great distances, and they could drink huge amounts of mescal and the Mexican *aguardiente*—without getting drunk like the Chihenne men. And while the Nakai-ye spoke reverently about the sacred rock formation above Santa Rita, the Godammies laughed about it. They all called it the Kneeling Nun.

But to Lazaro, what was most different about these Americanos was the way they fought among themselves. Instead of wrestling in the Apache way, or even using knives if the fight was important enough, they balled up their hands and struck each other with their fists. He asked Old Man if he should learn to fight that way and was sharply rebuked. The Chihenne way was the only way for a future chief, his mentor insisted.

Old Man also grumbled about the Nakai-ye mines, and was one of the few Chihenne who refused to go to their town. Even the Mexican drink could not lure him there. Another person who refused to go to Santa Rita was Tze-go-juni; she constantly designed fetishes with which to work her Power against the Nakai-ye, and never ceased to rail against them. And though scalping was a practice almost exclusively Nakai-ye, she treasured a dried and shrunken blond scalp that had reportedly belonged to a hated army captain.

When the day of his first novice raid approached, all the months and years of training and looking forward to being a warrior seemed a blur. At fifteen, possessed of superior speed and agility, the tall Lazaro barely remembered the cold childhood morning when he crawled out from his blanket well before dawn to run up a nearby mountain and back. Or that he had often done it with a mouthful of water, so he could learn to breathe through his nose. He had learned to use his first old mulberry bow with the crooked little arrows that wouldn't kill a fly, and then the slingshot with tiny pebbles that fell out. And there was his first fall from a pony, and the hundreds of days of learning every iota of tracking that led to his being able to read a three-day-old trail like the lines of Old Man's palm.

Only recently he had gone on a two-day scout, without food for the full period. The scar on his shin attested to the skin-burning ordeal that he had suffered without a sound, and he would forget how, to make himself brave, his eyes had been swollen shut by the stings of two dozen hornets. But all of it was past and meaningless in the face of his apprenticeship. For four days—to be Apache is to be four—he had undergone intensive novice training inside Old Man's wickiup. He had learned the ceremonial language of the warpath. He will wear a special war hat; he must drink from a hollow wooden tube—for if water touches his lips, unwanted whiskers will grow; he must use the scratcher made from the wood of a fruit tree or his skin will grow soft. If he eats warm food or the entrails of any animal, he will not have good luck with horses; he will not have intercourse nor speak obscenely of any female; he will at all times be respectful and not talk unless told to do so.

There was more, but Lazaro wasn't worried. He had asked for his apprenticeship a year earlier than normal so his older rival, Bacho, could not get to manhood before him. Despite his usual calm, the idea of still being a boy while Bacho was a *man* was unbearable. They were taking their first novice raid together. It was to be a livestock raid far up into Navajo country where the chief of a large village had violated a treaty with the Chihenne.

Lazaro felt the excitement as the ceremony began at first light on the small knoll above the village. Both his mother and father watched proudly, as did Old Man on his crutch. Since it was not a war party, but merely a raid with eight warriors and two novices, there had been no war dance the night before. But to Lazaro it could have been the warpath against the entire Navajo nation. On his head he wore a wide turkey-red bandana. A one-inch-wide strip of white paint crossed his nose and cheeks immediately above the strip of red clay paint.

A warm breeze rustled the high eagle feather atop her gaudy medicine cap as Tze-go-juni screwed up her black-and-white-painted face and began to chant as she did a short dance in front of him. Moments later, he bowed his head low for her to present him with his novice's warbonnet, a round hat with long sides, adorned with large eagle feathers and those of the hummingbird, the quail, and the oriole.

It was the signal for the others to break into the four happiness songs as Tze-go-juni sprinkled hoddentin over him and handed him the cane drinking tube and skin scratcher. She chanted loudly as she reached high to remove the old amulet she had given him at the time of his blood-father's death. In its place she hung a new pouch that contained a sliver of riven wood and the claw of a monstrous black bear she claimed had spoken to her. "Keep this, my son," she sang. "With it, you will find the far reaches of your Power."

As the shaman sprinkled hoddentin over him once more, he saw tears in his mother's eyes and the quick approving nod from Roberto. Old Man stumped off down the slope without a single show of expression. Lazaro felt awkward, wanting to reach out and touch his mother, for from this time on, their relationship would be more restrained. But he knew Bacho would be watching from below as the raiding party formed. He didn't believe it, but he was hanging on to the last shred of his detested boyhood as he felt the warmth of his love for her.

Nodding brusquely, he hurried toward his manhood.

The novice raid, like the three that followed in rapid succession, was essentially uneventful. As was the custom, the novices were made to stay back as much as a thousand paces to remain out of harm's way. For one of them to be in any way injured would have been a discredit to the war leader of the raid. The last two apprentice raids were against Mexican ranchos to the south, and it had been difficult for Lazaro to sit and follow orders like a lamb when he could have been doing something important.

But he didn't have long to wait.

The Navajo chief whose livestock they had raided on this first novice mission had struck a small Warm Springs village and cut the feet from the legs of the chief's wife. It was the worst crime Lazaro could remember. The Navajos were of the People and they also believed that when one died, one would have to go about the Happy Place forever in the form in which one departed this world.

The chief's wife would never have any feet!

Both Lazaro and Bacho were part of the nineteen-man war party that joined the Warm Springs warriors for a major retaliatory attack three weeks later. Following an enthusiastic war dance the night before, the combined force of thirty-one rode into an assembly position the next day. And on the following morning, just after dawn, the Chihenne struck.

Lazaro, riding the dun-colored pony his father had given him in his fourteenth summer, threw a blazing fagot into the first hogan he neared, then wheeled back to ram his lance into a Navajo man who was charging toward him with a war club. The Navajo's scream died on his lips. Lazaro heard Bacho's piercing wolf cry and responded with a louder one as he brought his bow into play and loosed an arrow into another enemy brave.

The village was burning in every direction. The screams of women, children, and horses echoed through the dust and smoke, mingling with the cries of pain and death. The barking of dogs added to the bedlam. Lazaro spotted a lovely young Navajo woman standing in bewilderment outside a hogan. What a fine slave she would make! But just as he urged his pony forward, Bacho rode in front of him and with a loud laugh, jerked the girl up onto the front of his saddle. She struggled only briefly because her captor slapped her so viciously across the face that she slumped into unconsciousness.

Lazaro turned back to the dying battle. A large brown cur snarled and jumped at his leg, but Lazaro ignored him. Unlike most Apaches, he felt a special warmth for dogs and couldn't bring himself to hurt one—even in battle. After dealing a severe blow with his war club to the head of a younger Navajo, his part of the fighting was over. All that was left to do was to get their horses and cattle.

Apparently the Navajo band had just recently made a successful raid on its own; there were a large number of horses in its corrals. And there were twenty-nine mules, so Lazaro guessed they had raided the Nakai-ye haciendas near the big town called Albuquerque. When the war party returned to the Willows, his share was three ponies. Not only was he a man, but a man of property! He gave the gentle mare to his mother and the black colt to his father. He kept the young brown-and-white colt, but only for two days. Then he remembered Old Man.

"What can I do with that horse?" the Old Man asked, lighting a cigarette made from native tobacco.

Lazaro shrugged. "I don't know. Maybe buy some good tobacco."

Old Man didn't even look at him. "It's your first one from battle."

One didn't usually speak of gratitude, but Lazaro didn't care. "It's yours. You were the one riding there, in my moccasins."

Old Man looked the paint over, feeling his foreleg. "Not a very strong looking colt," he said flatly. It was a beautiful animal.

"No," Lazaro agreed apologetically. "Spindly legs."

Old Man frowned. "Maybe I could fatten him up and get a jug of mescal for him."

"Maybe."

* * *

Since Bacho lived with his mother and father, the pretty Navajo captive became a servant in his mother's tipi. Sixteen summers old, she was slender and had the large brown eyes of a young antelope. They called her Dineh, the name for the Navajo, and Lazaro often saw her about the village. One morning when he was returning early from his river bath, he saw through the bushes that she was bathing by herself in the women's area. He stopped, moving closer and staring. She was more shapely than any Apache girl he had ever seen! He could hear her singing in a low tone, something in Navajo. When she climbed out of the water to shake herself off, she was completely naked.

He almost fell into the bushes.

Watching her dry herself, he breathed in short gulps. The disturbance between his legs was a full erection. He should pull away—what if he got caught? But she was so beautiful . . . and so tempting the way she gently dried the inside of her thighs and the tips of her breasts. He knew his mouth was wide open, but he couldn't close it. He had never been with a girl; it wasn't usually done before marriage. It was the Way—

She glanced up, and right through that opening in the bushes she looked directly into his eyes. And then she smiled, holding his gaze for a few seconds before she slowly slipped into a blanket and walked away.

Lazaro's day was ruined. No matter what he did, Dineh's attractive brown body filled his thoughts. And the excitement in his loins lingered. Once, when he was making arrows with Old Man, he got another full erection and was afraid to move for fear his mentor's sharp eyes would notice. He had trouble sleeping that night and the next morning he spotted her bathing again. This time she was with Bacho's sister. And they wore petticoats.

He saw her twice walking through the village, and each time she smiled with her eyes before casting them down. But it was useless. If he so much as talked to her, the watchful Bacho would ridicule him. He had to do something to get his mind back on manhood—he volunteered for the next war party. And when he returned, he owned two horses, which would be the beginning of his herd.

On the day of the first snow, Bacho made Dineh his wife.

The next day, Lazaro sat outside Old Man's wickiup whittling on a bow. He had a headache from too much tiswin the night before, and the idea of Bacho being between the beautiful Dineh's legs was a horrible thought he couldn't get out of his mind. Finally, Old Man said, "Go see a widow."

"For what?"

"You know. Find a widow who has not remarried. No so bad as if you get caught with a young girl. Father or brother won't shoot you."

"How do you know I want a woman?"

"I know. You are crazy for one. You are a boy who walks on three legs."

A week later, Lazaro visited his cousin in his mother's former village. His cousin was two summers older and he was married. After a long talk, he finally told his cousin what he was looking for. He spoke haltingly and before he could finish, the cousin broke in, "You should meet Nadzeela. She is an exciting widow who turns down every man who asks for her. Her husband was killed seven moons ago in a Nakai-ye raid."

"How old is she?"

"Young, maybe only twenty summers."

She sounded old and exciting to Lazaro. "How can I meet her?" he asked, adding, "And why would she be interested in me?"

His cousin shrugged. "Everyone knows you have the blood of Silsoose. I will tell her. Come back in three days."

"Can I see her?" Lazaro asked eagerly.

"No, come back in three days."

The three days seemed like three moons, but at last Lazaro was back in the village of his mother. His cousin took him to a nearby high hill when the sun was at its midday peak. Leading him into a shelter of rocks that formed a small room, he pointed to a tall young woman in doeskins who waited on the edge of a rock. "This is Nadzeela," he said, and left immediately.

Lazaro felt a sudden rush of heat on his cheeks. The woman had a whimsical smile on her face as she watched him. She was laughing at him! She nodded. Her voice was low, but seemed to roll over the words. "And you are Lazaro, son of Roberto and Adala." She lolled against the rock like a lazy mountain lion. "You are very tall," she murmured. "I hear you are a successful warrior already."

He shrugged, unable to think of anything to say. His cheeks burned even more. *Where were his words?* She looked just like a Navajo— almost. No, she looked better.

Nadzeela chuckled. "Your cousin did not tell me you lost your tongue to those terrible Navajos."

"I have a tongue," he blurted out. Her skin was flawless, and what white teeth!

"I hear you will be a great chief some day, perhaps like Silsoose."

Lazaro shook his head—he disliked the burden of such an idea. "I am only a warrior."

She crossed her arms and he could see she had full breasts, even though she wasn't thick-waisted at all. "Why did you want to meet me?" she asked directly. "Aren't there many girls your age in your village?"

"Of course!" he answered too quickly. "But I, they are . . . just little girls. I want to be with a woman!"

She smiled again. "And what do you intend to do with a woman?"

That was it! She was insulting him—no wonder she hadn't remarried. Her tongue was too sharp. A decent woman didn't make fun of a man, not a decent Chihenne woman! "I just want to talk to her," he replied lamely.

"All right then, I have brought a blanket and some nuts to eat. If you will make a fire, we'll sit and talk."

He had completely forgotten how cold it was. "Enjuh!" he replied, seeing that the fire makings were already piled in the middle of the place. He knew that she had gathered them and felt a grudging respect for her. If only she would quit *laughing* at him.

A few minutes later they sat across from each other in front of the crackling fire and slowly began to talk in a more casual manner. "My husband-of-whom-I-am-not-speaking was not so much of a man," she replied frankly when he asked her why she had agreed to see him. "And the rest of the men in my village are little better, or else they have too many wives, or they are too old. You, my young giant, are like a fresh colt splashing in the quiet pool—a big, pretty colt who might amuse me."

He was embarrassed by her talk; he should get up and leave.

She laughed, a light sound that reminded him of the deep tones of a wood flute. "I don't like being only with women and children." She talked on about how she had never had a child, and how she had considered becoming a medicine woman. She chuckled. "But that would have meant I had to be ugly and who wants to be ugly?"

He watched her in the shadows and bit of sunlight that played through the rock room. What high cheekbones and expressive dark eyes! That skin and that voice! How she aroused him just talking like this . . . would she really want him, really do it with him? How should he— Was there an Old Man to teach lovemaking?

She asked him about his raids and the war party, and at last he could unwind and talk about something he knew very well. Soon his enthusiasm sparkled from his eyes and he made wide gestures with his hands. A Spanish word here and there flavored his descriptions, and she listened with wide eyes until she suddenly jumped to her feet. "I must get back to the village," she said without making an explanation.

He couldn't believe it! Wasn't she supposed to remove her clothes about now? He reached for her hand, but she was already striding out of the rock enclosure. "Wait!" he cried out. "What about—"

"Come back one week from today, if the snow is not deep. Same time."

He jumped to his feet, but she was gone.

It was the longest week of his life, and he was there nearly an hour early on the appointed day. He had a roaring fire going when she arrived and greeted him with a warm smile. Again, they sat by the flames, nibbled on the nuts she had brought, and talked about different things. He was worried that it was too cold to make love, so he had brought a deerskin robe. But she just sat across the fire from him as they talked. Finally, he blurted, "Should I take off my clothes?"

Her eyes widened momentarily and then she laughed. "Why—are you too warm?"

That was rude! he snapped angrily to himself. Jumping to his feet he grabbed her hand and pulled her up. The humor was still in her eyes as he pulled her close and hugged her. *One does not kiss in public,* he reminded himself. What about in a wintry room of stone? She was looking up at him with those mocking eyes—but no, they were soft, not mocking after all. "Let me loose," she said softly. And he relaxed his bear hug, even though he was totally aroused and wanted to throw her on the robe.

Her hand came gently to his cheek and she drew his face down to hers. Her kiss was warm and sweet—the first he'd ever experienced. She kissed him again, long and searching, and then slowly drew him down to the robe. Placing his hand on her breast, she began slowly to wander over his hard young body with her knowing fingers.

Lazaro went on four raids and two long warpaths that winter and early spring, and when the snows melted he had eleven good horses and other things of value, such as finely embroidered buckskins, a special hand-carved bow of the finest willow, three pistols, and two muskets. It was already being said at the campfires of all the Chihenne villages on the Willows that his Power and good luck on a raid or the warpath was greater than anyone had ever known. Even seasoned warriors wanted to go on the trail with him.

And he had not yet seen his seventeenth summer!

Chief Roberto was thinking back to the Catholic services of Easter, when his son came and told him about Nadzeela. He told his stepfather he wanted her for his wife. Roberto nodded; he had known for some time of the meetings. And when Lazaro had finished he said, "You are a warrior and a man, my son. By custom, you are permitted to select any woman of your choice to be your wife. Still, I must say something. As you know, this woman is many years older than you, and she has had no children in her earlier marriage. This is a most important thing when you are a chief. And you will some day be a chief. Also, as you know, I have been unable to get my wives with children and it is a deep sadness with me. I thank Ussen for you every morning in my prayers."

Lazaro listened quietly as his mother entered the wickiup and sat silently behind her husband. Roberto continued, "If you persist in this desire, you should consider one other factor—this woman was free and immoral with you, a boy barely out of his apprenticeship. Will she be true to you, or will you someday have to be a chief with an adultress wife—one perhaps with a face that you have had to disfigure by cutting off her nose?"

Lazaro had listened respectfully; now his face hardened. "She loves me," he said coldly. He didn't have to get their approval.

Roberto nodded. "I have said what I had to say, my son. I am sure you will have a good marriage."

His mother found a smile. "And I, too, my son."

It was customary for a newly married man to go to the home of the bride, where—although the groom was not supposed to see or have contact with his mother-in-law for the rest of his life—the new husband became a member of his wife's family. Lazaro and Nadzeela broke with tradition and returned to the large village of Roberto, where they set up their wickiup apart from any family. Lazaro had given five horses to his wife's father, not in payment, but as a symbol of the high regard he held for her and also as a sign of his status.

The Chihenne whispered and giggled behind his back about the marriage, but for only a few days because he was their good luck amulet in war. And everyone sang his praises, everyone except Bacho.

The next five years were filled with a special zest for the two young lovers. The wise Nadzeela provided just the right degree of maturity and mothering for the growing Lazaro as he crossed the difficult bridge into actual manhood. He continued to find good fortune on his raids and warpaths, and in his twentieth summer he became a war leader who commanded his own forays when not involved in a large war party. The enigma that was his Power continued to elude him, manifesting itself in strange ways now and then, and totally obscuring itself for long periods.

When Nadzeela finally became pregnant, Lazaro brought Benita into his life. It happened after a raid into Old Mexico. One of his warriors had taken as a captive a Mexican girl of seventeen summers. Her face was quite ordinary, round when she smiled; and her eyes, though small, were darkly bright. She had a sturdy figure that tended to be thick-waisted, and a strength suited to life on the frontier. What was noticeably different about the girl named Benita was her attitude. As the raiding party hurried north toward the Willows, she refrained from any tears and any cowering. In fact, she watched the efforts of the men with unabashed interest, and the movements of the tall Lazaro in particular.

When they were only one day's ride from the Willows, Lazaro spoke to the warrior who was her captor. Without haggling, he bought her for a fast horse and a very good battle shield. The price was high, but Lazaro guessed she would be well worth it.

"But I don't need a servant!" Nadzeela insisted.

"You are the wife of a Chihenne leader," Lazaro replied archly. "And you are with child."

"A Chihenne leader's wife does not need a Nakai-ye to help bring a child to life."

"I spoke with her on the trail. She knows about childbirth."

Nadzeela coolly appraised the captive. The girl stood a few yards away, taking in everything around her in a strangely calm way. A smile even touched her lips, as if this were some great new game she was about to play. Nadzeela sensed a warmth about the girl, and wondered: Could her lusty husband have need of another woman on his blanket? No, she quickly decided, he was too scrupulous for that.

Surely there was something. Lazaro had taught her to speak Spanish—she would talk to this Benita first.

Lazaro shrugged. "I have already bought her."

With the help of one of her friends, Nadzeela showed Benita how to construct a wickiup. Before sunset, the Mexican girl's house was finished not far from her own. In halting Spanish she explained, "It will do no good to try for escape. The men will catch you and beat you. No captive has ever escaped and lived. Tomorrow—"

"But I don't want to escape!" Benita exclaimed.

Nadzeela regarded her blankly. Was this strange young woman loco?

"This is a big adventure!"

"You have no Nakai-ye husband?"

"Oh, no." Benita's smile was disarming. "My village had only a few young men—all ugly. Definitely no husband for me."

Nadzeela's expression didn't change. There was more that this girl wasn't telling . . . something. She would keep an eye on her, particularly with Lazaro.

As the weeks passed and Nadzeela approached her delivery day, she and Benita became closer. Except for a secret she was certain that Nakai-ye girl was keeping, there seemed to be no guile—just a willing cheerfulness on Benita's part to do anything to help or please. She caught the girl casting a longing glance at Lazaro now and then, but her husband seemed not to notice. Once, when they were washing clothes at the river's edge on a crisp spring morning, Benita suddenly asked, "If Lazaro were chief, could he have more than one wife?"

Nadzeela answered carefully after a moment, "Lazaro could have more than one wife now, if he wished. But normally a Chihenne man marries more than once only to support the widow of a relative or close friend." She shook her head, feeling the child kick within her huge belly. "But one wife is the Way of the Chihenne."

Tze-go-juni was keeping a close eye on the Nakai-ye girl, as well as on Nadzeela. All through the pregnancy, the shaman had provided potions and charms to ensure everything from comfort to the long life of the powerful chief who might be growing in Nadzeela's stomach. And now she insisted the fetus would be a boy—due to its being highly active in her stomach. Most important, the medicine woman had safeguarded the pregnant woman against clashes with other women, since nearly any one of them could have been a witch.

* * *

Shortly before midday, Nadzeela went into labor. Tze-go-juni arrived at her wickiup immediately, and Lazaro was sent on his way. Since the husband was not supposed to be near the birth, he rode off to the rock formation the Nakai-ye called the Kneeling Nun and prayed to Ussen. A runner was dispatched to Nadzeela's village to summon her female relatives; Adala called the midwife and Benita hung back anxiously. Since it was a mild, clear day, a bed was prepared on the ground in front of her house. The wooden birth post had been driven into the ground two weeks earlier by the midwife as part of the service for which she would receive a fine horse.

As the pains increased in severity and frequency, Nadzeela ate four small pieces of the narrow inner leaves of yucca that had been dipped in salt. Next, a concoction of water in which the root of the birth plant had been boiled was used to bathe her genitals. And over all, Tze-go-juni, her face painted vermillion and green, chanted and implored her private Powers to bring about a safe delivery.

When the pains were close enough together, Nadzeela knelt before the wooden birth post, gripping it firmly with both hands. Spreading her legs as far apart as possible, she closed her eyes, bit down on the strip of thick leather in her mouth, and began to force the baby out of her womb. With the midwife's exhortations and the shaman's chants ringing in her ears, she used all of her remaining strength to keep up the pressure. The midwife's firm hands massaged the baby downward until, in a sudden burst, the dripping child was born. Instantly, using a sharp knife of black flint, the midwife adroitly snipped the umbilical cord and tied it in a knot.

It was a long boy, but he wasn't making a sound.

Tze-go-juni immediately splashed a pan of cold water over him, receiving a swift little cry in return. She beamed, reminding everyone that a baby that did not cry loudly at first would grow up to be a powerful warrior. Placing the baby on a soft robe, the midwife quickly bathed away the blood with warm water, then rubbed his tiny body with a paste of red ochre and grease to keep him moist.

"Hai, ya, hi, ya, haida, yi, yi!" the medicine woman chanted as she joyously sprinkled hoddentin to the four directions.

The other women ministered to Nadzeela, but she weakly pushed her mother aside so she could watch the midwife ritually hold her baby up to the four directions and add further prayers. This done, she closed her eyes and let them carry her inside the wickiup. She did not see Adala gather up the afterbirth and the umbilical cord and wrap them with the blanket on which the birth had taken place. Placing the bundle under her arm, Lazaro's mother marched erectly up a nearby hill to a large stand of berry bushes. Turning to the east, she held her parcel high and prayed, "Great Father Ussen, because this bush gives life every year, may this child also have his life renewed." Turning to the bush she added, "May this boy live a strong life and watch you bear fruit forever."

Unless some characteristic or event dictated it, the naming of the newborn child seldom took place for several months. But Nadzeela was by no means a conventional mother.

She called him Taza.

>> 4 <<

June 6, 1839

As the Cardenas party topped the ridge that overlooked the de Gante hacienda, Carlota gasped. Below, winking back in soft tints of pastels, lay a sprawling collection of buildings nearly as large as the last town they had visited. But then it should sparkle—wasn't it the place of her dreams? *La Reina*—The Queen—was what the de Gante family proudly called their largest and northernmost possession. The Queen sparkled in the bright sunshine as if she truly had a diamond tiara on her proud head.

Fidel de Gante and her father drew their horses up beside Carlota's. "La Reina stretches from its center where you see the main buildings to over three leagues in every direction," Don de Gante said proudly. "We have been on her land for the last two hours."

Carlota wanted to stand in her saddle and reach out to the power of this wild and beautiful land. *La Reina!* Finally! The giant hacienda over which she would one day be mistress was like a great fief to her, stretching out of sight beyond a low range of hills to the east. She smiled quickly at her mother.

"Much of La Reina is untamed," de Gante continued. "In places it is barren and nearly impassable, and much of it is nearly unusable as grazing land. But there is still enough grass for a few thousand head of cattle."

"For you or for the Apaches?" Andres de Cardenas asked. At forty-seven, he was showing gray in his beard as well as at his ears. He had been a colonel for over a decade, but the still-shifting sands of capital politics had kept him from the rank of general despite the machinations of Fidel de Gante.

"Good question," de Gante replied with a frown. "It has been said that those bastards have their own form of farming—they steal a certain amount of livestock, but always leave enough so the rancher can raise more for them to take another day. I hope when you get to Santa Fe, you'll put a stop to this damned practice."

Andres shook his head. "I'll never have the strength for an offensive against them. Besides, they're never there when you go after

them." After five years in Washington as military attaché at the
Mexican embassy, he was returning to the same job he had held
during the early twenties in Santa Fe. Now, with the troublesome.
Texans claiming part of New Mexico as theirs, the assignment was far
more vital.

Carlota blocked out the unpleasant talk. This was *her* day and she
didn't want anything distasteful to mar it. She had not seen Agustin
de Gante since she was ten years old, and now he was waiting for her
down there in that shimmering beauty of La Reina, waiting for his
future bride. She sighed deeply. Her handsome, dashing Agustin!

At fifteen, Carlota was already fulfilling her midwife's predictions.
As tall as the average man, she had a willowy figure that had been
turning men's heads for two years. When it wasn't her figure catching
their eyes, it was her striking face with its laughing blue eyes and fair
skin. In venal Washington, many would-be swains had mistaken the
quick smile that lurked around her lips as an open invitation, only to
be quickly disappointed. "Oh, Papa, I can't wait," she exclaimed in her
surprisingly deep voice.

Andres smiled indulgently. "The princess wants to meet The
Queen."

Carlota's smile flashed back as she urged her horse forward.

Agustin de Gante at eighteen was not quite pretty, but he was close.
Tall and slender, his long face was accented by large dark eyes under
bushy black brows, eyes that were at one moment alert and humorous,
and at another, distant and moody. His stylishly thin nose watched over
a black mustache and a mouth that Carlota thought was the most
sensual she had ever seen. He was the de Gantes' only surviving son,
and had recently been commissioned a second lieutenant in a militia
regiment headquartered nearly seventy leagues away in Chihuahua
City.

As Carlota sneaked periodic looks at him across the white linen of
the dinner table, she couldn't believe her good fortune. Arranged
marriages often involved some very unpalatable mates, and she could
easily have been promised to a sniveling little snot nose, or to a
greasy fat bully. Instead, this delightful young officer with a warm
gentleness and wide smile was to be *hers!* She would marry him
immediately if they would permit it—after all, many girls were married at her age.

At the lower end of the table, Gregoria de Gante was holding
court. Prematurely white-haired in her middle forties, Señora de Gante
was the epitome of the wealthy Creole Mexican mother. Nothing was
too insignificant for her attention, and she let go of nothing. Carlota

had sensed her cool animosity the moment they had climbed down from their horses. And she knew why—while the Cardenas family had the requisite background, and particularly with Rosa's direct Spanish blood, Andres de Cardenas simply could add little to the de Gante fortunes. And the match had been made between her often foolish husband and his boyhood friend—without even consulting the most important person involved!

But she could not intimidate the sophisticated Rosa. Gossip from Madrid and Washington were far too juicy to let an air of superiority preclude their telling. Carlota smiled to herself. Señora de Gante would never have complete control of life on this hacienda as long as her mother was visiting. And in the same moment she wondered how difficult she would be as a mother-in-law.

"I hear life is exciting in Santa Fe these days," Agustin said abruptly. "But then when you have a sheep thief for a governor, it can't be too dull. I understand you were born there."

Carlota nodded with her quick smile. "Yes, but I don't remember it too well."

Agustin laughed. "Very good, Señorita. And what of the world of politics in the great City of Mexico? Did you hear any good gossip during your visit?"

"Santa Ana will be president again. His heroics against the French at Vera Cruz makes it a certainty."

One of Agustin's thick eyebrows shot up respectfully. "Hmmm, you do stay informed. Are you aware that we aren't in his favor? It all goes back to my father's support of the Liberator when he returned from Europe."

Carlota wanted to laugh at his foolishness. Of course she knew. "Isn't that why the de Gante family is in the north of Mexico?" she asked pleasantly.

"Very good. But not exactly correct. I am staying here to manage La Reina, and that could be a permanent occupation. There is so much . . . " Agustin went on enthusiastically describing at length the potential of the hacienda.

Carlota hung on every word, for wasn't this to be her domain?

When dinner was finished, Agustin asked permission from Rosa to take Carlota for a walk. Since the girl had never had a *duenna*, it seemed a hollow request, but Rosa was nevertheless pleased at his good manners.

The couple strolled leisurely through the darkening shadows of the warm April evening, each a bit self-conscious at suddenly being alone together. The soft music of a guitar drifted toward them. He told her about the tall cottonwoods, the main house, and the chapel; about the families and the priest, and about the cattle and horses that made La Reina the equivalent of a complete town. "All that is missing," he added with a smile, "is the *cantinas.*"

Instantly Carlota pictured him sitting in a noisy cantina, his sombrero on the back of his handsome head, and a broad grin on his face. A beautiful girl with castanets is dancing in front of him, closer and closer, and then suddenly she drops on his lap and kisses him!

"Do you go to the cantinas often?" she asked, pushing the horrible scene from her mind.

"There are no cantinas for a don," he replied easily. "Only for those who are subject to him." He went on, "We even have our own fiestas here, complete with our own music, weddings . . . "

He moved close, touching her hand for the first time. Her breath caught as she looked up into his eyes and detected his appealing scent. His voice was gentle. "Carlota, would you mind very much being married here? I mean, I know it is normal—that is, I can easily come to Santa Fe when it is time, but—"

"I would love to be married here," she whispered, moving her fingers against his.

The Cardenas party stayed at La Reina for one week, and when it was time to leave, Carlota was not only gloriously in love with her *desposado*, her fiancé, but also with the magnificent life and hacienda that would one day be hers. Tears filled her eyes as she took one final look at the buildings from a nearby ridge while the party proceeded north toward Apache country. For extra safety, and since he had been there before, Agustin brought five dragoons from the small presidio that guarded the hacienda and accompanied the small column as it rode north. Following the water, both active streams and springs, it was nearly sixty leagues from the hacienda to Santa Rita—a five day trip at a pace comfortable to Rosa.

Santa Rita was one of the seven scheduled presidio stops on the way north for Andres. As the new commander of the New Mexican military department, he was performing a double duty—introducing himself to the troops and commanders, and giving them a long overdue general inspection and opportunity to air their complaints. Little would be done about their grievances, but it was procedure. The presidio at Santa Rita was not large—two officers and nineteen enlisted men—and it had not been inspected in over five years. He guessed it would be in unfavorable condition because he knew the commander. It was the same unsavory Padilla, still a captain, whom he had once suspected of being involved in a slaving operation on the Jornado de Muerte. He didn't look forward to the visit with any pleasure.

With Agustin commanding the escort, Carlota was in a festive mood. Riding mostly at his side, she plucked away at him like a biographer— organizing a full picture of this delightful young man who would be her mate. And he welcomed nearly all of her amusing questioning, adroitly sidestepping any pitfalls that might someday cause him or her discomfort. He was especially careful about her probing questions regarding his experience with other girls.

In the firelight of the evening campfire, he quoted his favorite poems to her and listened while she translated her choicest English poems. She had been tutored to a nearly flawless command of that language during the five years in Washington, but sometimes wondered if she would ever use the tongue again. As the days rushed by, their newfound love blossomed like a sunflower opening its broad fresh petals.

While her mother was hardly happy with the hardships of being on the trail, Carlota exulted in it. An expert horsewoman, she wore pants and rode with a man's light saddle. Her father had taught her not only about horses at an early age, but the use of firearms as well, and sometimes during a halt she was permitted to fire a rifle. On the third morning, accompanied by a scout, she killed a young buck deer that soon found the spit above a campfire, making her even more enchanting to the soldiers of the escort.

And at night she and her mother shared the day's happenings, sometimes giggling like sisters in the small tent that Andres's orderly carried on one of the pack mules. Although strict security was maintained, there was no sign of the dreaded Apaches on the entire trip. It was as if this great beautiful desert, with its periodic mountains and special blooming vegetation, was all hers . . . hers and her beloved Agustin's.

Carlota rose from the crude bench in the rear of the little church and stepped out into the fresh early morning air. Removing the scarf from her head, she glanced at the small plaza and the millions of minute, diamond-bright reflections the nighttime shower had left behind. She sniffed. Despite their fresh sparkle, they did nothing to disguise the ugliness of this forsaken little mining town.

Two older women, bent under their drab shawls and the life they were forced to endure, moved past her and soon disappeared inside the dried-mud hovels they called home. She shuddered—go to Mass and make do; the life of a poor Mexican woman. An ugly yellow dog stirred himself from a puddle and growled at some imagined antagonist before giving her a bored look and limping away. And in front of a nearby cantina, a man in his *serape*, still drunk, sat snoring against a stained adobe wall. Eyeing the foul-smelling garbage and broken drinking jugs that littered the plaza, Carlota couldn't imagine staying in such a dismal place. Three days was enough!

"Ladron!—Thief!"

Carlota jumped back as a man, a tall American with a heavy black beard, was pushed from a doorway just a few feet from her. A plump woman with unbrushed hair wearing a dirty chemise screamed as she followed him outside. "Cheat a poor working girl, will you, *Yanqui* pig? I'll tell everyone! You won't get another woman or a drink in a single cantina, you'll see! Pig! *Ladron!*"

The big man threw Carlota a quick glance, jammed a filthy sombrero over his eyes, and weaved across the plaza. She shook her head as the whore slammed her door—what a terrible place! Moving quickly up a crooked alley, she was soon outside of the horrid little town and turning up a slope toward the early morning sun. Loosening the single chignon, she let her long black hair stream out behind, a symbol of her unbound love.

It was such a beautiful morning, so fresh, just what she wanted to treasure, to hold clearly in her memory until she could be with Agustin again. Sleep had evaded her most of the night, and tears had dampened her pillow at times as she had tried to push their parting from her mind. It was so foolish, but she just couldn't help it. When they went their separate ways in a few hours, it might be *ages* before they saw each other again!

She stooped to pick a cluster of yellow and white daisies to stick behind her ear—Agustin would like that. Ah, how spring and love blended together! Gazing up the mountain at the remarkable rock formation known as the Kneeling Nun, she drew in a sharp breath and felt the sorrow flood her heart. For legend had it that a nun had broken her vows with a handsome Spanish comandante and the Lord had turned her to stone in a kneeling position to forever repent the sinful act where the entire world could be reminded of her transgression.

Even a cowl seemed to shield her romantic, tragic face.

Carlota felt her eyes brimming and wondered how she would ever be brave enough to bear being separated from Agustin.

Lazaro dismounted silently and tied his pony to a scrub pine near the side of the knoll, unaware that anyone was near. Staring down with melancholy at the slowly stirring town below, he found he still had no reason for coming so early. Yet *something* had awakened him long before first light, some unknown force had pulled him from his blanket and drawn him irresistibly to this hill overlooking Santa Rita del Cobre. He stroked his smooth chin, trying to clear his mind and be receptive to any influence that might make itself known. It was another of the ways in which he tried to understand his Power. If he could detach himself, leaving his mind totally unobstructed, sometimes information or decisions were unmistakably thrust upon him.

It was utterly still in the clear morning, and he could feel the nearness of whatever it was that was plucking at him. But he couldn't draw it in. Slowly he held out his hands, palms up, and looked toward the sky to the east. "Tell me," he whispered fervently. "Give me your sign, Father." But nothing came to him except a stronger sense of anticipation and the sound of his own breathing. He waited, unblinking, as a tiny breeze stirred the air. He thought he saw an eagle gliding over the hill that held the Kneeling Nun. A sign! It was something important. . . .

He thought about the fiesta that would begin in a few hours in the grassy bowl between his position and the edge of the Nakai-ye town. A party of White Eyes, led by a trader named Brant-son, had arrived the day before. His father had known Brant-son for some time and traded Nakai-ye mules to him for ammunition on occasion. Now the American was giving a fiesta for Roberto and Santa Rita's inhabitants to celebrate the special peace terms it was said he brought with him from the City of Mules, Chihuahua.

There would be barrels of both mescal and aguardiente, it was promised, enough to please all. And there would be presents, *socorro*—the corn meal—wheat flour, blankets, sweet molasses, and other pleasures. There would also be music and dancing in both the Apache way and the Nakai-ye way, with their bright-eyed señoritas.

Roberto's whole family would be there, as well as many of his friends and their families. Nadzeela was excited about coming, and had spent part of the night finishing a new pair of beaded moccasins for their son, Taza, to wear.

As Lazaro stared back down the grassy bowl, he felt a sudden uneasiness. He didn't like the dark-bearded Brant-son, nor the other White Eyes with him. A new treaty—why should the Nakai-ye nantan send a White Eye? They already had a treaty with the Santa Rita nantan that had lasted for many years. And only because his father was chief did he not speak against it. He seldom came to this Nakai-ye town—it was a place where these intruders stole Chihenne Power with their fiery drink. Today both the men and the women would drink. . . . He would listen closely and drink only a little.

Above, on the crest of the knoll, Carlota brushed away a tear. She would be strong and gay these last hours with Agustin. She would laugh—and the fiesta, she loved a fiesta, yes, they would dance, pretend— She hadn't noticed the spotted pony before. It had an Indian saddle. Drawing in a sharp breath, she quickly glanced around but saw nothing. Who could be there? Something was moving by the thick stand of bushes near the pony! Her eyes widened as she saw a head appear, a red bandana holding the hair—an *Apache!*

Lazaro nodded, deciding the Power just would not reveal anything in this place. Perhaps higher up in the mountains— What! How could someone be so close, no more than ten paces away, staring down at him?

His hand went instinctively to his knife.

No, it was a woman, a tall *white* woman with eyes that stared back at him without flinching. She was startling! Something from the mountain gods? White Painted Woman? No, impossible—yet the early morning sun made her face glow as if Ussen were touching her. Tall, with the high cheekbones—she looked exactly like his Nadzeela, but pale. His breath caught at her beauty.

Was this what the Power had brought him to see?

Carlota braced herself, fighting down the fear. She liked to think that nothing ever scared her. His eyes held her, so black and bright, like two piercing coals, magnetic! A sudden weakness invaded her knees. He was the most imposing Indian she had ever seen, taller than her father or Agustin, with those penetrating eyes that were somehow— even over the short distance between them—somehow mournful. It wasn't possible for a heathen Indian, she told herself sharply, but with his sharply defined nose, his high forehead and strong jaw, and the thick black hair that fell over his faded red shirt to his waist . . . he was actually handsome!

* * *

Lazaro continued to stare at her, not moving. If the Power had brought him for this, what should he do? Where had this young white Nadzeela come from? Brant-son had brought no women. He'd heard the Nakai-ye military column had two, but she was so white! She looked so young, so special.

Carlota finally dropped her frank gaze, feeling the burn on her cheeks. She felt so disconcerted—no man had ever looked at her like that. It was unseemly. But then he was only an Apache . . . she had to get back . . . he might— She looked up for one more glance into those compelling eyes, then turned and walked erectly down the slope.

Lazaro followed her with his eyes, still frozen as if in a spell. He wanted to run after her and touch her soft pale cheek, stare into her strange eyes of the summer sky. A tiny gust of wind brought him suddenly to his senses. He felt peculiar, out of breath. Inhaling deeply, he shook his head. What kind of a bizarre day had begun for him?

Colonel Andres de Cardenas stared out the window of the *alcalde's* office at the dusty little plaza. He would have left early in the morning, but the mayor had asked that he stay until after the fiesta began—after all, he was the highest ranking person ever to come to Santa Rita del Cobre, and it would add to the prestige of the event. So he had reluctantly agreed. Watching as the residents light-heartedly moved about the plaza, he noticed that the American—Brantson—was engaging in some kind of an argument with Captain Padilla. At least he was frowning and gesturing as if they were in disagreement. Suddenly Padilla nodded vigorously and patted Brantson on the back. As they separated, Andres shook his head. "What connection is there between Captain Padilla and this illustrious Señor Brantson?" he asked.

The alcalde shrugged. "They are old acquaintances. In fact, the capitan readily suggested approval of the fiesta. And you know how drab our life is here at Santa Rita, Don Coronel."

Andres disliked this obsequious little official nearly as much as Padilla. The inspection had gone about as he expected: sloppy records, undisciplined and filthy soldiers who stayed drunk whenever they had the money; an unscrupulous commandant who most certainly was supplementing his income with any possible illegal activity. He would relieve Padilla on the spot, but he could prove little, and frontier officers of any kind were hard to find. "I will depart at noon so we can get a few hours on the trail today."

"Si, Don Coronel. All of the speeches will be finished by then."

"Has this Brantson mentioned this treaty to you?"

The alcalde shrugged again. "No, not a word."

Andres frowned as he reached for his hat. "I heard nothing about it in Chihuahua City when I was there three weeks ago." Something was wrong, he could feel it. But he had to get on toward Santa Fe and his other inspections, not get involved in politics.

Lazaro returned to the mining town with Nadzeela and his son, Taza, at midmorning. His wife was dressed in a new, richly beaded doeskin dress with blue-dyed fringes. Long turquoise beaded earrings hung to her shoulders and several different necklaces were suspended over her breast. Lazaro knew she had brushed her long lustrous hair from before dawn to sunrise. Her animated smile brightened her speech as she again cautioned Taza to play close to her.

Lazaro nodded approvingly as he looked into her eyes. She was the most beautiful Apache woman Ussen had ever created.

The fiesta was split—the Mexicans were mostly in the town plaza, while Roberto's family was grouped around a low wooden platform in the grassy bowl outside. Lazaro's father, wearing his finest ceremonial headdress and the special ochre paint of his office, sat on the dais with Chihenne and Nakai-ye leaders and a beaming, black-bearded Brant-son. Even the Nakai-ye coronel was there, listening quietly as Roberto spoke at length. His mother sat behind the chief, having a fine time with the other women as they sipped the rich aguardiente.

As Nadzeela made her way to the other women, Lazaro felt a return of the morning's urgency and a sense of detachment. The sun reflected brightly off a concho necklace, and the loud music of the Nakai-ye musicians blasted into his eardrums. He watched Taza dancing his version of the war dance with two other small boys, but they seemed distant. As he forced himself toward the platform, a group of boisterous Nakai-ye men and women ran down into the bowl to dance, reminding him of mountain spirits. He shook his head and found a seat on the edge of his father's parley group.

Andres was relieved that the talk had finally returned from its meandering and approached the core of the parley. He was familiar with the Indian method of long-winded discussions over many draws on the long pipe, and the Chihenne Apache custom was no different. He listened carefully as Brantson said, " . . . so, Great Chief, in return for no further raiding by the Chihenne, the Mexican government will supply fifty horses, two hundred head of cattle, two hundred bushels of socorro, and five barrels of aguardiente, every three months. And—"

Andres shrugged inwardly, it sounded like a fairy tale. He still didn't believe this coarse American, but he wouldn't get involved. As far as he knew the states of Chihuahua and Sonora were still paying the bloody bounty for Apache scalps—one hundred pesos for a male, fifty for a woman, and twenty-five for a child.

He looked across the bowl to where his daughter stood hand in hand with Agustin on its far rim. He had had enough.

"Who is that tall Indian with the bright red bandana around his forehead?" Carlota asked carefully as they made their way to the floor of the bowl.

"I think he is the son of the chief," Agustin replied.

Carlota looked briefly into Lazaro's surprised expression as she passed the leaders, then quickly turned her attention to the dancers, where two cantina girls were whirling around in the arms of two soldiers—one a dragoon belonging to their escort. Suddenly she grabbed Agustin's hand. "Dance with me, darling!" she laughed.

He bowed low with a broad grin. "My pleasure, Señorita."

Seeing the handsome couple, the half-drunk musicians switched to a lively number. Round and round the newcomers whirled as everyone watched and began to clap hands in beat with the music. Carlota loved it—she loved any fandango, and how she loved this beautiful young man whose touch made her sing! Round and round! *Guadalajara!* Once her laugh seemed to go right into the eyes of that impudent one in the bandana.

The Indians were all nodding heavily to the beat. Suddenly a fat woman pulled herself to her feet and began to vigorously shake her fringed doeskins. Laughter poured over the platform and Carlota held Agustin even tighter.

But too soon it was over. Her father rose from the center of the dais and gestured that it was time to leave. Reluctantly, she squeezed Agustin's hand. The terrible moment had arrived, and they must find a secluded place for their final goodbye. Already her eyes were brimming at the thought.

Forty minutes later the Cardenas party rode east toward the Rio Grande.

* * *

"Hola!" the half-drunk, heavily painted whore shouted. Sitting on a rock with her legs spread and crossed at the ankles, she was fanning herself with one hand and holding a cup of aguardiente with the other. "You want a little diversion, big brave?" she said loudly.

Lazaro ignored her, moving to a group of pine trees to get away from the noise and hopefully to relieve the feeling of sadness that was smothering him. The babble of drunken Chihenne and Nakai-ye, combined with the blaring music, had finally become too much. Lifting the nearly empty jug of mescal to his lips, he thought that not even drinking seemed to affect him this strange day.

Two small Chihenne boys ran by, each wearing a young antelope skin. He watched them morosely, thinking he should just get his pony and ride into the hills. But he couldn't leave Nadzeela and his son. He looked back into the bowl where he caught a glimpse of her. The huge pile of socorro, bags of flour, and the other gifts were still stacked behind the platform. Weren't they ever going to pass them out? The roasted oxen in the pits had long been eaten and the lengthy speeches finished. He could see the eagle feathers of a headdress, trampled like the white flowers of the morning. The paint of celebration was now smeared over rubbery faces.

He flung the mescal jug away.

He *hated* what the drink did to the People!

A loud blast from a musician's horn pierced the air, and Brant-son stood, holding his arms wide and shouting in Spanish, "It's time for your gifts, my friends! Come for your rewards!" And the Chihenne began to stir, those who were not drunk, like his mother and Nadzeela, shaking the others and heading for the piles of bounty.

Suddenly Lazaro jerked to full alertness. The premonition, the sadness, the strangeness of the morning—it was all a warning! He felt the same tension he always sensed just before a battle. There—at the top of the bowl, Brant-son's men and that Nakai-ye commandante of the presidio . . . *kneeling over their muskets!*

No!

He saw Brant-son move to the pile of socorro, and the Nakai-ye who had been around the platform suddenly scrambling up the slope toward town. One of the musicians dropped his guitar, leaving it as he madly hurried away.

No!

He wanted to throw himself into the bowl to stop what was coming, but he couldn't move.

His people were converging on the socorro heap, women in front, carrying empty bags for their gifts. *No!* His hand went to his knife, but his feet refused to budge. "No!" he screamed. *"Get back!"*

But his words were drowned out by a rocking explosion from the center of the socorro. Horrified, Lazaro saw fire and smoke belch from the pile. Chihenne who were closest to the blast were tossed into the air or smashed into the ground, already bleeding from the jagged pieces of metal that had ripped into their bodies. Instantly a fusillade of musket fire from above stabbed into the stunned mass of humanity.

Screams of the women and children shattered the air.

Again there was a terrible explosion from the cannon in the socorro pile, and another flash of fire and smoke. A second wave of Chihenne was cut to the ground, bodies hideously ripped apart. The musket fire was deafening; smoke and dust filled the air. Lazaro looked frantically for Nadzeela and Taza, and suddenly, with a mighty effort, he broke free and dove over the rim into the screaming, struggling death below. A wide-eyed woman in her blood-spattered white doeskins staggered past him. More followed, an old man whose face was a mask of blood, words of anger trickling from his lips; a little girl crying over a shattered arm.

Quickly reaching the bottom, Lazaro frantically stepped across moaning bodies, turning over those of women—looking, not wanting to see, knowing . . . Hands tore at him, blood spattered into his face as a woman screamed at him, more bullets crashed around him as the terrible uproar continued. And suddenly he found her, lying on her side, already dead from a vicious scarlet wound that had torn away part of her chest. Her eyes were open, staring. His beautiful Nadzeela. He dropped his face to her bloody breast, choking off a wrenching sob. He barely heard Taza screaming at his side.

He saw her teasing smile that first day in the cold rock room, a beautiful young woman commencing her love for an arrogant boy. It was a bright sunny day, like this one.

But quiet, with no smoke.

More bullets thudded into the bodies around him.

Taza!

Tearing himself away from her body, he grabbed his hysterical son and rushed up the slope toward the ponies and away from the nightmare behind him. But something stopped him at the bowl's rim, and he turned back for a final look. There, in the middle of the carnage, Brant-son and his White Eyes, accompanied by a few Nakai-ye, were bending over Chihenne bodies with flashing knives. Swiftly, as if they knew their grisly business well, they slashed scalps from the heads of dead and wounded alike. Women, children, and men. His mother was down there, as was Roberto. He started to go back, but Taza screamed again.

The last thing he saw was one of the dark-beards holding up an infant. With a roar of laughter, the White Eye cleaved off the top of the baby's head, then deftly dropped the bloody hair into a bag at his waist as he flung the tiny corpse away.

It was the largest bonfire Lazaro had ever seen. Not even when he was still a boy and Roberto had returned from his biggest victory near Janos had there been such a blaze. But never before had such a sudden and horrible disaster struck the People, nor had such an important decision faced the remaining leaders of the Chihenne.

As he had done all evening, Lazaro stared rigidly into the fire and refused to enter into any of the speeches. It had been four days since the massacre, yet all he could see was the still face of his Nadzeela and the mutilated bodies of his parents. And all he could hear was the sound of screams mixed with shrieking Nakai-ye music.

The beat of the drums had been incessant since shortly after the fall of darkness. Nearly as steady had been the monotonous tones of the singers as the shamans moved through variations of the ceremony. They had been dancing wildly for over three hours now, the painted colors of their bodies casting off different hues in the bright flickering light of the flames. It was the spirit dance, the *cha-ja-la*, their most powerful medicine.

Leading it, because so many of the victims had been women and children, and because she was the most powerful shaman, was Tze-go-juni. Although she looked ancient, Lazaro knew she had actually etched tiny criss-crossing lines in the skin of her face and neck to give it the appearance of having existed forever. Her bright eyes were sunken below bushy black eyebrows and above stark, high cheekbones that shot out from sharply recessed cheeks. Painted white was the vivid scar that slanted down over her squat nose from right to left where the big cat had slashed her face.

Her Power had been enhanced only a few months earlier when she was struck by lightning, and it was evidenced by an amulet she wore constantly around her neck. Spear-shaped and made from fused quartz, the talisman came from the base of the pine tree that had been hit by the same bolt of lightning.

Tonight, the hideous Tze-go-juni wore a vest over her ochre-painted upper body, a doeskin garment cut so deeply that her sagging breasts were barely contained. Over her quartz amulet she wore the most powerful of her fetishes—the necklace of human fingers. On a round collar of buckskin and tiny blue and white beads, eight dried human fingers were interspersed with a wide assortment of teeth and strands of human hair. She claimed all eight were the third finger, left hand, of the enemies slain by her medicine.

Sprinkling hoddentin toward Lazaro from several feet away, she chanted in the language of her special world and turned back to the three medicine men. Each was still dancing energetically to the beat of the drums and the chant of the singers; each was naked to the waist, while wearing fringed buckskin kilts and elaborately decorated moccasins to the knees. On the head of each was a domino or mask of blackened buckskin on which distorted faces had been painted. And atop the misshapen masks were headresses of rich plumage from the eagle, the hawk, and the owl.

The flames lit their twisting bodies and reflected from the eyes of the hundreds of Chihenne who sat back from the dancers, watching solemnly and lending their voices to the chanting. As the volume of the music rose, the dancers' pace became more frenzied. They jumped about the circle, pretending to search for an enemy, muttering, singing, leaping and swaying, whirling and building to a great crescendo.

Suddenly Tze-go-juni darted from the fire to Lazaro, her arms outstretched, babbling loudly, the spirit dance headdress low over her forehead. In her hands she held a four-strand medicine cord with a hoop of eagle feathers fastened by pieces of the sacred green chalchihuital. Dancing around him, she held the long medicine cord high in one hand and sprinkled liberal amounts of hoddentin over his head with the other.

And then abruptly she stopped and the music ceased with her.

The dancing medicine men froze and all eyes were on Tze-go-juni.

Slowly she turned in the sudden silence and hung the cord over the right shoulder of the still-seated Lazaro, draping it across his back to his left hip in the time-honored custom. "Lazaro," she intoned in her shrill voice. "The spirits have spoken and the People have agreed. You are the new chief of the Chihenne who will guide our brave warriors to supreme vengeance and great victories. May Ussen be at your side forever as an example for all the lesser spirits." Abruptly she turned back to the fire and lapsed into a forceful chant.

Slowly Lazaro unlimbered his long legs and got to his feet.

It was time.

He felt the Power surging through his body. It was finally clear and meaningful. There were new things to be done, new strengths to be gained. Always it had been the clans and the smaller bands, even the larger groups like the Willows Chihenne and the Warm Springs Chihenne. There were the Nednhe and the Bedonkohe, the White Mountain and all of the Chiricahua; the Gila, the Jicarilla, the Lipan, and the Mescaleros. And more. All were the People. All were Apache.

Always there had been such independence that even the smallest chief could walk out of the council of the strongest. And always the treaties were like the summer wind—one day the fighting was side by side, the next day against each other. His father, Roberto, had brought about much unity. But even Cuchillo Negro of the Warm Springs paid him only tentative allegiance.

Now it was time for wholeness.

The great Silsoose had given the Chihenne oneness—now it was his descendant's challenge to return it to the People. With unity, the Apache could withstand anything. It was his call, what his Power meant.

He cleared his throat as the hundreds waited. The only other sounds were the soft chanting of the shamans and the crackling of the freshly replenished fire. "My people," he began slowly in his deep voice. "A terrible sign came to us four days ago, but it was as unmistakable as the lightning strike, as the sudden snow upon the mountain in midsummer. We have been losing the Way of the People by trying to live with the way of the Nakai-ye and listening to the White Eyes. . . .

"Now we must start anew. From this moment, our smallest sons will begin training such as none of us has ever known. They will be sniffing the track of the lion at the first light of every day. Our warriors will forget the raiding trail and think only of war." His raised fist drew every eye. "But first, the place of the copper must be emptied of all but the spirits. Every Nakai-ye must pay! Their leaders will hang upside down over our fires! Then we will return to the south, raiding and killing the enemy as never before. No town, no hacienda, no caravan, no *single* Nakai-ye will escape our mighty lance until vengeance is ours!"

Lazaro nodded as the leaders scrambled forward, their eyes shining, their fists raised. Promising young warriors followed. Coletto Amarillio, Delgadito, Nana, Ponce, Cuchillo Negro. Already they had smeared the white paint of the warpath across their faces; their blood was hot and nothing would stop them. But it would take patience. The only leader missing was Bacho.

The vigorously beating drums joined their shouts as the new Chihenne chief, still in his twenty-sixth summer, turned abruptly from their clamor and disappeared into the darkness.

Benita stared up at the monstrous pilasters of stone in wonder. She remembered the priest from her village reciting a story about castles in Spain, and thought these huge pillars could be the battlements. But the Chihenne legend was more descriptive—the columns were the massive fingers of the ogre, Giant. She could just imagine five of them curling out of the floor of the bowl to make a huge fist. A sad smile touched her lips as she watched Taza race around an exceptionally wide spire with two other boys. Except for his shortened hair, one would not know that he had lost a loved one. Five-year-olds seldomed grieved, she thought.

She grieved; at times Nadzeela had been like her big sister. And she grieved terribly for her tragic Lazaro. He had barely spoken to her since that horrible day, but even he could not hide the acute anguish that hung over him like a blanket. Whenever he wasn't talking to others, he seemed to slip into a trance, staring unseeing off into the past. She had watched him cut his hair the morning after the tragedy, wanting to help, but afraid to break into his pain. Instead of snipping off the customary length for mourning, he had continued to chop with his sharp knife until it was little more than an uneven inch long.

He looked so strange.

And she sensed other changes in him. It was as if becoming chief had also aged him considerably—not in appearance, but in his bearing. He was firm, yet quiet in his decisions with the People, and for one so stricken with sorrow, it seemed that he had planned his actions for a long time.

As in moving the People to this strange place of spires. Giant's Claw, he called it, with a special touch of respect as if it were his private retreat. It would be for the summer, and the women were to make caches of dried food in the event they should have to return at times of emergency.

She led the horses to a small knoll across from where the narrow trail opened into the bowl. She had two wickiups to build—the one in which she and Taza would live, and one for Lazaro. She sighed as she hobbled the horses, wishing they needed only one.

* * *

Old Man was now deserving of his name, having passed sixty summers. But he was still active on his one leg, and at last his time had come. His charge had lived up to his promise, and now, as chief, needed him as a close advisor. It was a singular position of pride for him, since Lazaro had announced that Old Man would be in command of the village and of any moves during the chief's absence. In fact, his new status had prompted him to begin whittling a special wooden shaft that he could bind to his stump of a leg so he could have more mobility and ride a little better. He sensed that great things were ahead for the Chihenne under his son—for that was how he regarded Lazaro—and he was eager to be a part of the leadership that would direct them.

Lazaro assumed that the traitorous Brant-son and his White Eyes were already in Mexico, so he wasted no effort in trying to get at them. Pragmatically, he doubted they would ever meet. But the Nakai-ye were at hand. They were partners with the White Eyes; their nantans paid for Apache hair. He put his copper mine plan into effect the day after he became chief, sealing off the three main trails into Santa Rita—the one from El Paso del Norte, the one from Sonora, and the one that led east to the great river.

His people had disappeared like the mist, but they would return like the thunder. It was only a matter of time.

"But the pack train always arrives by the middle of the month," the fat alcalde insisted. "You know that, Don Capitan. It was due three weeks after the . . . the fiesta." He didn't like to talk about the day of the Apache slaughter.

Captain Padilla shrugged. There wasn't anything he could do about a missing pack train. This sniveling civilian seemed to think it was *his* fault, muttering about the Brantson incident like he did. He was more concerned about the courier from Chihuahua who was also overdue—after all, how was he to get his scalps to the government bounty office if that bastard didn't show up? One hundred and seventy-five pesos he would get—over five months' pay! He should have gotten more scalps, but those damned Americanos had been just too quick with their big knives.

"We are low on food, you know."

"Of course I know, you fool!" Padilla snorted. "But the *conducta* will be in for the ore this week, and the problem will be over. Besides, it won't hurt those damned miners to eat less for a while."

The alcalde shook his head—before that terrible day in the bowl, the Apaches had provided fresh meat. Now the only way it could be obtained was to slaughter the stock. And if things got worse . . . how he hated to think of it . . . they would need all the mules and horses to go south. He had queried the mine superintendent, and none of the miners had any hunting experience. And Padilla was afraid to send his soldiers out into the hills—even if they could find any game and shoot it, which he doubted.

And the priest was complaining.

And the mothers, and the whores. To say nothing about his scolding wife. The cantina operators were also whining, for the supply of alcoholic beverages was nearly gone. In fact, he would welcome closing this morbid place and returning to Chihuahua—even if it meant going back to being a lowly clerk. "Maybe there will be no conducta," he said tiredly.

"I don't want to hear you say that again!" Padilla said darkly. But he was merely covering his own doubts.

Over a month had passed since the People moved into Giant's Claw. In that time, Benita had run a dozen plans through her head, examining them, trying the words, acting them out in her imagination. But when it came time to implement one, she lost her courage. So much was at stake—she loved him so much, and any day he might take another woman. Finally, one night after Lazaro returned from a week's absence with his war leaders on the trail, she made up her mind.

It was a night of the three-quarter moon, warm and still in the high bowl. The tall spires stood guard like majestic knights standing a silvery sentry tour, attended only by the highest ponderosa. It had rained late in the day, and the nearby brook ran hurriedly, creating the only noise except for the cry of a solitary baby that was quickly hushed, perhaps by a warm nipple. It was a night for love and she touched her own nipples in anticipation.

He had walked about the village in the early evening, inquiring about health and offering advice on several matters. Later, he stopped by a campfire where a storyteller was holding the attention of several small children with vivid Coyote stories, and finally he talked at length with Old Man. At last Lazaro had gone to his own wickiup. Soon after, she heard the deep breathing of his sleep.

She waited, unsure, finding a dozen reasons to change her mind.

And then she stimulated herself by thinking of the hundreds of times she had fantasized over him in her wickiup in the middle of the night, of how she had imagined his tall, powerful body embracing her, hard against her breasts, and powerful inside her moistness—how she had kissed and kissed his strong, sucking mouth, and wrapped herself around him, lost in his powerful erotic smell. And every time, he had picked her up when they were finished and held her in his strong arms as if she were a melted leaf. And he had said softly, and then loudly for all to hear, "I love you, Benita. *I love you!*"

Her breathing increased with her pulse. Yes, now! She threw off her robe.

Crawling slowly inside his wickiup, she drew up beside him. He was naked, she knew. He always slept that way in the summer. Gently, she touched her lips to his cheek. As he started to stir, she whispered in Spanish, "I'm here, my darling, your little Benita. Let me make love to you and drain the pain from your warm body, my love, my beauty." And her fingers found his penis.

He started, then his hand touched her smooth buttocks, and his other arm drew her to his chest. Her lips hurried to his mouth where she alternated between kisses and bubbling words of love. He was already becoming aroused—*he was hers!*

The huge moon was well below its zenith when she awakened, it was still shedding ample light for her to see Lazaro's still form seated erectly outside the wickiup. She cleared her throat as she went to him, on her knees, searching his face, waiting for his words of love.

At length, he said in a low voice, "I will make you my wife, woman."

She nodded, smiling gently, hiding her disappointment. Where were the words she so craved?

"You are already my son's mother."

She nodded again. His eyes looked so darkly mournful, she wanted to reach out and take his head in her arms and rock him at her breast.

"A chief needs to be married."

He would grow to love her, she knew it!

"I will announce it today."

It was on the sixth day after the forlorn column departed from Santa Rita that Lazaro struck.

The leaders had held out in the mining village until late July—over two months after the massacre—but when none of the scheduled arrivals from Mexico reached the town, Santa Rita's fate was obvious. Twice, early in the month, hunting parties had gone out to find game. But they never returned. Strict food rationing had been in effect for over three weeks. Continuous prayers went unanswered. There was only one solution.

With the last remnants of food carefully guarded, a ragtag train of wagons, carts, and the remaining animals was loaded with bare necessities. Early one morning, men, women, and children trudged into the hot, glaring sun as the procession headed south toward Janos. By the end of the third day, two women and three infants had perished from exposure and malnutrition. Four emaciated horses had been butchered, but they didn't go very far in the pot of nearly two hundred starving and weary people. By the night of the fifth day, there were twenty-four fewer mouths to feed.

It was shortly after four in the afternoon of the sixth day that Captain Padilla led the column into the deep *barranca* where one of his soldiers looked up at the skyline and let out a scream of alert. Silhouetted against the bright sky was a tall figure on a large black horse. In his hand was a lance from which fluttered a single red pennant.

Hurriedly, one of the soldiers fired at the figure, but the horseman sat rigidly still. Word flashed back down the column: *Apaches!* Panic struck as more horsemen began to appear on the ridgeline, and then on the opposite crest overlooking the refugees. More hasty shots were fired. Women screamed. A child was trampled to death under a startled horse. The column bunched up, pressing, mashing together like a giant, wriggling pile of bugs.

And still the horsemen sat unmoving, awaiting a signal from the motionless figure on the black horse.

More shots rang out, and more people were crushed in the roiling, terrorized mass of humanity in the barranca. A riderless horse came galloping out of the dust cloud that was beginning to obscure the terrified Santa Ritans.

And then the leader's arm went up with the red-bannered lance. When it came down, two hundred war cries split the air as the same number of arrows darkened the sky like a sudden raincloud. A volley of musket fire joined the next shower of arrows, and then there were no more soldiers alive or without wounds. The rest went down quickly. In less than five minutes, it was over. When the dust settled, sixteen skinny mules, twelve oxen, and nine horses had survived, and the trail in the barranca was a sweltering, blood-stained pile of corpses and crying wounded.

Throughout, Lazaro sat rock-still on the ridgeline.

There had never been many women or children at Santa Rita. Most of them, thirteen women and twenty-six children survived. They would be sold or bartered throughout Apache Country, or kept and—in the case of the children—taken into the families of the People. All of the men except four died in the onslaught or in the brutal follow-up by Lazaro's white-painted, screaming warriors. They were the alcalde, the mine superintendent, the priest, and Captain Padilla. Bound with rawhide strips they were thrown at the feet of the tall leader.

His eyes narrowed, cold, as he spoke in Spanish first, then in Apache: "I am Lazaro, who rose from the dead at Santa Rita. I sentence you to die by the fire."

At his signal, the protesting, crying prisoners were led to four large posts that stood beside four roaring bonfires. In moments they were tied and suspended upside down over the fires, hanging no more than two feet from the flames. As the fires burned down, their bodies were lowered. Lazaro went to the one in the uniform and stared down into the bulging, blood-red eyes of Captain Padilla, who was choking out unintelligible words. Chihenne vengeance had been exacted to the fullest.

"Enjuh!" he said.

Since the column's half-starved animals would have had a hard time making it back to the Willows Country, they were all butchered for a huge feast. The wagons and other goods that Lazaro's men did not want were hauled into the hills and broken up or burned. All of the Mexican bodies were also pulled high up from the trail. Some were buried, others were hidden in the rocks. The buzzards flying overhead would take care of everything once the Chihenne left the site.

The people of Santa Rita simply vanished.

When they arrived at the Willows, Old Man had completed the move of the village from Giant's Claw. Word quickly spread to all the tribes of the People that a powerful new leader had avenged a terrible wrong by the most well-planned and violent of retributions. It was also said that this new nantan was to conduct a war to equal no other against the Nakai-ye. Within the next six weeks, all of the major chiefs came to meet with Lazaro and to make new treaties.

It was by no means an answer to his dream, but it was a start.

≫ 5 ≪

June 6, 1841

"Carlota!"

Her father's voice echoed across the valley below, breaking the early morning stillness and causing a nearby deer to snap up its head in alarm. Carlota laughed as she jerked back on the reins, forcing the spirited white Arabian to rear and paw the air. The magnificent horse was her wedding gift from Agustin. What a marvelous morning the Heavenly Father had provided for this great day, she thought, wanting to shout like a vaquero and tell the world that all of this splendid, brutal landscape was about to become her royal domain.

Her La Reina—she savored the phrase.

"You ride this recklessly and you may never get to the chapel today," Andres de Cardenas panted as he reined in his big roan.

She shook her head, laughing. "No, I'll be there, Papa. *You* may not make it." She moved her horse closer to the edge of the escarpment. "Just look at those glorious rock formations across the valley—it must have taken a million years for water currents to form them. They seem to have all the warm colors of the rainbow. And what sheer power. Don't you think, Papa, that such an atmosphere will mold your grandsons into powerful young gods?"

Andres nodded, indulging in this moment and thinking of the abrupt change his life would take without her sleeping in a nearby room, eating at his table, waiting for him to come home so she could greet him with a warm hug and a kiss. Silhouetted in the sunlight as she stood up in the stirrups, she seemed to him to glow as if encased in a mist of gold. My God, how he loved her! And already she was talking about the young princes she would bring him from this place. Suddenly, he saw her as a little girl of six, sitting on her first pony and asking him if he wanted to race. He couldn't remember a single moment of her life when she hadn't been the most beautiful creature in the world. *Holy Mother,* he prayed silently, *give her happiness in this new life.* He made the sign of the cross.

Again rearing her horse, Carlota shouted, "I'll race you back!"

His eyes flashed. "For a peso!"
"Of course!"

Carlota enjoyed strolling around the rancho headquarters early in the morning before it swung into operation. The freshness of the clear morning air, cool and somewhat moist before the ever-present sun took over, stimulated her. And the sounds of a country settlement coming alive—the crow of a rooster here and there, the braying of a mule, a dog's bark, even the soft baritone of a vaquero singing as he shaved—played a stirring melody as she moved slowly around the compound.

She smiled at a boy of twelve, moving sleepily toward his chores, and nodded pleasantly at a grinning vaquero carrying his sombrero. Two soldiers, lounging over their first cigars, stopped a saucy-eyed housemaid to flirt with her. The girl's clear laugh rang over the other rancho sounds, and suddenly Carlota wondered if she made love to any of these aggressive young men. Making love had occupied her mind these last few days, or at least it had taken over her fantasy world. Nearly any private thought or contact with Agustin seemed to produce an erotic stirring. Just a few more hours, my darling, she sighed to herself as she passed by more vaqueros coming sleepily out of the bunkhouse.

Going by a corral that held over two dozen fine horses, she called out to her beautiful white wedding gift, but the animal didn't yet recognize her. Now she was at her favorite vantage point for viewing the magnificent greathouse. The huge one-story building had been built thirty years earlier, incorporating like sentries a dozen mature Siberian elm trees that stretched to nearly seventy feet in height. Its many rooms enclosed a courtyard inhabited by exotic plants, while its nearly windowless exterior was fortresslike and gave her a sense of invincibility.

Moments later, she moved on to the small chapel where the ceremony would take place. Like the other buildings, the tiny church was made of adobe walls nearly three feet thick. It had a richly decorated altar, the pride of Agustin's mother, and benches for eight dozen people. Along the wall, ornately carved wooden statues served as stations of the cross. Because of ample donations from Agustin's father, a Franciscan priest managed to be on hand each Sunday, all feast days, and for special occasions—despite the long ride it might entail from Janos or another settlement.

As Carlota savored the peaceful setting of the tiny church, a small boy ran up and gave her a sheepish smile before hurrying inside. In a moment the overhead bell began to peal vigorously, announcing to one and all that the master was to marry on this wonderful day. She smiled again and made the sign of the cross. She should hurry inside and offer her thanks to the Lady of Guadalupe at once—

"Good morning!" Agustin said brightly as he came outside the chapel, blinking into the sunlight and smiling broadly as he nearly ran into her. "How was your ride?"

She stopped, startled. She simply could not get used to how his dark good looks affected her! She suddenly wished she were wearing a rebozo so she could draw it around her face. She wasn't supposed to see him until the ceremony. "Exhilarating," she finally said, breaking their gaze. "But we shouldn't—"

His hand touched hers, gently moving over her fingers. "I love you very much this morning," he said softly. "More than any other, but less than I will tomorrow."

She quickly pulled her hand back, feeling her breast swell. Just the thought of being in his arms at the next sunrise devastated her! She nodded, looking back into his beaming eyes. "I know," she replied, trying to find a calm voice. "I love you more than any decent woman should love anyone, Agustin de Gante. Now get away from me before anyone clucks a tongue."

He grinned, touching his forehead in a salute. "As you command, my princess." And he was gone.

Except for the boy ringing the bell incessantly, the chapel was empty. Moving to the altar, she crossed herself and deftly lit a candle to the Virgin before kneeling and commencing her prayers of thanks for having been brought safely to this wonderful place to marry this magnificent man. And as she prayed, her heart grew even fuller and tears filled her eyes. She promised to curb her willful ways and try gentleness, to treat all of her new subjects with the tenderness she would accord a sparrow with a broken wing.

She promised fervently.

" . . . nor will God be wanting in your needs; He will pledge you in the lifelong support of His graces in the Holy Sacrament which you are now going to receive." The voice of the priest seemed far away, though he stood directly in front of them at the altar.

Radiant sunlight flooded through the narrow windows on the chapel's south side, brightening the festive but quiet congregation. One shaft of light rested directly on the bride and groom, she in the fragile old lace and satin wedding gown her mother had brought from Spain twenty years earlier, he in his blue dragoon uniform with its glowing gold buttons and medals. The gown had graced her grandmother's wedding in the great cathedral in Madrid, and those of three generations of her forebears prior to that. And now, in the custom of the frontier, *el lazo*—a finely woven thin lasso—was draped from her gown to Agustin's broad shoulders.

Carlota's gaze flickered to the altar and then to the niche that held the Holy Virgin in the north *crucero*. The altar table was draped with off-white linens trimmed with Spanish lace, while the polished wood floor at her feet was partially covered by a deep crimson *jerga*. The entire chapel was filled with early summer white roses, including the one behind her left ear. And draped over an extremely high comb, the long mantilla of Chantilly lace reached below her waist.

"Agustin, wilt thou take Carlota, here present, for thy lawful wife, according to the rite of our Holy Mother, the Church?"

Agustin's voice was firm as he smiled softly at her and replied, "I will."

"Carlota, wilt thou take Agustin, here present, for thy lawful husband, according to the rite of our Holy Mother, the Church?"

"I will," she whispered.

She and Agustin dropped to their knees in front of the altar.

"Ego conjungo vos in matrimonium, in nomine Patris et Filii, et Spiritus Santi. Amen." The priest sprinkled them with holy water, then blessed the ring. *"Oremus. Benedic Domine, an-ulum hunc. . . . "*

Her heart was so full. It was nearly perfect, even to the thirteen old Spanish gold doubloons Agustin had given her for the customary *las arras*, the pledge.

Sprinkling the ring with holy water in the form of a cross, the priest handed it to Agustin. It was time. She turned partially to her right and extended her left hand. Placing the thin gold band on her third finger, he said, "With this ring I thee wed, and plight unto thee my troth."

"In nomine Patris et Filii et Spiritus Sancti. Amen."

Carlota blew out a deep breath as the strains of the waltz ended. It was only her second dance with Agustin during the entire reception and she felt excited by his touch and smell. She was flushed and the satin slippers were beginning to pinch her feet, but it didn't matter. Nothing so insignificant mattered, for shortly it would be time for the *entriega*—the moment when those in attendance would release the *novios* to their new life, when she and Agustin would leave the reception and retire to their privacy. When they would finally— She mustn't think about it! And touching him like this was no help. "I must freshen up, my darling," she murmured.

"Yes, this nonsense is about to end for us." His eyes shone. "Soon I will have you in my arms with nothing between us but your perfume."

She felt her cheeks grow warm. *She wanted him so much!*

Minutes later, she stood before the floor-length mirror in the huge master bedroom. Making a repair in the side of the old gown, the aging seamstress asked her to hold her breath. Drawing in her tiny whalebone-enclosed waist, she started to say something cross, but remembered her vow in the chapel. She even found a smile for the young hairdresser who waited her turn.

Her mother sighed as she rose from a nearby chair. "There's nothing more I can do, my dear," Rosa said, heading for the doorway. "I've lost my beautiful daughter to this provincial squire and I might as well get used to it."

"Ha! He's going to be president of Mexico someday!"

Rosa stopped, turning a warm smile. "Don't forget to invite me to Chapultepec. I *love* palaces."

Carlota sobered as her mother departed. That was another of the changes she would have to adjust to—not being with Rosa all the time. They were such good friends. But she could visit and—

"Forgive me, Señora, but please stand on your toes for a moment," the seamstress said quietly around the pins in her mouth.

The hairdresser stood on a chair, quickly removing the lace mantilla and the high comb. As she deftly arranged stray wisps of hair, she said, "You are the most beautiful bride in all of Mexico, Señora."

Carlota nodded. She would have to give the women a gift, something—

Were those shots?

No, impossible.

More sharp explosions, just like the crack of muskets! Were some of the vaqueros already beginning to celebrate? The soldiers? She frowned. Indeed! Wedding reception or no wedding reception, they had no business firing their weapons. Agustin was too lax!

There were more shots, combined with wild yells. Could someone important have arrived? No, all the honored guests were already present. "Go see what is happening," she told the seamstress in a sharp tone.

She heard a horse scream.

The seamstress's hand flew to her mouth, stifling a shriek of fear. *"Apaches!"* she cried out from the window, her dark eyes wide.

Impossible! Carlota snapped to herself as she started for the window, but a loud grunt from the doorway stopped her. Coming toward her, brandishing a musket, was a squat, menacing Apache with white slashes of paint across his cheeks!

Her hand flew to her mouth as the hairdresser screamed. Watching in horror, she saw the barrel of the Apache's rifle catch the woman flush in the mouth. The next swing of the weapon knocked the shrieking seamstress senseless. Instinctively, Carlota bent quickly to the floor, grabbing a large pair of scissors. But before she could stab the intruder, his fist crashed into the side of her head. White lights exploded. She saw herself falling, saw the leer on the Apache's ugly face, heard more screams and a barrage of gunfire. And suddenly it was silent. She was asleep but awake. Faces danced before her, her father with wild eyes and blood streaming from his forehead, a priest clutching his scarlet breast, wide-eyed children running, screaming. Shouting Apaches with their terrifying war whoops . . .

What a terrible nightmare!

And it continued. Dead vaqueros. Flames licking at imported Chantilly Lace curtains, women shrieking, more animal-like shouts from the long-haired painted attackers on their rearing horses. Knives flashing in the too-bright sunlight and swirling dust, dogs barking, more gunfire.

And then utter silence.

Lazaro wasn't sure what urged him to go into the hacienda's building area during the height of the raid, but it was sudden and compelling. Normally he stayed apart from the actual fighting during a raid, remaining in a position to control the action. But once there, he had excellent opportunities to try out his White Eye shooter, the new gun called a re-volv-er. Riding into the center of the conflict on his big black horse, he fired the five-shot pistol well—hitting two soldiers and one vaquero before he had to reload. After two more shots, a tall officer in a bright uniform came at him with a flashing sword. He shot him between the eyes.

He jerked his head around as Placero, one of his ablest young warriors, shouted to him from the front of the large house. Swinging his mount around, he rode close enough to see a young woman in white being held by the hair by Placero. "I found a White Eye!" the warrior yelled.

Lazaro nodded and was about to turn his attention elsewhere when the woman opened her eyes and stared at him. *Nadzeela!* He blinked, disbelieving. Yes, it *was* his Nadzeela! "Woman—" he shouted before he realized with a jolt that this white-skinned one could not be her. He stared, swinging his horse around. *It was unbelievable!* And then a picture of a girl with eyes the color of the summer sky came back to him, a tall girl on a small hill outside of Santa Rita on the most terrible day of his life. A girl with the whitest of skin. And the sight of the killing in the grassy bowl returned, a picture he had tried to blot out for all these moons. His beautiful Nadzeela, her smooth breast slashed open and pouring blood . . .

The white one continued to stare up at him.

"Bring her!" he shouted, whirling to shoot a vaquero who was coming at him with a musket. Shortly he was outside the compound, waiting on a low hill, trying to control himself. The raid now meant nothing. All that mattered was *her!* It was the most excitement he had felt in years.

The violent dream continued for Carlota. She saw herself kneeling at the altar of the tiny chapel, her beloved Agustin beside her, resplendent in his uniform, her mother and father beaming . . . but no, there was no music, and no priest, no Agustin . . . she was bouncing, draped over the hindquarters of a horse, her face slapping his sweaty coat. The brilliant sunlight made her dizzy, hurt her eyes. Her head shrieked with pain as the dust caught in her throat. And the thong cut into her wrists. There were other horses, Apaches' legs, voices.

They stopped. She thought she would retch, but strong hands jerked her to the ground and held her steady. Through the hair streaming over her face, she looked up to the tallest Indian she had ever seen. He was sitting above her on his dark horse on a knoll ten feet away. He was Apache, and there was something about him—

The one who had struck her in the bedroom thrust her forward, speaking in their strange language. Her hands caught at the lace of her torn wedding gown as she stared upward into the stern expression of the tall Apache. His dark eyes bored into her with steady intensity, holding her. Her breath caught. And then his eyes seemed to soften and show a fleeting glimpse of compassion, of tenderness. And slowly he nodded to her before turning away.

He reminded her of someone—who? A dream? *No, a quiet early morning, the Kneeling Nun! He was the same Indian—*

She was given a rude order and jerked toward her horse. Tearing away the lower part of the wedding dress, they thrust her atop the animal and lashed her to the saddle. She looked around frantically as the Apache column pulled out of its position a half mile north of the main ranch buildings. Smoke was rising from the greathouse, but she could see no flame. Choking dust hung over everything. She wanted to jam her heels into the horse's flanks and somehow steer it back to her loved ones, but the Apache on the horse ahead held its reins.

Except for the piercing headache, she felt numb. How could this terrible thing be happening? Where were the soldiers? How could these horrible Apaches just ride in and do what they wanted? With a sharp pain in her breast she thought of her mother—*what had happened to everyone?* She heard the Apaches always raped and murdered. Was her beautiful mother— Oh, *My God!* Her brave father— surely he would have fought back! *Agustin!* Were was Agustin? He must have been wounded, yes, that was it—stunned by a blow right at the beginning, unable to stop it, staggering, trying to save her, save everyone. She could see him now, shaking his head, a trickle of blood from a minor wound on his cheek.

Suddenly she realized she had seen no other prisoners. Not one. And for the first time, fear gripped her—rigidly, sapping her strength and making her nauseous. She stared ahead, trying to stop her shaking hands, stifling the scream of utter terror that wanted to burst from her lips. Closing her eyes, she somehow contained it until the panic passed.

Settling into the rhythm of the trotting pace, she concentrated on the top of the bay horse's head. She wanted to cry, but there were no tears. Only a feeling of terrible loss, which slowly turned to anger. *They had stolen her wedding!*

Slowly the rage began to ebb and she instinctively thought of survival. She had to somehow keep her head. Surely *some* way to escape would present itself. Then she'd rush back to La Reina and find everyone patching up their scratches and cleaning up the mess. They would cry with joy at her safe return and continue the wedding celebration. Certainly! Or her father and Agustin would overtake them with a huge patrol of soldiers and vaqueros and rescue her. Yes, and kill every one of these hideous Apaches!

Why weren't there any other prisoners?

She glanced at the soiled and torn part of her wedding dress that remained above her bare knee, and the tears finally welled up in her eyes and streamed down her dirty cheeks. This magnificent gown, this work of art and link to her grandmothers in Spain . . . it could never be replaced. They had ruined her beautiful wedding. *It wasn't fair!* she sobbed inwardly, they were *animals* and they had no concept of *anything* civilized. They had no more place on this earth than *vipers*, than— She sobbed loudly, then jerked herself erect as the Apache leading her horse turned and looked at her as if she had done something terribly wrong. Shaking her head, she tried to see through the moisture and hair in her eyes.

They stopped in a box canyon and rested late in the afternoon when the sun was still boiling down. The brave who had led Carlota's horse handed her a skin bag of water. At first she wanted to throw it at him, but her better sense and demanding thirst prevailed. When she finished drinking, he untied her bonds and gestured for her to get down and exercise her legs. Disdainfully, he handed her several kernels of corn from his pouch. But she knocked his hand away. *She wouldn't eat in such a heathen manner!*

The brave looked down at the kernels in the dirt and turned back to her with an angry growl. He drew his fist back to strike her, but at the same time Lazaro approached. His knowing eyes quickly glanced at the ground and back to his angry warrior. "No," he said softly. His eyes locked on Carlota's but only for a moment before he walked away.

Soon they were back on the trail north, following an invisible route that provided both cover and water as the war party continued to move briskly. At dusk, the column turned into yet another canyon that led upward and provided walls from which a handful of defenders could hold off any kind of pursuing force.

Carlota could never remember being so totally exhausted. And she was ravenous, but she knew her rashness over the corn kernels could mean the end of receiving any kind of food. She tried to occupy her mind by combing her snarled hair with her fingers. The gown was virtually destroyed, now torn all the way to her hips. Her upper thighs were exposed to the greedy eyes of the warriors, but she had too many real problems to let that worry her.

At last light, she looked up from where she sat by a large mesquite shrub to see the tall leader watching her from several feet away. The brave who had taken her from the bedroom nodded as the leader spoke, then came to her and held out some hard grass seed bread. It looked like a feast to her, but she reached for it slowly, holding the warrior's amused gaze through slitted eyes. And then she nibbled slowly, using all her will not to cram the tasteless hardtack into her mouth and gulp it all down at once. When she finished, the warrior said, "Come," in Spanish and led her to a deserted place by the running stream that was guarded by bushes. In moments, she was splashing refreshing water over her face and hands.

Minutes later, walking back to her mesquite bush, she tried to get some information from her captor. "Where are we going?" she asked. But he ignored her. When she asked him the chief's name, he looked at her strangely, then threw his head back and laughed loudly. Then he tied her to the mesquite bush. She was in for a long, uncomfortable night on the hard ground.

The sun burned her badly on the second day, but she ignored it as she continued to glance over her shoulder for the inevitable pursuit that would be indicated by a telltale cloud of dust. A body of heavily armed dragoons would make up such a column—one led by her angry husband and her relentless father. She knew they wouldn't sleep until they rescued her.

They would come.

By that night her faith had begun to weaken, but she replaced it with scorn and began planning ways of escape. Her anger was never far from the surface, but she managed to control it and ignore her captors in spite of her condition. Her lips were now cracked and blistered from the sun, and most of her exposed skin was badly burned. Before collapsing in sleep, she managed to make some mud at the edge of a narrow stream and smear it all over her body. She didn't even care about bathing; she didn't care much about anything except getting even.

And escaping.

On the third day, she occupied her mind by dreaming of different ways to do both. In her fantasies, she shot her captors, and especially that monstrous leader, in different parts of their bodies. The one she liked most was right between the eyes, blowing away their grotesque painted faces. By that afternoon she was reeling in the saddle, dizzy and ill from the merciless rays of the desert sun. It seemed there was a fuzzy, ultrabright halo encircling her face, a brilliance that distorted everything coming into her swaying vision.

Twice Lazaro rode back to look at her closely, but he never made a sound and each time rode away expressionless. And twice she remembered the brave in front turning around to give her a queer look when she caught herself laughing. She couldn't understand what made her laugh, but she knew it had to be something ridiculous. Maybe it was the fact that these ugly heathens were no longer leering at her lily-white thighs that were mud-caked and filthy where they weren't bright crimson from the damned sun.

Another day in its murderous rays and she wouldn't be appealing to a vulture. God! she thought, how terrible she would look when Agustin and the soldiers caught up and rescued her. *What would she do, cover her face?* The new Señora de Gante with her face covered? . . .

She threw back her head and roared with laughter.

They didn't stop at dusk, but continued the hurried pace into some hills when the last trace of daylight was gone and the moon slipped over the eastern horizon. It was then that she developed a sudden sense of clarity. Shapes of trees, of rocks, even the horse and rider in front of her, seemed to dance with sharp lines of definition. And she felt a wild elation—a silly, uncaring euphoria that lasted for only a few minutes. For then, just as suddenly, she slumped forward and dozed. When she awakened, the horse was still and the brave was slapping her raw bare thigh and grunting something insistent in Apache. He loosened her bindings and she slipped to the ground, her legs rubbery, her ears pounding.

And then she collapsed.

Opening her eyes, Carlota knew she was in some kind of room, a round room with a tiny fire in the middle and a hole in the ceiling that let in some moonlight. She could make out the brown features of a woman dressed in Indian clothes, a woman who reminded her of her hairdresser sitting cross-legged four feet away by the fire. Was it another of her strange dreams? The woman nodded as she leaned forward, saying in normal Spanish, "Good, I'm glad you are awake. My name is Benita. What is yours?" There was nothing warm in her expression.

Carlota continued to stare, finally moving her cracked lips to reply.

Benita nodded, turning to the fire to ladle warm broth into an earthen bowl. "Sip this," she said. "And tell me about yourself."

The broth had a pungent taste, but it awakened her hunger. She spoke awkwardly. "Where am I?"

"In the main village of the Chihenne, near the copper mines."

The words sounded familiar, bringing back visions of a journey with her parents, with Agustin. A dirty little village, her Kneeling Nun rocks. "Are you . . . Apache?" she asked.

"No, I am from Chihuahua. I am the wife of Lazaro, the great chief."

Carlota shook her head, the woman had to be lying. A woman like this couldn't be proud of being married to a savage. Surely—

"I have been here a long time."

Carlota drank the last of the broth. "What will happen to me?" she asked softly.

Benita's face was rocklike as she replied, "You, too, will become the wife of Lazaro."

Carlota blinked at the bright moistness of the Chihenne village as she stepped outside the wickiup the next morning. Rising on both sides of the valley were high silent hills, while a hundred yards down the slope a running stream was marked by a long strand of green willows. Wickiups, perhaps sixty of them, dotted the wide hillside, joining the tall aspens in a haphazard arrangement. She noticed that all faced to the east, as if in some ritualistic manner. And here and there a wispy fire in front of one of the huts announced that its occupants were ready to commence the morning labors. A tethered brown and white pony looked up at her in momentary curiosity. And except for the barking of a solitary dog not far downstream, an ethereal silence blanketed the area.

It was gently peaceful, she thought, but with a rush of returning anger she rejected the idea. How could these murderous savages even understand peace? And then Benita's words came back, *"You, too, will become the wife of Lazaro."* Even remembering made her shudder.

She was Señora de Gante!

Oh, Mother of God, she silently cried. Oh, where is my beloved Agustin? Where is my husband? Holy Mother, please bring him to me soon, please, Holy Mother. The anger drained away completely as she dropped to her knees and broke into tears. She could see Agustin lying in bed with his hateful little mother bending over him, tending to his blood-soaked wounds. Was that a priest, that dark figure standing in shadow near the foot of the bed? "Ooohhh!" The moan tore loose from the pit of the deepest anguish she had ever known.

She looked up to see a small boy of perhaps seven staring at her. And a man with a peg leg watched her with disdain from a few feet away. Her wet cheeks suddenly burned. How wretched to be such a spectacle! She got quickly to her feet. Her mother would be so embarrassed if she were to see her daughter like this. Her mother. More tears streamed down her cheeks. Closing her eyes, she prayed, "Oh, Lord Jesus, heal her if she has been hurt."

The sight of Benita approaching forced her to regain her control. Benita had given her a change of clothing to replace the tattered remnants of her ill-fated wedding dress. Clad in old knee-high moccasins, a worn buckskin skirt and frayed blue cotton blouse, she walked stiffly behind the Mexican woman toward the stream. The Apaches who were stirring at this early hour, mostly curious women and running children, stared at her openly. She was much taller than most of them, and she felt even more like a freak in the hideous green ointment Benita had given her to apply to her scorched skin. Reaching the water, she wanted to quickly undress and plunge in, but she was not about to show her bare body to these heathens. She asked Benita if there was a place of privacy, but the woman just glared at her.

She had to keep up this anger, maintain her superiority—otherwise she would break down and cry and she would be lost. She *had* to be strong . . . but logical.

She glanced at Benita as she washed her sore arms. "How were you captured?" she asked.

Benita looked up from where she was splashing cold water on her naked body. "I don't consider it as capture," she replied coolly. "I was saved."

"What do you mean—"

"Those warriors brought me to a life and a man I love every waking moment. Here, I have a position of honor."

Carlota stared at her. "You, a civilized Mexican woman, you call living here with these savages *honor?*"

Benita's voice was harsh. "The People in many ways are more civilized than you." It was the end of the conversation.

Following a breakfast of a hot corn tortilla, Carlota fell into a deep sleep in the wickiup. When she awakened two hours later, she jerked upright at the sight of the tall leader staring at her from his sitting position a few feet away. "I am Lazaro," he said quietly in surprisingly good Spanish.

Her hand flew to her mouth. She wanted to throw herself at him and tear his eyes out, but she caught her breath and managed to glare back.

"You will be my wife," he said gently.

"No! Never! I'm already married! You saw the—"

"You are not married to an *Apache.* You will be my wife soon."

Carlota shuddered with repugnance. Feeling suddenly nauseous, she had to steel herself from breaking down. But it was no use. With a shiver, she dropped her face into her hands and sobbed uncontrollably. It was all so outrageously impossible!

"Enjuh!"

She looked up, startled at the sight of a wrinkled old woman with a hideous scar running diagonally across her face. She was wearing a strange hat of small animal heads that looked like rats as she leaned through the entrance. Her eyes were bright and she seemed pleased at what she saw. "Enjuh!" she said again with a grin that revealed her black teeth. When she withdrew, Carlota immediately sensed it was her own discomfort that seemed to gratify the old woman. Again she shivered. The old hag! she cursed to herself as she wiped away the tears.

"I see Tze-go-juni has inspected you," Benita commented as she entered.

"Who?"

"Tze-go-juni, the medicine woman."

"Holy Mother! She looks like a witch!"

"There are those who think she is, and she has the Power."

Carlota knew of the Indian belief in special powers from the Pueblos at Santa Fe. "What does she want with me?" she asked quietly.

Benita shrugged. "Who knows? Only one thing is certain—it won't be pleasant."

As Benita watched Carlota stare vacantly at the floor and fight back more tears, she felt sorry for her—but only momentarily. This too-pretty Spanish *lady*, this pale girl—this overbearing, spoiled intruder, was taking her Lazaro from her. She knew, she had watched his eyes when he told her about the marriage. And she knew why—any fool could see Nadzeela in this white girl's face, and in her tall figure. Even she had been startled when she first saw her. But this was not the noble Apache Nadzeela. This was her enemy.

The boy, Taza, scared Carlota. The first time she saw him, he stared at her so hard she thought something was wrong with him. And now, as he gathered brush for the new wickiup, he continued to look at her openly. She finally ignored him, telling herself the boy had the same impudence as his father. Benita and another woman were busy building the new wickiup some thirty yards back in the edge of the tall pines. "If you don't know how to prepare food and care for yourself, your highness," Benita warned, "you'd better learn quickly, because I'll not be your handmaiden."

Lazaro stopped by in the early afternoon to observe the construction and add to Carlota's discomfort by watching her in that disconcerting manner of his. Holy Mother, why did he always look at her like that? After Agustin kills him, she'd have those bold eyes torn right out of his head!

The thought of her husband brought tears to her eyes, but she fought them back. She knew now that *something* had happened to him, but she also knew it was only a wound, some kind of a minor wound that kept him from riding, from joining her father in the rescue. No, something had to have happened to her father, she was sure of it now—but she just couldn't think about it. No—everyone was all right! They would come for her soon, she knew it.

She shifted her attention back to Lazaro. She had heard of his terror, his raids, the murders, rapes. But she hadn't seen any raping. She shouldn't think about such a thing. He was naked to the waist except for a necklace of turquoise beads and another with a charm of sorts. Like all Apache men, he wore a breechcloth over his trousers. The buckskin moccasins reached to his high knees. And though his torso was not muscular, she knew it had to be powerful. She turned her eyes away. A half-naked savage was her captor and tormentor and it was coarse of her to even look at him.

She felt her pulse quicken as he moved toward her.

"They make a big wickiup for you," he said softly. "You will like it."

She glared at him, refusing to speak.

"You'll laugh there. We will have much love."

"No!" she cried out. She would never laugh again. "The only love I have is for my *real* husband, and it isn't inside some brush hovel! Can't you understand that, you stupid beast?"

A brief expression of pain crossed his eyes. He nodded, then turned and walked away. And again she felt belittled.

Carlota was startled the next morning to find herself alone in Benita's wickiup with the sun already well up and and the women of the village busy at their labors. Again she thought about rescue—she couldn't accept the fact that it wouldn't happen. Surely a day and a half was ample time for even the slowest of columns to catch up. Her father and Agustin wouldn't let them tarry—

No, she couldn't think about it anymore!

She was Carlota de Gante and she would just have to fend for herself, that was all there was to it. Survive and escape, that's what she would do. And if, in some way, they came after her—then that would be fine. But it was her against the Apaches, and she would show them! She brushed away a single tear as she walked to the stream.

She had nearly finished washing when a shadow fell over her. Looking up, she was repelled by the black-toothed grin of Tze-go-juni. "What do you want, crazy woman?" she asked angrily.

The medicine woman shook her head, then laughed out loud—a piercing cackle that caused the other women to turn their heads. "You are not worthy of him," she said in Apache, raising a charm made of a dog's eye and shaking it toward Carlota. And in guttural Spanish, she added, "Lazaro no want dead woman."

Carlota looked at her sharply. "Go away, hag!" she shouted. "Go scare your heathen and leave me alone!" But she felt a stab of fear.

When she returned to the huts, Benita announced, "Your wickiup is ready. It is furnished with cooking ware, blankets, and new clothes, including your new wedding dress. Come, I'll show you how to light a fire."

Carlota started to protest, but shrugged and followed the other Mexican woman.

For her evening meal, she picked at some of the dried venison and fruit of the *nopal*, the prickly pear. When she finished, she decided to go for a walk outside the village to see what would happen. Climbing the grassy slope to the tall pines of a nearby ridge, she stopped to look back in the fading light. Escape would be ever so easy! Why, she could—

The small figure stopped moving. Some twenty yards away, little Taza stood staring at her. And she knew—*she had a seven-year-old guard!* She wanted to laugh, but the grim expression on his young face stopped her. And then she remembered what Benita had said about the boys learning how to track and hunt as soon as they could walk. She nodded to him as she headed abruptly down the slope. He stepped aside, waiting until she was several yards away before following. Shaking her head, she thought about the glance they had exchanged. It told her one thing—this warrior child, this proud son of a chief, would take his assignment as seriously as any grown man in the tribe. And she shivered.

Arriving at her wickiup, she was startled by a noise and the movement of a large animal. Tied to a tree fifteen feet away, was the black horse Lazaro had ridden on the raid!

"It is the custom," Benita said caustically, stepping from a shadow. "Normally, a man leaves his horse at the house of a girl he wishes to marry as an offering. If the prospective bride decides to accept the suitor, she feeds and waters the animal, then returns it to the wickiup of the future husband. It is the Way."

Carlota's eyes flashed darkly. "Ha! As much as I love horses, I'd kill him before I'd do that! How many times do I have to tell you I am *already* married? When is this madness going to end? Answer me, Benita—you know I was married in a formal wedding mass before God! Surely, you haven't forgotten what that means, have you?"

Benita shook her head. "I know only the Apache way now. He's merely being polite and affording you the honor."

"Honor indeed!"

As Benita turned away in the darkness, Carlota moved closer to the handsome animal, stroking its soft nose. She wondered where he'd stolen it. And now the madman was being terribly unfair to the creature—making him go without water while he forced himself on a woman who hated him!

Quickly, she untied the horse's tether and slapped him on the rump.

"Woman!"

Carlota was awakened by the insistent shout from Benita shortly after first light the next morning. She stuck her head outside to see a stern looking Lazaro standing beside his Mexican wife. "Where is the horse?" Benita asked sharply.

Carlota thrust out her jaw as she glared defiantly at Lazaro. "I turned him loose. He had nothing to do with me. I am the wife of Don Agustin de Gante and no ridiculous Apache foolishness will change that!"

The tall leader glared back for a moment, then turned and walked heavily away.

"That was stupid, woman," Benita snapped. "That horse is much prized by him and could have been lost."

"I didn't ask for the animal to be tied there."

"You have no choice in the matter."

Carlota placed her hands on her hips, glaring down at the woman. "I will *always* have the choice. Now go away and tell your great savage that I'll die before I'll be his mate!"

Benita moved closer, the dislike raw in her angry dark eyes. "Listen closely, you spoiled bitch. Before you came, *I* was the only woman and wife of Chief Lazaro. He may not have loved me with fire, but

I kept him happy on the blanket. And now you come along and stir his blood and make him blind. And the women are laughing that you are stealing him away. I hate you and your haughty manner, but my lord has charged me with teaching you our ways and watching over you." Benita's eyes narrowed as she suddenly drew her forefinger across her throat in an obvious gesture. "Otherwise, I would kill you in an instant!"

Carlota's eyes widened.

"The marriage feast will take place in three days."

No! Carlota turned away only to see Tze-go-juni scowling at her from a few feet away. She raised her right hand, holding it out toward Carlota; a dead snake dangled from it. Following some gibberish Carlota didn't understand, she spoke angrily in Apache, then in Spanish. "You no come back. Big birds eat you." She came closer. "You go away die!" The snake came closer, its dark skin hideous to Carlota. With a sharp cry she spun around, dropping her face into her hands.

"You go away die," the shaman repeated, then strode away with her snake.

Turning back to the watching Benita, Carlota asked softly, "What does she mean?"

"She thinks you are bad for the People. She wants you dead."

Lazaro stared into the dying fire. It was late, and except for the boys walking guard, no one else in the village was stirring except Old Man, who sat across from him smoking a cigarette of real tobacco taken from the de Gante hacienda. Old Man had already spoken against the marriage, now he dropped into his storytelling voice. "You know about Coyote, my son. Since you were old enough to listen, you have been learning from Coyote's mistakes. It is the Way." He inhaled from the shortening cigarette. "I want to remind you of when Coyote married his daughter."

Lazaro nodded. He knew the story, but it would be impolite not to listen.

Old Man began, "When the earth was made, at the very beginning of time, there were just animals. They spoke like human beings." He shook his head. "You know Coyote. He always did wrong, he did wrong everywhere on the surface of the earth.

"He had desires toward his daughter. 'When worms have fallen, you will go,' he said to his children. 'You will give the oldest girl to the first person you meet,' he said.

"Then, the worms having fallen, the children started out. They were going along some distance off. The smallest child looked back. 'My father has jumped down,' he said.

" 'My little one, do not speak so. We have long ago left him.'

"But the father had jumped down. From there, in a roundabout way, he came to meet them where they were going along over yonder. And they did not know him.

" 'What did your father say to you?' said Coyote.

" 'Give the oldest girl to the very first person you meet,' he said to us.

"Then he married his oldest daughter. He did not go away, and she did not know he was her father.

"Then she was searching for lice on him. A wart lay on the side of his head. His wife who was his daughter found a wart on the side of his head while she was looking for lice on him.

"Then the girl went back to her mother. And she spoke thus to her mother, 'When I am searching for lice on him, I will move my hand about the side of his head where there is a wart.'

"Then her mother spoke thus to the girl, 'You will search for lice on him again. Put him to sleep quietly. A wart was on the side of your father's head.'

"Then the girl put her husband to sleep. And she saw the wart on him while he was sleeping. Then she pushed his head away. 'It is indeed him! It is indeed him!' the girl cried. 'My mother, it is indeed him!'

"She picked up a small axe. Then she ran toward him with it. And he ran away from her."

Old Man relit the bare remains of his cigarette.

After several moments, Lazaro said, "She is not my daughter."

"She is bad for you. Poison, like the worst arrow. She has Power, a medicine so strong the woman shaman fears her."

Lazaro laughed. "Tze-go-juni is afraid of no one."

"It is not to make fun, my son. Send her away, sell her, give her to your Apache brother, Cochise—but do not take her as a wife."

Lazaro replied softly. "My heart was once torn from my chest, Old Man. Now it is healed and it's new like a fresh bud in the spring. It soars like the eagle and sings like the warbler. She is my path, my father, I cannot change the direction."

Old Man nodded into the fire. He had spoken.

≫ 6 ≪

*Ussen, one day lonely
in his Sky,
Smiled upon his People
and chose
Mother Earth to be his Bride*

The drums began to beat shortly after daybreak, announcing the marriage feast of the Chihenne chief, Lazaro. While it was a day of zestful celebration for most, it was one of dispute for others. Several chiefs and war leaders came to pay tribute to the leader and drink to his happiness, but others like Cuchillo Negro refused. Many of the People were displeased that Lazaro would make yet another Mexican woman his wife, instead of keeping her as a servant. But all who came were ready to gorge themselves on the huge amounts of food and drink the chief's tiswin as long as it lasted.

It was another bright, clear day, promising more uncomfortable heat, even at this high elevation. Dogs barked louder than usual, excited by the noisy laughter of children as they dashed around, infected with the spirit of the holiday. The women, too, were buoyant, dressed in their finest doeskins or now and then a brightly colored dress that dated back to the mining days of Santa Rita. They would drink their share of the tiswin.

Carlota was ready when Benita came for her at noon. She had first thought she would refuse to wear the Apache finery and go disheveled to make a sham of the whole sordid affair, but such a thing would have been degrading and would not have befitted her plan. The off-white, richly beaded and fringed doeskin dress matched the bright moccasins and fit her quite well. She refused to wear any of the jewelry and she fixed her hair in one long braid on the side—fully contrary to the Apache custom. She had also vehemently refused to have her eyebrows plucked or to have crimson paint applied to her cheeks.

Benita explained the simple ritual. "You are to bow your head to Lazaro and sit directly behind him in the circle of men. And you will remain silent as they resume their discussion, smoke their tobacco, and drink."

Carlota didn't reply. She'd bow her head to no one and speak to whomever she pleased.

Sitting behind Lazaro as the hot afternoon wore on, she held herself erect and expressionless, refusing food or drink. Around the circle, dark, stern faces of the leaders stared at her over tiswin cups, strange hostile faces etched with deep lines from thousands of days of sun-frowning. Some of the faces were cruel, others with wide slack mouths were openly lustful, but mostly they ignored her as if she were a sack of socorro Lazaro had stolen.

The chant of dancers, the incessant drum beat . . .

Outside the ring of men, in a shimmering maze of heat and color, were the faces of the women—curious, sometimes mocking or hostile faces that stared, whispered, or now and then laughed rudely. A few even pointed as they openly talked about her. Many of them became even more forward as they drank more tiswin. It was obvious they disliked her as much as she despised them.

But none of it mattered. All of that had been on her mind since realizing there was no escape from the Willows or from the incredible physical encounter that lay ahead. She had her plan, but she was uncertain that it would work. The thought of copulation with this savage had plagued her, keeping her awake and dominating her dreams. Always she shuddered with revulsion, but once she awakened with a horribly erotic feeling like she had known before her wedding. How frightening! She was the lawful and spiritual wife of Agustin de Gante, and her body and all of its passions belonged wholly to him!

Those terrible drums, beat, beat, beating . . .

They departed an hour before sunset. Lazaro was cheerful, excited, showing no effect from the tiswin he had sipped throughout the festivities. He led the way on his favorite black horse. Carlota followed silently, into the slanting rays of the reddening sun on the brown and white mare he had given her. They rode through the cooling hills until only a faint amount of light remained, stopping by a grove of tall ponderosa pine that contained a single sheltered wickiup of recent construction. Dismounting, Lazaro spoke quietly, "We sleep here."

She climbed down from the little mare, feeling her heart begin to beat faster. It was beginning. Even the darkness and slight noises of the woods were suddenly ominous, the tall trees forbidding.

He quickly unpacked the large roll of supplies and built a small fire just outside the wickiup. He nodded meaningfully toward the food. Silently, she placed strips of fresh raw venison on the fire and opened the mescal. There was also a container of rare honey to celebrate the occasion. Even the bread was fresh and made from wheat flour that had been taken on some raid. She frowned, wondering if it could have come from La Reina.

Later by the firelight, he watched her as he ate. She refused to join him, sitting still and staring into the fire, trying to find some thread of new hope, of confidence—any miraculous means of a last ditch reprieve. His deep voice filled the stillness as he spoke to her of the mountains, slowly at first, in gentle tones and words of love. He told her of the friendly spirits that resided in the mountains, and how they protected the Apache. He spoke with a soft reverence of the worshipped White Painted Woman and Child of the Water.

But she barely heard, thinking only of the coming ordeal on the floor of that dreaded wickiup. She could sense the tension and lust mounting in him—it wouldn't be long now. But it wouldn't do him any good, not a bit. No matter what. Her eyes dropped to his knife lying by the fire. Maybe she could kill him and ride away to the south.

She continued to eye the knife, but her resolve melted. She didn't even know where she was, let alone how to get anywhere safe. Where would she find water? No, she knew she didn't have a chance—she would never survive. And survival was her only thread of sanity. Besides, he had fought and slain too many to let a woman kill him.

He was watching her with those haunting eyes. Could he know what she was thinking? No, he wouldn't die easily; no, it wasn't the answer.

He was leaning toward her.

In the flickering firelight his strong features looked as if they were hewn from rock. Except for the eyes. He reached slowly for her hand, but she pulled back, eyes wide. "No!" she cried out. "No . . . you have other women. Not me. I couldn't because I am married." The words tumbled out. "I'm cold, you won't— It would be terrible. I, I'd be sick. You see, God—your Ussen—He doesn't approve. I'm not—" The words trailed off.

He moved closer. She could smell the tobacco, feel his shortened breath as his fingers closed over her wrist. "You are my wife," he said huskily. "I have looked on you so much, even in my dreams, and always my heart beats harder when I think of you, my precious pale-eyed fawn. A look from you is like the water, silvery over the fall of the mountain in the sunlight. I—"

"No," she begged, shaking her head. It was suddenly so hot in the high mountain air, suffocating.

"Come to my blanket," he said softly, drawing her close as he got to his feet. "It is time."

She turned her face, fighting the tears, but it was no use—they tumbled down her cheeks and she was afraid she'd sob. *What had he said about White Painted Woman?* "Hail Mary, full of grace," she began fervently. "The Lord is with thee—"

"Come, my fawn, my light." He drew her closer.

"Blessed art thou amongst women and blessed is the fruit of thy womb, Jesus."

He reached for the fasteners on her dress.

"Holy Mary, Mother of God, pray for us sinners now and at the hour of our death. Amen." With a sudden lunge she broke his embrace and burst away from the fire and into the nearby brush. Branches slapped at her face and she stumbled, but she caught herself, dodging a large pine tree before tripping and rolling heavily down a steep bank and banging into a boulder at the bottom. She lay still, panting, her lungs burning—trying to be quiet, listening fearfully, her ears pounding, afraid to open her eyes.

She heard nothing.

Light from the early rising moon kept the gulch into which she had stumbled from being totally dark. Moving slowly around to the back of the boulder, she found room to wedge her body into the deep shadow. It would do, he could never find her here. Suddenly with a start she thought of the animals of the ground, and sucked in her breath. Benita had told her the reason Apaches seldom fought or ventured out at night was their fear of snakes. Snakes were normally night creatures, that was what Benita had said, they slithered around at night. And in dark cool places. *No!*

She jumped to her feet and spun away from the boulder. Looking frantically up the hill, she wondered if he had heard. She stood stock still, not breathing. It was so silent. Maybe he had given up, finally realized it was— "*Ayeeh!*" she screamed as Lazaro encircled her arm with his huge hand.

She kicked and flailed fruitlessly as he carried her up the slope. His strength was amazing, his chest as hard as a rock and his arms like leather. He murmured to her in Apache as she struggled and shouted at him. Shortly they were back at the fire, where he placed her on the ground. Pointing to her heaving breast, he said, "Your clothes," and began to undress.

She stood there frozen, knowing it had come down to the final moment of truth; there were no more boulders left. Drawing herself up, she summoned as firm a voice as she could muster. "No," she said coldly. "By the Holy Church, I am not your wife."

His red shirt was off and he was undoing his trousers.

"I do not belong to you!"

Without a word, he leaned down and picked up a thick bough of wood. Holding it before her face, he snapped it in two pieces as if it had been a twig. "Your clothes," he said firmly. "The dress is too pretty to tear."

She stared into the excitement in his eyes and knew she had only one choice. She could fight him with every ounce of her strength until she was unconscious and then he would take her. And he would win and she would lose. And whenever he wanted her in the future, it would be the same. So she had just one choice, only one way of holding the upper hand and winning out. There was no, absolutely no, alternative. That was her plan, her last resort.

She stifled a shudder; she *must* maintain control.

"Your clothes," Lazaro insisted, reaching for her.

Her shoulders came back even farther, her chin thrust out as she narrowed her eyes and glared up into his gaze. She pushed away a final wave of fear and fed her anger. She would humble the beast as he had never before been humbled. With every iota of her will power she would remain aloof and in control. She reached for the fastener on her dress. Her voice was low, even. "You are a thief, Lazaro. You wish to steal my most precious possession, but I won't let you."

She saw his glint as she undid more fasteners and more of her white skin was exposed.

"No, you are lice, Lazaro, and I will make my body available only in pure contempt. I *loathe* you, Apache. I detest you and will spit on you when you finish. And above all, remember this—regardless of what you do, you cannot touch one iota of the *real* Carlota de Gante!"

She pulled the doeskin over her shoulder and threw her head back in the rage she had built. "I hate you!" she snarled, standing rigid in her nakedness.

His expression was wary as he undid his trousers and moved closer.

"The ultimate weapon!" she screamed to herself, fighting back the panic, forcing herself to not waver. He was so huge—

Suddenly she made a bitter face and spat at him.

His open palm crashed into her cheek, knocking her head sideways and bringing an instant taste of salt. And then he was on her, lifting her high in the air with a loud growl and swinging her back to the ground. Closing her eyes, she gritted her teeth. She had to relax! Opening her legs, she cursed to herself. She would be nothing, flaccid flesh, nothing, a stolen urn, an old shoe. Her body would humiliate him beyond anything in his entire life. She would control it and make it do so. Control, yes, control. The pain, *God! the searing pain* . . . Holy Mary, Mother of God . . . Oh God! the pain! She locked her teeth together, *she would not cry out!* Control and contempt, control, contempt, control. . . .

Later she lay in her blanket by the fire, staring listlessly into the darkness. The terrible ordeal had left her drained. She knew she was torn and bloody, and should probably take care of herself, but she wasn't up to it—not yet. She was simply empty, and nothing seemed to matter, nothing except the hate that was now a dull ache. He had robbed her—and no matter how she colored it, he had marked her. In spite of what she had told him, deep down she knew he'd had at least a partial victory. But she would never let him know it. She would never speak to him. Ever. It was one of the means of control. And she had to keep control—*it was her only means of prevailing.*

He had walked away when he was finished, saying nothing, not even looking at her. Now he was back. Dropping to the ground across the coals from her, he selected a thick branch and placed it on the fire. He stared into the slowing growing blaze, saying, "You are my wife, and I love you."

But she refused to even raise her eyes.

They arose early and rode westerly, up and down ridges and along streams. At one place in a clearing of tall pines, he pointed to two peaks sitting side by side a few miles to the north. "The Twin Sisters," Lazaro announced. "We see them all the way from Mexico." After eating some dried beef, they descended to a narrow valley where a vigorous stream ran off to the south. This they followed for over two hours, picking their way carefully, sometimes having to ride in the water when the ledges were too abrupt for passage. Once she was startled by a large black bear that looked at them balefully before disappearing into the heavy undergrowth. She wondered why Lazaro didn't shoot him, and he seemed to have read her mind. "The Apache never hurts the bear," he grunted.

They camped that night on a high ledge by a small fire, eating in silence and ignoring each other. Dreading another ordeal on the blanket and wondering if she could cope with it, she was much relieved at his brooding. Shortly after dark, she rolled up in her blanket not far from where he sat staring into the fire. She was afraid to congratulate herself, but she knew she was succeeding. Whether he was actually humiliated or just piqued wasn't important.

They passed the next morning in silence as he led them up another stream with rough, steep banks along each side. From the sun's location, she guessed they were moving northwest. It was time for her to begin noticing such things, she told herself, if she were ever to escape and survive. As they proceeded, the country grew even rougher and less passable. Twice her mare stumbled, nearly throwing her into the cold, swirling water. *Where was he taking her?*

In midafternoon, with her enemy the sun beating down from a cloudless sky, they suddenly broke out of a steep trail into the edge of a wide basin filled with the most awesome rock spires she had ever seen. Her breath caught as she stopped the mare and stared up at the imposing pinnacles. Never before had she seen anything so totally raw and massive.

"Giant's Claw," Lazaro announced tersely. He urged his horse forward into the bowl. Following closely behind, Carlota continued to gape at the huge stone turrets. They reminded her of huge chess pieces. And then all at once she felt a sense of elation, of a strange new strength that was somehow pouring into her body. She nearly called out to Lazaro to tell him, but caught herself in time.

She shook her head—was this madness, too much sun? She felt as if she could reach out and strangle Lazaro with no trouble. Was it some kind of power? Benita had spoken of people who had power. Could this strange sensation have something to do with—no, she was beginning to think like these savages!

Could this be some kind of a place of destiny for her?

Telling her to build a fire, Lazaro went off to find some fresh game. A short while later, still feeling a sense of stimulation, she wandered from where the horses were hobbled toward the western side of the bowl. Seeing a large eagle glide into the top of one of the spires, she sat on a small boulder to survey this strange place. It was then that she noticed the cave opening, a dark space behind a very large boulder. For no particular reason she walked over to look at it. The entrance was a nearly perfect arch with edges broken only slightly by vegetation.

A tiny reflection at her feet caught her eye. Bending, she saw it was a stone the size of a wild strawberry. It was heavy and cool to her touch, and looked as if it were all bright yellow metal. She stared at it—she had never seen a nugget before. Could it be gold? She felt a flush of excitement as she stared into darkness past the opening. A mine, a real gold mine? *She had to find out!*

She was soon back with a flaming branch from the fire. Inside the entrance was an arched tunnel. Taking a deep breath, she moved through the opening. How smooth and clean the surface was, she marveled as she gingerly stepped forward in the flickering light. Only a few hanging mineral formations broke its conformation. Suddenly she thought of snakes and other crawling creatures and shuddered. But she was drawn on. In moments the tunnel opened into a large round room with a higher ceiling. And there on the floor, a dozen reflections stared back at her.

Oh! she cried out, picking up a large nugget.

Placing it in the pouch on her belt, she eagerly selected another. They were *huge!* It would take a big sack just to get what she could see! Hurrying around the large room, she stared at the reflections, laughing, feeling giddy, thinking about what it would be like to bring Agustin and her father here. And her mother—they would—

"Woman!"

She jumped as Lazaro's voice cracked like a whip in the small cavern.

She dropped the torch as he grabbed her wrist, knocking the nugget from her hand and dragging her to the tunnel. It was the first time she had ever felt raw fear with him. Struggling to bring it under control, she blinked at the bright light as they reached the outside. Drawing back a fist, she started to strike out at him, but remembered her vow and just stood rigidly staring past him.

The anger drained from his face. Releasing her, he said evenly, "That was oodo, the tears of Ussen, woman. It is sacred to the Chihenne and must remain in the ground always. It is said that long ago, a whole people perished here in a great turning of the earth because they disturbed the oodo and made ornaments from it. You are forbidden to ever touch it again in this place."

"I must speak to you, woman."

Carlota sat staring into the fire as Lazaro returned from a long walk. His expression was troubled as he twice started to tell her what had been so difficult to determine. "I know this other man is in your mind."

She didn't move. The crickets were the only night sounds as she waited. Could he possibly be relenting? No, it would be too much—

"I know this feeling. I know pain in the heart."

She clenched her fingers into her palms.

"I know it takes time to change."

Now what did he mean? She held her breath.

"But I cannot be treated disrespectfully by you. I am a Chihenne chief, the father of his people. And they cannot see a woman act like you. I would have to beat you, and I cannot do that. Therefore, I will wait for you to find a place in your heart for me. I will come to your house, but will not force myself." He paused struggling for the right Spanish word. "But I know sooner or later your heart will open to me. So even if it takes until there is winter in my hair, I will wait for you."

7

"How," Carlota asked, "could it be possible in one time?"

"Ha!" Benita replied with flashing eyes. "You were with him four days. Do you think I'm stupid? Your time was ripe, that's all."

An Apache *bastard!* Carlota cried to herself. Losing her virginity by rape to an arrogant Apache was one thing, but bearing a bastard half-breed child by him? She blinked back hot tears. "Is there a way to stop it? Many women have—"

"I wish you would! Go jump off a cliff and kill yourself."

"But I can't *have* it!"

"Then talk to your God about it, not me." Benita laughed. "Say a few thousand Hail Marys, pray for crop failure."

Carlota slumped over the bread she was making. "It's impossible. I'm not his real wife. I—"

"Then talk to the medicine men. Tze-go-juni might take care of it for you—she'd be glad to cut it out with that big knife of hers." Benita laughed again. She had been more friendly since she found that Lazaro ignored her rival and never went to her wickiup at night. Her status among the women had improved as soon as she told them her lord had found his new wife distasteful and incompetent on the blanket.

"You have to help me get away!" Carlota blurted.

"Ha! Lazaro would throw *me* over a cliff. Besides, you'd never survive out there in the desert. It's too far, too many dangers. No, that idea is even crazier."

As Benita walked away, Carlota felt a rush of panic. Hurrying inside her wickiup, she went to the bag that held her personal belongings and withdrew her prize nuggets. She clutched them tightly to her breast and closed her eyes, picturing the place Lazaro called Giant's Claw. "Come back, whatever you were!" she pleaded, trying to recapture that strange sense of strength she had experienced high in that forbidding place. Holding the gold close to her stomach, she cried out, "Help me, help me kill this monster that has started inside me! Drive it away, kill it. It isn't mine . . . it isn't *mine!*"

And suddenly she slumped to the floor, repelled by what she was doing. "My God," she whispered. "Now I'm even praying to the devil."

"Enjuh!"

She looked up to see the hateful Tze-go-juni standing over her. The shaman nodded, closing her eyes and saying something in Apache.

"*Get out!*" Carlota screamed, rising to her knees and hitting the medicine woman in the shins. "Get out and stay away from me, you witch!"

Tze-go-juni's eyes glittered as she suddenly jerked a sharp-pointed knife from her waist and jabbed it into Carlota's face. More Apache words tumbled from her lips. "*Too bah ghees chin en, Too bah ghees chin en . . .*"

Carlota stared at the bright tip of the knife, then at the old woman's excited face. She was truly crazy! "What do you want?" she cried out.

The medicine woman nodded, abruptly replacing the knife in her belt. "Child of the Water," she said, pointing to Carlota's waist.

"She's going mad," Benita said, shaking her head. "She thinks because you survived the trip with Lazaro and came back with child that it will be a new Son of Ussen."

Carlota blinked, trying to find some plausible reason. "Who does she think I am, the Virgin Mary—that Painted White Woman, or whatever they call her?" She laughed nervously.

"The Apache religion is not humorous, woman. In many ways it makes much more sense than that of Rome. There are no priests or other intermediaries; Ussen is among us, and we pray directly to Him. You've seen the People standing in front of their wickiups in the early morning, arms uplifted to the east—they are praying to Ussen. And He often answers—sometimes through ancestors, now and then through those with the Power. We too have a great Happy Place, but it is a four-day journey."

Benita's expression was animated as she went on. "Apaches do not steal from each other, only the enemy. And they never lie. Have you seen the woman whose nose is missing? She was unfaithful and it was cut off. Do these things remind you of the Commandments? The Apache believed in them before the first Catholic came to the new world, woman! Since before the rocks were hard. Even your vaunted purgatory has a parallel. The unworthy cannot always go directly to the Happy Place when they die, but must sometimes be brought back in the body of a bear first.

"And finally the parable of White Painted Woman who conceived

Child of the Water without a mate. The only difference is He outlived all his enemies. Will you sneer at the religion of the People now, woman?"

Carlota quietly shook her head. "But the old woman's nonsense. How?"

Benita shrugged. "Maybe she got into the tiswin. Who knows? At least she won't be trying to kill you for a while."

As the weeks passed, Carlota settled into a routine. Periodically, when he wasn't off on a war raid, Lazaro would come to sit by the fire in her wickiup and stare into the flames. Only once did he attempt physical contact with her, but her cold contempt quickly dissuaded him. She tried to become friendly with his son, Taza, who was still fulfilling his role as her sentinel with sober dedication, but he remained aloof. When she rode her paint mare farther and farther from the village, she could never get very far away from him as he followed doggedly on his little pony. One day she rode westerly, trying to recognize the trail Lazaro had followed on their so-called wedding trip. But she had little luck, not even picking out Twin Sisters up in the higher mountains.

"What do you know about Giant's Claw?" she asked Benita one day in October.

"It is a special place to Lazaro. That's all," the Mexican woman replied from where she was bathing in the icy water of the stream.

Carlota finished wringing out the wet skirt she had just washed. "I've heard there is much gold there," she said casually.

Benita stepped out of the water, drying herself briskly. "I don't know. It means nothing to me."

"But think of how it could ease your life. I mean you could have all the good things money can buy, you—"

"I have everything I need," Benita bristled.

Carlota decided that approach wouldn't work. But if a successful escape were to be made, she had to keep picking away, storing information.

By Christmastime Carlota felt as big as a wickiup. She had long since given up hope of being rescued and refused to even consider the possible reasons anymore. Cross and usually disconsolate, heavily uncomfortable, she no longer even rode her pony. To pass the time in the winter cold, she made elaborate escape plans, often bringing on sleep at night with one scene after another. And sometimes she missed her parents so much that she simply cried herself to sleep. She even began to learn Apache, but found the language difficult and yet another symbol of what she so hated.

It was on New Year's Day that she finally admitted that Agustin was dead. It was a terrible thing—surrendering the hope that he would ride into the Willows with a huge cavalry command and wipe out the Chihenne—but it was an obvious fact. Over six months had passed, plenty of time for him to do something, had he been able. And had there been even an attempt to reach her, a failed effort, Benita would have heard and told her.

She grieved dreadfully for over a week, but she knew it had to be faced if she were to be realistic in her single-minded commitment to escape. Benita told her no woman had ever escaped from the Chihenne, or any other Apache tribe as far as she knew. Now, she only had one goal—to get away when she could safely travel, and claim her great hacienda.

The baby boy was born on March 7. He was long, weighed at least eight pounds, and had an abundance of downy black hair on his perfectly formed head. He also had a lusty scream that was part Apache and part Carlota. All the threats she had made about killing the fetus, and later of abandoning the newborn child, were immediately forgotten. She took one look at the wriggling package of tiny hands and feet that went with the round little face and Carlota Evangelina de Gante was suddenly and overwhelmingly in love. She had never felt anything so complete, so rich, in her life. She wanted to rush out to the middle of the village, holding him aloft, and shout, "This is mine—you can't steal him from me!"

She named him Andres, for her father.

Tze-go-juni, who camped outside Carlota's wickiup for days, named him Child of the Water and chanted in Apache night and day.

Lazaro rushed to the wickiup three days later, having ridden hard from a meeting with Cochise off in Chiricahua country to the west. This new son had a special meaning to him—it was from her. How his love for her swept over him as he sat in the wickiup and watched her nurse the tiny boy-child. He felt at once tender and aroused. The baby was his answer, through him she would relent and gradually come to her senses. Come to him. He was certain of it. "He is a fine son," he said softly. "He will make a good leader."

She ignored him, as usual.

He wanted to touch her cheek and tell her that he would wait all the days of his life, if need be. For she was so firmly driven into his heart that she could be an imbedded arrowhead. These months had been difficult for him. To have the woman he worshipped so close, and yet so untouchable, was the most difficult problem he had ever encountered. Even mourning The-woman-whose-name-he-could-not-speak had not been so excruciating. He had loved that other woman so very much, but this woman, this Carlota was a *goddess!*

He would bring her the riches of the world, if she would only let him.

But he knew he would have to act out this game by her rules if ever she were to relent and take him to her heart. And it wasn't easy; he knew the People were aware that she continued to reject him. But he had long ago cast away any concern over what *anyone* thought when it came to her. Yes, he would have to continue the game with the patience of an old man who had no arms or legs, but knew he would live a hundred summers.

It was the way of this thing that was so much of his life.

"I have another fine pony for you," he said gently. "It has the look of one that can run all through the day."

Carlota didn't even look up.

Benita's reactions were mixed. She had helped deliver the baby and showed a special mother's warmth, but as the days passed she grew jealous of the attention being paid to Carlota's wickiup. She noticed Lazaro's interest and was reminded sharply that she had no sons. And sons were a mark of status, as well as a future source of security. Sons could, if they became chiefs or important war leaders, become another means of power for a woman.

Five weeks after Andres's birth, she told Carlota she might consider assisting in an escape.

Throughout the spring and summer, Carlota alternately chafed at being held back by Andres and finding sound reasons to delay her escape attempt. The child had become the center of her existence and she was afraid to expose him to any possible danger. What, she constantly asked herself, would he do if something happened to her while they were fleeing? He was still nursing and couldn't even walk. He wouldn't survive a day. And survival would be most difficult even for her, if everything she was learning was accurate.

Young Taza had ceased to follow her about halfway through her pregnancy. So now, with little Andres strapped to her back in his *tsach*, she was able to ride farther and farther away from the village on periodic tours. She ventured south and east, often staying away until nearly dark. Most often, she went to the deserted village of Santa Rita, where she liked to wander through the dusty buildings and play mind games about what the former residents might have been doing. She remembered the sloppy whore the morning she came out of the church, and the alcalde's pretty wife, and a fandango at the palacio. And she busied herself keeping clean the altar of the little church with its two stumpy belfries.

But most of all, she liked to climb the hill to the Kneeling Nun rock formation. She was able to recapture her earlier fascination because now the alleged tragedy touched her most vividly. Once a sudden rain squall caught them sitting below, and she had to dash up into the base for shelter. It was then that she thought of baptism.

The next day, wearing her best dress, she brought Andres to the small Santa Rita church at shortly before noon. She had invited Benita to come along, but the woman not only refused to enter a church, she scorned her for interfering in the sacraments. After saying the rosary for thirty minutes, Carlota raised her son's wriggling form high to an imagined priest at the wooden altar and said, "Baptize him spiritually in the name of the Holy Mother, oh Father . . . and the Son and the Holy Ghost. Should I not survive what is ahead, protect him as Your own. And if death should come to him, please accept his innocent soul into Your loving arms. Amen."

She felt warm, as much at peace as any time since her capture. She thought of how pleased her mother would be. "Mama, your grandson is a proud son of the Church," she said softly. She saw her mother standing at her side, smiling warmly as she reached out to take her grandson in her arms. "Be patient, Mama, we're coming."

She often spoke to her mother and father in an abstract manner. It provided an edge against the troublesome loneliness that prevailed when her child was asleep. Agustin had also been a part of the soliloquy, but the thought of him lying in a grave had proved too much to bear and she no longer included him.

It was on the next visit that she found the knife, a beautifully crafted stiletto with a nine-inch blade in richly engraved Toledo steel. It had gone somehow unnoticed in the dust under the alcalde's desk in the palacio. Its tip was as sharp as a needle and its blade seemed to gleam back at her with a special significance once she cleaned and burnished it with the soft buckskin of her skirt. It was to her a sign of strength, or armament, of coming good fortune. She made a buckskin sheath for it the next day and hid it with her precious gold nuggets.

It was early October and as much as she detested the thought, one more winter in the Willows lay ahead.

In her nearly two years of captivity, Carlota had never before seen an adult male captive. There had been a handful of women—all mestizos who worked on the ranchos—brought in after raids. Two had come to the main village in the past month when the raids resumed, but she had little to do with them once she found they knew nothing of La Reina. And several children that had been acquired soon melted into village life, learning the language and the Way of the People. But this man was a soldier, a sergeant with graying hair and a downcast look. She saw caked blood on the side of his face as he was led toward her position, stumbling on the end of a rope. He was a dragoon, she could see, and there was something familiar about—*he was from Agustin's command at La Reina!*

He fell almost directly in front of her, but was kicked viciously by two braves from behind, and staggered to his feet. Carlota's hand flew to her mouth in shock. *She knew it! He was Agustin's first sergeant!* She started to cry out, but caught herself. *He was from La Reina!*

It was shortly after dark when Carlota approached the wickiup where Sergeant Quintero was being held. With the victory dance in full sway at the campfire in the center of the village, the prisoner was unguarded. Who worried about a captive bound hand and foot in the great Willows stronghold of Lazaro? Carlota slipped quietly into the hut and softly introduced herself to the dark form on the dirt floor. "Did you serve my husband, Don Agustin de Gante?" she whispered.

Quintero squinted, wondering if this woman were another hallucination. "Yes," he replied hoarsely.

Carlota drew in a sharp breath. She didn't know if she could ask the question. Her heart pounded. Clasping her hands tightly together, she spoke softly, slowly. "I have been a prisoner since my wedding day." That part was easy. "How . . . how did my husband die?"

Quintera shook his head. "But, Señora—he is alive."

Carlota stared, blinking. *The words were foreign, impossible. This man was addled, he didn't understand.* "No, my husband—Don Agustin."

"I saw him at the hacienda only a week ago. Before the patrol."

She shook her head—was this some kind of a dream? Could she

believe it? Agustin was alive! But suddenly a sobering thought struck her. Why hadn't he come for her in some way? Something was wrong. He must be crippled. "How is he? Badly injured?"

"No, Señora. He was wounded that day, but he soon recovered. Do you have water?"

"I'm sorry," she whispered, kneeling beside his face and holding a small bag of water to his lips. She felt terribly weak, confused. It was hard to think. "I thought he would try to rescue me."

"He heard you were dead."

"Tell me about that day."

After several gulps Quintero began, "It was a terrible day, Señora. Many people were killed, including the Don's father. The priest, a dozen soldiers, many vaqueros, some women. I—"

"What about my parents?"

"Who?"

"Colonel de Cardenas and his wife?"

Quintero cleared his throat. "I'm sorry, Señora, they were both killed."

Carlota stumbled unseeing into her wickiup and dropped to the floor. The tears streamed down her cheeks and over her lips, but she wasn't conscious of them. "—they were both killed." The words crashed over her, resounding, stabbing. She had known it all along, but now the tiny hope had perished. "—they were both killed."

Unstrapping her son from his tsach with numb fingers, she began to sob, harshly and uncontrollably. Her beautiful gentle mother and her handsome brave father . . . she remembered every detail of their splendid clothes as they sat behind her at the wedding. Her fine gown, his fancy medals . . . and their proud smiles—

All splattered by their bright blood.

By the hand of a hideous Apache!

"But our Agustin is fine, my darling. Your legal father, your new father." She choked over the words. Agustin was alive, that was all that mattered. But there were things she couldn't blot out. Pulling the curious Andres tightly to her breast, she began to rock him and whisper soft words through her tears. She saw her mother and thought of the times when she was a little girl and had been held just like this, and comforted. Her beautiful, wonderful mother. And her dear father, towering over her, holding out the reins of her first pony, his smile broad as he said, "Your very own, my little one." And when she was older, whirling gaily in his arms to a waltz, the envy of every girl in the ballroom.

She saw a vague form in a bright uniform lying on the ground, unmoving, never to love her again.

Her wet lips found Andres's cheek. "You must comfort me, my darling," she whispered, holding him desperately tight. "You must always be my love and comfort. Always. For you are the only other Cardenas now."

"Mother in Heaven!"

Carlota stared in disbelief at the savage scene that greeted her as she rode into the edge of the village and heard the uproar. Sergeant Quintero was standing in the middle of a tight circle of howling women, holding his arms helplessly over his head to defend himself from their flailing clubs. Only strips of his army trousers remained, the rest of his body was bare and covered with blood streaming from his head. His eyes looked hunted, desperate, as he tried to find a way out. The loudest and most violent of his assailants was the wild-eyed Tze-go-juni, who kept screaming, "*Yizilhee!*" over and over. *Kill! Kill! Kill!*

Surrounding the circle of maniacal, raging women was a shouting, frenzied mob consisting of the rest of the village and a Warm Springs war party that was passing through from another raid. Carlota saw Lazaro standing back on a small knoll, watching coolly, seemingly detached. She wanted to get her dagger and stab him between those terrible eyes!

But she was mesmerized by the horror unfolding before her, unable to believe what she was seeing. Everyone was treating the murderous event like a big game, a play on a natural stage. She saw Taza and two of his friends struggling, trying to push inside for a better view. Their faces were as excited as the rest. With a flash of horror, she thought of Andres—*Could any of this bloodthirstiness be in his soul?*

A shattering war cry caused her pony to start. "*Da'itsaahii Nakaiye!*" *Death to the Mexican!* It reverberated through the warm mountain air, becoming part chant, part clamor.

Suddenly, in a frantic burst of reserve strength, Quintero burst through the ring of shrieking attackers and, lowering his bloody head, smashed through a weak spot in the surrounding crowd and ran wildly toward the stream. But like a pack of howling mad dogs about to lose their prey, the screaming women ran after him.

Carlota urged her pony forward, but a fleet-footed woman knocked

Quintero sprawling, and in a moment the whole swarm was on him again, pounding, hammering him mercilessly. By the time the mob caught up, Carlota knew it was over. Quintero had stopped moving. Slowly, the club swingers drew back, panting and suddenly quiet. Tze-go-juni, a crazy leer on her white-painted face, jumped forward to drag the lifeless body to a nearby boulder on higher ground. Pulling the dead sergeant's head up by the hair, she looked around the crowd like a victorious gladiator in ancient Rome. *"Santa Rita!"* she screamed. *"Dh'-itsaahii Nakai-ye!"* And with her flashing knife, she ripped off his scalp.

Carlota leaned over the side of her pony and retched.

"Don't tell me about how civilized your damned Apaches are!" Carlota ground out savagely to Benita a short time later in front of her wickiup. "That was the most barbarous, insane murder any group of beasts that walk on two legs could possibly commit!"

The other wife shrugged. "I admit it wasn't pretty, but you forget the ways are hard here. It isn't the first time a man captive has been given to the women, and—"

"A scrap of meat to the howling wolves—is that it?"

Benita shook her head. "Grown enemy males are never permitted to live, it's the Way. And you also forget what happened at Santa Rita. Every one of those women with a club lost a loved one at that massacre. Many saw the top of a child's head chopped off just like that sergeant's. And you must remember how the Apache feels about dismemberment."

"What about the soldier?"

"Pure revenge."

"And your great lord Lazaro—doesn't he respect an enemy soldier any more than that? To turn him over to such a barbaric death at the hands of a savage swarm of banshees—is *that* honor?"

"It's the Way—a periodic reminder to all, including the children, that Santa Rita will never be forgotten, but avenged to eternity."

Carlota dropped her face into her hands. She was still shattered by the death of her parents, and now a thing like this. She had to do something before she lost her reason. "I can't stand it any more, Benita, I have to leave soon. Tonight, tomorrow night. I have to get away from this hideous place forever."

Benita nodded. The plan was for Carlota to go in three weeks when it was warmer, but the last few evenings had been mild and the moon was nearly at its fullest. Besides, she knew Lazaro was spending more and more time moodily watching her rival's wickiup and it would be only a matter of time before he went to her blanket. "Then take your weak stomach and go!" she said sharply.

Carlota watched the older woman stalk away. Yes, it was time, she told herself, forcing away the depression. Yes, Andres had been walking for over a month and could eat normal food. She smiled sadly to where he watched from his tsach. "Would you like to go for a long ride tonight, *Chiquillo?*" she whispered.

He laughed as he reached out to grab her fingers, saying *"Dah."* "No" in Apache was his favorite word.

Carlota laughed with him, but only for a moment. It was time. The water bags—dried calves' stomachs—were hidden in the Santa Rita palacio, as were the grain for the pony and dried venison and fruit for themselves. She had tried vainly to get a gun all winter, but it didn't matter. *They were leaving at last!*

As near as she could figure, it was May 6—precisely twenty-three months since that horrible day at La Reina, twenty-three months of discomfort, sadness, hatred, and terror. Her hand crept to the pouch of her belt. Through the soft doeskin she could feel the strength of the nuggets she now carried at all times.

A shadow fell over them. "I go to Ojo Caliente to meet with Cuchillo Negro today," Lazaro said quietly. "When I come back, we will go again to Giant's Claw. You and me and the baby. It is time he touched the stone of Silsoose." He nodded. "And it is time for us to sleep on the same blanket."

She didn't look up, knowing for sure, now—it had to be tonight!

The timing was going to be delicate. She would have to be out of the village before the moon came up if she were to avoid detection. And that would give her less than thirty minutes from last light until the first sign of the moon. At sunset she went to Benita's wickiup to find her former adversary sewing beads on a new dress. Benita regarded her carefully for a few moments before saying, "So you are finally leaving." There was no emotion in her voice.

Carlota nodded. She never thought she would be saying this. "Thank you, Benita. I might not have survived . . . without you." She reached out tentatively to touch the other woman's hand. "I wish you well." She turned and slipped away; there was nothing more to be said. Benita would tell them the fleeing woman had spoken of heading southwest in her escape attempt—a lie, because she was going southeast. She would tell them in the morning, or whenever they discovered she was missing.

Horse was the only name by which Carlota had ever called the hardy little mare Lazaro had given her. At first she had rejected the animal as a constant reminder of her ordeal with him, and had considered her unworthy of an affectionate name. By the time she had grown to love the strong little animal, the name had stuck. Just as darkness fell, she led Horse outside the corral and swiftly saddled her. Placing the blanket roll with their belongings behind the saddle, she tethered the pony and hurried back to the wickiup. Andres laughed from his tsach as she gathered up the last of her effects and some additional food. This was a grand adventure in the dark for him.

Stepping back, Carlota tried to think of anything she might have forgotten. She was so excited, so nervous, it could be anything. No, she had to hurry, it—

"*Basta, puta!*"

She whirled to see who was calling her a whore—it was Tze-go-juni, standing directly behind her.

"*Ladron!*" the medicine woman snarled, pointing to Andres. Thief!

"Get out of the way!" Carlota snapped.

"*Too bah ghees chin en!*"

"He is not Child of the Water, you witch!"

Tze-go-juni made a sudden lunge for the tsach, but Carlota whirled, facing her and whipping out the sharp stiletto. With a low scream the older woman hurled herself forward again. The arc of the knife had every ounce of Carlota's strength behind it as it rammed into the charging crone's stomach. Tze-go-juni's scream died in her throat as her eyes rolled and she suddenly went limp.

Carlota shook off the leaden form, spinning, looking frantically around. *Had anyone heard?* What a terrible turn—why hadn't the old hag stayed away just another two minutes? It didn't matter now. *They'd find her body!*

Quickly she unslung the tsach and placed it against a tree trunk while she dragged Tze-go-juni inside the wickiup and covered her with an old blanket. Until someone looked closely, the inert form could easily be taken for the sleeping occupant of the dwelling. She felt the old woman's weakening pulse and saw the blood spurting from the wound. She would certainly be dead in minutes.

Hurrying outside, she patted Andres's cheek and returned the tsach to her back. She listened quietly, hearing nothing but the pounding in her ears and the bark of a dog in the distance. She would have to hurry.

Five minutes later the pony was picking her way through the dark down the river trail toward Santa Rita. Carlota breathed normally for the first time. They were clear of the village. Shortly, the crest of the huge yellow moon began to rise above the hills to the east and visibility quickly increased. In another hour and fifty minutes they were in Santa Rita, where she gathered the rest of her belongings, filled the water bags and took leave of her last source of known shelter. Then it was due east for five miles, where she hit the Mimbres River again and headed south toward her first night's stop. It was slow going, but she couldn't take a chance of Horse stepping in a hole and going lame on her.

Some four hours later she struck a sharp bend in the river and stopped to rest for a few hours in a willow thicket close to the water. She hadn't relaxed a single moment since their departure. Drifting into broken sleep, she was pleased with her progress on the first leg. And though killing Tze-go-juni had created added danger, she felt exultant over finally striking back. She would kill a *thousand* Apaches if she had a chance.

She was up at dawn, feeding a sleepy Andres and securing him in his familiar tsach for the next leg—a ten-mile trek that would take her south of the Willows Mountains to the northern slope of the next range, the one with the high peak. It was here, east of Antelope Plains, that the land flattened out considerably. It was also on this stretch that they were naked, vulnerable to any sharp eyes following them. She was sure there would be no pursuit until well after daybreak, and then, she told herself, they might not search in the right direction. But deep down she knew better; those warriors could track *anything*, track it and describe its activities en route. After daubing Benita's green ointment on Andres's face and her own, she pushed Horse along through the bright sunshine that would bring a hot day. She couldn't resist glancing over her shoulder nervously. *He* might not be back there, but his finest trackers would be.

At shortly after midday, she stopped in a concealed arroyo and gave Horse a rest. The pony seemed to be holding up well, but she couldn't take any chances. After letting Andres scramble around for a while, she overrode his loud protest and strapped him back in the tsach so she could take a much-needed nap. The strain and effort were beginning to tell.

Two hours later they were underway again, heading as directly as possible for the tip of the next range of hills. Again she rode with her head twisted backward half the time. *They were back there somewhere now!* But maybe her luck was holding—maybe they hadn't discovered her departure until late in the morning. *Ha!* she told herself, don't count on it! The sun's rays were unrelenting as they bore down, further sapping her strength and that of her pony. She wrapped the sweat-drenched bandana more tightly around her forehead and rode on. At shortly before dark, they reached the south flank of the hills and she stopped again to rest. But when the moon came up she had to be back in the saddle. That was when the Apaches would stop somewhere and hole up for the night as they always did. That was her advantage, her only advantage.

"Oh my God!" she cried aloud, abruptly sitting up in the blanket and seeing that the moon had moved over halfway across the firmament. She had overslept and no more than three hours of moonlight could possibly be left! Quickly she saddled the pony, loaded up, and moved out blindly toward what she was positive was southeast. This was the biggest guesswork of her entire plan. Benita had been unable to give her any further information from this point on, and it was highly possible for her to actually start riding in a circle and head right back toward her pursuers! But she had no choice. They were back there ready to ride at first light.

As she had done the night before, she settled in just before the moon disappeared over the western horizon, then arose shortly after daybreak to continue. By looking back at the last hill mass and coordinating it with the rising sun in its due easterly direction, she was elated to find she had held a relatively straight course during the night. But the jubilation quickly passed; she was extremely tired and little Andres was vigorously protesting against being cooped up in his ever-present tsach.

But they had to hurry on.

There was so little time left.

Over two hours passed. And with them went the last of the water—a couple of spoonfuls to Andres, the rest to Horse. She rubbed her own parched lips with the last drops. Her throat was raw and she felt giddy. She imagined a crystal-clear pool, saw herself diving in and drinking deeply, tossing a laughing Andres high in the air. He was covered with huge silvery drops of cold water. And she drank some more, gulping down huge mouthfuls.

Enough! She had to think about something else to get her mind on another subject. Yes, Agustin—how proud he would be to find how stalwart she had been. Yes, how many women could do what she was doing—escape from the damned Apaches?

The thought gave her a touch of added strength. "Just a little longer, chiquillo," she said softly as she remounted. But as she stared ahead to the east, the newfound confidence began to ebb. Was the great river really there somewhere? Could Benita have lied to her just to get rid of her? Was all of this a hoax, a terrible mistake that would have them dying of thirst, choking on cactus for the last drop of desert moisture? No, his trackers would get to her first, his terrible trackers.

No! They'd never get her!

Once more she stared over her shoulder, knowing they were closer. Adjusting her damp bandana, she dug her heels into Horse's flanks and squinted into the blazing sun.

"Oh, thank God! Oh, thank God!"

It was all Carlota could say, over and over, when she reached the top of a ridge that looked down into the lushest, greenest looking valley she could ever remember. "It's the Rio Grande, chiquillo, the river, the *river!*" Tears streamed down her cheeks through the caked ointment and dirt. Her hands shook. She wanted to get down from the hardy little pony and kneel in prayer on the spot, but she couldn't take even that much time. They were closer behind her; she *knew* it, she could *feel* them.

Glancing to the high hill on her left, she remembered from her last trip down the King's highway from Santa Fe that the village of Doña Ana should lay almost due east. In fact, she could see some smoke and the reflection of something man-made on the far side of the river. That had to be her destination. She was about to ease Horse forward when she heard a sound behind her, down the backslope of the ridge. Jerking around, she saw them—three braves, strung out in single file and urging their ponies along at top speed toward her! *They were no more than a few hundred yards away!*

Instantly ramming her heels into her pony's flanks, she screamed, "Go, little Horse, go. Just a little more!" Andres cried out from her back, but she barely heard him as they raced down the hill, dodging rocks and shrubs. "Just a mile, little Horse," she pleaded as the pony slipped, then recovered. They wouldn't dare follow her into Doña Ana!

She brought every bit of her superb horsemanship into play as she kept the tired mare going down the rough slope, sliding, pawing, dodging, and yet eating up ground. She gambled one backward glance and saw the first Apache break over the crest of the ridge in full pursuit. *"Eeeyaah!"* she shouted to Horse as they hit a stretch of open ground with less slope.

Suddenly, in wide-eyed horror she felt Horse's head dip and saw the ground flashing toward her face—Oh, God!

The rest was a blur—flying from the saddle, crashing into the ground, rolling with the tsach pounding into her back in the swirling dust; gritting her teeth and riding it out until she finally slid to a stop. She was on her side, tasting salt in her mouth, salt and dirt. Her body felt numb, burning. Vaguely, she saw the mare pull herself to her feet a few yards away and stand with her head down as if she had done something terribly wrong.

Andres! Sitting up abruptly, she tore at the tsach's straps, all stiff thumbs and fear. In a moment his wide, scared eyes blinked back at her from under the little canopy, and suddenly he screamed in terror. Anxiously, she started to remove him, but the loud beat of pounding hooves interrupted her. She looked up in horror as the first brave came reining in through the choking dust. Instantly he was hurtling to the ground and running toward her, an exultant Apache shout on his lips.

Before she could dive away he grabbed her roughly by the wrist, jerking her to her feet. It was Placero, the same hated warrior who had stolen her from the bedroom so long ago on her wedding day! Instinctively her hand went to the stiletto at her waist. The Apache sneered as he drew her close, drawing his other hand back to slap her. But suddenly he froze, the sneer turning to a startled grimace as she rammed the long blade into his stomach. As his grip relaxed and he started to slump, she jerked the knife free and turned to face the others.

The second and third warriors came pounding toward her, yelling loudly. Sucking in a harsh deep breath, she drew herself erect. *They would never take her back!* She held the bright blade in front of her at arm's length. *Never!* The first rider pulled his horse to a jarring stop, his sweaty face creased by a triumphant grin. She wanted to slash him, cut off that hideous face. A knife flashed in his hand! "No!" she screamed.

She barely heard the shots.

The Apache jerked convulsively in midstride, then slammed forward to the ground, his hands groping at a gaping wound in his chest.

The second Apache pitched screaming over the neck of his spotted pony as it flashed by, down the slope.

Carlota stood stiffly still, staring around in shocked wonder, unable to cope with the sudden change. She turned sharply to face the sound of—

"I am sorry we were so late, Señora," a tall Mexican under a large sombrero said as he trotted up on a mule. He had a mammoth black mustache and a protruding belly. His tall son, also on a mule, followed him. The man shrugged, smiling sheepishly. "This stubborn mule, she is not so fast."

Lazaro stood quietly on the small knoll outside of Santa Rita and stared down into the grassy bowl that had been the massacre scene four years earlier. Sadly, he recalled the screams of terror and death, the roar of Brant-son's cannon and the crash of muskets. And he saw the blood running wild in tiny rivulets through the white spring flowers, the blood of his laughing wife.

He pushed the uncomfortable sight away, turning toward the Kneeling Nun and picturing a remarkable young girl. She was erect, her skin clear and pale in the early morning sunshine—her luminous eyes hauntingly curious, exciting, as they went directly to his heart.

And he recaptured other memories of her. Although unkempt in her torn clothes after capture, she was the most beautiful creature the land of the People had ever seen. Or at least the second most beautiful. He recalled how, even in her anger, she had graced his village, his heart, and once, his loins. She was a breath, a white dove—

"They were killed," the war leader said abruptly. "The sign showed two were shot from horse, the other on the ground. The Nakai-ye have the woman and boy, Nantan."

Lazaro nodded silently. Somehow he had known it would be this way. Her Power was too strong. He had hoped she would surrender long before this, but inwardly he'd known otherwise. In a way, he respected her remarkable escape. She simply could not be held.

"We can raid the Nakai-ye village, Nantan."

Lazaro shook his head. She would die before she would come back now. Maybe another time. "No," he said softly, and turned away.

Once more he glanced at the hillock where he had first encountered her and he saw a final glimpse of her frank expression, her youthful beauty. And the sadness flooded over him.

8

"There should be a military party through here in a few days," Pablo Martinez explained. "It comes from Santa Fe twice a month, sort of a mail and supply train, not nearly as large as a conducta, but able to hold off any damn Apache attacks."

Pablo Martinez was the heavy Mexican with the huge black mustache who, with his son Patricio, had rescued Carlota the day before. He owned a small rancho on the west side of the big river, not far from Doña Ana, where he and his large family—he had seven sons—raised cattle, trapped for furs in the nearby hills, and grew enough crops to survive. Pablo Martinez punctuated his speech with frequent hearty laughs, and he liked to brag that all of his tall sons were crack shots. "How else could we survive these murdering Apaches?" he asked frequently.

Carlota felt better after a long sleep and some of Señora Martinez's good food. Except for the heavy bruises and scraped skin on her hands and knees, she was all right—sore all over and so stiff she could hardly walk, but all right. And Horse had apparently survived the fall without any damage, so she still had transportation. "No," she said, "I can't wait. Not now, not with El Paso del Norte so close." A two-day ride would be nothing after the last two years! She told Martinez where La Reina was located, and he agreed the only route of any safety was through the city to the south.

"Señor Martinez, you get me and my baby safely to the hacienda La Reina and my husband will pay you three hundred pesos."

The big man made a face as he pulled at his large mustache. He hadn't seen more than a hundred pesos at any time in his entire life. "It's planting time, Señora," he said quietly.

"Four hundred, but I want to leave tomorrow."

Martinez shrugged, spreading his palms. "My neighbors and one son can watch my great hacienda." He smiled at his favorite little joke. "Señora, you have just hired a private army."

Carlota held her head high as the small column splashed through the knee-deep ford of the Rio Grande. She had wound her long hair into a large chignon the night before, and now rode bareheaded in the late afternoon sun. Señora Martinez had offered her best dress, but the woman was short and much broader and Carlota decided she would look ridiculous dressed that way with Andres's tsach strapped to her back. And there was no other way her child could travel. The doeskin dress had been scrubbed clean and would serve as her badge of honor until she stepped through the door of the Pass's finest dress shop.

After that, no one would laugh at Señora Carlota de Gante.

As a woman riding in a passing carriage stared at her, Carlota looked ahead to the dusty maze of buildings that was El Paso del Norte. She had been taken prisoner by the Apaches two years earlier, and had held herself morally correct, worshipping the Holy Trinity and the Virgin Mother through the entire period. What other woman of gentle birth had single-handedly escaped from the dreaded Chihenne? Her famed white skin was tanned darker than normal and her hands were rough and unkempt, but her carriage was erect and her spirit not only intact but filled with pride and anticipation. And her beloved son chirped happily on her back. The mistress of La Reina was returning from the wilderness and no one had dare utter even a snicker at how she looked.

Pablo Martinez glanced back from his big black mule, a wide grin creasing his face as his horse stepped out of the cool water. There had been no trouble coming down from Doña Ana, not even a hint of an Apache. And if they had merely a touch of luck, the additional hundred and twenty miles to the señora's hacienda would present no problems he couldn't handle. His main concern would be collecting his sons after a night in the Pass's cantinas and bordellos when it was time to ride on. And he couldn't blame them—life at Doña Ana offered little in the way of diversion for lusty young males. Already they were grinning and prodding their mules, returning the curious smiles of the first señoritas they met.

El Paso del Norte in 1843 was roughly the same size as Santa Fe, if one counted the small farms and ranchos that sprawled down the lush green valley to the other towns. The city's name was derived from the giant slash the river or some other force had at one time worn through the line of mountains that ran to the east of the Rio Grande and continued south into Mexico, where the valley turned southeastward. The Pass, as it was commonly called, was the only major stop between Chihuahua and Santa Fe for the caravans carrying goods north and south. It was the first city in Old Mexico to greet American traders of the Santa Fe trail.

But unlike its sister frontier city to the north, the Pass was a hodgepodge of adobe structures with no major palacio to give form to its rambling streets. Its inhabitants on the whole enjoyed life, comfortable in the knowledge that their valley produced excellent winemaking grapes and other fruits, as well as many staples that kept hunger away. Troubles with the Mescalero and Lipan Apaches had waxed and waned in the nearly two centuries of the town's existence, but were now a matter of history. The sun shone all but a couple of days of the year and if one could overlook some dry hot days in the summer, the only disconcerting element in the weather was a capricious wind that could sometimes bowl one over.

Carlota wanted to leave El Paso's comforts behind as soon as possible. By now, Lazaro could be planning anything to recover his lost property and she didn't want to give him time to react. She had a relative in the city, a smaller nugget to sell, and clothes to buy for her grand entrance back at La Reina. But more than anything, she didn't want to waste a single moment in getting back to Agustin. All the memories of her bridal fantasies were as vivid as they had been two years earlier. She had been reliving them down the trail from Doña Ana, and could almost *feel* his touch.

Her great-aunt's name was Magdelena Medina. A tall woman with dyed black hair who smoked incessantly, she was still managing the small hotel her deceased husband had left her. Aunt Magdelena stared at her blankly when she opened the door to her apartment to find a tall young woman in an Indian dress holding a tiny boy. Blinking at the apparition, she suddenly crossed herself and cried, "Jesus, Mary, and Joseph!" When she caught her breath, her face was white. "Is it truly you, child? I heard—"

Carlota patted her hand. "I am your niece, Carlota, *tia*. And this is your new nephew, Andres."

An hour later, Carlota had told her Aunt Magdelena as much as she wished. "And now," she said abruptly, "I have to go out and get some money." She pulled the small nugget from her pouch. "This is a souvenir of life among the Apaches."

Magdelena lit another cigaret as she glanced at the sleeping Andres. She didn't mention the obvious.

The assayer was still in his little office when they got there. A short, rotund man of about sixty, he took his time examining the nugget. Twice he made pricks into its surface. "May I ask generally where this came from, Señora?" he said quietly.

Carlota smiled. "Let's just say it came from Ussen."

The man looked at her blankly. "You realize that an accurate estimate would require its dissection, don't you?"

"Yes, but I need to sell it as soon as possible."

The assayer nodded, drilling a fine hole and examining the nearly one hundred per cent gold particles that came out of the nugget. He pursed his lips. "It is almost pure gold." After some hurried calculations, he announced, "I will pay you six hundred and forty pesos for it."

After selling the nugget, Carlota and her aunt entered a store that advertised the latest fashions from New York and Paris. Carlota quickly selected a close fitting Redingdote dress of white Indian muslin with a pale blue silk lining. It wasn't the wonderful old lace wedding dress she had been captured in, but it would convey the spirit. She could see herself in it now, across the small table from Agustin in romantic candlelight. No! she wanted to dance in it. Whirl and sweep to the waltz, dazzlingly beautiful in the striking gown, tingling at his touch. She'd have him summon the musicians and declare a second reception that very day. And everyone at La Reina would dance until dawn! Excluding the bride and groom, of course. It would be her second wedding day—

"I still mourn your beautiful parents," Aunt Magdelena said sadly.

The comment abruptly sobered Carlota. Their graves would be her very first stop. She pushed the sadness aside. They had to go on to another store where she could buy men's clothing for riding and a sombrero to keep the sun off her head. It was time to start thinking of her complexion again.

"There, Señora, is your hacienda," the Lipan guide told her, pointing down from the ridge where the party had drawn to a halt.

Carlota looked off to the southwest. There, shimmering in the late afternoon heat stood the tall cottonwoods that marked the hacienda headquarters. She could see spots of light color that marked the buildings, friendly forms reaching out to her in curiosity. Were they groping in their memories and finding a greeting for their mistress? She smiled, fighting off the sudden nervousness. How many times had she lived this scene in her dreams? Two cows and one large bull stood a hundred yards away, indifferent, chewing on the sparse grass. And on the slope of a knoll, a young buck stood staring at them, wondering how soon he should bolt.

It was not much more than a mile away—could she contain herself? Her La Reina . . . her Agustin . . . oh, Mother of God. She wanted to shout her thankfulness to the sky!

Gregoria de Gante hurried to the front veranda when the maid told her of the stranger's arrival. One glance at the small column and she knew. She couldn't believe it, but she knew. Only one young woman could ride so confidently at the head of an escort. She felt a chill and automatically crossed herself. *How had she come back from the dead?* And what was she holding in her arm—*a tiny child!*

Instinctively, Gregoria's hand went to her mouth. A child! She had a small child with her. Mother in Heaven! Drawing herself up to her full five feet, she marshalled her emotions and braced herself for the encounter.

Carlota tried to control her excitement while savoring every yard of the final approach to the buildings—she even wondered if the handsome white horse Agustin had given her waited in the corral. Clutching Andres tightly, she whispered, "This is it, my son, the beautiful home I've been telling you about."

Moments later, she dismounted and hurried toward the veranda. In spite of herself, the tears of joy spilled shamelessly down her cheeks. The stern face of her mother-in-law swam in the bright mist. Holding Andres even closer, she managed, "Hello, Mama," and ran to embrace Gregoria with her free arm. "Where is Agustin?" she asked, glancing quickly around.

The graveyard behind the chapel was enclosed by several young elm trees that provided a bit of respite from the heat. Carlota had been kneeling before the graves of her parents and praying the rosary for nearly an hour when she heard the footsteps behind her. Whirling to her feet, she brought her hand up to reach out and touch him. He was so tall, so strikingly handsome, oh God in Heaven, he was finally— "My darling," she cried, running a few steps to his arms. Her lips found his, hurrying on to his cheeks and back to his mouth as she reveled in his taste and smell. "Oh, my love," she whispered, dropping her head to his chest and hugging him as tightly as possible. "You have no idea, my darling. I have missed you terribly."

"Dah."

Andres stepped out from behind a bush, holding up an amulet of small turquoise beads. He smiled. "Dah, Mama."

She felt Agustin stiffen, then realized he hadn't said a word. The expression on his face was pained as he stared at Andres. His hands dropped to his sides.

"Mama," Andres said, tugging at her skirt.

She watched Agustin's eyes. Raw anger exposed itself briefly before he looked away. "Darling," she whispered, reaching for his hand. "This is my little Andres. I, there is so much I have to tell you—"

"Dah."

He pulled his hand back as he took a deep breath and blew it out. "Your son?" he asked tonelessly.

"Yes. You see, it's an involved story. I want to sit down with you and your mother and tell you the whole—"

"He's an Apache, isn't he?"

The fear clutched coldly at her heart. She had expected some kind of a problem, but—

"Isn't he?"

She blinked at the accusatory look in his eyes. "Yes, but you see it isn't what . . . " How could he be like this? Her voice wavered. "I was . . . " She knew she couldn't say raped, he wouldn't understand. "I was taken once. I told you I would tell you all about it. I couldn't help it, my darling. You don't know, a person has no choice and—"

"Why didn't you leave the boy with his kind?"

It was as if he had slapped her with an open palm. Her hand went to her mouth. "I—he is my son, Agustin."

"He is an Apache, an animal. His kind are no better than the coyote, or the rattlesnake. They are predators and should be exterminated. If anyone should know, it's you. Your parents are lying right there near my father."

She had never seen such dispassionate hatred in anyone's eyes. Her voice was barely audible. "He is a baby, Agustin."

"How could you do this to me?"

The tears burst from her eyes as she shook her head and tried to find an answer. "Mother of God, Agustin, surely you must know I had no control, no desire to hurt you." She reached out to touch his cheek, but he stepped back. "I love you so much, my darling. You have no idea how many nights I prayed for you in a brush hut so mean you wouldn't let your dog stay in it."

The mask of disdain slipped, permitting his anguish to show momentarily. "I just don't know how you could do this to me, Carlota," he said, and then turned on his heel and headed for the big house.

* * *

Carlota finished brushing her hair in front of the mahogany dresser. The lacy peignoir was the one she had intended to wear on her wedding night. She glanced in the mirror at its low bodice—had it been kept around for two years to haunt her? She sighed, it was time—the tears were gone. She could brush her hair until the end of the world and nothing would change unless she tried. She hadn't begged in Chihenne country, not once. But now she would do *anything*.

She had been informed that there would be no formal dinner, and her meal had been served three hours earlier in her room. Gregoria de Gante had not spoken to her since her arrival. As the Apache said, it was the Way.

She went to where Andres was sleeping in a crib that a thoughtful maid had provided. Touching his soft cheek, she shook her head. She couldn't believe there could be so much hate over such an innocent, lovable child. Then she remembered with a pang of guilt how she had been ready to deny the unborn child when he was barely a fetus. She had been ready to kill him. She blessed herself and turned to her confrontation.

Moments later she stood before Agustin's open bedroom door. He was seated in a wingback chair close to the four-poster bed that would have been their wedding couch. A brandy bottle sat on the floor and in his hand he held a half-empty glass. She didn't knock. "I must talk to you, Agustin," she said softly. "You can't shut me out like this."

Reaching the chair, she dropped in front of him at his feet. She looked up into his tormented face, but he avoided her eyes. She touched his hand, wanting to squeeze it with all her strength. It was so hard on him—she could feel the torment that was going on inside his body. Yes, she would beg. "Hold me, Agustin," she whispered. "Hold me close and let me tell you about it. Please. It's not what you think. I love you so desperately. Please, darling, give me a chance."

He looked at her briefly, but said nothing and finished his drink.

She put her hand inside his thigh. "Please, my darling, I am your wife. Take me to bed and make love to me. Take me and do what you will, but don't close me out. Do anything, but please listen to me when you are finished. I beg of you."

Agustin just stared at the rug under his feet. His expression didn't change and he didn't say a word. After the longest few moments in Carlota's life, he got slowly to his feet and walked from the bedroom.

* * *

The priest was named Father Ferdinand, and with the growth of La Reina, he had been assigned full time to the hacienda. Carlota had sensed immediately that he was firmly under the thumb of Gregoria de Gante and would do precisely as she told him. He adjusted his eyeglasses as he glanced at the statement of settlement. Agustin, his face a mask, sat across from Carlota at the long oak dining table. The overhead chandelier was not lit. Behind Agustin de Gante, Doña Gregoria stood stonefaced, her hand on her son's shoulder.

The priest cleared his throat and began reading. The first page was filled with procedure and high sounding phrases that meant nothing to Carlota. The next page went straight to the heart of the matter:

" . . . *a generous settlement of five thousand pesos to be paid in full when Carlota Evangelina de Cardenas presents herself at the aforementioned bank in the City of Mexico. . . .* "

Carlota could hardly follow the words. For three days she had been in a daze, unable to feel or function properly. If one of the maids had not taken Andres under her wing, he might not have eaten. She had ridden for hours each day, but the La Reina she had dreamed so vividly of returning to merely mocked her. She had tried to pray, but it was impossible. And she had groped toward suicide, but Andres's survival had obviated that madness. For two years she had kept herself going because of her love for this man and this magnificent place where he lived. And now, in the space of a few words, it was all being taken from her.

" . . . *You will at no time personally use the name of de Gante, nor will you permit any offspring to use it. . . .* "

Now it was all so clear—the failure to rescue her. He had simply given her up in the beginning. He was weak, shallow, and thought only of himself. Or what Gregoria wanted. He was still a spineless boy, an emotional child with few values . . . but Mother in Heaven, how she still loved him!

Agustin looked at her, the pain raw in his eyes for a moment, but the blanket of hidalgo coolness quickly returned. She couldn't take her eyes off him, not for a second. She didn't want to forget a single element of this moment, nor the terrible coldness that clutched at her heart. The memory would be her only salvation. Her nails dug into her palms. She would not break down!

" . . . *The Holy Mother Church will see fit to announce this annulment at the earliest convenient time.*"

>> THE OLD WOMAN'S JOURNEY <<

The white-haired lady stepped down from the train, glad to stretch her legs while the engine took on water. Off in the distance she could make out Cooke's Peak. She sighed, remembering how it had often been a guidepost to her.

"Are you tired?" the reporter asked as he lit a cigarette and blew the smoke to the side so it wouldn't bother her.

"No," she replied, holding her large hat so the slight breeze wouldn't blow it away. "I want to tell you about the Mexican War. As you know, Texas became a republic in 1836, leaving a bitter taste in the mouth of many Mexicans. There was a distinct cultural clash between the two nations that would grow in the next decade. Many Mexicans were beginning to think of themselves as *la raza*, a cultural philosophy and heritage they felt extended all the way back to Rome—a value system that was symbolic and mystical, and entirely in contrast to the practical and aggressive Americans.

"There was already a boundary dispute, and when the United States decided to annex Texas and make a state of it, the Mexicans reacted strongly. But there is much more to it. California and New Mexico were huge and attractive Mexican provinces, and there was a strong desire among American leaders to acquire them as part of a plan to extend their borders from sea-to-sea.

"Also you have to remember that the mid-1840s was a time when the North and the South were beginning to agitate the political pot. So there were many undercurrents at work when James Knox Polk became president in 1845. Some historians have referred to that time as America's imperial period, and Polk as its most noted imperialist. The war that followed has also been called Polk's War, but many other avid jingoists in Washington were involved.

"And in Mexico, where anti-American fever reached the boiling point, one must remember the instability of government. Revolution was common, and coup was a household word. Not to mention the ubiquitous General Santa Anna, who popped in and out of the presidency like a bad penny, a dozen other would-be dictators lurked on the fringes and fanned the flames of nationalism to further their own ambitions.

"Not only was Mexico unstable, it was bankrupt. Polk offered more than fifty million dollars for those western territories, but there wasn't a leader willing to accept it.

"In short, an American army under General Zachary Taylor marched into Mexico in 1846. And from Fort Leavenworth, Kansas, General Stephen Kearney brought a column with his First Dragoons to capture New Mexico. The governor and commanding general at Santa Fe, Manuel Armijo, fled before the invading army's arrival, and the capital as well as the province was handed to the Americans on a silver platter.

"Of course, this was all very confusing to the Chihenne Apache—the Americans being at war with the hated Mexicans. It is said that Lazaro offered to fight alongside Kearney, but the general demurred. Regardless, the chief in his wisdom could tell that such a vast number of White Eyes soldiers would only bode misfortune and the eventual loss of Chihenne hunting grounds and, in the end, perhaps even the Way.

"Meanwhile, in Mexico, the army fought surprisingly well against the Americans—considering how poorly trained the underfed and unpaid common soldier was. But it was only a matter of time. In the fall of 1847, the final battles at the City of Mexico were drawing down the curtain. . . . "

9

Chapultepec Castle,
September 13, 1847

"Where are the goddam ladders?"

Everyone was shouting it! With storming parties piling into the fosse—the deep ditch that surrounded the castle—it seemed utterly impossible that the scaling ladders could not be there. More curses filled the smoke-filled air as sharpshooters picked off any Mexican head that showed itself over the parapet above.

Captain Rafael Murphy stepped out of the fosse briefly to look up at the castle. It was fortunate, he thought, that the Mexican guns couldn't be depressed over the rampart to rain fire down on the rapidly growing assault force. What he could see through the bright smoky sunshine didn't look promising—going over that wall would be brutal. He still wasn't sure the expense of taking the castle had been a wise decision on Scott's part. But Scott was the commanding general, and he was only a brevet militia captain from Texas.

"Where are those goddamn ladders?"

The din increased as more troops crowded into the base of the Chapultepec's western wall. Musketry rattled, mixing with human shouts and the crash of artillery. Captain Murphy wondered if Tom Jackson's guns were still blazing away. Rockets flashed through the thickening smoke. And faintly, somehow, the strains of "Deguello," a Mexican no-quarter song that reached back to Moorish days, drifted down from above. And then came troops from the New York and Pennsylvania regiments, from the Ninth and Fifteenth, and more from the Voltigeurs. And suddenly Murphy could feel the deadly drain of emotion as the soldiers in the clogged fosse began to lose their momentum. *They had to get up the wall!*

Gray-and-blue uniforms, sprinkled with a bright kerchief here and there, intermingled with the brilliant and clashing rainbow of flags and sparkling weapons as the assault force continued to grow. Captain Murphy caught glimpses of determination on the faces of veterans who had survived the horror of Molina del Rey and before that, the

Pyrrhic victory at Churubusco. They had to keep going! He nodded to a sergeant. "Keep the men alert! It won't be long."

And then suddenly the men with the ladders appeared under heavy covering fire. He guessed there were over fifty of them. *"Make way! Make way!"* As men scrambled to provide room, the tall wooden ladders were set up and at once the first scalers began to clamber up toward the parapet. Shouts of encouragement shook the fosse, a bugle sounded the clear and exciting notes of the charge!

Along the line, many of the scalers fell wounded. Others came crashing down as their ladders were knocked over. Some stayed. Other ladders went back up and held, soldiers pouring over their tops and onto the castle grounds above. Murphy was nearly at the rampart when he caught a glimpse of Lieutenant George Pickett struggling up a nearby ladder with the colors of the Eighth Infantry. Between the shouts of the attackers and the wave of musketry, the noise was deafening. Over the top, Murphy waved his gleaming saber and encouraged his men to keep going. Bodies of the defending Mexican soldiers were everywhere, many of them victims of the artillery, others dead, some wounded for only moments, their cries joining the tumult.

He hurried toward the disorganized Mexicans as they broke and ran to the walls of the castle. It wouldn't be long! He threw a glance up to the top of the main building where the tricolor of Mexico waved in smoke. It had to come down! Now the attackers were a swarm of cheering, violent bees streaming into the heart of the castle. Murphy suddenly spotted a Mexican colonel and raised his pistol, but a smashing blow to his right knee hurled him to the ground. The pain was instant and overpowering. Blood spurted from the wound, evidently torn by a large-caliber bullet. He gritted his teeth to keep from crying out. Jerking a scarf from his neck, he fashioned a tourniquet for his thigh.

He had to hold up, had to see that flag come down. . . .

Carlota liked to bring Andres to the Alameda in the middle of the afternoon. It was to her the most delightful place in the entire City of Mexico. She had heard there was no promenade its equal in all the world, not even in Paris. Hyde Park in London supposedly came the closest. Surrounded by a breast-high wall, the Alameda de Mexico formed a long square that was a virtual paradise of color when its many varieties of flowers, shrubs, and trees were in bloom. An iron gate at each of its four corners afforded admission to carriages, horsemen, and pedestrians alike. The drive itself, a perfectly level sandy thoroughfare, was comfortably shaded in season by poplars, ash trees, and willows.

But mostly, Carlota liked to amble aimlessly up the alleys that converged into large common centers, paths that were ornamented with fountains of sparkling water jets and bright clumps of myrtles, roses, and jasmines. It was all a special alchemy to her—the noises of the people, the horses, and the noble carriages; the murmur of the water; the sighing of the wind through the trees; the buzzing of the bees and hummingbirds; and the laughter of a child here and there.

The Alameda was never without its prancing steeds and luxurious equipage, whether it be a gilded carriage or European chariot. She found the beautiful women amusing, often stretched languorously on the silk pillows of their carriages, or adeptly speaking the special fluttering language of their fans at the window. Seldom seen were the *saya* or *mantilla;* rather, the latest gowns of silk that were only a few months behind the latest Parisian mode. Extravagant jewels were commonplace.

She usually came by providence, a hackney coach, and then had the driver wait while she walked about with Andres. On more than one occasion she had been forced to dissuade the bold eyes of a would-be lover with a cold expression. She knew that assignations took place in many of those fine coaches, but tried to push the thought from her head each time it intruded. Surely such meetings, ignored by yawning coachmen, were of a totally common or desperate nature!

Romance of the cheap variety had been available—in fact, she had been propositioned at least a dozen times by attractive married men. But serious, legitimate relationships had passed her by in the four years since her arrival in the capital. It was only natural for a woman who had been befouled by the Apache and had a five-year-old son from the encounter.

She had strongly considered creating a fictitious story and another name—as the widow of a dashing young officer killed outside of Santa Fe in a heroic act against the dreaded Navajo. And with Andres's relatively fair skin, it might have been accepted . . . by some. But both her father and Fidel de Gante had been so well known that the massacre had been big news in the capital papers when it happened. And in claiming her Cardenas inheritance, she had to make her true identity known.

She was simply the tragic young woman who had escaped from the barbaric Apache after being sullied and impregnated—the tainted beauty who had to be cast aside by a bereaved Agustin de Gante.

She and her bastard Apache child.

How she gloried in her zestful little Andres. Tall for his age, he was already coming out of his pretty stage. And as if his eyes were a compromise between mother and father, they were hazel with flecks of dark brown. He was bright and quick with a generous sense of humor, asking sometimes difficult questions, like the perfectly natural, "Where is my papa?" On this one point, Carlota adamantly refused to tell him the truth. She simply replied that his father had gone away, and refused to elaborate on the lie.

Besides, she had no intentions of remaining permanently in the city. As soon as this war was finally settled and she could sell her largest piece of property, she intended to move elsewhere—to California, perhaps Spain, possibly even the United States. Then she could escape the stigma that besmirched her life. It would be time for the fiction.

"Mama!"

From where he stood by a bubbling fountain a few yards ahead, Andres was holding up a bright coin. "Mama, look what the soldier gave me!"

Standing near her son were two American officers in campaign dress uniforms with their dark blue coats and bright sashes. Both were smiling warmly. The taller one closest to Andres held a wooden cane. As she approached, she could see pleasant brown eyes greeting her from under the visor of his high cap. In flawless Spanish, he said, "I hope you don't mind, Señora. It's only a Texas penny."

She didn't know why she spoke brazenly in English, perhaps because of his superb Spanish. Perhaps because she was tired of scrupulously avoiding the crude Americans who occupied her city. "You should not present gifts to strangers, Captain."

He switched to English. "Not even to a little boy?" His grin was pleasant, slightly crooked. She noticed he had a thin white scar on the left side of his jaw.

"Come, Andres," she said in Spanish as she took his hand. "Tell the man 'thank you.' We must be going."

The tall one with the cane removed his hat and bowed. "Please allow me, Señorita. I am Captain Rafael Murphy and this is Lieutenant George Pickett. I hope we might—"

He didn't get a chance to finish. Carlota towed Andres away as coolly as if the two Americans weren't there.

"It certainly pays to know the language. Right, Rafe?" Pickett laughed.

Captain Murphy smiled ruefully. "I wonder if she could have been his governess? Perhaps his aunt?"

"C'mon, Don Juan, your success with the ladies is only exceeded by your good fortune at monte. Let's find a game."

"Maybe his big sister?"

Carlota nodded her thanks as the butler removed her cloak. The City of Mexico was quite warm for the Christmas holidays, but the nights were still brisk enough to require a warm overgarment. She smiled as her Aunt Magdelena led the way toward their hostess at the end of the large vestibule. The lady was Señora de Anaya, the wealthy widow of a former judge and an old friend of Magdelena. It was the only time Carlota had been out for any kind of a social affair during the holiday season—in fact, since the previous summer—and she had spent too much money on a new gown of soft gray silk. But she felt it was worth every single *real*—enhanced by her mother's finest pearl necklace and earrings, it was a fitting raiment for her gay mood.

Heads turned as she moved into the large reception room. Drawing herself a bit taller, she imagined their thoughts, if not their asides behind the fluttering fans . . . *the Apache woman!* But tonight she didn't care; she felt precisely like what she was—the most beautiful young woman at the large dinner party.

From a corner of the room, Captain Rafael Murphy agreed. He, too, had accompanied an aunt to the affair—his mother's sister, another widow of substance who was a friend of the hostess. He stared at the tall beauty in gray silk with her hair piled high in a lustrous black diadem, unable to believe his amazing good luck. She was the same exciting young woman he had seen on the Alameda only three weeks earlier! He hadn't been able to get her startling blue eyes out of his mind, and here she was—live and unescorted, in all her radiance right before his eyes!

"She is Carlota de Cardenas, the unfortunate young woman who was with the Apaches," his aunt said coolly, watching her nephew's admiring eyes. "That one I told you about last fall . . . with the Apache child."

"Introduce me, Tia," Rafael said urgently.

"There is plenty of time. You know she is practically an outcast. Why—"

"So am I, Tia. Please do it now." Rafael's hand gripped his cane tightly. What a remarkable young woman!

Her expression held a touch of humor, her voice was charmingly low. He was completely fascinated as the introductions were made. "My lady of the Alameda," he said with a broad smile. "And how is the handsome little boy?"

As the small talk developed, she found his warm brown eyes unreserved and apparently unsophisticated—actually forward. Tall and rangy, there seemed to be a certain wiry tension about him that contradicted the sense of security he emanated. "Your Spanish is excellent, Captain," she said as the two aunts slipped into their own conversation.

"Yes, my mother was a perfectionist."

Carlota glanced at his aunt. Probably an old family from the capital—certainly not a Murphy. She knew about the Irish from those days in Washington.

"My father was a fair Celt who spoke Spanish like it came from a potato," Rafael Murphy grinned.

"In Texas?" She wondered about the cane.

"Yes. They met when they were both very young at the time the American Volunteers under Magee and Lockett came into Texas on the 1813 filibuster. Five years later, she ran away with him to New Orleans."

Carlota raised her eyebrows. "How interesting. And you were born in Texas?"

"Yes, but my father is from the state of Ohio, by the Great Lakes—"

The signal for dinner interrupted.

They were seated separately, but Rafael ignored the cigars and brandy, and went directly to her after the long and involved dinner. She was pleased. Holding her with his direct gaze, he asked if he could call the following day. She smiled—there was simply no sense in playing the coquettish delaying game. She wanted to see this boyish, honest American again, and the next day would suit her just fine. In fact, as he bowed over her hand, she wished it were already tomorrow.

The forbidding Customs House in San Domingo Street had once been the Palace of the Inquisition. From where Rafael had stopped the buggy across the street from its entrance, the old building seemed to sag from the suffering that had resulted in its chambers. "Isabella certainly was a paradox, wasn't she?" Carlota said quietly. "She did so many wonderful things during her tragic and glorious rule, and yet she could mother an Inquisition so brutal that it defied any logical reasoning . . . and so thorough that it could reach across the great ocean she helped discover to inflict great wrongs on her colonists."

Rafael nodded. "Perhaps the tragedies that befell her children were acts of retribution."

"But it was done in the name of Rome and the Holy Father."

Rafael snorted. "I wish I had a silver peso for every wrong committed under the guise of religious justification." He tapped the reins lightly on the horse's rump, urging it forward. "Or, for that matter, in the guise of doing *anything* deadly that is 'best for the people.' Look at what Santa Anna has done to the Mexican people, or what President Polk and his confederates have done. Who or what is right? Santa Anna butchered my father at Goliad, along with three hundred and eighty-nine other victims of his treachery. But for what reason did *Los Ninos Heroicos* die in the last-ditch stand at Chapultepec—six young cadets who had so much to live for?"

And why should there still be warring Apache? Carlota thought bitterly. Why should a whole area the size of an average European country be threatened by savages who could steal a young bride away from her proper life? She pushed the unanswerable questions aside like always and turned to watch the sure manner in which Rafael drove. It had been five weeks since the holiday dinner party, and they had seen each other nearly every day. He was the most persistent, yet gentle man she had ever known.

"It is a certainty they will sign the treaty in Guadalupe Hidalgo soon," he said. "Then we can all go home and pick up our real lives." He said it so quickly she barely noticed: "I think we should be married soon so that hurdle will be crossed before the orders are issued. There is paperwork, of course, but I'll dispose of that. And then there is the matter of getting you and Andres to San Antonio, since I will probably have to return with the troops. Now I have—"

She caught his hand. "No, Rafael, don't."

"What do you mean? I've told you over and over how much I love you. I thought possibly a quiet service with just a few friends—nothing big."

How dare he do this to her so suddenly? It wasn't fair at all. "No, Rafael, my dear Rafael, I hardly know you. It would be out of the question. I—"

He kissed her, dropped the reins and kissed her right there in the middle of the street as the horse continued to trot along. "And now, my dear," he said softly as he released her, "Is a month enough time for you?"

"Stop right now, Rafael Murphy! I won't be treated like this! I can't marry you and I won't." She couldn't go off to Texas, not with the Apache horror hanging over her head. He would always have it in the back of his mind, always . . . it would always be the Apache brat thing, no matter what or where . . . Spain, Paris, California—those were places to go, not Texas. She and Andres.

Slowing the horse, he gripped her hand tightly. "Now you listen to me, Carlota. I know what's pounding through that pretty head of yours, all that nonsense about the Apache. I know about ostracism in this provincial society. By the Virgin in her seven sorrows, I know. But it doesn't matter."

She dropped her head, refusing to look at him.

"Look at me! What do you see—an American, a Texan? Yes, but something else. You see a man of double blood—half Mexican, half Anglo. Do you know how much hate was fostered between the two in Texas in the past twenty-five years? I own a sizeable piece of land south of San Antonio, and my father was a hero of the revolution, but those hard-nosed Anglos will never forget that my mother was a Mexican. Never."

He kissed her hand, his eyes wide and caring. "Already I love Andres. I know he will have some problems before his life is over, but I want him to be my son so perhaps the name Murphy can shield him a bit. I want to adopt him as soon as we reach Texas, give him everything possible. That's what I want. But mostly, I want you, my dearest."

The tears streamed down her cheeks, but she didn't care. She just stared at him, stared and blinked and nodded her head. *Could she lead a normal life?* "A month will be enough," she whispered.

Six days later, while shopping on Tacuba Street near the Plaza Mayor, Carlota bumped into a tall man in the uniform of a Mexican cavalry colonel. His dark good looks washed over her like a sudden wave of pain. "Hello, Carlota," he said quietly. It was the first time she had seen Agustin de Gante since leaving La Reina.

Drawing in a sharp breath, she tried to quell the sudden pounding of her heart. She had often dreamed of meeting him again, particularly during the first months when she frequently had to cry herself to sleep. And how she had practiced the words of hate and contempt she would rain on him. But now they had deserted her. Summoning a mask of indifference, she nodded curtly. "Colonel de Gante." She had read in the papers that he had been captured after fighting bravely at Chapultepec. He looked so strong, not like the weakling from the hacienda.

"I was told you were living here," he said with a tentative smile. "I must say, you are even more lovely than I remembered."

"I didn't know you remembered," she replied coldly. She knew her hand was shaking. *Why did he have this effect on her?*

"Oh, yes," he said, holding her eyes. "More than you could imagine. . . . I have wished so often that things could have been different. We could have—"

"How is your wonderful mother? Has she selected a proper wife for you yet?" The words were bitter.

He nodded. "Yes, well, I'm engaged to marry. The war, you know."

Carlota stepped to the side. "I hope you will be very happy. Now, if you will excuse me, I must be on my way." She threw a harsh look at him. "I have a handsome young son waiting for me at home."

His hand caught her arm. "May I see you again?"

"For what?"

"I, well, I want to tell you how sorry I am . . . I just want to see you."

She didn't answer as she walked away.

But she couldn't walk away from the emotional disruption Agustin had caused. No matter what she did, he was on her mind. And Rafael couldn't help—he was serving on a courts-martial board in Puebla for a few days. Following a light dinner at which she merely picked, she tried needlework. But it was the same thing—Agustin, over and over.

As the final ringing of the Angelus bells faded out, a messenger arrived with a dozen roses. Inside the box was a note from Agustin:

> My Dearest Carlota,
>   I have thought of you every moment. I must see you as
> soon as possible. There is much for me to make up. I love you.
>   Agustin

She tore up the note and angrily threw the flowers in a waste container. How dare he? What did the arrogant fool think she was—

some kind of baggage who would run to him the moment he called? He was *nothing*, a shallow nothing who had ruined her life! But no, *Lazaro* had ruined her life. Could Agustin be blamed for Lazaro's raid?

She grew angry and went to her bed. Why couldn't she just cast off the supplications of this arrogant weakling? She should laugh at him—caught in a betrothal arranged by his mother, at his age? Why, he was pitiful, not a *fraction* of the man Rafael is. The thought of Rafael made her feel guilty—because Agustin had unsettled her? No, because she was weakening!

She pounded her pillow. No matter how she denied it, she *wanted* to see Agustin. She could fuss and fume and feel as guilty as she wanted, it all boiled down to that. She wanted to see the man who had been the center of her life for all those years—no matter *what* he had done to her!

And that made her nothing but a repulsive weakling.

His house was on San Francisco Street, a two-story affair that was nearly two hundred years old and elegantly furnished. It was not the de Gante house she remembered from nine years earlier, but the family could easily have owned several such residences. The supper had been a superb meal of tender steak, complete with champagne and candlelight. Agustin had even provided a violinist who played Gypsy music from the seclusion of a shadowy corner. The table was abundant with bright flowers. Seated across from her between tall silver candelabra, he wore a dress uniform and spoke gaily as if they had been together forever. In addition to battle stories and anecdotes about Santa Anna, he related enjoyable tales about other government figures and their foibles. She waited for his deep apologies, but none were forthcoming. Only the full intensity of his considerable wit and charm filled the room.

And she was entranced.

She wanted to ask about his mother; but it would have been out of place in such a beguiling setting. In fact, she didn't want anything to interrupt the romantic allure of the entire evening. This was the handsome Agustin de Gante she had married so long ago, and she had finally reached her wedding night. His white teeth flashed in the light as she lifted her second glass of brandy. All the nights of longing seemed to hang over her like an overpowering mantilla of seduction. She barely heard his words, thinking only of how it would be next to his warm skin, held tightly in his arms, kissing him, being totally aroused by him. . . .

And finally they were alone. Quietly, he arose and rounded th table. Taking her hand, he drew her from her seat and into his arms He was so strong, his scent so attractive. She melted against hin drawing in his inquisitive and then demanding tongue. Without inte rupting the long kiss, he picked her up and carried her toward th door. It was her wedding night with her beloved Agustin, and at las they would be one. Nothing else mattered.

He lowered her to the huge canopied bed, murmuring, "Hurry, m darling, your clothes." His voice was husky as he pulled at the buttor of his uniform coat. "Hurry, oh hurry, my darling. I want you beautiful, creamy white body for the entire night, I love you s much."

She watched him fumble with his cravat through wide eyes, b suddenly he was no longer standing before her—he was seated in wingback chair in another bedroom, and she was on her knees be ging, begging to be loved and he was staring hopelessly at the floc . . . she was in her white wedding peignoir that had waited two yea for her return from a terrible ordeal, begging.

His tone was urgent. "Your clothes, my darling. I—"

"*Aaaheeeee!*" Her scream was terrible. "*Aaaheeeee!*" She rushed pa him and out of the bedroom, still screaming, tears running down h cheeks. She tripped, nearly falling, but caught herself and ran on dow the long hallway to the dining room. Slumping at the table, she crie uncontrollably, releasing the dreadful pain she had been carrying f so long. And finally she heard his voice. "What is this nonsens Carlota? Are you crazy? Is this some kind of Apache foolishness, something?"

She looked up at him through the tears. Never before had sl loathed herself so much. Her hand closed over a steak knife and sl saw an old hag coming at her, a wickiup, a sergeant with a face beate to a bloody pulp . . . an Apache hurtling toward her and jumping fro his pony . . . Lazaro covering her, taking her . . .

Slowly she shook her head and dropped the knife. "No, Agusti it isn't Apache. But you wouldn't understand." Her voice was fl "Now, get my coat and order your carriage. I'm going home."

He frowned as he stared at her. "I don't believe this. You love m Carlota looked right through him. "I know," she said softly.

"Ego conjungo vos in Matrimonium, in nominee Patris et Filii. . . . "
There was no quaint *lazo* draped over them, no family chapel, a no wedding gown from Spain. Only a handful of people attended t

short ceremony, including her Aunt Magdelena and Lieutenant George Pickett. It was a late Saturday afternoon, and after a short reception at Carlota's house, the newlyweds would leave on a short wedding trip to Cuernavaca.

Carlota had been to confession, but she still felt highly guilty about her visit to Agustin. She had nearly told Rafael about it in a rash moment of contrition, but decided it would be unfair to wash her wrong off on him. She thought back to the other wedding, then forced it from her mind as the priest continued with the words of the service. A vivid memory of sitting behind Lazaro on that terrible day he made her his wife flashed back to her. All those hideous, staring faces, her near panic . . . another marriage. No! That was a crime inflicted on her, no marriage. How ridiculous to even think about it!

It was time.

Rafael took her left hand and placed the gold band on her finger. His brown eyes were full of love. "With this ring, I thee wed . . . "

10

Lazaro glanced up at the darkening sky. The sudden drop in temperature indicated the possibility of the first winter storm. He hoped it would pass; he didn't need bad weather to interfere with his conference. Pulling his lynxskin robe more tightly around his throat, he fastened his gaze on the back of the Chiricahua guide who was leading him up to Chochise's stronghold. He liked the location. The trail was narrow and crooked, and his experienced eye had already picked out several positions from which large stones could easily be rained down on any column of enemies trying to get up to the natural fortress.

It would be nearly as easy to defend as Giant's Claw.

He glanced back to where Delgadito followed him. The Lean One had become his most able war leader in the past two years. Just behind him rode Cuchillo Negro, the Warm Springs chief whose band roamed through the Black Range to the holes of hot water northeast of the Willows Country. Cuchillo Negro was his strongest brother Chihenne and the most important ally to pledge his loyalty. Then came Tze-go-juni, dressed as a man and heavily painted in the face. She had healed from Carlota's terrible knife wound in remarkably short time, due, she claimed, to her special Power as the greatest shaman since her forebear, the legendary Gagi-tash. Only six of his top warriors made up the bodyguard. His most promising young war leader, Victorio, brought up the rear.

They had ridden three days to the southwest from Willows Country to meet with the Chiricahua in their homeland hills. Lazaro's dream of uniting the People had never diminished since his dedication on the night he became chief following the Santa Rita massacre. But while he had made loosely tied treaties with various tribes and bands such agreements were usually temporary and did not serve to bring the Apache any closer together than they had been in the days of Roberto. A compact with Cochise and his closest chiefs could be a huge step toward his goal.

Cochise was actually a subchief under Narbona, but the chief was recovering from a wound and was ill as well. And Cochise was stronger than any of the others.

Topping a sharp crest, a grassy slope dotted with over a hundred drab brown wickiups greeted them. Wisps of smoke here and there marked low-burning fires where food was being kept warm for the occasion. The entire band of Chiricahua and other visitors were gathered near the entrance to greet the arrivals. Cochise, wearing two eagle feathers in his headband as a ceremonial gesture, strode forward as Lazaro swung down from his big black pony.

The Chiricahua chief was two years younger than Lazaro and some six inches shorter—still tall for an Apache. The son of Pisago was erect, slender, and wore the role of leadership as if he had been born to it—which he had, for the blood of chiefs that ran through his veins went nearly as far back as Silsoose. Hollow cheeks rose above a strong jaw and flanked a wide mouth that could fluctuate between a grim and pensive expression. His wide-set eyes were black and guarded a large, sharp nose. In fact, a stranger would have thought the two strongest leaders of the Apache were identical twins—except that only one of such a birth was ever permitted to live.

"Welcome, my brother," Cochise said as the two leaders embraced each other by the arms. He inclined his head toward several visitors. "Our brothers from the Nednhi, the Chokonen, and from the Bedonkohe, are here."

Lazaro nodded to the other leaders. "Enjuh!" He glanced at the threatening sky. "Is your Chiricahua Ghost Face about to descend on us and chill our bones?" Ghost Face was winter.

A smile touched Cochise's lips. "My most powerful shaman has assured me that Ghost Face will not drop his white blanket until the son of Silsoose has departed."

"Enjuh!" Lazaro followed his host toward a central fire as the others followed.

Cochise and Lazaro sat side by side on their blankets, smoking rolled cigarettes of real tobacco that the Chihenne had provided as a gift. The other visitors and Chiricahua leaders sat around the fire, speaking in small groups. Tze-go-juni, who had cast off all rivals as Lazaro's head shaman, sat directly behind him. The black-and-white paint that she customarily wore for ceremonial occasions formed a swirling pattern on her ugly face. She stared straight ahead as if in a trance, whispering a chant to add Power to her nantan's mission. In the background a soft drumbeat began and all voices ceased except for that of the Chiricahua chief, who launched into the ceremonial speech of the People. The words were poetic as he referred to the land and animals about them, to the sky, and the whispering breeze.

When he finished, all eyes turned to Lazaro. He waited, perfectly at ease, to gain effect. Twelve years had passed since the Santa Rita massacre, when he had vowed to bring the Apache together, and he had spoken before many a campfire. He was confident, eloquent, as he began the formal phraseology of the Apache. He spoke of the eagle and of the antelope; of the alder, oak, and buckthorn; he sang the praises of the lark and the dove, and of the mescal the Creator had given them for food and drink.

He drained his cup of the fermented drink.

Finally as dusk descended lavender over the stronghold's guardian hills, he worked into his topic. He recounted the centuries of war with first the Spaniard and then the Nakai-ye, of their faithlessness and their atrocities. He told of the coming increase in the scalp bounty that had been reported—a doubling in value of the hair of the People. His voice was clear, ringing: "I believe it is time, my brothers, to slacken our raids in the land of the Nakai-ye. We have done too well. If we lessen the frequency of our attacks, they will have time to fatten their herds for us. And then, my brothers, when the talk of more soldiers and high payment for hair has diminished, we will ride out of the morning sunrise like the flash of the Thunder People, and they will know the fury of the Apache lance once more."

He raised his hand in warning. "While the Nakai-ye grow complacent, we must think of the new threat to our hunting grounds. I have spoken with the White Eye nantan of the soldiers, and they have come to our homelands to stay. Their war with the Nakai-ye is long over and he says our land belongs to his great nantan in a stronghold in Wash-in-ton.

"He also says the Nakai-ye who stay are now Americanos, and that many more White Eyes will come in the years ahead." Lazaro paused, looking around for effect before adding, "And this nantan says we must no longer raid to the south—never, no more."

Guffaws and jeers from the entire gathering followed.

When the noise diminished, Lazaro continued, "These White Eyes do not understand that we *always* fight and raid in the south . . . since before the rocks were hard. They do not know it is the Way, but they will learn.

"He also speaks of giving us food in the Willows Country . . . food and other goods in return for the peace. The White Eye nantan says there will be a White Eye who will live among us, and give us these things, and speak for the great nantan in that place called Wash-in-ton. . . . "

Lazaro spoke on of the strength in banding together in mutual support for not only war but times of hardship. He talked of a loose alliance that would be like a soft string connecting the tribes, clans and bands from the south to the White Mountain, from the sunset to Tejas, where the Mescalero and the Jicarilla homelands formed the boundary of the People.

He watched the faces of those gathered in the thickening night, and he knew they agreed, but that their minds were wandering to their personal futures with the White Eyes. It was as he had expected—when he was finished with the parley, he would accept the same old verbal agreements, and they would go on their way. Still, the firm pact with Cochise was more important than any other.

Lazaro squinted into the shady wickiup to where Dineh lay opposite from the doorway. Benita was changing the bandage on her forehead. The Navajo beauty who had so many years earlier created the arousal in him that had led to Nadzeela was nearly unrecognizable. There was a deep gash over her right eye, which was a swollen mass of blackened tissue. Although she could see through the slit that was her left eye, the cheekbone below also carried an open gash. He had been told that her nose was also broken, as well as ribs.

She cringed when she saw him crawl inside.

"Do you feel better, woman?" he asked softly.

"Yes," she replied through thickened lips. Her voice was barely audible.

Lazaro nodded. It was an Apache man's right to beat his wife, and he never interfered in such matters. But Bacho had long carried his wife-beating too far—it seemed that Dineh had been unable to leave her wickiup or else had been a walking mass of bruises for over a year now. Benita had brought up the man's cruelty on several occasions, and now she was furious. Perhaps because both had come to the People as captives, they had become close friends.

"What are you going to do about it?" his wife asked sharply.

"I will speak to him."

"Words mean nothing to a beast!"

Lazaro found Bacho at the hoop-and-pole ground, where the Wolf spent most of his time. The hoop-and-pole ground was a secluded area of smooth grass and slick pine needles that was surrounded by a ring of thick alder to keep the prying eyes of females from even seeing the games in progress. Women were strictly forbidden to go near the place; it was said that any woman who did so would get swollen joints and pains in her legs. In fact, the hoop-and-pole ground was the universal fraternal meeting place of the Apache—where everything from pranks to war planning, from wrestling to heavy gambling took place. Music was made from such instruments as the musical bow, the flute, or the one-stringed violin in that special men's retreat.

But naturally the main activity was the hoop-and-pole game, a contest between two men with thin poles nearly thirty feet long that were slipped under a rolling hoop at the instant it fell. The accuracy in which this maneuver was executed determined the number of points awarded to the winner on each roll. Sometimes the stakes were exceptionally high between good players or heavy gamblers.

And nearly all Apache loved to gamble.

Bacho was the best player in Lazaro's huge band, and possibly the best of all the Chihenne. He made most of his living at the game. Bacho had been a thorn in Lazaro's groin forever, it seemed. Since their warrior apprenticeship together, and particularly since Lazaro's election as chief, the powerful rival known as Wolf had struggled against him—criticizing, opposing, at times openly defiant. But Lazaro always accepted these actions with stoicism. Bacho was a powerful warrior in combat, an excellent war leader, and somehow—in spite of his meanness—a kind of kinsman in spirit. And besides, the fierce independence of every Chihenne was his most treasured possession.

Lazaro had warned him before about his ruthlessness both in his wickiup and with weaker men. But each time, the Wolf had either laughed or snarled back at him. It was time.

He waited until Bacho finished the game in progress—in which the Wolf won a fast spotted pony from a visiting Warm Springs. And then he drew him aside. "What you have done to your woman is too much," he said quietly. "You could kill her with such beatings."

Instant anger flashed over Bacho's handsome features. "That's my affair!" he snarled.

Lazaro's voice remained calm. "The well-being of every Chihenne is also *my* affair."

Bacho's anger continued to mount. "She is a worthless *Dineh!*" He paced back and forth before the chief, scowling darkly, working up a frenzy. "And you, mighty Nantan, you are a *disgrace* to our warriors. Talk, talk, talk! Make treaties like a *woman!* Your mother's milk still runs through your cowardly veins!"

The many men who had been gathered in the hoop-and-pole place quickly gathered round in a circle as Lazaro's cheeks began to burn. He could walk away and maintain his dignity, assuming they would all understand the meaninglessness of Bacho's bluster—

"You piss your pants when the White Eye wiggles his finger!"

Bacho had gone too far. The confrontation that had been brewing since childhood had arrived, and he couldn't walk away from it. Victorio was watching him from a few paces away. Old Man had gotten to his good leg and fingered his knife as he glared at Bacho from eyes shaded by a low-brimmed old hat. Delgadito's face was a patient mask; others seemed not to breathe as they wondered how much more abuse their chief would take.

"Begone from my camp," Lazaro said quietly. He had used the dreaded words. An Apache could leave any band and join another, but to be banished was a terrible disgrace. "You are no longer of the Willows people."

"Aaarrrggh!" Bacho roared, drawing his knife and springing back into a fighting stance. His eyes glittered, as if reflecting the early winter sun that was giving the day such an unnatural warmth. He jerked the knife in an unmistakable taunt and began circling to Lazaro's left.

Instantly, the chief's knife was in his right hand—a broad, heavy blade that he had gotten from a passing Texan who claimed it was named for a hero in a far-off place called the Ala-mo. Man named Boo-ey. Dropping to a crouch and rising on the balls of his feet, Lazaro blotted out all else but the combat in front of him. His mouth was suddenly dry, his vision sharp and his hearing muted. He felt added strength course through his veins and for a brief instant wondered if it was his Power coming into force. The faces in the ring of men faded into haziness as he picked up the hypnotic pace of Bacho's methodical circling.

His shorter opponent was much thicker in the body, and with his long, powerful arms he had dismantled many an enemy. In fact, Bacho's prowess with a knife and willingness to use it had long added to his fearsome reputation. Now, his lips were parted, moist, his tongue moving around them as if eager to taste his enemy's blood. With his free hand, he tore open his shirt, briefly fingering a fetish on his bare chest.

He made the first feint.

Lazaro barely acknowledged the fake thrust as he continued to glide in the small circle to his right. He pitched slightly sideways as he stepped, weight on the balls and toes, ready to instantly plant a foot for power in any kind of sudden move. The years of practice in his youth came back to him sharply, though he had never used such a heavy blade. And always they had worked with a shield over the free arm; today the arm was the shield.

Bacho's long Daga dagger, a prize from a Mexican raid, flashed upward, slashing through Lazaro's sleeve and drawing the first spurting blood. A fleeting smile crossed the Wolf's lips as he nodded confidently. "I should have cut your heart out years ago!" he snarled.

The next minute was filled with feints and missed thrusts by both. Then suddenly, their knives locked momentarily. Pushing his chief back, Bacho nicked Lazaro's knife hand, and taunted him again. But Lazaro was completely under control, holding his emotions rigidly in tow. He was coldly aware that he was in the deadliest position of his life, and that survival would require every iota of his skill. He watched Bacho's quick moves, trying to pick up a pattern. Weaving from side to side, the Wolf began to force him backward to the cordon of excited onlookers.

A sudden flick of the Bowie knife opened a thin line on Bacho's cheek that swiftly turned crimson as rivulets of blood ran down his jaw and the side of his neck. He wiped it off with his free hand, and lunged forward, only to miss again. A long sideswipe from Lazaro missed, and they swung back toward the middle of their pine needle arena. The blades clashed together in a sharp *rrrring!* as both thrust toward each other's midsection simultaneously. And then Bacho's thinner blade caught the chief in a stinging slice on his left side.

At that instant Tze-go-juni burst into the ring of frontline spectators, her face contorted in hate, and a loud chant on her lips. *"Na-do-none, chido-dona, na-da-dona, bacho-na-do-nana. . . . "*

The pain was sharp from the wound in his side, and Lazaro knew he had to end it quickly or the better fighter would soon cut him to pieces. Avoiding another wide swipe, he missed a counterthrust to Bacho's stomach. His fingers went to the wound in his side, telling him of profuse bleeding. The sun seemed brighter and it was hot; sweat ran into his eyes. Blood drenched his left arm.

With a heavy lunge, the Wolf crashed into him, forcing him backward with his burly shoulders. *This was it!* Applying every ounce of leverage his tall body could summon, Lazaro twisted over his locked right foot and threw Bacho crashing to the ground. Instantly he was on him, pinning his knife arm and raising his own blade for the final, killing stroke. His old adversary's eyes were burning black slits, conceding nothing. The roars of the crowd and Tze-go-juni's shrill screams shattered the air. But something stopped him. Slowly, he brought the wide blade down to Bacho's throat, where he held its tip under the Wolf's chin. "Be gone from my camp," he panted and pushed him back.

Bacho's face twisted hatefully as he spat, "Some day I will kill you, woman-chief. If it takes forever."

11

Santa Fe, New Mexico
June 20, 1852

Carlota paused as the bugle notes of "Retreat" being blown from in front of the palace accompanied the lowering of the large American flag from its high pole in the center of the plaza. Early in their marriage, Rafael had convinced her that it was not only a military courtesy, but one of basic respect for her adopted country. Besides, there was something ceremonial, even mystical, about the flag being raised or lowered to the strains of traditional music. After all, she was the daughter of a soldier—it *should* stir her.

As the final note drifted away toward the snow-covered peaks of the Sangres de Cristo, the two soldiers folded the flag. She smiled as she nodded to them and hurried on toward her house on San Miguel Street. She wanted to hear Andres's lesson before he ate his evening meal.

They had gone to Rafael's house in San Antonio de Bexar in Texas the summer following their marriage. He also owned a tract of land south of the city that was fertile and grassy enough to support a fair-sized herd of cattle. But the war had done something to Rafael— or Rafe, as everyone called him. He described it as "having learned to love a parade." A wide strain of soldier blood had been exposed, he decided, and he would never be happy watching over cud-chewing beef cattle for the rest of his life.

Because of the medal he won at the Battle of Monterrey, and for having been mentioned in several dispatches during other campaigns, he was granted a regular army commission in the grade of first lieutenant, and sworn into active service in November 1848. Following several months of duty at the San Antonio garrison, he received orders assigning him to Colonel Sumner's Ninth Military Department in Santa Fe. His fluency in Spanish had also been the reason for his duty as a staff officer at the department headquarters there.

His meager salary of twelve hundred dollars per year was hardly enough for any kind of a decent life. Other than the ordinary staples of life, existence was expensive because other goods had to be shipped so far to reach the historic old capital. But fortunately the Murphy family had other funds to supplement the army pay—added to the money he realized from the sale of his properties in Texas was the remainder of Carlota's settlement from the de Gantes' and the money she had inherited from her father's estate. She had kept one large gold nugget from Giant's Claw in the event of an emergency. Actually, the Murphys were quite well-off relative to most regular officer families.

Carlota had found the house on San Miguel Street following a one-month stay in a two-room apartment at the Fonda Hotel. She had readily adapted to the city of her birth, with its sometimes absurd ways, and with over four thousand people trying to confuse the energetic Americans with their *mañana* customs. She even liked its frontier aspects, and had framed the first newspaper to be printed after their arrival. It was the Santa Fe *Republican*, and its front page announced that it was "Devoted to Science, Literature, Agriculture— The Earliest News from The United States and the General Movements of the Army." She had to chuckle at its motto: "We Die but Never Surrender."

Her first purchases had resulted from the advertisement that stated "J.M. White & Brother, Cheap Merchants. Calicos, Jeans, Lawns, Muslins—Officers and Soldiers about to return to the States can purchase suits here as cheap as at home."

Now she was practically a native Santa Fe-an, equally at home with the Americans and the Hispanics; as welcome at the table of the governor and the wealthy and influential old families as that of a poor army officer. Her social calendar was always full. At twenty-eight, her full-blown beauty was just beginning to take on a fine edge of maturity; there was a bit more definition to her high cheekbones, and a couple of tiny laugh lines at the corners of her still-sparkling blue eyes. And it was not only the forward Hispanic men who turned to stare in open appreciation as she passed by on the street; now and then a woman or a passing Indian did so.

The only element of Santa Fe life she couldn't bear was the Indian influence. Mostly Pueblo, with touches of Navajo and Jicarilla Apache, it was a constant reminder of her ordeal in the Willows Country.

It was such a pleasant day, and she found Andres finishing his lesson in the patio at the center of their house. He spoke brightly as she entered, "I have done my ciphers and my writing, Mama."

She placed her hand fondly on his shoulder. "Good. But you know what I want to hear you recite—your poems."

He nodded, opening his lesson book to the short but elegant Castilian verse that she had given him the week before. As he began, she smiled warmly. This wonderful son of hers would amount to far more than these uncouth, half-educated louts who were considered his peers. He would be a linguist, a mathematician, *and* a scholar before he reached university age. Already, he could read and write better than most of the boys who were three or four years older. Tall and athletic at the age of ten, his cheekbones showed signs of prominence and his nose already looked as if it would make itself known. Everyone remarked about what a handsome boy he was becoming.

Rafe entered the patio from the *sala*—the salon—kissing her cheek as he greeted them. "And how are the rest of the Murphys this evening?" he asked warmly.

Andres quickly told him about a spirited colt with Arabian blood that he had seen that morning.

"Was he white with a cream-colored mane and tail?" Rafe asked.

"Yes, Father, and he arched his neck like a proud prince. Will you buy him for me?"

Rafe smiled down into his adopted son's earnest eyes as he patted his head. "No, my son, you're still too young for such a horse. But I might consider a pony when I get back from the copper mines."

Carlota threw him a sharp look. "I thought you weren't going there."

"The colonel changed his mind."

"You've always wanted to meet him, I know." She meant Lazaro, of course, but she couldn't be too vehement in front of Andres. She didn't want him asking any questions.

"I won't deny that. He's the major chief."

She wanted to snap, "He's a thief and a rapist!" but she controlled her tongue. The idea of the upcoming meeting between the army commander and the Apache leaders annoyed her. Why they couldn't simply go on a major campaign and defeat the heathens—kill or capture the leaders and hang them—she could never understand. End it. And most importantly, *kill Lazaro!* "What does the colonel hope to accomplish?"

"The usual, a peace treaty. Actually, he has told the War Department that we should give this part of the country back to the Indians. It was theirs to start with, and the Mexicans in their centuries of strife here have never done anything of real value."

She wanted to retort that the Mexicans represented culture and civilization, but she was already acting shrewish and she hated to be that way. Rafe was such a warm and caring man. Their love was so good—and continually exciting in many ways. He was the dearest man and she had no right to be so contentious about the Indians. But she couldn't help it. "It's too late now," she said quietly. "Where would all of these New Mexicans go?"

"Oh, he meant the wild territory below the Gila. But it'll never happen, not with settlers and miners swarming like locusts."

She changed the subject. "Everything is in order for our dinner tomorrow evening. It will be *the* social event of the month. . . . "

Carlota leaned down and kissed Beatriz on the cheek. The seven-year-old orphan was her favorite in the group of sixteen in her poetry class at the *Castrénse*, or Military Chapel. The church had been built on the south side of the plaza by Governor and Captain-General Valverde y Cośio at his own expense and dedicated to Nuestra Señora de la Luz early in the eighteenth century. It had twin towers and an elaborate *réredos*, or fine altar carvings, that had been added in 1761. Her classes were held in the north part of the transept of the cross-shaped church. Actually, the church had been in disrepair for some time, but it was a central location in which some of the military wives—under Carlota's leadership—had chosen to educate the orphans in the arts.

"Beatriz," she said encouragingly in English, for that was the language that she was using, "Please recite Mr. Shakespeare's 'Fancy' for us."

The little girl smiled bashfully, then closed her large dark eyes and collected herself for a moment before beginning:

> *"Tell me where is fancy bred,*
> *Or in the heart, or in the head?*
> *How begot, how . . . nourished?*
> *Reply, reply.*

Beatriz closed her eyes again, then went on,

> *"It is engen . . . engin—"*

"Engendered," Carlota prompted.

> *"—engendered in the eyes,*
> *With gazing fed; and the Fancy dies*
> *In the cradle where it lies.*

> *Let us all ring Fancy's knell;*
> *I'll begin it,—Ding, dong, bell.*
> *Ding, dong, bell."*

Beatriz finished proudly with a bright smile and Carlota congratulated her. "Now, children," she added, "that will be all for today. Read your poems tonight and practice your recitation. Get *feeling* into it, like Beatriz did today."

On the way across the plaza, she met Father Benivedes, the pastor of Our Lady of Guadalupe, the church where she was a member. He lifted his round black hat as he greeted her. "How did your class go today, Señora Murphy?" He had offered his church for the classes, but Carlota didn't want to change location.

"It was fine, Father," she replied with her bright smile. "Now I must hurry home to make sure the cook has everything in the right pot."

The priest grinned back. "My stomach twitches at the thought of visiting your remarkable table this evening."

"Good. Don't eat a thing." She hurried on, thinking: For one who wasn't truly religious, she seemed to be very much involved with the church. Well, she wasn't alone in going through the motions. Her ordeal in the Willows was a better excuse though . . . how many of these other women who went to Mass at least once a week, confession and communion when it looked good, had ever been cast aside by the Heavenly Father?

Carlota had decided to buy the house. Nothing as nice was available for rent and she didn't care for the quarters Rafe's predecessor had used. Several things went into the decision: Santa Fe was her place of birth, she thought the value of the property would increase, and she just *wanted* to own the house. Rafe had agreed readily, since he also thought Santa Fe would grow along with the continuing influx of Americans to the territory.

Like all of the other houses in the capital, the structure had been built of *adóbe*, the thick mud walls that served so well in keeping out the summer heat and the sometimes severe winter cold. The style was a square, a fortress type carryover from the early days when protection from Indian attack had been necessary. Essentially, it was also a throwback from early Spanish and Moorish origins. All of the rooms opened on a central *patio*. The inside walls were lined with a bright patterned fabric that was mostly red to a height of four feet, then treated with a nearly white coating of calcined *yeso*, or gypsum. The heavy *vigas*, or beams, that supported the roof were one of the characteristics of the house that most appealed to her. They were ornately carved, painted a very dark red, and in the custom of the Pueblo Indians, connected herringbone style with pale yellow-painted willow shoots. Only the very best houses in the city had such bright ceilings. Each room had a low, mule-shoe-shaped corner fireplace trimmed with bright, patterned tiles. It was the floor that did it: Instead of the usual adóbe, this house had a heavily varnished hardwood floor, over which she had placed some attractive throw rugs purchased in the plaza from Navajo weavers.

She had brought from Mexico two elaborately carved wooden chests that had belonged to her mother, and from San Antonio an ornate dining room suite that had belonged to Rafe's mother. The rest of her furniture was strictly Santa Fe in style. Instead of chairs, she used *colchóns* or mattresses which were folded and placed like benches around the room next to the walls. These were covered with bright Chimayo and Navajo blankets. At night the colchóns were spread out and used for beds.

The sala was her pride. Quite large, with two kiva fireplaces, it held a large oil painting of her father in dress uniform, as well as several other good paintings that her mother had acquired or brought from Spain. The dining area was that part of the sala closest to the *cocina*, the kitchen. Dinner was in progress. Although Carlota loved to cook, she had brought in Maria Elena two days earlier to add her special skills to the repast. Maria Elena had been preparing the best meals in Santa Fe for some time and was the mark of a very special entertainment. The menu she and Carlota had decided upon could grace any table in New Mexico:

Crema de Elote
(CREAM OF CORN SOUP)

Arroz Blanco con Chili Verde y Piñones
(WHITE RICE WITH GREEN CHILI AND PINE NUTS)

Flor de Calabaza con Crema
(PUMPKIN BLOSSOMS WITH CREAM)

Loma de Puerco al Horno con Tomates y Cebolla
(ROASTED LOIN OF PORK WITH TOMATOES AND ONIONS)

Natillas y Empanaditas con Conservas de Duraznos
(SOFT CUSTARD AND LITTLE TURNOVERS WITH PEACH PRESERVES)

Spanish Sherry
Cigars for the men and cigarets for the women

The evening had begun without a hitch and the Flor de Calabaza had just been served. Carlos, the waiter from the Fonda she had hired on his night off, was keeping the wine glasses filled with *Vino de Borgoña* and assisting María Elena in serving the food.

The seating arrangement was excellent. Colonel Edwin Vose Sumner sat on her left, Señora Vigíl—the wife of the former acting governor—across from him, and next to her she placed the guest of honor: Christopher—Kit—Carson, the wiry little, soft-spoken hero of the Mexican War in California. Across from him sat Mrs. Sumner and next to her, the noted lawyer and publisher, Major Richard Hartman. Other guests down the table included Father Benivedes, Mrs. Josefa Jaramillo Carson, the famed scout's wife, and Don Donaciáno Vigíl. Rafe occupied the chair at the head of the table. As Mrs. Carson complimented Carlota on the delicacy of the pumpkin blossoms, the subject of slavery was brought up by Father Benivedes. His comments ended with, "How you Americans can continue so openly with slave-holding, I don't understand."

Richard Hartman gave him a stern look. A West Pointer from the District of Columbia, he was the epitome of a Southern gentleman— in fact his dueling was becoming legendary in Santa Fe. "Sir," he said softly, "you should not criticize a system that is open and honest while looking the other way at local slavery."

The former acting governor, Donaciáno Vigíl, spoke. "And what slavery is that, Señor Hartman?"

"The practice known as peonage, sir," the Southerner replied. "Don't tell me that doesn't qualify."

"Peonage is quite different. *Peóns* are not bought and sold in the market as chattels."

"There is little difference." Other conversations stopped as everyone at the table turned to listen. The West Pointer went on, "The law under which this system functions is called, 'Law regulating contracts between masters and servants.' Now while that sounds quite dignified, the statute is altogether one-sided and always favors the master. And don't even mention the wages a peón is paid—*five dollars a month?* To feed his family?"

"But he can leave the service of his master, if he wishes," Vigíl replied.

Hartman snorted. "Only if he owes the master no money. But he's required to buy his daily needs at the master's store—and you know they always pay more than market value. The peón is always in debt over his ears and is a slave for *life*. If fact, many of them have to bind their children over to the master, making *them* slaves for life."

Rafe spoke up from the end of the table. "And the master isn't required to take care of the peón or his wife in infirmity or old age. A peón gets too old to work, he's turned out to the hungry pasture like an old horse to die. Also, what about the Indian slaves?"

The lawyer nodded his head. "Yes. For years the Mexicans have kidnapped Indian boys and girls and sold them into slavery."

"But that's different," Vigíl said. "After all, they're just savages and it's a chance for them to become civilized."

Kit Carson broke in, giving the former acting governor a cool look. "Did you know that my first wife was Arapaho?"

Vigíl paused, obviously embarrassed by his gaffe. After a moment of total silence in the room, he lamely went on, "That's different. I'm talking about Navajos, Utes, and those damned Apaches. Now don't try to tell me you consider the Apaches anything more than savages!"

Suddenly Carlota felt a coldness. It was as if she had just said the same thing. How many times, in fact, *had* she uttered similar words? But these comments were cast in a different light—and all she could think of was her darling Andres back in his room. Would he ever get out of the shadow of his arrogant, savage father? There it was again—the word, savage. But Andres was *hers*, not his. He had *never* been an Apache. But she couldn't shake off the troubled feeling. She'd have to continue shielding him, have to keep cultivating his wonderful little mind.

She pushed the problem away and signaled for the Loma de Puerco to be served. This was too stimulating a dinner party to be spoiled by worry. She gave Rafe a meaningful look and he quickly broke into the conversation with, "Can you tell us about your adventures around San Diego, Colonel Carson?"

The colorful Mexican War veteran smiled wryly. "I hate to see a good argument get shut off, but since you ask—"

12

The Kneeling Nun
July 1, 1852

Lazaro stood below the rocks of the Kneeling Nun and looked down at Santa Rita. The sun was bright, like it was that terrible day, but the vivid patches of rust and its colorful cousins now dressed the familiar hills in their fleeting autumn coat. Why was he so often drawn back here to this place of sad memories? It seemed only yesterday that treachery had erupted in the midst of a fiesta . . . when he lost his beloved wife, and so many of the People were slain and maimed.

He recalled how, before the massacre, he'd ridden quietly to a meadow above the town, thinking about his Power, feeling a vague uneasiness about something elusive. That was when he saw her—the most beautiful young woman he'd ever encountered. Her pale skin and striking eyes the color of the noonday sky flashed back before him. She'd looked up, momentarily caught by his gaze. In that instant he'd fallen in love with her.

And then one day he'd found her, taken her captive on the huge Nakai-ye hacienda. Made her his wife, and encountered her unwavering hatred. Even when their fine son was born she never relented—froze him out of her very existence. It had been nine years since she'd taken his boy and escaped. He still secretly admired that feat. He was certain he could always find her at the de Gante place, but another woman prisoner from that same hacienda told Benita that she had come and gone—no longer a member of the family. She lived in Mexico City, the woman thought.

Nine years had fled, but nothing had impaired his memory.

She'd be back in Chihenne country with their son someday; he knew it as well as he knew the rocks were hard. She was part of his Way, part of his Power. Just having her in his memory made him strong. He would wait. He swung up on his pony. He had to meet the chief the Godammies called Sumner. . . .

Colonel Edwin Vose Sumner was tall and gaunt at fifty-five, with long legs and arms that dangled like pieces of lariat from his broad shoulders. Hazel eyes scowled below a high forehead that was usually covered by his well-worn campaign hat. His voice was deep, his Massachusetts accent still lingering. As military commander in the Territory of New Mexico, he was specific in his approach to the Indians: his soldiers would chase them when necessary, but it was the job of volunteers to guard settlements when that was required. He had opened a new fort near Santa Rita to let the troublesome Chihenne Apache know that he meant business. Now, as he sat on a stool for the talks with Apache leaders—he refused to sit on the ground—he listened carefully to his interpreter, Lieutenant Murphy.

"The great chief, Lazaro, says his people have always warred with the Mexicans. It is their way, and has nothing to do with us," Rafe said in English.

Rafe tried to keep from staring at Lazaro, but it was difficult. He was sitting quietly a few feet from a man who had kidnapped and raped the woman he loved. But he had steeled himself for this encounter well before arriving—in fact, he'd known as a certainty that he'd meet the tall Apache personally from the day his orders were cut assigning him to New Mexico . . . perhaps even from the day he'd decided on an army career. From a Jicarilla Apache in Santa Fe he'd learned about the custom of sometimes making a woman prisoner a wife, that it was sometimes a respectful thing to do in their culture. And he'd tried to accept that. But how does a man accept a *rapist?*

He didn't have to *understand* Lazaro, just wipe out the loathing and deal with him. That was the job at hand.

The man showed such keen intelligence, both in his dark eyes and in his poise, that it was hard to relate to the oft-used term "savage." Actually, one could almost feel his strength just being so close to him. Undoubtedly Lazaro had proven himself many times in his still-young life or he wouldn't be such a powerful chief. The Jicarilla had also told him that Lazaro was the most respected chief among the Apache. He guessed the man was about forty, although he could be younger. His long hair was still coal black.

"He says further that the Mexicans owe his people much."

He nodded again to Lazaro, who said in Spanish, "Many years ago, the Nakai-ye sent bad men to take our hair—the hair of our warriors and the hair of our women and children. . . . " He went into detail about the Santa Rita massacre, stopping now and then to give Rafe time for translation. His tone remained even, emotionless. "And only recently in Sonora, when some of our people went in peace to trade, the Nakai-ye gave them the firewater and when they became drunk and fell asleep, *fifteen* of them were killed by clubs."

Lazaro looked around calmly at the other Apache leaders seated around the small circle—Blancito, Negrito, Ponce, Placera, the strong Cuchillo Negro, and a powerful young subchief, Victorio—then said, "The People cannot forgive such offenses."

Colonel Sumner now spoke: "No one can live on vengeance. If the Mexicans send scalp hunters, our army will punish them. If other enemies attack you, we will defend you. You are our brothers."

Rafe translated and watched the skepticism flit through Lazaro's eyes.

Sumner went on, "For a period our government will feed your people. In addition, we will provide good breeding stock and provide instructors to teach you how to get different and better crops from the ground."

Once more Rafe translated and watched the eyes of the other chiefs. "For all of this," he added, "we ask that you maintain order. No more stealing of stock or any other raids on the American settlers." He saw Lazaro stare at the ground, not joining in the comments of the other Apache leaders. If Lazaro would not agree, the treaty was dead. Finally, the tall leader looked up and said quietly: "The Chihenne agree."

One by one, the others nodded their heads and indicated approval.

As the meeting broke up and the Apaches departed, Rafe watched Lazaro and noted his solemnity. The tall chief didn't speak with the others as he mounted his big black pony and rode away. Somehow he knew this was not going to be a permanent solution to the problem—and he didn't think Lazaro believed it either.

"I've spoken to the colonel, and he has agreed to let me go to Lazaro's camp," Rafe said at dinner a week after his return from the Kneeling Nun meeting with the Apache.

Carlota's eyes showed surprise, then concern. "But why should you go there?"

"I've told you that we don't understand these people. If I can spend a little time with them, perhaps I can better grasp how to deal with them."

Her look became incredulous. "Why do we have to understand them? They're our enemies, savages." There was that word again.

Andres had excused himself from the table to go study, so Rafe was able to speak directly. "Do you consider Andres part savage?"

Her response was angry, "Of course not! He has Castilian blood and I have raised him. He's educated and sensitive."

As usual, Rafe was gentle and patient with her. "There are people the world over who haven't had the advantages of your motherhood, my dear. In Europe, in Mexico, all over America. We don't call them savages."

"But they are *civilized.*"

"Meaning what? Were those civilized men who came to Santa Rita thirteen years ago and massacred Lazaro's people for scalp money?"

Carlota frowned into her coffee cup as she poured more from the sterling pot. "That was war."

"That was *not* war; it was a brutal act of treachery that coincided with the barbaric policy of the governments of two supposedly *civilized* Mexican states."

"I don't know why you want to side with them, Rafe. Sometimes you exasperate me beyond understanding. You know what they did to me."

Again his tone was soft, "But we must look ahead. Someone has to be logical if we are to deal with them. We've come here to *their* country and said it is ours. We tell them they can still live here, but they have to do it our way. And they have been here for ages longer than we have. Twice Lazaro used the term, 'before the rocks were hard.' "

Carlota shook her head as she got to her feet and began picking up dishes. "You'll never convince me."

"What are you going to do about Andres?"

"What do you mean?"

"He has to be told about Lazaro one of these days."

She shook her head. "Not now. The right time will come."

Rafe shrugged and sipped his coffee. It wasn't his decision to make.

Rafe arrived at Fort Webster on the twenty-third of July and, after reporting to the captain who was commanding the post, put his meager belongings in the spare room reserved for visiting officers. Based on his rather open-ended orders from Colonel Sumner, he sent a message via a half-breed named Gilberto to Lazaro. Orally it was:

> I wish to learn the ways of your People. May I come to you alone and spend a few days? I will pay for any food and for your time.

Gilberto returned late that afternoon from Lazaro's village site with the chief's reply. "Yes, you are welcome."

At nearly nine the following morning, Rafe followed Gilberto into the village. He looked around at the brush wickiups located neatly along a running stream. Greeted by curious looks from several women and a gaggle of children, he dismounted and let Gilberto take his horse. In moments, Lazaro appeared, striding toward him. The chief spoke in Spanish. "Welcome to my village, Mur-fee."

Rafe thanked him and followed him to an empty wickiup on the edge of the encampment, where Lazaro told him he could sleep. He gave the chief a box of cigars that he had purchased in Santa Fe a few weeks earlier. Lazaro smiled and grunted his thanks.

"What is it you wish to know?" the chief asked quietly.

Once more Rafe had to quell the disquieting thought of the Apache forcefully taking Carlota and raping her. He said, "I want to know about your way of life—how your people live, what they believe. If I can learn the essence of your ways, perhaps I can help us live together in harmony and peace." He selected his words carefully, not certain how extensive the Chihenne's Spanish vocabulary might be.

Lazaro nodded his head and led him to a shady place under some tall willows beside the stream. There, Old Man and Tze-go-juni waited with his son, Taza. "I must warn you, Mur-fee, that my advisors are suspicious of your intentions. They think you have come to spy on us so you will learn how we make war. There will be no training here during your visit. I will tell you of our war ways, but you will see nothing."

Rafe nodded as they met the other Apaches and seated themselves, cross-legged on the ground. Their expressions were stoic, their eyes carefully hostile. He produced three plugs of tobacco from his kit bag, offering one to each. Old Man looked off frequently, indicating his disdain. The medicine woman, the skin around her eyes painted black, flicked a fetish of what looked like two eyeballs of some kind of an animal back and forth from the thong that held them to her wrist. The young Taza was the friendliest looking of the three.

"Each of them speak the tongue of the Nakai-ye, so they will understand much of what you say, Mur-fee."

Speaking slowly, Rafe began, "We Americanos are new to your country. . . . " He told them about the ways of progress in developing a new land, and how it often infringed on the lives of longtime inhabitants. He spoke of machines and the iron horse, and of what the ways of the Americanos could mean to them. And when he finished their expressions had not changed.

Tze-go-juni waved her fetish at him and spoke in her gravelly voice. "You come to steal from us. You want our Power, but it will hold you off."

"Our doctors have new ways to save lives," Rafe replied, and instantly knew he had said the wrong thing.

"We have been saving lives for thousands of moons," the shaman replied testily.

"Perhaps we can learn from you," Rafe rejoined lamely.

"You aren't White Eye, you're Nakai-ye," Old Man said coldly.

Rafe glanced at Lazaro, who said nothing, and replied with an easy smile. "My mother was Nakai-ye, my father White Eye. I am Americano." He paused, then went on, "In America, most citizens are from other peoples—some from far away across great waters. You are Chihenne Apache, but also Americano because . . . " He made a sweeping motion with his arms. " . . . America is vast and Apache lands are inside."

"No!" Old Man snapped. "The land of the People is *everywhere*."

Rafe realized he was getting nowhere. He had come to learn and he was preaching. Turning to Lazaro he said, "Can you tell me of your People? How did they come to live here?"

Lazaro nodded his large head. "I will tell you of Silsoose. . . . "

Benita had fared well in the years since Lazaro had made her his wife. The Chihenne women had accepted her pretty much as their own and had come to accord her the respect of a great chief's wife. She had given him two daughters in those years, the eldest of whom—Gabriela—was now nine. She knew her position with Lazaro was also firm because of the warm affection he gave their children. With that faraway look he often got in his eye, he sometimes spoke of using them someday as connections in his dream of bringing the People closer together in one large band such as their cousins, the Navajo, had done. Now she regarded this Mexican-American officer suspiciously.

"Your husband has given permission for me to speak with you, Benita," Rafe said pleasantly. "As an adopted member of the tribe, you must have views that will help me to better understand the Chihenne way of life."

At first she refused to share her opinions with him, but sensing his sincerity, she finally broke down and told him her story. In the end, she glowed as she spoke of the Chihenne Way. "They—we—are very spiritual, worshipping Ussen the Father." She told him of White Painted Woman and Child of the Water, of Giant, and of some of the customs such as the Spirit Dancers, and the morals.

In each of her stories, Benita brought Rafe closer to the understanding he sought. As he suspected, the Apache culture was far more advanced than he had guessed—certainly far more than the average American could possibly believe. But how could the newcomers ever find this out?

Eventually he asked her *the* question: "I know a woman who was once a captive of Lazaro. Her name is Carlota. Did you know her?"

Benita's expression hardened and she waited a moment before answering. "Yes, I knew her. She was a spoiled young aristocrat—at least she *thought* she was an aristocrat."

"She told me he made her his wife."

"That's true. She was young and beautiful—I have to admit that— and she turned his head, made him lose all good sense for a time."

"She told me a Mexican captive named Benita helped her escape. Was that you?"

Benita nodded her head, frowning. "Yes, to get rid of her. I hated her airs." After a pause, she asked, "Do you know where she is now? Does she still have the boy?"

Rafe replied, "She is in the town of Albuquerque, married to an army officer. The boy is a fine lad."

Benita shrugged. "Well, I am glad for both of them . . . I suppose."

Rafe changed the subject and asked about the way Apache women treated captives.

Finally, just before Rafe's departure for Santa Rita on the morning of the third day, Lazaro led him on horseback up to the crest of the tall pines that was known as Pinos Altos and offered him some special tiswin. "I will tell you of the Chihenne warrior, Mur-fee. Perhaps that will help you, and perhaps you can tell your white father in Wash-in-ton why the People will never be defeated in war."

Rafe sipped the tiswin and nodded his head. "Please do, sir."

They sat cross-legged beside the trunk of a tall pine. "Our young men are warriors," Lazaro began, "who are trained to fight as no other warrior. We can travel huge distances in a day and be ready to fight. We can track nearly anything that moves, and live without food or water. We can also endure pain better than any other. All of this is a matter of training, but it is more. Since before Silsoose, being a great warrior has been the way of our young men. To be a great warrior is the highest goal."

As Rafe listened, he felt a distinct liking for this huge leader. Completely gone was his original animosity. Now that he knew more of the Apache culture and the policy toward prisoners, he understood how the man had offered Carlota his highest gift—marriage. And surely he could understand how a man could be crazily in love with that woman, it was as easy as watching the falling rain.

He had a terrible urge to tell Lazaro about her and Andres, but he quelled it. Certainly, such a revelation would serve no good purpose.

"You Americans are brave, but you lack shrewdness," Lazaro went on. "You build a great fire that throws out so much heat you cannot get close to warm yourselves. And when you hear a gun fired, you rush foolishly to the spot. But it is not so with us; we build small fires in secluded hideways and gather near them . . . and when we hear a gun fired we get away immediately to a place where we can watch to learn what caused it."

Rafe was surprised that Lazaro would tell him this. It bordered on fighting tactics, supporting the fact that Apaches never stormed a position unless the odds were heavily in their favor, but fought hit and run. He knew it was a matter of survival; he didn't know how many braves Lazaro or any of the other chiefs had, but he knew that in all of Apache country, the number couldn't exceed a thousand.

"You must also know that we are not always able to control all of our warriors," the chief added. "I am trying hard to unite all bands of the People, but the bands have been separated for so long that it is difficult. This freedom of spirit is part of why the People have such Power. For instance, Mur-fee, there is one named Bacho who recently broke the new peace. He raided in Sonora and burned a rancho, killing a big family. He is a wild one."

"A renegade wolf?"

"Yes. Some day I must kill him."

Rafe was surprised to hear such a statement, but then he realized he shouldn't be. Lazaro had made an honorable agreement that was being undermined by a treacherous minor leader.

They talked on over the tiswin until it was time for Rafe to get his horse and head back to Fort Webster. He reached into his saddlebag and withdrew a highly polished meerschaum pipe and a pouch of specially blended tobacco that he'd ordered from St. Louis. Handing it to Lazaro, he said, "This is a symbol of my friendship, Chief Lazaro.

Whenever you feel anger with us Americans, rub this and remember that there is one who wished to be your friend."

Lazaro took the pipe and looked at it, nodding. "I will remember, Mur-fee," he said quietly. "I will remember. . . . "

"Well, are you going to tell me about your stay with the savages?" Carlota asked. She had controlled her curiosity until after dinner the night of Rafe's return from Fort Webster. Part of her rejected everything about his foolish trip; another part was compellingly curious. She had told herself that even a casual curiosity was ridiculous, but it was there nevertheless.

"I find the Chihenne Apache a very interesting people. They are proud, clean, and adhere religiously to their beliefs. I feel richer for having gone to visit them."

She couldn't resist. "Did you meet . . . him?"

"Lazaro? Yes. I found him intriguing."

"After what he did to me?"

"He must have loved you very much, my dear."

"Ha! He was a *beast*."

"He acted quite gentle with his family. His wife, Benita, seems to care for him a great deal."

Carlota arched an eyebrow. "Wife, huh? Seems she has moved up. Last I knew she was a servant. What about his son, Taza?"

"A grown young man. Quite handsome."

Andres's half brother, she thought. No! She simply would not think in such terms. Taza was a *savage!*

"And Benita has two daughters."

"They'll probably be fat cows."

"I was surprised to find Chief Lazaro with a woman adviser, a shaman or medicine woman with a name like Say-?-huni, or something like that."

Carlota's eyebrows shot up. "Tze-go-juni! I thought I killed her with a dagger when I escaped. She must have nine lives. Ugly old witch?"

"Yes, with a scarred face."

"That's her. Hmmmm."

"Lazaro seemed to value her counsel."

Carlota caught herself staring at her coffee cup. She could hardly believe her ears when Rafe quietly said, "I like and respect Lazaro, darling. I have to tell you in spite of what you think of him. He is probably the greatest of the Apache leaders. And he's always treated with respect."

Her voice was cold. "I don't want to hear anything more about that rapist."

Rafe nodded his head slightly and changed the subject. "Colonel Sumner listened carefully to my verbal report, but he doesn't want to know anything about them except what will help him fight them. And what's so bad is that's normal official thinking everywhere."

Carlota didn't hear his last words. She was caught up in too many bad memories.

Tze-go-juni wound the horsehair around the rattler skull. Ordinarily snakes weren't a part of the Way, but she needed some especially strong medicine to hold off the premonition that had seized her a couple of days earlier. It had come to her in the middle of the night when a full moon was shining, and although she couldn't define it, she knew it foreshadowed severe ill for someone important to her. It had taken the shape of Giant in her dream, an ugly, violently angry Giant who was wearing a coat of snakes and chewing on a mouthful of tarantulas that kept spilling out of his mouth. Any dream she'd ever had involving an angry Giant preceded an unhappy incident.

She carefully tied off the horsehair, leaving the eye holes uncovered. Pricking her finger to draw blood, she wiped it on the bald spot on the top of the small skull and intoned, "Die, evil thing, go away from my fire and die!"

Next she took an arrowhead that she'd stolen from Lazaro when he was a boy and held it high to the moon. "White Painted Lady, I offer up the will of your Lazaro in this hardened stone of his brave heart. Protect him, Mother, against all enemies and let him lead his proud people forever."

The shaman then lifted a lock of black hair attached to a piece of worn wood from Taza's first tsach. "White Painted Lady, if it be Taza who is threatened, keep him safe so he can someday be a great chief with his father. Guide him in finding wisdom and good judgement, but keep him safe from harm, oh Mother. I beg of you."

Leaning into the small fire she withdrew a burning stick and rammed its glowing tip into the palm of her left hand. She tossed the stick back in the fire and picked up the rattler skull. Holding it high to the moon, she screeched, "Giant, if you harm my men, I will *destroy* you! I will bring the sun and the moon down on you and Child of the Water will shoot the fire arrows of death into what is left! And our

God, Ussen, will sprinkle your ashes in the waste of all that is hated."

She sank to her knees, chanting unintelligibly whatever sounds that came to her. After several minutes she lifted her hideous, black-and-white-painted face once more to the sky and said softly, "White Painted Lady, also look over our young Child of the Water, wherever he may be."

She had prayed daily for Andres all these years, never losing her belief in his true identity.

13

At seventeen, Taza was slightly under six feet in height, still quite tall for an Apache. He had his father's nose and intense look, his handsomeness. But the boy was still too full of himself, Lazaro thought as he turned to watch the young warrior follow him up the narrow ledge toward Giant's Claw. But it was time. If Taza were ever to become chief, he would need to know the secret of Giant's Claw so he could lead the People to its safety if the requirement arose.

He was not satisfied with the treaty he had signed with the Godammies. The White Eyes could come out here and talk about the White Father in Wash-in-ton and how much he cared for the People, but it sounded hollow. Protect the Chihenne from their enemies? How could soldiers protect against raiders from Sonora or Chihuahua when they couldn't even go there? But he had been unable to say "no" to the offer of free food and perhaps a new way of growing it. Still, it wasn't the Way of the People. It wasn't the way of proud warriors and hunters. . . .

After climbing up the well-hidden trail for another six hundred paces, they suddenly reached the rim of the huge oval bowl. Lazaro nodded as he looked at the ragged rock walls of rich earth tones and the dozens of massive rock formations against the summer sky. He felt something special, like when he prayed to Ussen. He had been in this awesome place only a few times, but it always moved him, made him feel clean or in the presence of something greater than life. It shouldn't be called Giant's Claw, he thought, rather Ussen's Claw—for surely it was spiritual.

They proceeded on to the base of a huge rock. "Here," Lazaro said, "is where Tze-go-Juni told me the great Silsoose confronted the evil *oodo* worshipers. It is said that he talked for two days and nights to the leader of the bad people. And then he spoke to Ussen, who was already angry about his tears being used for evil, and then Ussen tore the ground apart in a thunderous ripping that destroyed the houses of the evil ones and killed many of them."

Taza looked up in awe at the tallest spire. For some reason, his voice had not developed with the growth of his athletic body; it was still high-pitched. "It is like a giant White Eyes' fort, but with no houses."

"Yes, which is why I brought you here. In case of extreme emergency, this is the haven of the People. The Nakai-ye and the White Eyes know nothing of it, and they could never attack it successfully if they did." Lazaro reflected for a moment; *one* Nakai-ye knew about Giant's Claw—his wife, the beautiful Carlota. But she would never be a threat to it. She probably hated the memory of the place—if she even remembered it. He sighed softly.

Carlota.

A short while later as they continued to explore the sunlit bowl, a dull glint caught Taza's eye. He leaned down to find a gold nugget the size of a misshapen plum. He rubbed it. It had to be oodo, since the old story about Silsoose said the bad people had plenty of it. He looked up at his father, but the older man was praying some distance away.

Oodo. He'd heard how the Nakai-ye were always looking for it.

He looked at the nugget again and rubbed it against his legging. It felt strange, slightly cool. He knew he should leave Ussen's tear where he'd found it, but perhaps he could get something for it sometime; maybe the White Eyes would trade something of value for it if they, too, wanted it. He slipped it in his pouch and looked around for other pieces of the pretty metal.

He liked the White Eyes' firewater, whiskey they called it. It made him stupid and sleepy, but it also made him feel good and made him laugh. He'd had it only twice, and his father always talked against it, but sometimes the chief was an old woman about such things.

Well, someday he'd be chief, and then he'd do as he pleased. Enjuh! There was another oodo stone, somewhat smaller than the other one, but still as large as a big cherry. And an even smaller one lay beside it.

Just as he slipped the other two stones into his pouch his father approached. "Come, let me show you where I would place the large rocks and hot water," Lazaro said. "Because of the steepness of the walls, the path is the only logical approach. We should pick one place and let no enemy pass it. But I've heard that soldiers are trained now in the use of what they call *ropes*, which let them climb straight up. So we have to make other plans. . . . "

* * *

It was three weeks later when Taza rode into the town of Santa Rita with another young brave named Ramon that he decided to try the balls of oodo on a White Eye. It was late on a warm afternoon and a thunderstorm was building to the northwest. He looked around the sky, wondering if it would rain before he finished his business. The Mexican government had resettled the village and reopened the copper mine a few years after the massacre. And in the intervening years the garrison town had grown to a bustling little community. Lazaro, admitting that the present inhabitants were not to blame for what had happened years earlier, had finally told the Chihenne they could go to the town.

Taza liked to come here, even if this was where his mother had been killed. What he had in mind now was exciting, perhaps a bit dangerous. But he liked the thrill of doing something even the older men didn't do well—trying to beat the White Eye at a trade. They went into a general store operated by an American by the name of Crowder. Taza spoke in Spanish, which Benita had taught him well. "I want some of the tobacco."

"You got some dinero, Injun?" the proprietor asked in Spanish.

"No money," Taza replied. "But I have some trade."

"Whatcha got?"

Taza pulled the smaller of the middle-sized nuggets from his pouch and placed it on the counter. The proprietor looked at it casually at first, then with more interest. But he managed to control his expression. Picking the nugget up, he held it to the light and examined it. "How much you want for this, Injun?"

Taza had been trying to figure out how brazen he could be in his price, but he still had no idea. A good deer hide could get three plugs of tobacco or five of what the Godammies called *yards* of some bright cloth like cal-i-co, maybe some bullets if no one was watching, or two White Eye *dollars*. Other animal coats varied in value. He just didn't know. But he knew this oodo was special; he could see it in the storekeeper's eyes. "You tell me," he replied.

Crowder held the nugget up again and looked at it closely. "I'll give you five dollars for it," he said.

Taza wanted the tobacco, but his instinct told him to wait. "No, I get more." He held out his hand.

The storekeeper handed the nugget back. "Tell you what, Injun, I'll make it *eight* dollars."

Now Taza knew it was worth more for sure. He shook his head as he put it in his pouch.

The greed in the storekeeper's eyes glinted. "I'll make it *ten* dollars *and* give you a plug of tobacco."

Taza looked at his friend, then shook his head at the storekeeper. "No."

"Can you tell me where you found this little pebble?" Crowder persisted.

"On ground."

"Where on ground?"

"Not here. Far away."

A thickset man with a bushy blond beard, an American named Tom Waugh, sidled up and listened.

Crowder dropped his voice to a conspiratorial tone. "You suppose you could show me where?"

Taza shook his head, suddenly realizing he'd made a mistake; this was more than just trying to win a bargain. Lazaro would be very displeased if he heard *anything* about this.

"I could give you tobacco *and* whiskey," Crowder said. "If you'd take me there."

"No," Taza replied, turning to Ramon. "Come, we must go."

The storekeeper grinned, pulling a plug of tobacco from a case. "Here, to show you my heart's in the right place, have some on the house. We can talk later about this."

As the two young Apaches walked away from the front porch of the store, Tom Waugh turned to Crowder. "I was watching. What was that he showed you—gold?"

The storekeeper nodded his head, raising an eyebrow. "Uh-huh. Very *good* looking gold. Pure. I'd say that little nugget was worth maybe a *hundred* dollars. Maybe more."

"Wouldn't tell you where he found it, huh?"

"Nope."

Tom Waugh tugged at his beard, his eyes narrowing. "I might be able to tease it outta him with my knife. He's just a young buck."

Crowder and Waugh had owned the store for over two years, and were always alert to a way to capitalize on the gullibility of the Chihenne. They had gotten their stake in the California gold rush in '49, and Waugh had sold more than one Apache scalp to the government of Chihuahua after getting out of the Army in Mexico City in '47. The storekeeper, who was cleanshaven, said, "I don't know. I think I've seen him come in here with that big chief, Lazaro. Might not be too good an idea to carve him up."

Tom Waugh shrugged. "For enough gold, I'll carve up the god-damn chief too."

The storekeeper's eyes also narrowed as he watched Taza and his friend disappear around the corner. "There might be enough where that nugget came from to carve up the whole damned tribe."

Taza couldn't calm the excitement the oodo gave him. The store-keeper, Crow-der, had told him what he needed to know. The stones were worth more than a little tobacco or cal-i-co. He also knew he could not let the Godammies know anything about Devil's Claw. But what to do with the stones? They were no good to him in his pouch. He had decided to go back to Santa Rita and ask Crow-der for twenty White Eye dollars for the small one. He also decided he didn't want to trust his friend, Ramon, any further. Ramon had chided him for even having the oodo, since it was against the Way of Ussen. Now, two days later, he again entered Crowder's general store. After wait-ing until the storekeeper finished with a Nakai-ye customer, he said, "I want twenty Godammie dollar for the stone."

Crowder glanced meaningfully to his partner, who was reading an old El Paso newspaper from where he sat next to a cracker barrel. Looking back at Taza, he said, "How much did you say, Injun?"

"Twenty dollar."

Crowder shook his head. "Naw, I couldn't pay that, but I'll give you thirteen for it."

Taza shook his head, pulling out the nugget and holding it up to the sunlight that flowed in through a nearby window. "Twenty dollar."

"Tell you what, Injun, you show me or Mr. Waugh, there, where you found it and I'll pay you the *whole* twenty. Is that a deal? No, I'll throw in a big plug of tobacco *and* when you've finished showing him, he'll give you a jug of the best whiskey in Santa Rita."

Taza tried not to show his pleasure. He really didn't expect to get that many Godammie dollars—and now the tobacco . . . and *whiskey!* Imagine what he could get for the *big* one! He thought quickly. Of course he wouldn't take them to Giant's Claw, so he had to think of another place. The high place with the tall pines—*Pinos Altos!* Yes, that'd be good. It was far from Giant's Claw, at least a day. He could continue to get oodo from the Claw, but never give away its location. "Yes," he finally replied, "I take Señor Wa in four days. I come here again. You give me the tobacco now."

"You've got a deal, Injun." Crowder gave him a large plug of chewing tobacco and wrapped it in a yard of cheap red cloth. "There," he added with a grin. "You can give that to your mother."

Taza's eyes narrowed ever so slightly. A Godammie named Brantson had killed his mother. But he would give the cloth to Benita. "I will come in four days." Before there could be more talk, he picked up the red cloth and moved quickly toward the open door.

Pinos Altos, the Spanish name the People sometimes called the high place where the *nilchí ndeez*—the tall pines—grew, was a place of mystery. There were springs about that bubbled to the surface and arroyos that ran with abundant water. A few ruins of ancient pit houses and bits of broken earthenware and other artifacts not of the Chihenne indicated that people from long ago had once inhabited the place. It was also a place that Lazaro's people sometimes frequented in the summer. Now it was rich with the tall pines that would one day be called ponderosa, with juniper, scrub oak, and pinion that were crowding into the high crest over seven thousand feet above sea level. In fact, this place straddled an imaginary line that would in a few years be known as the continental divide.

It was here that Taza led Tom Waugh. Riding down over the crest to the west, he stopped his spotted pony by a slowly flowing stream that was quite shallow and about twenty feet wide at one point. Its bed was a combination of rock and sand at this point, its water tossing off little silvery reflections as it worked its way downhill. "It was here in the ford that I found it," Taza lied in Spanish. "The water was very low and I saw the sun on it."

Waugh's eyes glinted in anticipation. "Show me exactly where."

Taza stepped into the shallow water and walked a couple of steps, looking carefully at the bottom. Slipping the smaller nugget from his pouch, he continued to stare at the stream bed. Finally, he said, "Enjuh!" and leaned down to remove his "find" from the water. Holding it up, he looked at it closely, then handed it to Waugh.

Tom Waugh grinned as he examined the nugget, exclaiming, "Good. Good!" Still clenching the stone in his hands, he leaned down and stared at the water. His search became more frantic as the minutes passed. Finally, after covering an area of some ninety or a hundred square yards, he looked up and scowled. "Maybe I need to dig."

At that moment, he jammed his hand into the water where it was only about two inches deep and pulled out a handful of light gravel. In it, were some tiny particles of a *shiny yellow substance*. "By God, it's here!" he exclaimed. *"Look!"*

Taza didn't know anything about the tiny particles, only that they were a total surprise. From the way Tom Wa was reacting, his ruse had apparently turned out to be *true*. He nodded, even smiled. Perhaps Ussen had changed His mind about the tears. . . .

It was then that Tom Waugh pulled out his pistol and shot Taza in the chest.

Benita walked down to the stream where she found Tze-go-juni beating the hide of a ground squirrel on a flat rock. "Have you seen Taza?" the Mexican woman asked.

The shaman shook her head.

"I have not seen him for two days," Benita persisted.

The medicine woman shrugged.

It was midmorning. "It isn't like him. He went to Santa Rita then, but said nothing about going anywhere else. I thought perhaps he may have gone with his father to the meeting with Cuchillo Negro, but Ramon told me he didn't."

This time, Tze-go-juni grunted, but when Benita turned away she grimaced.

Benita sighed and went on a few yards where she asked another woman if she had seen Taza. The reply was negative. She shrugged and kneeled to wash her bundle of clothes. At that moment she saw Lazaro ride into the area where the horses were kept with Old Man. She would ask him.

She wrung out the clothes she'd just washed and hurried to meet her husband.

"No, I haven't seen him since he went to Santa Rita," Lazaro replied, pulling the blanket from his second favorite pony. "Maybe he went on a long hunt. Ask Ramon to come see me."

The stocky young warrior who was his son's best friend stood before him a few minutes later. "No," Ramon said. "We had a small quarrel and he went back into Santa Rita. That's the last time I saw him."

Lazaro sat cross-legged and grunted. "Why did you quarrel?" he asked.

Ramon looked pained, obviously not wanting to tattle on his friend.

"Tell me," Lazaro persisted softly.

The words tumbled out. "He found some oodo when you took him to Giant's Claw and showed it to Crow-der at the store. Crow-der wanted to give him something for it, but Taza refused." Ramon told him the rest.

"Then you say he went back to sell Crow-der oodo?"

"I'm sure he did."

"Hmmm." Lazaro stroked his chin thoughtfully. "I think we should ride into Santa Rita. Come along."

The store was empty except for a Mexican woman when the two Chihenne entered. Lazaro waited until she paid for her few purchases and departed before saying, "Señor Crow-der, I am Lazaro. My son, Taza, a tall young man, came here two days ago. We have not seen him since. Can you possibly tell me anything about his visit?"

Crowder slowly shook his head. "I don't know any Taza."

Lazaro studied his face a moment, then turned to Ramon and said in Apache, "Is this the man Taza spoke to about the oodo?"

Ramon replied quietly, "Yes, and the other man who is often here was listening."

Lazaro turned back to the storekeeper and spoke patiently in Spanish. "My son was with this young man and he tried to sell you a small rock of oodo, the yellow metal."

Crowder shrugged. "Sorry, you Injuns all look alike to me."

Lazaro stared into his eyes.

Crowder slowly nodded his head and pursed his lips. "Yes. Come to think of it, I kinda remember him now. Tall brave, right?"

Lazaro nodded. "With rock of oodo."

"Yes, I recall now. Four, five days ago. I offered him a few dollars for his nugget. Wasn't worth too much, but you know I like to give you Injuns what you want."

"You haven't seen him since?" Lazaro's expression was blank.

Crowder shook his head as a soldier walked in. "No, Chief, can't say as I have. Sorry." He turned to the young American, asking in English, "Help you, trooper?"

Lazaro and Ramon waited patiently until the soldier finished buying some fishing line. As he walked out, Lazaro said, "If you or your friend, Tom Wa, hear of anything about my son, please send word to me at once."

Crowder smiled. "Oh, don't worry, Chief, I'll be sure to do that."

Outside in the hot, dusty street, Lazaro turned to Ramon. "He's lying."

The young man nodded. "I know, but what can we do?"

* * *

Lazaro went to Tze-go-juni as soon as he returned to the village.

"I will see if my Power can find him," she said, frowning, not showing her fear. She didn't mention the dream of Giant.

Lazaro had thought about the possibilities during the ride back from Santa Rita. The boy could have been hurt and be lying somewhere. He could have been captured by the Navajo, or some renegade White Eyes or Nakai-ye. But he was certain his disappearance had to do with the oodo. If Taza had sold it to Crow-der and Wa, they would probably want to know where it came from. They always wanted more. Would he take them to Giant's Claw? Probably not; the boy did rash things, but he knew the importance of secrecy when it came to the Chihenne haven. Therefore, where would he take them? Any number of places. . . .

Still, the first obvious place to look would be Giant's Claw. He would personally go there. Simultaneously, his search teams of two trackers each would commence scouring the area.

The shaman's spells and conjuring produced nothing more than more bad forebodings until the third night. Then, in a dream, she saw a glimpse of Taza's body in some kind of a small cave near a running stream. Wide-eyed, she immediately reported this to Lazaro, who had returned empty-handed from Giant's Claw.

He weighed her report carefully, not discrediting it. When his search teams began coming back in on the fifth day, he told them of the shaman's dream and sent them out again.

That night, Tze-go-juni dreamed of tall pines punctuated by Giant's laughter. She awoke in a sweat, unable to conquer another feeling of foreboding. She would go search for the boy by herself, she decided. Shortly after dawn, she rode her coal black and quite ugly little pony in a direction that some unknown force seemed to pull her—to the place called Pinos Altos. There, she sat down and smeared yellow hoddentin over her entire face. Removing her medicine hat from the bag, she placed it firmly on her head. Over the years the stained hat had grown quite ripe with its many adornments, but she never paid any attention to the smell. On its black painted buckskin sides, stitched into the hide of a particularly savage mountain lion, hung the dried testicles of four bobcats. Pieces of abalone shell and the blue-green stone, chaltchihuitl, were fastened around the hat in random fashion. "Enjuh!" she said, as she picked up a lance decorated with streamers of black-and-white dyed swallow feathers, and began to look for her lost godson.

For three days she searched from daybreak to dusk, and then she prayed until she fell asleep. On the third night Giant laughed at her in her dreams, and on the fourth day she knew her quest was useless.

But she did see a White Eye working with a pan in a shallow creek just a short way down from the crest at the place called Pinos Altos. He had a dirty tan tent pitched nearby, with both a horse and a burro tethered next to it. After watching him closely for several minutes, she recognized him: the man called Wa from the store in Santa Rita.

This time Lazaro entered the general store in Santa Rita alone. But a Mexican woman greeted him. He looked around, asking, "Where is Crow-der?" in his deep voice.

The woman clerk replied, "I don't know, but I think he is somewhere in the mountains panning for gold."

"And the man called Wa?"

"I haven't seen him in nearly two weeks."

"Where did he go?"

"Off somewhere with a burro and some provisions. He was with one of your young braves, Chief."

"A tall boy of maybe seventeen summers?"

"Yes, I saw them ride out together."

Lazaro nodded his head and left the store.

His next stop was Fort Webster, where he was shown in to see the army captain commanding. He told him about the disappearance of Taza and the connection with Crowder and Waugh. He would play by the White Eye rules to honor his agreement with Sumner and Mur-fee.

Returning to the Chihenne village, he went directly to Tze-go-juni's wickiup. The shaman was sitting, her face solid black, staring into the sky and chanting something he couldn't understand. He told her what he had learned from the woman at the store. She described seeing the man, Wa, and his small camp. She also told him harshly of her dream of Taza's body being in a small cave.

Lazaro had long ago learned that much of Tze-go-juni's information was reliable; such was her Power. In this case, it merely matched his own feeling of apprehension. Just as he was about to tell her he would send his searchers out again, Old Man came hobbling up on his crutch, a wild look in his eye. "Taza's spotted pony came trotting into the camp several minutes ago," he said excitedly. "No bridle, no blanket. No sign of Taza."

* * *

It was shortly after ten the next morning when Lazaro led his small party to the wide spot in the stream west of Pinos Altos where Tom Waugh had his camp. Tze-go-juni, Old Man, three of Lazaro's war leaders, and Ramon filled out the small band. The American was busy panning for gold in the shallows as they watched quietly from above. Neither Crowder nor anyone else was in sight. In complete silence, they watched for over fifteen minutes. Finally, Lazaro gave the signal and the four younger men slipped away to surround the American. Several minutes later, Tom Waugh looked up in surprise as the Chihenne splashed into the water on a dead run headed straight for him. He was immediately overpowered and dragged, dripping wet, from the stream.

It took just over fifteen minutes to get the small fire blazing, the small fire that burned just below the head of the American. Tom Waugh was hanging upside down from a sturdy, low-hanging tree limb. All of his clothes had been removed.

"What have you done with my son?" Lazaro repeated for the tenth time in Spanish.

Tom Waugh's long hair had been crudely chopped off with Ramon's knife. His eyes bulged, his mouth hung open. He shook his head and managed, "I know nothing of your son," in a strained voice.

Lazaro nodded his head slightly to the war leader holding the rope that was tied to the American's feet. Ever so slightly, Tom Waugh was lowered toward the fire. "*No!*" he shouted, his voice panicky.

Tze-go-juni moved close, holding a smelly dead rat close to Tom Waugh's face. The American's eyes bulged even more. A strand of hair that had survived Ramon's knife dropped into the blaze and burned quickly to the scalp, causing Tom Waugh to scream. The pungent smell of the burning hair lasted several moments before being blown away on the light breeze.

"I will have your balls here on my belt!" the shaman snarled. "*Tell me where the boy is!*"

One of the war leaders placed another piece of dry brush on the fire just as the one holding the rope lowered Tom Waugh another half inch. The flames were now flicking to a point only three inches from the American's head. Finally he shouted, "*Cut me down! I'll tell you!*"

It took a couple of minutes for the prisoner to quit shaking as he sat off to the side of the fire, sweat streaming down his face. At last he said jerkily, "I was panning for gold and he was sitting on the bank watching. I, I heard a shot . . . and he fell into the water. I pulled him out and he was dead. I—" his teeth chattered for a moment as he looked at the fire. "I took him to a small cave over there—" He pointed down the hill. "And buried him. You can find him there."

"Who killed him—Crow-der?"

"No, it was a man I'd never seen before. Said he hated Injuns. He just rode on and I haven't seen him since."

Lazaro stared at him as Old Man snapped in Apache, "You lie! You killed him!"

"Show us where he is," Tze-go-juni said coldly.

Several minutes later, the dirt-covered, partially decomposed body of Taza was pulled from its shallow grave. Tze-go-juni threw herself on the corpse and shrieked in sudden grief as Lazaro stared down at the remains of his first son, his beloved boy born from the womb of his beautiful young Nadzeela. He sighed and fought back the emotion before nodding to the senior war leader. They would take the body to the Willows for a decent burial.

Tom Waugh's body, impaled on a sharp stake by the water's edge, would greet whomever came to the site first. From it, the black-and-white dyed swallow feathers from Tze-go-juni's lance moving gently in the light breeze would finish the unmistakable message.

But Lazaro knew the White Eyes and the Nakai-ye. When they heard of the oodo find, they would not be intimidated for long. It was just one more nail into the Way of the People.

He looked again at the slightly deteriorated, but still handsome face of his son as the shaman brushed the last particles of dirt from his mouth. *This* was a massive nail into the heart of the nantan who led them.

>> THE OLD WOMAN'S JOURNEY <<

The white-haired woman pinned the wide-brimmed hat with its big blue feathers on her head as the train began to slow for the city of El Paso. She looked out the window and smiled her quick smile. My, but the place had grown in seventy years! Of course, the coming of the railroad in 1880 had been a big factor. That was when the American side of the river became a big town.

As the train lurched to a halt at the station, she looked out the window through the cloud of white steam. It was another of those hot days that marked the summer down at the Pass of the North. The reporter reached for her cloth valise as the other passengers began to file down the aisle to get off. "We have nearly an hour before we catch the other train," he said. "Maybe we can find a cool place to get something to eat."

The little Mexican café just down the street from the station was called "The Burrita." Over a cold glass of lemonade, the woman told him, "In the next few years life was relatively peaceful for the Chihenne. They continued their war against the Mexicans and tried to change their way of life to what the white man wanted. But it wasn't in any way easy for Lazaro. His people just weren't meant to be farmers, and the more strangers who came to the Willows Country, the harder it became to find enough game for survival.

"At this time the Territory of Arizona was all a part of the Territory of New Mexico, which ended at the Gila River. In 1853 the United States purchased a large area of land to the south extending the territory and the Union to its present boundary. In the north the Jicarilla Apache joined the Utes in fighting, and in the mountains to the east of the Rio Grande, the Sierra Blanca Mescalero Apache were blamed for depredations they didn't commit and became the target of increased settler hostility. The new part of the United States, called the Gadsden Purchase, had no direct influence on the Way of the People. Their blood enemies still lived to the South and no treaty or border would ever change that.

"But there was other trouble on the distant horizon. Already dissension was growing between the northern and southern American states, a rift that would continue to grow and finally erupt into a civil war more terrible than anyone in America could have ever dreamed possible.

"Lazaro continued to try and bring all of the People together, but you have to realize that the Apache essence was individuality, utter independence. Their society was perhaps the closest to a true democracy in the world, and they rejected any change that might threaten it. The chief made a great stride in achieving a semblance of unity in the summer of 1859. That was when he decided his oldest daughter was a means. . . . "

>> 14 <<

July 14, 1859

Lazaro had mourned the death of Taza deeply but silently, turning more affection on his daughters. The oldest, Gabriela, was his favorite but he tried not to show it. She was a mix of his strong, handsome features and the dark loveliness of so many young Mexican women. Although Benita was not a beautiful woman, there had been some attractive women in her family. At sixteen, Gabriela was taller than the average Chihenne man, with some of her father's prominent nose, and dark eyes that could dance in mischief. More than once, Lazaro had found it necessary to punish her for her wildness. Now it was time for all of that to end.

She was about to go through the sacred puberty rites—or the Ceremony of the Young Maidens as some called it. It was the night before the four-day ritual and Old Man was telling the ancient story of its origins to all of the Chihenne who were gathered around a flickering campfire in the middle of the village close to the huge ceremonial tipi. "Long ago," he intoned, "the Chihenne encountered a wise and good medicine woman named E son kñh sen de hé, who had heard of a special cave that she decided to visit. They went with her to the foot of a big hill where she told them to wait.

"While she was gone to the cave, they heard drums and songs sung by unknowns. They were afraid, but they knew these sounds did not come from Earth People. At last, just as they thought her dead, she appeared with a lamb cradled in her arms. From that day forward, her cures were better and her good deeds increased.

"The medicine woman told them that Ussen had ordered her to go to the wall of a sheer cliff and climb it, then pray to the Creator of Life.

" 'But that's impossible!' the People said.

" 'I will do as Ussen commands,' she replied. 'Stay at the foot and pray for me.' And they watched her go to the base of the cliff, where she lifted her arms and prayed fervently. Then she took her first step, finding a toehold, and then another and another. Twice she slipped, almost falling, but she continued upward. Now and then it seemed that she could go no farther, but she always found one more bush, one more rock to help her climb. Suddenly an opening appeared in the solid rock and she went inside. The entrance was guarded by a huge ferocious bear on each side, and past them she encountered two snarling mountain lions, and then two huge, coiled snakes. Even though she was terribly afraid, she murmured a prayer, bowed her head, and passed between them into a bright room where the Mountain Spirits awaited.

" 'What does our daughter wish?' they asked.

" 'That which will most help the People,' the medicine woman replied.

"All of the Mountain Spirits had different Powers. The last Spirit was an aged woman and she said, 'When your young girls reach womanhood, you are to make a feast for the good and chaste. It is to commemorate the sanctity of producing new life. The ritual will last four days, during which the medicine men will sing at least one hundred and seventy-four prayers. You will teach them these songs and instruct the maidens to dance every night. On the fourth night the singing and dancing is to continue until dawn.

" 'Four groups of four men each will impersonate the Mountain Spirits after darkness has fallen. Through the minds of the Spirits, messages will be sent to the maidens, who for four days partake of the qualities of White Painted Woman. These messages must be told to the medicine men by the maidens, and they must be obeyed to benefit the entire tribe.'

"With that, she gave the medicine woman symbols and songs and instructed her to return to the People. And to this day our pure young maidens honor us with this blessing from the Mountain Spirits."

Old Man nodded his head in solemn fashion to signify the end of his story.

It was time for the ceremony to begin. Lazaro stood, tall and powerful in his best breechclout and heavily beaded buckskins, the scarlet blanket that Cochise had given him over his left arm. With a gentle look at Gabriela, who was seated with five other maidens on a blanket in front of the tipi, he said, "Let the ritual that is such an important part of our Ussen's love for the People begin."

Gabriela was lovely. Since Lazaro's mother had died in the Santa Rita massacre, the task of making his daughter's ceremonial attire had fallen to Benita. It consisted of long beaded buckskin moccasins and a two-piece skirt that was trimmed with long fringe, plus beads and dozens of tiny cone-shaped tin jingles. Like the skirt, the upper garment was made of soft white buckskin. It was adorned with fringe fifteen inches long hanging in graceful rows along both sides and covering her arms, and many ornaments of silver and turquoise. Her long dark hair had been washed by Benita with fragrant suds made from the root of the yucca during her bath, and was now adorned with three eagle feathers. She carried some tiny pieces of uncut turquoise in her moccasins.

She was just lovely, he thought. A wonderful prize for his friend, Cochise. The marriage of his Gabriela to the Chiricahua chief would take place on the day of the second full moon following the maidens' ceremony. He would miss her very much, but the marriage was part of his plan. He glanced to the fringe of the crowd where his second daughter, Auraria, watched with bright eyes. Just fifteen, she would marry Victorio, chief of the Warm Springs at Ojo Caliente in another year.

Tze-go-juni stepped forward to assume command of the ceremony. Four men, representing the Mountain Spirits, but sometimes called the Crown Dancers, appeared. They were dressed in buckskin skirts, high moccasins and big masks with a high crown of bright ornamented sticks; symbols were painted on their blackened torsos. They came from four directions, symbolizing the sacred number, and prepared to dance at the shaman's signal.

The favorite celebration of the Chihenne was ready to begin.

February 3, 1861
Cochise's mountain hideout village
near the Sonoita River

Lazaro listened quietly as Cochise told him about the affair at Apache Pass. The Butterfield Stage Line had a station there. While making a friendly visit to the station agent, the Chiricahua chief had been accused by a second lieutenant named Bas-com of the kidnapping of a boy named Felix Ward from his stepfather's squalid ranch in the area of Fort Buchanan in Arizona Territory. His camp was at a cave high in his homeland.

"I believe it may have been a band of Pinals who took the boy," Cochise said, "because my people have been at peace with the settlers. This Bas-com ordered his soldiers to take me prisoner, but I slashed my way out of the tent with my knife and escaped with bullets flying all around me. But three of my braves were still prisoners.

"I returned with many warriors and tried to convince this Bas-com to give up the prisoners. He refused and fired on us. We took three prisoners and attacked a passing wagon train. Again I tried to get him to release my warriors, but he still refused. Then a large number of soldiers arrived—about seventy. In the end, my people killed their agent and two others, and they hanged my three braves and three other warriors. All three of mine were relatives and I take their death harshly." Cochise looked grimly into Lazaro's eyes. "I will never forgive the White Eyes for that! Already half a hundred have paid with their lives."

Lazaro had heard about the fight at Apache Pass, and the subsequent raids by Cochise—which is why he had come. "What do you wish from me?" he asked.

Cochise's handsome features set in a scowl. He recrossed his legs. "I want your Chihenne to combine with my Chiricahua in all-out war."

Lazaro nodded. With an alliance, this was a normal request. "Of course," he replied quickly. "What do you want them to do?"

"Raid, raid, raid. No White Eye or Nakai-ye will sleep at night in all of our land without worrying about whether he is safe."

Lazaro nodded again. He thought of Taza, then of his beautiful daughter Gabriela, with whom he would eat the evening meal. But mostly he thought of Taza. That wound had never healed. "Agreed," he replied softly.

The rashness of one West Point second lieutenant named Bascom at Apache Pass would enflame the frontier. Within sixty days, over one hundred and fifty whites were killed. Lazaro and Cochise cooperated on several raids, the major being a standoff attack on General Carleton's California Column in the same Apache Pass. Additionally, devastating raids were made into Mexico. Arizona was no longer part of the huge New Mexico Territory, but a territory of its own, with its own peculiar problems—mainly a white population of castoffs, drifters, criminals, fortune hunters, and outcasts from other places of opportunity. Gold was the usual attraction, and the Indians were not only despised but considered subhuman by the flotsam that roamed both territories.

But suddenly, after April 1861, White Eye soldiers became a rare sight. The name "Fort Sumter" would have meant nothing to the People, even if they heard it—and terms like "secession" and "slavery," "North" and "South," "Union" and "Confederacy," were just as foreign. Nor did they know that grandiose plans to bring all of the New Mexico, Arizona, and California territories into the Confederacy had been initiated by rebel leaders. What they did know was that a mass exodus of bluecoats had occurred.

Fort Bliss at El Paso was abandoned. Mesilla was attacked and briefly occupied by the soldiers in gray. General Sibley moved on and took Santa Fe for the Confederacy. Colonel John Robert Baylor led his Texas Mounted Rifles into Apache country and proclaimed himself governor of Confederate Arizona. He then organized a special military contingent called the Arizona Guards and issued this order: "Use all means to persuade the Apaches to come in for the purpose of making peace, and when you get them together kill all the grown Indians and take the children prisoners, and sell them to defray the cost of killing the Indians. Buy whiskey and such other goods as may be necessary . . . allow no Indian to escape."

But the Union wouldn't allow this incursion for long. Colonel Canby retook Santa Fe, defeating his brother-in-law and former subordinate, General Sibley. And General Carleton was on his way to deal

with Baylor. But the frontier was still open to the People, for, as
Americans killed Americans, there was no concerted effort to combat
them.

Berea, Ohio
June 28, 1861

Carlota went to the hotel window for the eighth time. *Why was that
boy so late?* She glanced at the clock again. He should have been at the
room twenty minutes ago. He was always so prompt; could something have happened to him? It was bad enough that she had to tell
him. She couldn't lose her resolve now. She'd rehearsed it over and
over, trying to find the right words.

She should have told him much earlier back in Santa Fe, and other
times when Rafe had urged it. In fact she'd promised herself each New
Year's that she'd do it. But it was too painful. He was such a stalwart
young man, so proud, so intelligent. She'd done so much to make sure
that he was superior to his peers, and he'd proved it here at Baldwin-
Wallace College. For one year he'd made a top grade in every one of
his subjects; and he was then barely eighteen!

But she had to be honest; it was her reflection, she'd molded him.
His grandfather would have been so proud.

In spite of his natural father's dark looks—she still hated to even
think of it—Andres's skin was lighter than most mestizos. She even
hated the word mestizo. He was *her* son and so much had she blocked
out the truth of his conception that she considered him *hers* alone. He
was her work of art. He had a strong nose and bright hazel eyes, and
girls turned their heads wherever he went, an occurrence that wasn't
lost on him.

Baldwin-Wallace College in northern Ohio was a natural pick for
the boy because Rafe's father had grown up in the town of Berea,
where that strain of Murphys had roots. He had picked the school
over several more prestigious eastern schools, even though she'd
been keen on Harvard. She had come to Berea as soon as she received
his letter saying he was about to enlist. Andres had come to her time
after time in his boyhood, and particularly once in Santa Fe after he
got in a fight at school when a boy called him a half-breed, and had
earnestly asked her about his real father. But each time she'd told him
the fictitious story about a young Mexican officer whom she'd married, a dashing captain who'd died in one of the first battles with the

Americans in '46. And then she'd told him his name had also been Cardenas. But when Rafe legally adopted him, it became Murphy.

Rafe had warned her that she could get tangled up in her stories, but somehow she'd managed to keep them straight, even though he went through a more persistent period when he was twelve. That was when she finally got firm and told him Rafael Murphy was the father who was alive and *cared* for him as no dim face in the past could ever care.

Now she had to tell him the truth. Rafe had insisted and he was right. A boy simply could not go off to war without knowing a major truth such as who his father really was . . . even if it *was* that despised savage.

The knock on the door startled her.

Andres looked handsome in his cavalry uniform, even if it was the coarse private's issue.

"Hello, Mother. I got caught by my favorite history professor wishing me well in the war. Sorry." He grinned that infectious smile of his.

She loved that smile. Showing a touch of his bright teeth, it promised warmth and ready good humor. Flanking his hawklike nose, his hazel eyes looked at times piercing when he wasn't smiling, but they usually held a hint of curiosity, often accompanied by traces of mischief. Tall and erect, perhaps because he'd grown up as the son of an army officer, his manner was proud without being in the least condescending. And how she loved him!

They hugged as she asked, "Do you mean Mr. Ambercrombie?"

"Yes. He tried to enlist, but they told him seventy-one was just too old." He laughed.

Carlota sobered. "What time do you leave tomorrow?"

"My train leaves Cleveland at eight-thirty in the morning."

"I'll go there with you."

His tone was serious. "No, Mother, I'm going into Cleveland tonight with two other new troopers. This is our goodbye."

They went to a small restaurant down the street. It was warm in the tiny dining room with its blue-and-white gingham curtains, more so because Carlota was having trouble reaching the point of her concern.

"I think Father will get his regiment soon," Andres said. "Wouldn't it be something if I could join it?"

"I think he'll get an infantry command," Carlota replied absently. *She had to say it now.* "Darling," she began softly, taking his hand across the table. "There's something I must tell you. And it's very difficult for me to do because I . . . well, I have to confess to a big lie." She paused, trying to build her resolve.

He regarded her soberly as he waited.

She sighed. "It's in regard to your real father."

"Yes?"

She made the plunge. "His name wasn't Roberto de Cardenas and he wasn't a Mexican officer. . . . "

Suddenly the dining room was utterly silent.

She gripped his hand tightly, holding his surprised look. "I was married to a very rich young man named de Gante, but on my wedding day—"

He still waited quietly.

"—I was kidnapped by Lazaro."

One of his dark eyebrows went up. "The big Apache chief?"

"Yes." She thought she'd be able to control herself, but she felt on the verge of tears. Abruptly, she plunged on, pouring out the horror of her captivity, her revulsion for everything Apache and particularly Lazaro. "You were born after I was taken prisoner," she said quietly, suddenly wondering if her explanation sounded like a confession.

He continued to stare into her eyes, saying nothing.

"If it's any consolation, I was told that Lazaro was descended from a great chief of his people, a leader named Silsoose, who brought the Chihenne—that's the name of that clan of Apache—to southwestern New Mexico centuries ago."

Andres nodded his head slowly. "You should have told me before."

Her eyes were pleading. "I couldn't, my darling, I just couldn't. You don't know what it has been like—the pain, the loss. . . . " She told him about being rejected by Agustin, the annulment. "I survived by hating Lazaro and his people, and I just couldn't bring myself to tell you—"

His voice was still low. "You couldn't admit that your only son was an Apache, isn't that it?"

The tears were blurring her eyes again. "You are mostly *Spanish!*"

He nodded, reflecting. At length he replied, "Does it really matter?"

"It does in our world."

"Do you think it will be important on the battlefield?"

At times he was *so* mature, almost superior. Why should he reduce such a major problem to such a simplistic question? "I, well, I guess you'll have to decide that for yourself," she replied limply.

He looked away, obviously weighing this new development in his life.

"Will you forgive me for lying to you?" she asked in almost a whisper. God, could she lose him over this?

He looked back, his expression softening, his hand tightening over hers. "It must have been a terrible time for you, Mother. Now, that I know the truth, I suppose I can. What does Father—Rafe—have to say about this?"

"He has long urged me to tell you the truth."

His smile was soft. "Then I guess we should get on with everything, shouldn't we?"

She heaved a huge sigh of relief. This time there was no holding back the tears. "Oh, son, I love you so much."

≫ 16 ≪

January 18, 1863

Of the many adventurers streaming around the West during the Civil War, some forty had banded together under a veteran mountain man by the name of Joseph Reddeford Walker. Captain Walker, a white-maned prospector, trapper, guide, and opportunist of sixty-five, had led his motley, but well-armed and provisioned band through northern Arizona and Colorado in search of gold, and was now in the Willows Country, camped at deserted Fort McLane, southwest of Santa Rita. After making some kind of a deal with General Carleton, now the Indian-hating dictatorial military governor of the New Mexico Territory, the Walker party was proceeding back to Arizona. But, whether Carleton had offered him a reward for capturing Lazaro, or whether, as he stated, it was necessary to take him as a hostage for the period his band would be moving through Apache country, it was never clear. Whatever the truth, Captain Walker had decided to effect his capture.

The white-haired captain took a heavily armed party to trap the Chihenne leader near his village close by Pinos Altos. Accompanying him was a squad of blue-coated troopers under the command of a captain who had just arrived at Fort McLane as the advance party from the First Cavalry of California Volunteers under General Joseph R. West.

The Walker party rode to a grassy place beside a stream some five hundred yards from Lazaro's village, hoisted a white flag on a tent pole, and made camp for the night.

As soon as word came to Lazaro that the large group of White Eyes had stopped to make camp so close to the Chihenne, he hurried to a point above their camp where he could observe them. Tze-go-juni and Old Man joined him. "What do you think?" he asked them.

Old Man spoke first, "I say they come for no good."

The old shaman agreed. "They are evil. You should attack them at first light, while they are in their blankets."

Lazaro stroked his chin. "They fly the white flag to parley."

"I don't trust them," Old Man muttered.

Tze-go-juni nodded her head defiantly. "Kill them."

"Old Man," Lazaro said quietly, "have the warriors spread out on the slope above the camp at dawn."

Rising well before sunup the following morning, Lazaro bathed where the water ran through the ice in the shallow part of the stream. Finishing, he donned a fresh checkered shirt, his best high buckskin moccasins, a freshly tanned pair of leggings and a red breech cloth that was from the same bolt of cloth as the bandana around his head. Kneeling, he secured the large knife that was strapped inside the left moccasin. The last thing he checked was the short dagger that was held by a sheath in the top of the flat-crowned, wide-brimmed black hat that he so prized and wore on all major occasions. For some reason, probably from his Power, he felt a premonition about this morning. But it was undoubtedly just part of the experienced alertness that he had developed over the years when dealing with strangers, and particularly enemy strangers.

But what had to be done couldn't be averted; if the White Eyes wanted to talk, it was his responsibility to listen. Somewhere in this struggle called life there had to be peace. He thought of the old saying *"Niyaa gozhoo doleel*—Let there be joy and peace over you." Yes, there had to be peace for the People; their numbers weren't large enough to continue fighting forever.

Still, they were the People, and they would bow to no one—not the hated Nakai-ye and not the White Eye. Not ever.

Old Man and two good war leaders rode with Lazaro to meet the White Eyes at midmorning. "Don't go!" Tze-go-juni had insisted. "I had a dream—they're not to be trusted."

"My warriors outnumber them," had been his reply.

Now, as his small party slowly approached the White Eye leaders, he observed them warily. Like all Godammies the nonsoldiers wore thick beards and heavy clothes. There were five of them, sitting on their horses, one holding a white flag on a staff in the open space where they waited. There were three soldiers, one wearing the yellow shoulder boards of an officer. He glanced up the hillside. His warriors were well situated among the rocks in the shallow bright snow. The sun beamed down, seemingly extra powerful. It was the warmest day in at least two moons.

The leader with the white beard held up his hand and spoke in

Spanish: "We have talked at a distance, now let us parley like brothers. Please share my tobacco." He held out a large plug.

Lazaro watched his eyes, but he couldn't read them. He nodded and slowly dismounted, as did the white beard and the officer. "I am Lazaro," he said clearly. "You speak of parley about peace. What do you wish?" His war leaders also dismounted, but Old Man remained seated on his pony. Mounting and dismounting was too difficult for him. Lazaro accepted the tobacco with a nod of appreciation.

"My name is Captain Walker," the white beard said. "We have many men and soldiers at the unused fort called McLane. This is Captain Shirland. And we want to—" He stopped and nodded to the army officer as he pulled a long-barreled revolver from his coat and pointed it at Lazaro. At the same moment, the other White Eyes pointed guns at the Chihenne war leaders. "All right!" the white beard said loudly. "You are our prisoner, Lazaro. Tell your braves to behave. We are taking you with us as a hostage until our party passes completely through this here part of the country. If everything is peaceful, Chief, we'll let you go when we reach Tucson. If not, you'll be killed. Simple as that."

Old Man cursed in Spanish as both war leaders looked about angrily. At the flash of a hand signal, the warriors on the hill would open fire. Lazaro looked at the revolver pointed at his stomach. "No," he said in Apache. "I'll be all right with them. I'll do as he says, while you take the warriors back to the village. I should be able to escape with little trouble."

Old Man protested. "They lie like the coyote!"

"We have no choice. Go." Lazaro turned to Walker, his voice cold. "You are so far a liar, but I am your prisoner."

As the Walker party rode into Fort McLane, several hundred eyes greeted them. The rest of the First Cavalry from California had arrived and was camped around the little post. As Captain Shirland ordered Lazaro to dismount from his pony, a handful of men moved toward them. Striding ahead was the short figure of Brigadier General Joseph West, a Louisianan and Mexican War veteran who had been working as a newspaperman in San Francisco before the outbreak of the war. Just behind him, wearing yellow corporal's stripes on his blue uniform shirt, was a familiar face. Lazaro stared into the cold eyes of his longtime enemy, Bacho. He was an *army scout!*

The Wolf's face twisted slightly as he slowly nodded his head. "This is Lazaro," he said to the general in heavily accented Spanish.

General West stared up at the prisoner. "You and your savages have been raising hell long enough," he said angrily in Spanish. "What do you have to say for yourself?"

Lazaro looked away, saying nothing, taking in the large number of soldiers and rough-looking civilians who had closed in to watch.

The general bristled. "I'm talking to you, Injun! And I don't care if you are supposed to be a big goddamn chief! You are my prisoner, and you will afford me the courtesy of my rank!" He turned to Bacho. "Doesn't he understand Spanish?"

"He understands. He just thinks he's too important to reply."

"Tell him in Apache."

Bacho turned, glaring, to the person he'd hated since boyhood. "Nantan West says you are a man of no importance and that you are his prisoner. You must kiss his hand, *dog!*"

Lazaro looked away, ignoring the Wolf.

Bacho jerked his arm. "I'll tell him you should die."

Lazaro continued to ignore him.

General West turned to Captain Shirland, speaking in English. "He is an army prisoner now, Captain. But I'm sure he'll attempt to escape. In that event, I want him dead in the morning." No one within earshot missed the general's intent, least of all Bacho.

Lazaro was dozing by the fire of logs where the two enlisted guards who had been assigned to watch over him sat with their rifles. He stirred, pulling the blanket around him, and rolled onto his side where he could watch them through veiled eyes. He, too, knew what Nantan West had said. And he knew that Bacho would come to do the job before the night was over. One of the guards, the one called Mead, rose from where he'd been stirring the fire with his bayonet. "You awake, Big Chief?" he asked derisively, sticking the hot tip of the bayonet against Lazaro's foot. "Don't you want to escape, Big Chief?"

The acrid smell of the buckskin being singed reached Lazaro's nostrils just as the heat penetrated to his foot. He pulled the leg back, grunting. But his fingers found the wide-brimmed hat behind his back. His captors had discovered and taken the large skinning knife from his moccasin, but had failed to look inside his hat. In moments, he had the small knife working on the cord that bound his wrist.

"Whatsa matter, Big Chief, you don't like getting your toes warmed up?" the guard taunted, pulling his rifle up into Lazaro's face.

Lazaro just followed his eyes.

Mead laughed aloud and turned to the other soldier. "He doesn't like roasting chestnuts, you know that?"

The last cord on his wrist snapped loose as the little knife slipped and caught the skin on his hand. But he didn't have time for such a minor problem, not with Bacho looming out of the dark.

The stocky scout shook his head in mock dismay as he came into the firelight. Speaking in Apache he said, "I thought you would be finished by now, Lazaro. Like Nantan West said, you're to be dead by morning. So that's the end for the big dreamer, the coward who thought he was a chief."

Lazaro sat leaning forward in the blanket, working unobtrusively on the rope that held his ankles. "How long you been a White Eye snake, Bacho?" he asked quietly. He could see the Wolf's eyes harden in the yellow light. "What does your son think about you being a traitor?"

Bacho's hand went to his revolver, pulling it from its holster on his belt as he squatted a few feet away.

"Hear, hear, what you Injuns talking about?" Mead asked, moving close.

"I'm going to kill him," Bacho replied darkly.

Mead laughed. "That's a good one. You Injuns even kill each other." He moved back to where the other guard was dozing and relit his pipe.

Lazaro's ankles were now free under the blanket. He wondered if the small knife would be enough. He doubted it. Edging closer to the fire, he made his decision. "Do you really think you are one of them?" he asked, inclining his head in the direction of the guards a few yards away.

As Bacho glanced toward the soldiers, Lazaro made his move. Grabbing a burning ember, he threw off the blanket and jammed the ember into Bacho's face.

"*Eeeowww!*" the scout screamed, jumping up and grabbing his eyes.

Instantly Lazaro seized the dropped revolver and cocked its hammer. As Mead grabbed his rifle, Lazaro fired, spinning the sentry around. The other soldier jerked up, eyes wide, as the .45 bullet crashed into his chest. The third bullet hit the screaming Bacho's thickset form as Lazaro spun out of the firelight and loped into the night.

17

Washington, D. C.
September 26, 1864

The mail held two letters of interest. Carlota eyed the crest of the Legation of Mexico with curiosity, but opened the envelope from Rafe first. She read:

> In the Shenandoah Valley
> September 23rd

My Dearest Carlota,

By now you should have heard the news of our routing Old Jubal Early's Army at Winchester on the 19th & again yesterday at Fishers Hill. My Army of West Virginia did themselves proud yesterday, for sure. While Sheridan had his other two corps bristling in front of Early's dug-in army, I moved before dawn to sneak my two divisions around the rebel left. It was an arduous march, with our flags furled as we did everything to keep from being detected, but finally at 4 o'clock (12 hours after we departed) we crashed down the mountainside & hurled ourselves into Early's flank. At that point, Sheridan threw his main body into a frontal assault & sent the rebs a-hightailing. I hate to criticize any of my fellow commanders, but if the two cavalry leaders had followed up like Sheridan wanted them to, we'd have bagged the whole army.

One of my staff rounded up some fine apples & my cook is making ice cream, so shortly I'm going to dine very well. Being a major general does have its points, altho the losses always weigh heavily on me.

How is our fine son? I'm pleased that he is going to Sheridan. You've kept him in that Washington abyss too long. A good soldier like him belongs in the field. I wish I had him.

I miss you terribly, my dear one.

> Always yours,
> Rafe

Carlota sighed as she put the letter back in its envelope. It had arrived by courier from Sheridan's headquarters with only a three-day delay. It was just like Rafe to talk about ice cream and apples when she knew he'd rather share his sadness over casualties. He had done so well in the war; appointed from captain to colonel of the Thirty-seventh Ohio six months after Fort Sumter was fired on, promoted to brigadier general of volunteers a year later, and given his second star seven months ago. His record was remarkable, with several commendations, but she knew the Mexican side of his lineage had held him back somewhat; there were numerous major generals both younger and with far less experience.

Nevertheless, he *was* a general, and only one other man had more stars than her fine husband—and that was Grant himself.

She sighed and reached for the other envelope, noting the tiny surge of excitement that made her hand quiver slightly. She knew who it was from. She'd read in the *Evening Star* of his visit. Withdrawing the embossed invitation, she read:

> *It is with great pleasure*
> *That the Foreign Minister*
> *Invites you*
> *to*
> *A reception for*
> *General don Agustin de Gante*
> *At the Legation of Mexico*
> *Five O'Clock*
> *October 4, 1864*

Inside was a short note: "Please come." It was signed simply, "Agustin."

Carlota's eyes blurred at the words as she stared at the signature she had once adored. It had been over sixteen years since she'd seen Agustin de Gante, and even today she remembered the horrible remorse she'd felt when she went to his dinner, ready to accept whatever crumbs he wished to offer . . . almost ready to be his whore.

She shrugged. As a Union general's wife, and an attractive woman of forty who looked closer to thirty, she received a number of invitations to different functions. In fact, because of her volunteer hospital work, she had been invited to Kate Chase Sprague's last gala.

To make *that* invitation list was an accomplishment many a general's wife would die for. And now this. It was a long way from a crude Apache wickiup in the mountains of New Mexico; or, for that matter, from being an outcast at a hacienda named La Reina. . . .

In spite of herself, she felt a flutter of excitement.

Of course she wouldn't go; the casual urgency of Agustin's "Please come" was a danger signal. But still, it was intriguing. No, it wouldn't be right. . . .

On the other hand, she was probably the only general's wife in Washington who had been a Mexican citizen of Castilian blood and a Mexican colonel's daughter. She *should* be invited to Mexican legation affairs. . . . She could have Andres escort her. He wasn't scheduled to depart for the valley until three days after the reception.

She really should go.

Yes, that's what she'd do.

As she combed her long, lustrous hair before retiring, Carlota couldn't calm the mixed feeling of excitement and guilt that hung over her. Agustin. God, how she hated him! She'd nurtured and built on that hate until he had faded from her thinking. And now he'd come crashing back into it. Crashing! She couldn't think of *anything* else. What would he look like now? She'd heard from her aunt that he'd married the daughter of another wealthy landowner some twelve years earlier. A blond beauty from Jalisco, the newspaper had said. Probably the one she'd heard about—the one his damned mama had picked out.

Living at her La Reina. *Her* beautiful hacienda.

No, this thinking was *silly*. She'd pushed that disappointment away a long time ago, conquered the pain, washed it into limbo. La Reina was merely a bad dream, just as Agustin was.

And now—

She thought of his handsome face. God, she couldn't do this.

Still, it would be harmless.

"Please come," were his words. "Time heals all" was probably his thinking. Wartime Washington, two one-time lovers, surely. . . .

No, she'd control it.

And perhaps she was just fantasizing. That was it, just a face out of the past wishing to say "hello." No, that was too simple. Or maybe the Mexicans wanted something from her. Could be anything. No, deep down, she knew. . . .

* * *

Andres fastened the high collar of his dress uniform and checked himself in the mirror. At an even six feet, he was far shorter than his father, but he had inherited Lazaro's lithe leanness. He shrugged; the pomp of political affairs, and Washington life in general, was distasteful to him. He would much rather be back in his regiment fighting with the confidence much of the federal cavalry had acquired in the past year. But Carlota had pulled strings to get him assigned as the crippled General Sickles' aide following Gettysburg. It wasn't long after he enlisted in Cleveland that he was in action, eventually serving under Phil Sheridan, when the aggressive little West Pointer commanded a regiment. His excellent horsemanship and natural leadership qualities had quickly brought him promotion to corporal and then to sergeant. Later, while serving as a replacement in Custer's Wolverine regiment, he'd caught the young cavalry leader's eye. Then came the Gettysburg wound and his commission as a first lieutenant—once more a result of his mother's manipulation as a general's wife.

But he was about to escape the web. General Sickles had arranged for him to go back to Sheridan's headquarters escort in the Shenandoah Valley. It still wasn't what he wanted—which was a troop of cavalry—but it was close to the action. Everyone knew that while Little Phil Sheridan commanded an army, he was *always* close to the action. Three more days; he couldn't wait to get back where he belonged. After all, the grandson of a Mexican colonel and the son of an Apache chief should be in the midst of battle, not playing fop in the capital.

He wondered if there'd be any attractive girls at the Mexican reception. It would be nice to have one last romantic fling before turning back into a soldier. That had been the saving grace of being in the capital: there were plenty of loose women around for a lieutenant who knew what he was about.

But mostly he was curious about General Agustin de Gante, the man who had treated his mother so terribly. She'd told him the whole story about being cast out by the de Gantes. She hadn't said it but he knew it was partially because of a little half-breed boy named Andres. It made his blood boil. He could never remember seeing the man, but he hated him instinctively. He'd asked how de Gante had become a general, but she didn't know. Probably another political promotion. He should be used to them; there were so damned many in the wartime Union Army. A rich man with connections in Mexico could probably be promoted to God. And this one had been his first step-father—at least until the annulment of the marriage to his mother.

For a moment he thought seriously about avenging his mother's honor. . . .

Carlota's voice interrupted his thoughts. "Are you ready, darling?" she called from the bottom of the varnished oak stairs.

Carlota wore a gown of yellow watered silk that set off her still raven-black hair. Her earrings were small sapphires that matched the large rectangular sapphire brooch dangling at her breast. The blue of the jewels enhanced her eyes. She had gained perhaps an inch and a half around her slender waist in the last couple of years, but her figure was still a point of envy among Washington socialites. She lived modestly, shepherding her money in a wartime capital where one could spend practically anything. This house on "O" Street in Georgetown was a rather narrow two-story with two bedrooms and an attic. She'd rented it furnished for four hundred a year; a bit extravagant, but she wanted to be somewhat near Rafe and Andres. It had worked fine for Andres. And Rafe did get to town once in a while. The location was respectable, reflecting her status.

Between the continuing growth of her investments and those of Rafe, which she continued to manage, their financial situation was quite comfortable. They still owned the houses in Albuquerque and Santa Fe, and the one in San Antonio, all of which were rented on long-term leases. And, of course, Rafe's pay as a major general was considerably more than that of a peacetime captain.

She'd decided against wearing her hair in the fashionable long curls of the day, instead drawing it straight back into a chignon with a small comb of artificial sapphire with tiny rhinestones. It would remind everyone attending that she was also Mexican.

As Andres came down the stairs, she smiled and reached for his arm.

He let out a small whistle and said, "I guess I'll be with the most beautiful woman at the party."

She loved his charm. "And every woman's head will turn when she sees my handsome escort."

The Mexican Legation was a modest, high-ceilinged, two-story house with a large parlor that permitted average sized receptions. There was a reason: President Lincoln had refused to recognize the government of the Intervention the French had installed. Maximilian, archduke of

Austria and younger brother of its emperor, had been crowned emperor of Mexico just six months earlier. The puppet of Napoleon III of France, Maximilian, along with his wife Carlota, had deposed liberal president Benito Juárez, but Lincoln still recognized the great reformer's democratic shadow government. Matías Romero, the handsome young envoy to the United States, was Juárez's foreign minister, though he had no official portfolio. His primary goal in the United States was to create financial and political support for Juárez. He had little in the way of money to spend for the mad Washington social whirl.

This crowded reception was being paid for by the guest of honor, General Agustin de Gante. His hair now touched with silver, Agustin was, if anything, even more handsome than when he was younger, Carlota thought as they greeted each other. Even after this many years, she felt the tension as he said, "You are more beautiful than ever, Carlota." He held her hand a moment too long.

"Thank you, General. This is my son, Lieutenant Murphy."

Andres's expression was cool as he shook Agustin's hand. "I understand you were almost my stepfather," he said directly, holding the general's eyes.

"Oh, you're . . . uh, yes, I believe . . . something like that."

"What brings you to Washington?" Andres asked, still watching Agustin's eyes as they went back to his mother.

"We are trying to secure both funds and government influence for our cause."

Andres nodded. "From what Mother has told me, de Gante money should be enough."

Agustin smiled smoothly. "I wish that were true. However, our meager resources are not enough to bring down the emperor and the power behind him." He turned to another guest, breaking off the conversation.

Later, as Carlota was eating an aniseed *bizcochito*, a cookie, Agustin took her elbow, saying, "It's such a pretty evening. Let's go out back so we can get some fresh air and talk privately."

It was one of those warm October days that had begun briskly, passing its sun through clear blue skies to the western horizon, heating everything in sight, creating the opening for thousands of conversations, and providing good autumn cheer. Now it was showing off its glorious reddening color as if to say, "Partake of my last charms quickly, for my blessing is about to fade into the purple past."

An overly eager cricket was sounding nightfall.

Carlota felt the strain the moment they were alone together. The resentment was there, but so was the attraction. Agustin was so very handsome in his maturity, the silver of his hair rhyming so strikingly with his dark, expressive eyes. In spite of herself, she felt a tug of excitement.

"I can't believe how unbelievably beautiful you are, Carlota," he said, taking her hand. "But I should have known. No flower as remarkably lovely as you were in your youth could do anything but blossom into rare radiance."

"I see you've learned even more about the art of flattery," she replied, withdrawing her hand and speaking over her fan.

He smiled engagingly. "But how else can one describe the exquisite?"

"How is your wife?" she asked directly.

"She's in Mexico. We're here," he replied just as directly, his eyes widening ever so slightly and boring into hers.

"And your children?"

"We never had any. She's barren."

Naturally, she thought. What normally assertive Mexican man, let alone a don, would ever admit that he couldn't father children?

He went on, "As I said, my dear Carlota, we're here now together."

"We're not together, Agustin," she said more softly than she wanted to. "We haven't been together since a day long ago when a priest read marriage vows over our heads and a lazo was draped over us."

"That was a wonderful time for us, until the Apaches struck."

"Yes, the most wonderful moment of my life." She sighed, pulling herself back to the present and forcing herself to change the subject. "I'm surprised that a don such as you would be supporting Juárez. After all, reform must have struck at many of the people in your world of wealth and influence."

"The people who have backed Maximilian are my enemies. I switched to Juárez when I saw the coronation was a certainty."

"What's going to happen in Mexico?"

Agustin scowled. "Mexico will once more be ruled by Mexicans."

"When?"

"Soon." He touched her hand again. "But let's get back to us. I want to see you as much as possible while I'm here."

"I'm married—remember?"

"I know. General Murphy has a command under Sheridan. But I

don't care. I have a suite at the Willard. Come there later. Let me show you that I still love you."

She shook her head, withdrawing her hand again. The idea was tempting. She wouldn't do anything with him, just be with him. No, how could she be thinking such a thing? This was the man who'd broken her heart. Still—he was so handsome, and not that weak boy whose mother had ruled so long ago. She couldn't believe how much she wanted to go to his hotel. It had started picking away at her the moment she saw the invitation, creating the temptation, the curiosity, the old desire and pain. She turned toward the door. "We must go back inside."

"Will you come to the Willard later tonight?"

"No."

"Will you have dinner with me tomorrow?"

She shouldn't encourage him at all. "There would be no purpose to it."

He arched an eyebrow and smiled. "I disagree, but it's the lady's prerogative." Taking her elbow he led her inside, just in time to run almost directly into her son.

A hurt look flashed over Andres's face, but he erased it as he said, "Are you ready to go home, Mother?"

She nodded her head, feeling a pang of guilt. "Yes, darling."

Agustin bowed over her hand and kissed it. "It has been a distinct pleasure to see you again, Carlota. I wish you well."

The dozen red roses arrived at shortly after ten the next morning, while Andres was gone from the house. The card read, "I can't wait to see you again. Can we have dinner at six at the Willard? Please reply by the messenger." It was signed, "Your Agustin."

Carlota had known all morning that she'd hear from him.

She reread the note. No, she just couldn't. She simply didn't trust herself. She'd written a long letter to Rafe the night before, hoping that it would take her mind off Agustin, but it hadn't. *Why was she so tempted?* The bastard! Her hand trembled slightly as she sat at her dining table and dipped the quill pen in the ink. She wanted to see him. . . .

Breakfast!

That would be a harmless way out . . . and *not* at his hotel . . . at some place where there were people. Where? Ah, the Café Rouge down a few blocks on "N" Street. If it's warm enough, one can eat outside at a sidewalk table. She did want to see him, and he had to go on to New York in a couple of days. Yes, tomorrow morning. At ten o'clock. Mexicans ate on a different schedule from Americans. Late breakfast, no lunch, late afternoon dinner, dessert late in the evening.

She wrote the reply and handed it to the waiting messenger.

The Café Rouge in Georgetown had been open since the second month of the war. The middle of three large row houses, its facade was painted a rich red trimmed in gilt. In front, surrounded by a thin, waist-high hedge, were four tables under bright scarlet umbrellas. The day was as clear as a mountain creek, the sun already a threat to make someone complain about so much heat in October. A short waiter with a bristling mustache hovered by the door, a white towel draped over his arm. Carlota was stylishly late, arriving at a few minutes before eleven.

Agustin, wearing an expensive brown suit, smiled as he rose to greet her. After seating her, he ordered a rich black coffee from the waiter and told her how much the gray silk dress she was wearing enhanced her light eyes. She thanked him and they went through the niceties of the morning.

Although she was a bit nervous, she was glad she'd come. He was even more handsome than she had thought the night before, and she felt a certain electricity with him. When he brushed her hand with his, she knew she'd have to be careful. "What are you going to do in New York?" she asked, breaking the spell of attraction.

"Speak to a number of wealthy men about money for Mexico."

"Why should they provide that kind of money?"

"Because if Juárez lets them build factories or mines, they can make fortunes—an opportunity the Maximilian government won't give them."

"Do you think you'll be successful?"

"I don't know." He took her hand, smiling into her eyes. "Why don't you come to New York with me?"

The idea was intriguing . . . a couple of days . . . she didn't have to do anything wrong with him, just be with him, enjoy his charm. After all, didn't she deserve *something* coming from him?

But how would she ever explain it to Rafe?

Suddenly the coffee tasted bitter and she felt a chill. The years fell away and she was in Agustin's house in Mexico City, ready to be his trollop. She closed her eyes, bringing her hand to her forehead. She—

"Are you all right?" Agustin asked with concern.

She opened her eyes. "Yes, I just realized I've made a terrible mistake in coming here. I—" She looked up and directly into Andres's eyes. *He was standing on the other side of the hedge, staring at her in disbelief.*

Her hand flew to her mouth. "Oh!" was all she could say. *How long had he been there?*

Woodenly, Andres pushed the wrought iron gate open. Its little bell tinkled, oddly, a brittle sound, the only noise in a rapidly unfolding moment of horror for her. His eyes were narrowed, dark in their cold fury. He pulled them from her and leveled them on Agustin. "Sir," he said sharply, "I demand satisfaction for everything you've done to my mother." He threw a leather cavalry gauntlet on the table. "And everything you *intend* to do to her."

Agustin stared at the big glove, then back at Andres's piercing eyes. Slowly he shook his head, saying softly, "No, my boy, I won't honor your challenge."

"Are you a coward on top of everything else?"

"No, I'm not a coward." Agustin got to his feet, turning to Carlota. "I must return to the Willard, I assume you will be all right with your son?"

Tears were already streaming down her cheeks, tears of hurt, tears of shame. She had never seen such violence in Andres's eyes. She nodded her head, unable to speak.

"You Mexican bastard," Andres said coldly, blocking the entrance. "I *demand* satisfaction!"

"Out of my way, boy," Agustin replied coolly. "I won't fight you."

Somehow, Carlota broke her trance and moved between them. "Let him go, darling," she said earnestly to her son. "It's nothing."

Andres glanced from her to Agustin, back to her, and after a long moment, his furious eyes settled on those of the interloper. "Someday, de Gante," he said in a voice that rattled with hate, "I'll see you again. I promise you. And you won't back down then."

Agustin drew himself stiffly erect, touched the brim of his hat in salute to Carlota, and walked through the gate.

18

Winchester, Virginia
October 19, 1864

Andres blinked at the sound of the bugle playing Reveille and rolled over under the thick comforter. There *were* advantages to being a courier for the commanding general: one stood reveille in a nice warm bed if one wished. And if he desired, he could stay up a little late the night before playing poker. That is, if the war was quiet; and with the rebs outnumbered two-to-one some fifteen miles to the south, there wasn't much going on. In fact, he'd gone down to visit some of the boys in Custer's 3rd Division the day before, hoping something might get stirred up. If anything *could* get stirred up, it would be around Custer. How that man loved to fight!

The war in the Valley was in limbo. Early's army, which Sheridan had trounced soundly exactly a month earlier in what was called the battle of "Third Winchester," was licking its wounds down by Cedar Creek, with Murphy's Corps of West Virginians keeping a close watch on them. However, there was a rumor that Longstreet's powerful First Corps may have reinforced Early—at least that was what an intercepted rebel signal had indicated. But Sheridan had tossed it aside as a ruse before going to Washington to see General Halleck, Grant's chief of staff, three days earlier.

What was that faint rumble to the south? Sounded like guns.

No, couldn't be.

He swung his legs out of bed and looked at his pocket watch, then went to the window. The sky to the east was announcing its early light. It didn't look like there could be any thunderstorms around—

That was the sound of guns! Distant, muffled. Maybe some kind of an artillery duel. . . . But why? Who? He'd also visited his father, General Murphy, the day before and everything had been quiet. There was no order for a Union venture. Would *Early* attack? Hardly.

Maybe an itchy artillery battery commander had started something.

He stretched and yawned. He was hungry. That was another advantage of being on an army commander's staff—good cooks and good food. Of course they weren't at their own headquarters, but at that of the brigade commander who was performing garrison duty in Winchester. Still, they wouldn't exactly be eating hardtack. Pouring some cold water from the pitcher into the white porcelain bowl, he splashed it on his face. He reached for the soap, hearing the distant thunder again. . . .

"Come in here and join me, boy!" Major General Philip H. Sheridan barked as Andres walked into the kitchen. More descriptive phrases had been tacked on thirty-three-year-old Little Phil than any other general in the army. Banty rooster, black Irishman, bandy-legged—even President Lincoln, himself misshapen enough to be poked fun of by nearly anyone—joked of Sheridan's long arms and duck legs on his five-feet-five-inch frame with: "If his ankles itched, he could scratch them without stooping." Combative, with dark brown eyes and wavy dark hair, the general had taken five years to complete West Point due to a year's suspension for a fight with a cadet sergeant. His complexion was florid, his gestures jerky and nervous; his voice at times sounded like it was raking off a file. Usually his face was cleanshaven except for his clipped mustache, his uniform always proper. Described by newspaperman James Taylor as a "little mountain of combative force," he could nonetheless issue orders softly and carefully, with measured care.

Above all, Little Phil Sheridan was a war dog. As a lieutenant, he had served with Raphael Murphy in Indian campaigns before the Secession. Now he was Rafe's commanding general.

Captain Sandy Forsyth, one of Sheridan's aides, pointed to a place at the end of the table. "Sit there, Murphy."

Andres murmured his thanks and told the orderly how he wanted his eggs.

Moments later, it seemed that the distant rumble was increasing in intensity. General Sheridan raised an eyebrow at the brigade commander, Colonel Edwards. "Do you think it's getting louder?"

"Seems so, sir," the colonel replied.

Sheridan sipped from his coffee cup and turned back to Forsyth. "I don't think that's just a demonstration or reconnaissance in force. I have a hunch somebody's a heap angry down there. Soon's you finish your coffee, get our people together so we can ride down and see just what the hell's going on."

Captain Forsyth got quickly to his feet. "Yes, sir."

Andres also rose from the table. "I'll notify the cavalry escort, sir."

Sheridan looked up at him as he lit one of his everpresent cigars. "No, eat your breakfast, boy. Sandy'll take care of that. I doubt there's any real hurry."

At that moment the orderly brought Andres's plate. It would be the last full meal the new courier would eat until after dark that night.

Andres watched from two dozen yards away as General Sheridan climbed down from his horse and put his ear to the ground. After listening for nearly a minute, he nodded his head and drew himself erect. Scowling, he announced to no one in particular, "Whoever's doing the shooting is moving this way."

Swinging quickly back into the saddle, he led his contingent down the pike at a brisk trot. Andres fell back to ride beside the cavalry escort's commander. Dense early morning fog had given way to the warm, hazy sunshine that gave promise of a most pleasant day. The turnpike, a pale line passing through fields, orchards and farm buildings that showed an occasional wisp of blue smoke, stretched away from them as if this oft-battled-for valley had never known anything but peaceful calm instead of continuing warfare.

In a few minutes they topped a rise and found the pike blocked; a large Federal wagon train was halted in complete disarray. Some of its wagons faced one way, some another. Forsyth galloped forward and was back quickly. "Sir," he said excitedly, "a major just ordered the train to turn around and head back toward Winchester. *Our army was attacked by the rebs early this morning and is smashing us back up the valley!*"

Sheridan sat there a moment, looking at his aide and saying nothing, then slowly climbed down and began walking his big black horse, Rienzi, around the confusion of the wagon train. Anticipating that he might be needed, Andres moved closer to him. He could almost feel Sheridan's intensity growing, his combative instincts rising. Farther away, large numbers of disorganized blue-coated stragglers could be seen heading toward them. Sheridan scowled, finally mounting. Turning to Sandy Forsyth, he said, "Tell the quartermaster to turn this damned train around and take it straight forward. Then get word back to Edwards in Winchester to form his brigade across this pike by Mill Creek and stop any stragglers running back this way." Turning to Andres, he barked, "Get me fifty of the best troopers in that escort, Murphy. We're gonna turn this army *around!*"

Sheridan urged his big black horse into a long swinging gallop, causing his entourage into a rush to catch up. Within the next mile, the flotsam of rear echelon elements hurrying to avoid capture was streaming toward them in full disarray. As Sheridan thundered on, battle-seared troops, heads low or eyes wide, began to appear. The general swung his forage cap with its two stars and shouted at them to turn around. They stared at him at first, then glanced at each other, many murmuring, "It's Sheridan."

Andres watched in fascination as Sheridan swung his little cap again and shouted, "C'mon, boys, let's go back and give them a licking!" Slowly the battered soldiers began to stand straighter and look to their rear.

Before long, the pike was full of stragglers, many of whom turned—a new light in their eyes—to cheer their little commander. Many of them waved their hats and began to follow, shouting to their comrades farther out in the fields, "Sheridan, Sheridan!" "Here's little Phil! We're going back!"

On Andres charged behind the general as Sheridan's amazing magnetism continued to draw the fleeing soldiers. When one officer told Little Phil his army headquarters had been overrun, the general's face turned even redder, the glint in his dark eyes sharpened, his expression becoming grimmer. Still he exuded enthusiasm. "Turn back, boys!" he shouted. "Face the other way! *I'm going to sleep in our camp tonight—or in hell!*"

Even the many retreating soldiers who had stopped to boil coffee joined the new tide as Sheridan and his small van cantered through the fields and past the now-clogged turnpike. Finally, bursting over a rise, Andres saw the wreckage of the battlefield spread out before them: guns, broken wagons, stragglers, wounded men and stretcher-bearers, small groups of men looking aimless, here and there a riderless horse wandering. The remnants of a division was taking a stunned breather as it waited for the graycoats' next attack. All around was the warm Indian summer with its haze spreading to distant hills practically ablaze with October foliage. And crowning all was the deep blue of the cloudless Shenandoah sky. But before them, the black smoke of battle hung in merciless sunlight, its acrid odor reaching out to the newcomers' nostrils like the scent of death.

Andres stared. An army that had been driven back four miles was gasping its last angry breath. Or was it?

At just that moment a strange noise reached the destruction of the battlefield. Andres thought he was hearing things, but as he turned back toward Winchester, from where it seemed to be coming, he heard a faint cheer. The weak north breeze was wafting a vague murmur of some kind of exultation. Defeated faces looked up, puzzled. The sound grew in volume, staccato at times. Suddenly, he knew—the stragglers! They were returning and cheering as they headed back. Little Phil had turned them around!

Andres stayed close as Sheridan met the Sixth Corps commander, and after a short discussion, rode briskly in front of the battle line. Exhorting the men, he shouted over and over, "What a twist we're going to put on them!"

No one could figure out why Early hadn't followed up on the rout. With the staggering Union divisions broken, he could easily have administered the coup-de-grace by driving them from the field and securing massive numbers of prisoners. The greatest rebel victory of '64 was in his grasp, maybe even the greatest of the war, because Lincoln needed to win a major battle to get reelected in the upcoming election and continue the war. Andres heard even Sheridan wondering what could be causing Old Jube's delay. Could Early be waiting for Longstreet to bring up his famed First Corps? Was there truth to that rumor? The general personally questioned several prisoners, the last a captain. But no one honestly knew anything about Longstreet. Still a ruse, Sheridan decided.

After establishing a new headquarters, Little Phil was now taking his time reorganizing his shattered but rejuvenated army. Suddenly Andres heard him say, "Murphy, I want you to take this message to General Custer. And then stay with him. If there's anything I need be apprised of, I know you'll get to me directly."

Andres took the message and quickly mounted. Fourteen minutes later, he loped into Custer's Third Cavalry Division headquarters and swung from the saddle. A major greeted him and took the message from Sheridan. Immediately, Custer called Andres inside his tent. The tall lean man in blond ringlets and fancy uniform looked at him with impatience. "What the hell's going on over there, Lieutenant? Does Sheridan think I want to sit here on my arse all day? Do we even *have* a damned army?"

Andres smiled. "General Sheridan has personally turned it around, sir." He told Custer about the ride and what was happening.

The twenty-four-year-old brigadier tore open the dispatch, his eyes narrowing as he read. He nodded, grinning at his chief of staff. "Little Phil just wanted to let his favorite cavalryman know that we'll be on center stage when we roar back into the graybacks in a little while."

"I'm supposed to stay with you, sir," Andres informed him.

"Very well. When I win this battle for him, you can take the news directly back to him." He looked at Andres more closely. "Don't I know you, Murphy?"

"I used to be in your Wolverine regiment, sir."

Custer snapped his fingers. "That's it—you're General Murphy's son!"

Andres's expression didn't change as he said, "I'll be on standby, sir."

Custer's opportunity came a while after Sheridan began his major counterattack at four o'clock in the afternoon. Actually it was at dusk when an angle of Early's front presented an ideal breach into which Custer could slam his eager troopers. With the flamboyant, grand-standing Custer in the lead, three thousand shrieking Federal cavalry-men roared into Early's void. Trying to keep up with the blond showman, Andres loved it. But suddenly the brown mare he was riding stumbled and pulled up lame. They were near a bridge on a stream that led off from Cedar Creek as he dismounted and walked her off to the side. It was her right front leg, but he couldn't tell what was wrong with it.

"Damn!" Andres exclaimed, looking around anxiously as blue-coated troopers continued to roar past in column. It was then that he spotted the rebel gun, probably a four-incher, being wheeled into place in a defile off to the right of the narrow bridge. He counted five gun-crew members with a mule and two soldiers apparently serving as escorts. Instantly he knew what they were up to: *they could slam explosive or grape shot right down the line of oncoming horsemen!* He pulled his horse around to get some help, but blood was in the eye of every one of Custer's emotional troopers and not a single one of them paid any attention to him as they thundered by.

A glance back at the gun told him the reb gunners were loading a shell. *There wasn't a moment to lose!*

Much as he hated to hurt his horse, there was only one thing he could do. He hurled himself into the saddle, jammed his spurs into her flanks and charged straight at the gun. He was good with the long-barrelled Colt revolver, even at a gallop, and hit one of the rebs on the first shot. The third round also crumpled one of the butternut artillerymen. The others jerked up in alarm, pulling their attention away from the gun and grabbing their muskets; a quick shot whistled by his ear as Andres urged the mare into a short jump over a stone fence and right into the middle of the gun position. The mare staggered and screamed as she came down on her bad leg, but she managed to stay on her feet. He got off another shot, knocking one more gunner down. As he wheeled the game little horse for another gun, he received a searing jolt on his left cheekbone that snapped his face back. He shook his head; it burned like crazy and everything seemed red below his eye. He blinked; he could still see all right. He spurred the animal again, getting off another shot and hitting yet another reb.

At that moment he was smashed in the left side so hard that he nearly came out of the saddle. Simultaneously, the mare let out another scream and pitched forward. He crashed into the ground no more than a yard from the right wheel of the artillery piece and on top of a dying rebel gunner. Pain tore at his side, nearly making him ill. He stared down at a spreading blotch of blood on his left hip.

"You Yankee bastard!" the voice of a tall figure in butternut shouted as one of the survivors towered hazily over him, pointing a musket.

Somehow Andres had hung onto his big revolver. Now, in the blur of losing consciousness, he managed to bring it up and fire its last round into the chest of the apparition looming above him.

Damndest thing I ever seed, General, suh," the wounded rebel soldier was saying. "This here fool came a-spurrin' his damned horse right into our gun position—a-firin' away with his big pistol just like he was a bunch of unarmed schoolboys. Yessiree, he was somethin', General. I knowed I shot him once, but he kept right on a-comin' 'til that horse of his plumb crashed right beside our gun."

"Are you one of the gunners he shot?"

"Yes, General, he got me with the last round he fired. If my musket hadn't-a misfired, I'd-a blowed him apart."

Andres squinted up from where he was being loaded into an ambulance. The stretcher bearers stopped at a soft word from the general. Golden light emanated from a lantern being held just above his head. All at once the tired face of Major General Raphael Murphy came into focus beside it. "I'm proud of you, son," he said gruffly. He took Andres's hand briefly. "It was a brave act, charging those gunners. Phil Sheridan said he's going to give you the Medal of Honor."

Andres found a wan smile, slowly feeling around below his painful hip. "They didn't cut anything off, did they?" he asked softly.

"No, Andres, you were lucky."

He next touched the bandage on his face, but for some reason he wasn't even concerned about that wound. He had all of his limbs, a rarity these days when one got wounded. "Did we—I mean, did we win?"

Rafe smiled at him gently. "We did, son. Early's finished here in the valley. Now we can move on down toward Richmond and end this whole damned war."

It was the last thing Andres remembered. . . .

≫ 19 ≪

ndres stood in the waiting room, looking up at an old oil painting
f the plaza. He stroked his bushy black mustache; he'd apparently
otten the facial hair passed down to him from his grandfather, since
dians seldom had much of it. His hip had healed well, leaving him
ith only a minor limp. But the wound on his left cheekbone—the
1e that had come so close to killing him—had left a thin white scar
at the doctors said might take several years to fade. His mother had
ied over it, but Rafe had told him it gave him distinction, adding to
s handsomeness such as a dueling scar might. And the man he was
out to see knew all about duels.

"General Hartman will see you now, Mr. Murphy." The wiry little
erk motioned with his finger from the doorway.

Andres went inside the spacious office, expecting to see mementos
the war, but there were none. Instead, a painting of West Point
cupied a wall and law books in bookcases, along with other books,
led the rest. He should have known that Richard Hartman wouldn't
re display any of the flags he'd served under during the war. They
ere all from the wrong side. He was surprised that the lawyer even
d the audacity to use his Confederate rank in mostly Yankee Santa

Hartman came around the desk to shake hands. In his late forties,
was gray at the temples and quite handsome with his otherwise
ndy hair, greenish eyes, and fierce reddish beard. He was of middle
ight and bore himself erectly, as if he were still a cadet on the plain
West Point. He had commanded two different brigades in the
onfederate army, and on numerous occasions had been cited for
avery, but he had never gotten along with his superiors well
ough to advance to senior command. First, challenging General
ce to a duel, and then none other than John Bell Hood—the fiery
ro of Gettysburg, Chickamauga, and Atlanta—hadn't helped any.
ally, a harsh clash with the troublesome General Braxton Bragg
d insured that he would never rise above the rank of brigadier. Two

months after the end of the war, he had shown up in Santa Fe, moved back into his old offices, and thumbed his nose at the populace. No longer owning a newspaper, he'd taken out an advertisement in the *New Mexican*, brashly announcing his return to the city and his intent to get on with his career. "I am a New Mexican," he'd stated defiantly. "Everything else is past."

Hartman smiled into his eyes. "How's your lovely mother?"

"Fine. She's still living in Washington, but she'll be coming here soon. Father—General Murphy—will be going to Idaho Territory shortly."

"Yes, I understand there's a big Indian problem out there as well. What kind of rank did they let him keep?"

A shadow crossed Andres's expression. "Only permanent lieutenant colonel, but he's still wearing his brevet major general's stars."

"Any reason? I'd have thought he'd be at least a regular colonel."

"I can't help but believe it's because of the Mexican blood and the fact that he's not a West Pointer."

Richard Hartman nodded his head. "Makes sense in the narrow thinking of a regular army." He switched brightly to another subject. "I read that you were quite a thorn in Early's side up in the valley in the latter part of the war. Quite an article in the *Republican*."

Andres shrugged. "I was just a lowly lieutenant. Phil Sheridan was the thorn."

They chatted randomly for several minutes before Richard Hartman asked, "What's the purpose of your visit here?"

"I just finished another year at Baldwin-Wallace College in Ohio and I've decided to become a lawyer. I'd like to learn the law as your assistant."

Hartman stroked his fiery beard. "Hmmm, that's interesting—a Yankee hero wants to learn the law from a traitorous rebel general."

Andres smiled. To be able to practice law in the Territory, he had to pass the exam, and the best way to learn what would be required was to work in an existing law firm and study as much as time permitted.

"Why do you want to be a lawyer?" Hartman asked.

"I think it's a good solid base for whatever might come along in this growing part of the country, sir. And both logic and rhetoric have been my strong suits for some time—although literature has my interest as well."

The general nodded his head. "I think we can work it out. Foster, the clerk you just met, is about to leave me. You can be his replacent. You can start by reading Bacon's *Abridgement of the Law*. When you wish to begin?"

Andres paused before answering, feeling that he was about to make onfession. "I have to go down to Pinos Altos, that gold mining vn, to see someone."

"Anyone important—like a girl?"

"More important—my father."

"But I thought General Murphy was—"

"He's my stepfather." Again Andres paused, taking in a deeper ath. It would be the first time he told anyone in New Mexico of true birth. "My real father is Lazaro."

Richard Hartman, for all of his aplomb, stared for a moment, then ted as Andres went on with a concise explanation. In the end dres said, "Of course my mother has never told anyone but me, I she would be mortified if she knew anyone knew her well-kept ret."

Hartman nodded his head. "The poor, dear woman. My lips are led. But why did you tell me? Surely, if people learn that you're t Apache, they'll make life miserable for you."

"Because I don't want to live any part of a lie. And I didn't want nter your firm without you knowing."

"Does Lazaro know?"

"He knows she had a son with her when she escaped, but nothing e."

"Ha, I'll bet the old rascal will be surprised. Maybe you can talk a e sense into his head when you see him. His band is one of the few won't come into the reservations, you know."

Andres cocked an eyebrow. "I doubt that he'll be interested in ng advice from a young son he's about to see for the first time in nty-two years."

Hartman nodded his head again. "That's probably so. I wish you I in that venture. May I make a suggestion? Keep this information er your hat for a while—at least until people get used to seeing around."

Andres frowned. "I can't do that, sir."

"Okay, the Lord knows *I* don't back up when it comes to where I d, so why should I be telling you to do so." The general chuckled. ait'll they hear about you and me: 'the Secesh and the Apache.' "

Andres also chuckled at the thought. But he knew there wouldn't nuch humor in it in the long run.

* * *

Both Tom Waugh and storekeeper Crowder had kept their mouths shut about their gold find near Pinos Altos, so the word never got out at that time. A few days after finding Waugh's body, Crowder sold his store in Santa Rita for the first low offer and made a midnight departure for Santa Fe. It was reported that he stayed there only long enough to catch the next stage east. He was never heard from again.

In May of 1860, three American prospectors camped by the same ford in the stream—later to be named Bear Creek—as Taza had pointed out to Tom Waugh. While getting water for cooking, the one named Birch discovered small particles of gold in the clear, silver stream. Scooping up a handful, he shouted to his companions, and the gold rush of Pinos Altos was on. By September the town of Birchville had sprung up and some seven hundred miners, several with families, were living in the settlement's huts. At first all supplies came in from Santa Rita and Mesilla, but soon a couple of saloons and then a hotel opened. The Bean brothers opened a store—one of them, Roy, would later become famous as the judge who became "the Law West of the Pecos."

With the coming of the war, the gold rush was over and the town settled into a somewhat quiet existence. Though prospectors continued to look for the ever elusive mother lode, the primary mineral became quartz. Just two months prior to Andres's planned visit, the town's name had been officially changed to Pinos Altos.

Lazaro's people had made life difficult for the mining settlement since the first lean-tos had been erected, but only once did he mount a major attack on it. And that was after the attempt on his life by General West and company. Now things had been relatively quiet since the arrival of winter.

Andres bought the horse, a black mare with a flash of white on her face, in Santa Fe just after arriving from Ohio. Her speed came from the eastern thoroughbred breeding in her; her hardiness from the cow pony side. He called her Empress. He'd saved enough money during the war years to have a large enough stake to get him through the year in college. Additionally, he earned a certain amount of interest from the goodly sum of money Carlota had given him on his twenty-first birthday. He also drew against that principal now and then. His mother had also offered to support him during his law studies, but he didn't want to accept her money unless he had to. He intended to do some tutoring in Santa Fe when he got back.

Now as Empress climbed the trail through the heavy snow toward Pinos Altos, he marvelled at the beauty of this wild country at the

Continental Divide. Such tall pines, standing starkly green against the cold blue sky! Mantles of heavy snow, stubbornly resisting the persistent New Mexico sun, were doing their best to bend their boughs. The snow on the ground was over two feet deep in places where it hadn't drifted; there it was far deeper. Several riders and some wagons had been up the trail from Santa Rita before him, so the going wasn't at all difficult. It was briskly cold, but he was warmly dressed and the exercise of riding kept him comfortable. Besides, he was excited. This was the country of his conception and birth.

And he was going to meet his own father.

There was something special in the anticipation, an eagerness after all these years that he thought only one who had grown to manhood without knowing his *own* father could experience. Rafe was as fine a man as he'd ever known, and he thought of him as his parent. But this was different, he was going to see the man whose blood he carried, the man who had *made* him, and had given him certain characteristics . . . yes, the man who had made him. That was about the simple truth of it.

Perhaps most people couldn't understand that—certainly not his mother. She considered him her *sole* product and possession. But she didn't know that he wanted nothing from this man they called chief, not a single thing. It was a matter of curiosity. He simply wanted to *meet* him and experience him. Yes, it was a curiosity that had been on him like a blanket since that day back in Berea when she told him that he was Lazaro's son.

Entering the edge of the little town, he noticed how its buildings spread around on each side of the street. They were mostly log cabins, although he saw a couple of frame houses. He glanced at the saloon, the hotel, the general store, stopped and tied his horse at the rail of the saloon. Adjusting his eyes to the dimmer light as he entered, he went to the bar, removed his gloves and ordered a whiskey. He knew all about the problem Indians had with liquor, but he had done enough drinking during the war to know that his tolerance was about average. Apparently his Mexican blood counteracted whatever strange element of Indian blood it was that caused the trouble. He thought grimly that most of the massacres of Indians over the centuries had taken place when they became stupefied by alcohol.

He sipped quietly, noting the two rough-looking men several feet down the bar. They were drinking and talking about a mine they thought might hold some gold. At length he spoke to the bartender, lapsing into the vernacular of the frontier. "How would a man go about finding the local Apaches?"

The bartender, a short, thick-waisted man with a heavy mustache, replied, "Whatcha wanta find them for?"

"Little tradin' maybe."

"They's kinda mean, you know."

"Uh huh, I know. You know anybody can show me where I can find that big chief—what's his name, Lazaro?"

One of the men at the bar, a heavy man with a black beard, spoke up. "There's a breed works over in the store what knows some of them Apache. Name's Natalio."

Andres thanked him, finished his drink, and walked over to the store.

Natalio was about his age, the son of a Chihenne Apache woman and a Mexican ranch hand from Arizona who had bought her. After hedging until Andres agreed to pay him well, the young man agreed to take him to Lazaro's village on the following day, a Sunday. He also made Andres swear he wouldn't reveal the location.

The village was on the edge of a stream in a valley north of Santa Rita in the Black Range. A few tipis were mixed with the wickiups on the snow-covered area that was heavily guarded by thick fir trees. Smoke drifted lazily toward the sunlit sky in the windless brittle air. Andres was surprised to see women washing clothes through holes in the stream's ice, but he had heard the Apaches preferred cleanliness over comfort. A large black dog barked, then came closer to examine them as they dismounted near the edge of the village. Several children playing with some kind of a ball on a string stopped their activity to stare. Andres felt a special shiver of excitement and wondered if he would ever remember anything from the days he watched these people from the confines of a tsach.

But he knew what he was feeling was more—it was unbridled anticipation. Part of him sprang from these people, and even though he'd grown up hearing about them as being savages, he knew better. Rafe had told him about them after his visits with Lazaro. And after his mother told him the truth about his heritage, he'd probed further whenever he'd met his stepfather in the war.

But he knew the keen anticipation came from one thing.

He was going to meet Lazaro.

* * *

Lazaro was talking with Old Man and a young war leader when Natalio approached his tipi. The discussion was about the food problem. The war leader wanted to raid locally, but Lazaro rejected the idea. "We aren't strong enough to fight off any kind of a large attack on our village," he said. "And our women and children must be our first concern. If we raid or even steal a few head of stock from nearby White Eyes, the pony soldiers will come." He looked up as the young visitor stopped and shifted self-consciously from one foot to the other. After a moment he nodded for Natalio to speak.

"A young White Eye wishes to see you, Great Chief," Natalio said softly. "He paid me to bring him here and says his name is Murfee."

Mur-fee. Lazaro frowned, remembering the name. There had been a young Godammie army officer many years ago by that name—the one who had come to stay with him and listen. But this couldn't be him. He nodded assent, saying, "Bring him to me."

Andres tried to walk unobtrusively, but the eyes of the villagers were all over him as he followed Natalio toward the large tan tipi to the rear of the encampment. The common noises had seemed to be stifled, amplifying the sound of his boots as they crunched on the cold, dry snow. He spotted the tall man almost at once. He was wearing a long yellow mackintosh and a flat dark cloth cap with an eagle feather on his head. Even from many yards away, Andres could tell he was quite powerful looking.

Andres balled up his fists and flexed them to relieve the tightness that had suddenly drenched him.

From what he had been able to piece together, the chief was in his early fifties. But he certainly didn't look it. Andres sucked in a deep breath as he drew closer, his eyes riveted on the man who had made him. Everything seemed a little too bright, as if the sun had cranked itself up another notch in intensity. He barely noticed the old man or the young brave. He could swear his ears were ringing. Just a few more steps. He'd rehearsed his opening in Spanish. Stopping, he looked up at the tall man's cool gaze, nodded his head in greeting, and said, "I am Andres Murphy, the son of Carlota de Cardenas Murphy and General Rafael Murphy, both of whom you know."

He saw the chief's eyes widen ever so slightly.

"My mother, who was a captive here many years ago, tells me she was made your wife. . . ."

* * *

Carlota! Lazaro believed it the moment he looked into the young man's unflinching eyes. *This was the boy!*

Out of the corner of his eye, the approaching figure of Tze-go-juni appeared. But that would only be natural. She'd know that the son she'd prayed for all these years was here. She'd sense it.

His son.

Light eyes, he remembered. And there was a mark of the woman about him. He was tall, erect, confident. Slight limp. Scar on his cheek, maybe from a knife. He heard the low words tumble from the young man's lips, "I am your son, great chief," and they pleased him immensely.

Lazaro studied him as Old Man moved close and stared. Tze-go-juni came even closer, walking around Andres with a wide grin, and cackling some of her private phrases. Benita arrived from where she'd been washing clothes in the creek, and looked on from a further distance. More villagers began to drop what they were doing and drift toward their leader's tipi. A surge of feeling swept over Lazaro—not only had his second son come to him, but he was an extension of his still beloved Carlota. The years had never dimmed the passion and longing he felt for his pale-eyed beauty.

Now her son.

His son.

Andres, yes, that was the name she'd given the boy, he remembered the time of the birth so clearly. Now maybe he could stop thinking about Taza. "Why is your name Mur-fee?" he asked quietly in Spanish.

"My mother married Rafael Murphy almost twenty years ago. He is the one who came with Colonel Sumner and then later to stay with you and learn your ways. He is now a general."

Lazaro wanted to put his arms around him and hold him close, but it was out of the question. He controlled his deep voice as he asked, "Why do you come?"

The answer was frank, the gaze unwavering. "To meet my real father."

Lazaro stood rock still, looking into his eyes. Slowly he stepped forward, reaching with both hands to put them on the young man's arms. "Welcome, my son," he said gruffly. After a moment, he asked, "How long do you stay?"

"I have three days."

"Enjuh! Have you slept our way before?"

"I was a soldier four years in the American war, Father."

"A good soldier?"

"Some think so. I was a pony soldier officer."

Tze-go-juni's eyes were like black diamonds as she touched Andres's hand and stared into his eyes. Her face seemed to have wrinkles on wrinkles, yet somehow the skin glowed where it wasn't painted black and white. He'd never seen an uglier old woman in his life, yet there appeared to be something special about her.

She cackled. "Enjuh! You are the one I prayed for from birth, Child of the Water."

Andres's research had included the Apache deities, so he knew about Child of the Water, White Painted Lady, and Giant. His mother had told him about the medicine woman, and how she'd had this obsession from the moment he was born. He didn't know what to say.

Old Man's eyes also sparkled. "You good warrior, huh?" he asked in bad Spanish.

Andres just smiled and looked back at Lazaro. What a handsome and powerful looking man. There wasn't a gray hair on his head, and not too many lines. He didn't look a day older than forty. Obviously a proud man. No wonder he was the strongest of the Apache leaders—at least that was what Rafe had told him, and newspaper reports over the years seemed to confirm that opinion. He sensed the welcome in Lazaro's gesture and felt warm and comfortable; he was glad he'd come.

They swung down from their horses on the slope near the Kneeling Nun outside of Santa Rita. Lazaro pointed to a nearby bush. "It was there," he said quietly, "that I first saw your mother. She looked up with her pale eyes and struck me like the lightning. She was young and so beautiful that I couldn't speak."

"What happened then, Father?" Andres asked.

"She just walked away and I didn't see her again until that raid of the Nakai-ye hacienda, when I took her."

They talked on as Lazaro recounted his love for Carlota. At length, as they skirted Santa Rita and headed north, back into the Black Range, Lazaro spoke of the many times the White Eyes had broken their word with him. He told of the time that General West had tried to have him killed. He spoke about Cochise and the perfidy of the White Eyes in Arizona, but mostly he spoke of the People and of their heritage from Silsoose. Andres hung on every facet of the history, asking pertinent questions and making mental notes. He was particularly keen about the warrior training.

Three times Tze-go-juni spoke to him of being Child of the Water, but each time Lazaro interrupted, sparing him her incantations. Benita was no problem; she cooked and served the plain food, saying little. It was obvious that she didn't like his coming. The years of hard living had taken their toll and her hair was streaked with many strands of gray. Her love of Lazaro was evident in the little things she did for him, and how she looked at him and spoke to him. Andres guessed that she had been good for him.

Lazaro told him of Taza and of his half-sisters and their marriages. He told him of Victorio, the strong chief of the Warm Springs to the north at Ojo Caliente; of Loco and Nana. On the last night, as they sat around the warm coals in the tipi and sipped tiswin, Andres asked him why he wouldn't move the Chihenne onto a reservation like so many of the other bands.

"Many years ago, Carl-ton sent Kit Car-son to defeat the Mescalero in the mountains to the east of the big river. They weren't even a very warlike band. And then he moved them to the terrible place called Bosque Redondo and made them live there—them and the hated Navajo together. It's a terrible place, with no trees and no way to hunt. The People couldn't even grow the White Eye's crops to survive. Finally, the Mescalero had to flee back to their mountains. If the White Eye wants to keep us in one place, he should send his agents to our homelands, and show us we can trust them. Then we can talk of a real peace. But always he wants to ship us off to some strange and bad place.

"No, my son, I won't let that happen to my Chihenne. We may have little here, but we're free. When the cold lessens and the snow is gone, we'll ride into Nakai-ye land and continue the war. Then the People will eat well. It is the Way."

Andres couldn't resist. "Have you ever gone back to the de Gante hacienda, the one called La Reina?"

"Yes, we have taken much of their stock. The man called de Gante has led soldiers to chase us, but always we have eluded him. Cochise tells me that he has taken the hair of Chiricahua women and children, and Lipan as well."

"I met him in Washington. He's a bad man," Andres replied. "Why don't you attack him?"

"His house is too strong, guarded by many soldiers. Remember, the

People lose more warriors than we can train. Always we must fight and hide."

When at last the conversation had run its course, Lazaro said, "When you go back to your town of tall houses, tell the White Eye chief what you have learned from your father. Tell him that Lazaro wants peace, but it must be in the land of Silsoose." He touched Andres's arm. "My son, I will be unhappy to see you go in the morning, but I know you must. I hope you'll be happy being a law-yer, and that you will come back often to see me. There will always be someone who knows how to find me."

Andres took his hand and held it for a moment, fighting back a wetness in his eyes. "I will, Father. I promise."

Carlota was in Santa Fe when Andres returned. Rafe had accompanied her there and stayed two days while she moved into the old house. Then he had continued on to his Idaho Territory assignment.

"I don't know why you had to go see *him*," she said to Andres, following their warm reunion. "He has nothing to do with your life."

"But that's not true, Mother," Andres replied. "I felt like a part of them while I was there."

"Well," she said a bit too archly, "I suppose your imagination *could* make you think such things. And it's sweet of you to care about their hard life. But you must remember that as long as they refuse to comply with our rules they must continue to suffer."

"Oh, Mother, you still think the same, don't you?"

Her voice was flat. "Shouldn't I? Didn't they steal my early life from me? Didn't that *heathen* make me a prisoner and violate my marriage?"

Andres shook his head, unable to control his sudden anger. "You'll never change, will you? You're just as bad as the rest of these bigots, even worse. You think life on that hacienda with that stupid de Gante would have been everything. I saw you falling all over him in Washington. In fact, I can't ever forget that picture of you and him in that place in Georgetown. I thought it disgusting!"

Her expression changed. "I've told you many times . . . it was nothing."

"I don't believe you."

Her voice softened. "You have to, my darling. I was just, just recalling some old times with him. A woman does that, you know. Sometimes she needs it."

"Just don't preach to me about the Apaches. If you say anything more, I won't be able to live under this roof with you."

"I'll try not to. It's just . . . " Her voice trailed off. She changed the subject. "Did he take you to Giant's Claw?"

"No."

"That's where the gold is, you know."

"I'm not interested in gold. He told me there was a high place that was the sanctuary of the Chihenne, but why should he show me? After all, I'm still part of the American order. Even though he welcomed me as a son, why should he divulge every secret? Supposing I had been sent by the army, that I was a phony? No, I don't think anything personal will ever affect his responsibility toward his people. Anyway you told me they consider gold the sacred tears of their God."

She shrugged. "That doesn't mean we can't put it to some good use."

He looked at her coolly. "Such as making you richer?"

She switched the subject again, handing him an envelope. "Rafe left this for you. He wishes you'd apply for a regular commission and come to Idaho to help him."

Andres quickly read the warm note from his stepfather. The gist was precisely what his mother had said. The idea of a career in the cavalry was appealing, and he'd given it quite a bit of thought just after the war, but he felt that his life was here in New Mexico with his roots. His meaning was here. And while the law seemed most inviting, he had a new idea.

Richard Hartman stroked his fierce red beard. "What makes you think you can be a newspaperman?"

Andres was sitting in a chair beside the general's desk. In the time he had been visiting in the Mimbres area, Hartman had begun a new weekly newspaper called *The Monitor*. Why an openly proud former senior Confederate officer should name his newspaper for the Federal ironclad that had defeated the rebel ironclad, the *Merrimac*, seemed incongruous. "It has nothing to do with that ironclad," Hartman had announced in its first editorial. "The purpose of this newspaper is to monitor life and politics in this city and the state of New Mexico."

Andres shrugged. "I always did well on my written compositions in school. I like to write and keep a journal. I even write poetry sometimes—just for my own satisfaction. It's a means of expressing myself. And I read voraciously at times."

"Do you honestly think you have writing talent?"

"I wouldn't presume to say that."

Hartman nodded his head, thinking.

"When you started your first newspaper—did you think you had writing talent, sir?" Andres asked quietly.

"Good question. I don't think newspaper writing demands too much talent. A reporter or editor just needs to know the written language and get it down in an orderly fashion. The facts are more important than a well-turned metaphor. Hmmmm, no I guess I just like having a newspaper because it gives me a forum, a chance to shoot off my mouth. Is that what you want to do?"

Andres paused a moment before answering. "Yes, I think so."

"About the Apache plight?"

"Maybe."

"You can't be a newspaperman if you're blinded by one issue."

"I'll keep it sorted out."

"You sure?"

Andres nodded his head. "Yes, sir."

General Hartman stood up, stuck out his hand, and smiled. "As a part-time reporter, your salary shall be four dollars per week. Don't let it interfere with your law studies."

Andres grinned and shook his hand. "It won't, sir."

20

Santa Fe, New Mexico
May 4, 1873

"Brevet Major General Rafael Murphy: During the past war I found that you were capable of performing diverse duties. Now I am entrusting you to a new and challenging assignment in the southwest. Your role as Special Indian Commissioner is primarily to settle the Indians of the Arizona and New Mexico territories on reservations," President Grant's letter directed. "You must further use your skills to induce the whites to treat the Indians with humanity, justice, and forbearance, preserving the peace between the whites and the reds and to consider the propriety of inducing the nomadic tribes to unite and accept a reservation farther east."

Rafe had reread this opening paragraph of Sam Grant's letter several times since receiving it in San Francisco. Now, as he ended his three-day stay in Santa Fe to head into the field, he thought of it again. "I may be gone for nearly a month," he told Carlota as they lay quietly in bed after making love.

"What's a month?" she replied. "We haven't been together more than three years since the war."

"You could have made it more."

"Andres needed me."

Always it seemed to be Andres, even after all these years. He'd accepted it when they married and through the boy's growth, but it was still an obsession with her. It was the same old argument; telling her Andres was a grown man now would have no effect on her thinking, it would only start another strain between them. "I need you too."

"I'll be right here whenever you come home."

"That sounds too dutiful." He got up and reached for his robe.

"I don't know what else to say, Rafe. That's a lot of what being an army wife is about."

"There's more. . . . Darling, I love you even more than when I was wild about you in Mexico City all those years ago. You have no idea how difficult it is to be away from you so much."

"Then why don't you retire? We have plenty of money."

He shook his head. "I'm only fifty-one years old. What would I do—sell insurance?"

Carlota smiled. "We could always go after that gold down in Apache country, dear. I know I could find the place if I looked hard enough."

He sighed. "I told you several times—that gold belongs to the Apaches. In their spiritual belief, it's not to be molested."

"Huh! They don't own it any more than they own the silver down there, or the copper, or the gold at Pinos Altos. What's the difference?"

"The difference to me is Lazaro. A long time ago he trusted me to understand the ways of his people, and I'm not going to violate anything sacred to them." He sat beside her, took her hand, smiled into her wide eyes. "You are absolutely lovely, my darling. If anyone could talk me into getting out of the army it would be you."

"Then do it."

"I have things to accomplish first. This Indian problem won't go away, and I'm one of the few general officers who understands both it and them. Now, with this assignment Grant has given me, maybe I can get something worthwhile done."

Carlota swung her shapely legs over the side of the bed. At forty-nine she was still a beautiful woman. The smile lines at the corners of her eyes were a bit more pronounced, and there was a slight frown line between her eyebrows. But her figure still turned men's heads on the street. The major change in the last couple of years had been the appearance of a thin blaze of white hair that extended back from her widow's peak. She sighed. "Well, I hope you get them all on a reservation and put a high, barbed wire fence around it."

He spoke softly. "Aren't you ever going to relent? They're a proud people who've had nearly everything taken from them. Why do you continue to hate them?"

Suddenly Carlota jumped to her feet, jamming her hands on her hips. "I'll *never* stop hating them!"

The party consisted of Rafe, Lieutenant Holloman, his aide-de-camp, a clerk named Bergen, and an ambulance with a team of horses. There was no cavalry escort whatsoever. Rafe's mule, the one named Mandy that he always rode, was tied to the back of the ambulance as the little party ambled along in the hot afternoon sun. Andres was the only civilian in the party, serving as both advisor and journalist. As the party headed southwest along the Rio Grande toward Albuquerque, Andres sat beside Rafe in the ambulance. They hadn't spoken much before departure because Andres had been down in the Sacramento Mountains gathering information from the Mescaleros.

"The problem," Andres was explaining, "is the homelands. Tularosa was selected as a primary reservation for the Apache without regard to *any* homelands. Certainly it's a long way from Chihenne country and a great distance from Cochise's Chiricahua country in southern Arizona. It's some seventy miles as the crow flies from Victorio's Warm Springs homeland near Cañada Alamosa, a lot more over the trail through the upper Black Range. Tularosa is simply a damned place that was picked by an idiot and now everyone's going to live with it come hell or high water."

"When did you last talk to Lazaro?" Rafe asked.

"Three months ago."

"And what will he do?"

"He'll move his people there for a trial period because they simply don't have enough to eat. But don't count on him keeping them there."

"What about the others?"

"Some of the smaller groups will stay, at least for a while. But Cochise and Victorio will follow the path of Lazaro."

"What added incentives would keep them on the reservation?"

Andres shrugged. "I don't know. Perhaps some extra ration items like coffee and sugar. Maybe some extra flour. But then you have to make sure the agent gets it to them and it doesn't get sold off first."

"Are you implying that the agent is dishonest?"

"No, but you know there are various ways to skim the rations."

"Do you know what the Apaches think of the agent?"

"Piper isn't liked, from what I've heard. He's old and often quite inconsiderate with the People."

They rode on in silence for a few moments as Rafe digested that information. Finally he asked, "Have you ever considered becoming an agent? You could be a remarkably good one, you know."

"Yes, I've thought about it," Andres replied. "But it just isn't the job for me. I can do more writing about the situation. I have a book in progress, you know."

Rafe raised an eyebrow. "No, I didn't. About the Chihenne?"

"Mostly, but the Apache in general."

"When do you think you'll finish it?"

A smile touched Andres's lips. "At the rate I'm going, about twenty years from now. I'm in no hurry."

"Does your mother know about it."

"No, I didn't see any sense in telling her. She'd just tell me to quit wasting my time."

Rafe nodded. It was good to have his stepson along. It seemed ages since they'd had any time together. And now it was truly of value to get his inside information. He was very proud of Andres.

Although he wasn't part of the group of chiefs, including Lazaro and Victorio, who were meeting with General Murphy, another war leader had joined their council. He was a medicine man, purported to have strong Power. In a treacherous raid near Janos in the state of Chihuahua, a Mexican army command in 1858 had attacked the camp of visiting Apaches who had come on a friendly mission to receive a peace tribute. Since the warriors and their leaders were all in the town at the time of the raid, the women and children were slaughtered in their camp like penned-in animals. The medicine man's mother, his wife, and their three children were all slain. The intense hatred created by this perfidy would convert this medicine man into one of the most noted warriors in all of Apacheria. His name was Goyalka—One Who Yawns—but the Mexicans called him Geronimo, and it had stuck.

Andres had heard of Geronimo's exploits, but hadn't yet met him. A stocky man of forty-four with a very wide mouth and no humor, the war leader had attached his small band to Victorio at Cañada Alamosa and had then made the move with the Warm Springs to the disliked reservation at Tularosa. Since Andres had worked hard on his Apache, he spoke the language fairly well and they talked in the language of the People. "We'll never stay here," Geronimo said emphatically. "You tell Mur-fee that I will return to the warpath in Sonora if he doesn't move us back to Cañada Alamosa."

"General Murphy knows the People are unhappy here," Andres replied. "But he must talk to the Great White Father in Washington before any change can be made."

"Always," Geronimo rasped, "it's the same—the Great White Father in Wash-in-ton."

"Be patient. I think General Murphy will get you back there."

"I'd rather be down in Mexico killing Nakai-ye anyway."

"I know. But this is best for your families."

Andres looked up to see one of the most beautiful young Apache women he'd ever encountered looking at him frankly from some six yards away. She was tall and slender, with much sharper cheekbones than the average Chihenne woman. And her eyes seemed lighter, a softer brown. But that could have been, he thought, because of the bright sunshine that seemed to be casting some kind of an aura about her. He blinked. She held his gaze for a few more seconds, then turned away. He watched, drawing in a deep breath and blowing it out. "Who was that?" he asked in a voice that seemed unnatural.

"Lizah," Geronimo replied. "The woman warrior."

"Who?"

"She's from Victorio's Warm Springs. She fights like a man and has great Power."

"Who is her husband?"

"She has none."

Andres drew in another deep breath as he caught a final glimpse of the shining black hair of the beautiful young woman in soft brown buckskins leaving the center of the village.

"Tell me about this Lizah," Andres said.

"She has great Power," Tze-go-juni replied in her raspy voice. "Never in memory has one been so skilled in locating the enemy. And she shoots better than most warriors. She's also strong and swift."

"How old is she?"

"Twenty-six summers."

"Why isn't she married?"

"There is a story," the shaman replied. "When she was a young girl, warriors reported seeing a man they called the Gray Ghost in the Black Range. He rode alone and no one ever got close enough to him to speak to him. He was of huge stature and very powerful. He wasn't Chihenne or Warm Springs. Once three Warm Springs warriors saw him pursued by White Eye cavalry into a canyon. They called out to him and pointed out a secret hiding place. He nodded his thanks, hurried into it, and stayed until the soldiers quit looking for him. He came to the Warm Springs camp near Ojo Caliente and stayed for a long time. He learned our words and told Victorio he was a chief from far toward the rising sun.

"One day a strange wagon, guarded by twelve men, came to Ojo Caliente. There was a driver and an old woman. All spoke the language of the Nakai-ye, but they were positively not Nakai-ye. The wagon carried a very beautiful young woman. When they moved on toward the mountains to the west, Gray Ghost followed.

"Lizah was too young for marriage, but she had the big eyes for his chief, and no other man ever interested her. She pushed marriage rom her mind and became a warrior. Now she is respected above all iving women——she is as sacred as White Painted Woman."

Andres shook his head. "Huh. Quite a story. I want to meet her."

"I can arrange it."

Tze-go-juni never seemed to age. It was if she'd been born old, at ome predetermined advanced age. The scar on her face was still vivid when she wasn't wearing some kind of paint over it; her teeth, always tained dark, were as strong as a lion's. And her carriage was erect. andres guessed from what Lazaro had told him that she must be in er late seventies, but no one would ever know. She still treated him s if he were the anointed one and often reminded him that he was hild of the Water. He bore this fixation of hers with gentle good umor, never commenting on it, or denying it in any way that might urt her. "How soon?" he asked.

"Tonight."

was just before the sun settled behind the purple hills to the west at the shaman brought Lizah to Rafe's sleeping tent. Andres smiled he nodded in greeting. The young woman was even more beautiful the lengthy evening shadows. Her long black hair reached well low her shoulders and although the faded blue shirt she wore vealed little of her figure, he guessed that she was well formed. It as her lovely brown eyes, now even lighter in the slanting rays of e departing sun, that captured him. They seemed almost hazel, like s own. She look directly at him with confidence and ease. Her voice as low, with a touch of resonance, as she spoke in excellent Spanish, ze-go-juni tells me you were a great warrior in the old White Eyes ar."

"Not like the Apache warrior," he replied quietly. "Besides the old oman always speaks too highly of me."

"She thinks you are very special. She told me about your birth."

He switched the subject. "How do you speak such good Spanish?"

Her reply was matter-of-fact. "I have a gift for tongues. I also speak White Eye words." She switched to English: "The white man tells what *he* wants us to do, not what is *right* for us."

He smiled. "Excellent! You could be invaluable as an interpreter."

"No, I would lose the Power. The White Eye is our enemy."

"I hear that you have other powerful medicine."

"There are things I can do."

"Locating the enemy?"

"It's a gift from White Painted Lady."

They strolled in silence around Victorio's village, talking about the general things that were happening at the talks and life at Tularosa in general. Finally, as the early moon began to throw its silver into the new darkness, she said, "We won't stay here, you know. Victorio will take us home and we'll go back on the warpath to Mexico."

He nodded, understanding. Victorio was a war chief. "Do you like raiding?" he asked at length.

"Yes. It adds to my strength."

"Tze-go-juni says you are as strong and swift as any warrior."

Her smiles were rare, but worth waiting for, he decided as her white teeth flashed at him.

"I am."

"When did you first notice your Power?"

"Sometime, I believe, in my sixteenth summer."

He wanted to ask her about Gray Ghost, but was afraid it would either hurt her or cause her to withdraw. Such a question would be far too indelicate. Instead he asked, "Can you tell me what it's like to have a Power?"

She thought for a few moments before saying, "It is sometimes a rich feeling, but mostly just an acceptance. One knows one has it and one never abuses it. One does not assume other Powers. For instance, I would never say how far the sun or the clouds are. I can tell you the rain comes from the clouds, but there are those who say they *cause* it to come. They believe *that* is their Power. There are shamans who have the Power to heal. Some have more than one Power—like Tze-go-juni—who also has the Power to counsel a chief. Victorio has war Power. Lazaro has great leadership Power. But always we who have a Power must be wise in its use."

He sensed some of the aura he had felt about her the first time he saw her—if not a glow, at least something special as she spoke so calmly of the supernatural. For that was the only logical term he could apply. "Do you intend to always be a warrior?" he asked quietly.

"What do you mean?"

"Never marry and have children?"

"Yes, that's what my *kan* has decided."

He knew that a kan was a friendly god. He decided to plunge on. "But won't that make you feel incomplete as a Chihenne woman?"

Her expression was cold in the moonlight. "You have no right to ask such a question. We have just met."

He watched as she spun away. He *had* gone too far. And he wa sorry. This remarkable young woman fascinated him. To see one so strikingly beautiful who was an accomplished warrior was highly intriguing. But there was more: he felt an intense attraction.

Andres saw Lizah only once the following day, and that was from across the village, a glimpse. When he finished sitting in on the afternoon talks, he looked for her again. Tze-go-juni told him she had left the village for some unknown purpose and that no one knew when she would return. He had a short talk with Cochise, who was ailing, one with Victorio, and one more with Geronimo. Finally, after the evening talks, he sat by the dying embers of the fire, alone with Lazaro. Following some general discussion about hunting, he asked what his father really thought about the reservation situation and the talks.

"Tularosa is a failure. Now that the air is warm, most of the People will leave. If Mur-fee has power in Wash-in-ton, he must use it. I have tried to hold the People here, but the chiefs grumble. Cochise says he'll stay for a time, but he won't. Victorio will certainly go."

"And you, Father?"

"My home is in the tall willows."

"But there are so many Americans and Mexicans there now, a new town south of Pinos Altos will bring even more."

"The mountains are huge."

"And the game is short."

"There is always Mexico."

"But won't the added rations General Murphy has offered provide plenty of food for the People?"

Lazaro's eyes narrowed. "I thought you would understand."

"I do, Father, I know the heavy pull of one's homeland. I'm just trying to be practical."

"Life is not always practical."

Andres escaped by asking, "What do you think of Geronimo?"

"He's a good warrior, driven by hate for the Nakai-ye. And a good medicine man. The combination makes him a successful war leader. The problem is that he does only what he wishes."

"He doesn't care for the good of the People as a whole?"

"Only his own small band."

"And that makes him dangerous to any treaty, doesn't it?"

"Yes, but he isn't the only one. Juh is down there in Mexico too. He's a war chief. But the most dangerous is Bacho."

"Bacho? Oh, yes, you told me. Your old enemy."

"Yes. He was a scout with the White Eye army when they tried to kill me ten summers ago. Then he got in trouble with them, got drunk and killed a sergeant. Now he has his own band down in the Sierra Madre. He raids *everywhere*. Some of the raids on friendly settlers in our country, the ones that have been blamed on the Chihenne, have been his. He loves to kill and maim. When you hear of men's parts being cut off, of scalping by Apaches, rape, or torture—you are hearing about Bacho."

"Why do you let him go on?"

Lazaro sighed. "Remember the Apache as a whole are independent. No leader tells another how to do anything."

"But he's a *renegade*. He hurts the People."

"I still cannot go to war with him. Besides, some of the People think he is doing what we should all be doing—instead of sitting on our blankets with the White Eyes."

Just before the scheduled departure time the following morning, Andres saw Lizah standing by a tree on the edge of the village. She appeared to be watching him in some detached manner. Breaking away from Rafe, he smiled as he approached her. "I was hoping to see you before I left," he said pleasantly.

"Why?" she replied coolly.

Her directness took him aback. "I'm sorry I intruded on your personal life yesterday. As you said, I had no right."

"It isn't important."

"Yes, it is. I want to know you."

"Why?"

"Because . . . " The right words were difficult to find. He was intensely attracted to her, had been awake half the night thinking about her. "Because I want to see you again and be your friend."

Her eyes held his as she weighed his words for several moments. "You are the son of the great Lazaro," she said at length. "But you really aren't Apache. You are Nakai-ye and you are White Eye, pretending to know the Apache. But you don't have the Apache heart."

A tinge of anger touched him. "How can you say that? You barely know me."

Her voice was even, collected. "I know such things."

At that moment the sun slipped from behind a small cloud and bathed her in its sudden glow. He was once more struck by her special beauty, her unique grace. "I'll see you again and prove to you that my heart is part Apache," he said, looking deeply into her lovely eyes.

She didn't answer, just held his gaze again for several moments before turning and walking away.

21

Santa Fe, New Mexico
August 12, 1873

"Aren't you the Apache lovin' bastard who writes nasty articles about New Mexicans?"

Andres looked up from where he was sipping a glass of beer near the end of the bar in the Cantina Coloradas. The place was quite full, mostly with members of the territorial legislature that was in session. It was just after dusk, and the place was noisy. Standing behind his shoulder was a man perhaps a year or two younger than himself and about his size. He was wearing the clothes of a well-to-do Mexican rancher, with a big white Stetson tipped back on his head. A huge black mustache dripped over his lips. Andres remembered that his name was Reyes, and that he wore his Hispanic blood like a badge of angry honor. Also that he liked to cause trouble.

Andres ignored him and turned back to his beer.

"I was talking to you, Apache lover!"

Suddenly the hubbub subsided. Andres turned, looking into the hot black eyes of his accoster. "Do you have a problem?" he asked softly.

"You're damned right I do. As a tenth generation New Mexican, I resent the accusations you made against men of my proud blood."

"I only wrote what was true."

"Damned lies!"

Andres felt his quick temper slipping, tried to hold it. The thin scar on his cheek had turned to red. "Sir, I don't lie!"

"You wrote that Mexicans are raiding along the Rio Grande down near Mesilla and spreading the word that it's the damned Apaches!"

"I have proof."

The bar had quickly grown silent. "Ha!" the rancher snorted, snapping a finger in Andres's face. "*That* for your lying proof."

Andres snapped, lashing out with his left fist, catching Reyes on the right cheek and knocking off his big white sombrero. Before his taunter could make a move, he smashed his right into the man's stomach. With a roar he threw an overhand left that knocked the rancher into a table and sent him sprawling. As he got to one knee, the rancher drew a long-barreled Colt .44 from its holster and started to aim it at Andres.

"Hold it!" Richard Hartman snapped, springing between them.

"Get out of the way, old man!" Reyes shouted. "I'm going to kill that Apache loving bastard!"

Hartman's foot deftly kicked the revolver out of the rancher's hand. Leaning down, he grabbed a handful of the man's lapels, jerking his head up to where he glared into his eyes. "If you want to kill him, do it like a gentleman, not a boorish fool. I have dueling pistols or swords."

Reyes scowled around his shoulder at Andres. "Pistols, you bastard."

The general raised an eyebrow at Andres. "Do you agree?"

"Anything."

"Tomorrow at seven in the morning then," the general said. Pushing Reyes back to the floor as he released his lapels, Hartman growled, "And don't *ever* call me 'Old Man' again or you'll have to fight *me*, and I'll kill you faster than you can spell *chile*."

It was cool even for a Santa Fe morning. And still. The surrounding mountains watched like curious but condemning custodians, tall, clean and majestic as royal green and tan battlements. The sheltered area by the river that Hartman had selected was lush with grass; a grove of junipers gave the area form. Only the light trickling sound of the slowly flowing Rio Grande broke the silence as the duelists loaded and checked their ornately engraved weapons. Andres had as his second a young man who had read for the law with him, while Reyes had a middle-aged man in a large black sombrero, his ranch foreman. The distance between them was about twenty-five yards. General Richard Hartman stood in its center, aloof, familiar with the rules of the duel, unused to being a nonparticipant.

A handful of spectators, including the sheriff, watched from the edge of the trees.

"You ever fired one of these?" the young lawyer asked with concern.

"No, but I fired plenty of others," Andres replied, eyeing Reyes. "But I suppose he has too."

"In the cavalry, right?"

"Yes, but that was several years ago."

"These are pretty fancy pistols, aren't they?"

"They're Belgians, the general's pride and joy."

"He's killed a few people, hasn't he?"

"In dueling? He's won about a half-dozen, I guess." Chuckling rather obviously to relieve the tension, he added. "Naturally, he hasn't lost any."

Andres was glad for the conversation. It took the edge off his nerves. Another glance at Reyes met his opponent's cold black eyes. There was no relenting on the rancher's part. He'd probably have to be killed. The general had cautioned him, "Shoot to kill on the first round. The secret to successful duelling is to live, not to *let* live. Besides, he's an asshole and doesn't deserve to keep on breathing."

"What are you going to aim at?" his second asked.

"His chest, the widest part of his body." Andres nodded to Hartman, then turned his attention back to Reyes. Killing in the war was one thing; this, this premeditated, cold attempt on a man's life was something far different. The passion of anger and effrontery was gone. He didn't like it. This kind of an attempt at some form of chivalry wasn't a part of him. Oh, he'd been an officer and a gentleman in the war, but that was an expedient, not a way of life. He didn't have a rigid code of honor that had to be settled by dawn's early light. He glanced back at the pistol. End this, quickly, cleanly—and never do it again.

For some reason, the Apache woman, Lizah, crossed his thoughts. What would the beautiful woman warrior think in this type of situation? But she'd never let herself get caught in something as stupid as this. Apaches had no such complicated idiocy in their Way. Yet, his father had once fought his old enemy, Bacho, with a knife. Benita had told him about it. Was that any different? His thoughts went back to Lizah. He might see her soon on his visit to the Willows—

"You will take ten paces from where I am now standing," General Hartman intoned, his voice breaking the morning stillness. "Please proceed to this point."

Both duelists proceeded to meet him, pistols hanging in their right hands.

"You will turn, facing away from each other, and commence slowly pacing in the opposite direction at my command. I'll count aloud your five paces. When you complete the last step, you are free to turn and fire. Do each of you understand?"

"Yes," Andres replied quietly.

"Of course," Reyes snapped, glaring, obviously keyed up.

"Good," Hartman said. "Now turn and commence pacing. One . . . " The publisher stepped back out of the line of fire as he counted slowly.

Andres barely heard the numbers as he paced, feeling the tension mount, bursting to turn and see what was happening. But he held his head still, counting along with Hartman. He'd rehearsed what was coming over and over in his head. *Three . . .* He inhaled, blew it out. *Four.* Inhale again, hold it. *Five!* He turned smoothly, bringing the pistol up and aiming steadily at the all-too-bright chest of Reyes, barely seeing the other aimed pistol that belched flame just as he pulled the trigger. Its bullet crashed into his left arm, but he stood still, staring, as Reyes slowly crumpled.

He knew he'd hit him in the chest.

In seconds the doctor and the other spectators had rushed forward and the doctor was bending over Reyes. After putting his head to the rancher's mouth, he slowly looked up and said, "This man is dead."

"So be it," General Hartman said solemnly.

Andres moved forward to stare at the body, blood slowly trickling from his left sleeve. Seeing it, the doctor hurried to treat his wound. "Get that jacket off at once!" he commanded.

At that moment a horse and rider came thundering down from the crest. It was a woman, her dark hair flying. As the horse skidded to a stop, the woman flung herself from the saddle. *"Are you all right?"* Carlota shouted at Andres.

"Yes," he replied.

"Why are you doing something stupid like this?" she demanded.

Hartman interceded, "It was a matter of honor, Mrs. Murphy. Andres had no choice."

"Honor? You call this—" She spotted the blood on Andres's arm as the doctor ripped back the sleeve of his white shirt. "Oh, dear God!"

"It's all right, Mother," Andres said.

Peering closely at the wound, the doctor said, "I think it missed everything but muscle and that'll heal."

Jerking back to Hartman, Carlota said coldly, "You arranged this, I know it. You and your duels. It's a wonder he wasn't killed."

The general spoke calmly. "There never was any real danger, because Andres is a dead shot. But I am sure thankful about one thing." He spoke gravely. "Madam, I thank the Lord that no one had to duel *you* out here this morning."

Andres stood, looking out the window of Hartman's office. "I just don't think staying here is doing me any good," he said quietly.

"But you've made a good start as both a lawyer and a journalist," the general replied. "It isn't easy to make a fresh start. Oh, you can do it as a reporter practically anywhere. But you know how low the pay is."

"I'm just not *doing* enough in regard to the Apache. My book is crawling along like the proverbial snail. Yesterday I had to kill a man who didn't like a story I wrote that told the truth. And there's so damned much I need to learn. I've really only scratched the surface of their culture.

"So what are you going to do?"

"I've been thinking about Silver City. They have no newspaper. If I could buy a used press, I could maybe make it profitable within a year or two."

"And how will you eat during that time?"

"A few law cases might tide me over."

"Do you know how many lawyers they have in the town?"

Andres shrugged. "No, but I'll get some cases."

"Not if you make too much noise about the Apaches. A lot's happened down there between the Indians and the settlers. It's not like Santa Fe or even Albuquerque; there's plenty of hate down there. You start sounding off about how the Apaches are getting the short end—or writing about it—and you'll be in a lot more trouble than you are here. It won't be any civilized duel like yesterday morning. No, they'll tar and feather you, and run you out of town on a rail—if you're *lucky*."

"A wrong's a wrong."

Hartman's face turned red in an instant. "Damn it, boy, listen to me. You won't be dealing with college presidents down there. Nobody cares about right or fair. Those white folks and Mexicans *hate* more than you've ever known. So, if you go there, you'd better make up your mind to keep your Apache feelings to yourself."

22

*Silver City is essentially an Eastern town, full of live, energetic
and intelligent men who have come there to stay. There is no
jumping of claims, no quarreling. The town already contains three
stores, one saloon, a boarding house, livery stable, two blacksmith
shops, one shoe shop, and a print shop; and situated as it is, in the
beautiful Cienega surrounded by rolling and picturesque hills
covered with pine, cedar, and oak, must in time become the most
beautiful town in southern New Mexico.*

—*The Las Cruces Borderer*
March 1871

Silverrrr. The word purrs across the tongue with elegance, reminding
one of finely shaped eating utensils and ornate goblets, of exquisite
brooches and elegant rings. The discovery of gold stirs men's blood;
the discovery of silver also makes it quicken. With the finding of rich
silver deposits in the area known as San Vicente Cienega in the early
summer of 1870, swarms of miners arrived. The quickly labeled
"Silver Flat Mining District" became a beehive of the usual tents, huts
and lean-tos. But it wasn't too long before the place had some more
permanent wooden structures and a new, more dignified name: Silver
City.

The new town was located just over six miles south of Pinos Altos.

In the following June, armed with a license to practice law in the
state of New Mexico, Andres moved into a small office in a building
on the east side of Main Street south of Broadway. In addition to the
sleeping room, there was a large storeroom to the rear of the office,
and in this he installed the small used printing press that had been
shipped in from Albuquerque. He found a drunken sign painter who
sobered up long enough to letter in gold leaf THE SILVER CITY GUARDIAN
on the front window. Silver City's first weekly newspaper had been
established.

Small letters at the bottom of the window also announced: Andres
Murphy, Editor and Attorney-at-Law. He had studied at length on
mining law while he continued to work for Richard Hartman in Santa
Fe during the preceding years, but his interest was primarily in the
newspaper. In his thirtieth year, Andres was still lean and even more

handsome than ever. He'd had his share of romances in Santa Fe, but nothing serious enough to bring him to the altar—much to the dismay of his mother. One fast affair had nearly brought him grief and had precipitated his departure for Silver City: it had been with the young and lovely wife of a prominent Mexican merchant, and it had almost brought him his second duel.

But no woman, regardless of how charming and lovely she might be, could erase the memory of a young Apache woman who had special powers and who lingered in his mind.

Rafe had convinced the head of the Indian Bureau that Tularosa was unfit as a reservation and also that, since Lazaro was the major Apache chief, and further, since several of the more troublesome bands would follow his lead, the Willows Country should be the new reservation for the Chihenne, the Warm Springs, Cochise's Chiricahua and some lesser groups. An area roughly ten miles long and five wide was set aside on the Mimbres River northeast of Santa Rita. It had officially become the new reservation in April.

Although Silver City was several miles to the west of the new reservation, it was to be another major nail in the wall that was pushing the Chihenne out of the way. More people meant even less game and less space for Lazaro's people. Minor raids into Mexico continued, and there were still unscrupulous traders willing to exchange certain food staples, ammunition, often whiskey and other nonessential goods for good Sonoran or Chihuahuan horseflesh and beef. But the United States government had become more difficult to deal with—particularly in its insistence that the reservation plan included a cessation of all forays below the border.

Though there was still a slight chill on the Black Range at night, the days were hot and often uncomfortable, even at the higher elevations. As Andres rode into Victorio's village, a couple of dogs barked and several children at play stopped their game and ran up to him. When he asked if the chief was present, one of them pointed toward a large wickiup. Andres handed the reins to the boy and asked him in Apache to take care of his horse.

The chief nodded and greeted his visitor warmly. Andres had met Victorio on several other occasions. The Warm Springs chief was fifty-four years old, a couple of inches under six feet tall, and had long, thick black hair that was liberally sprinkled with gray. His mouth was wide, his nose prominent, his dark eyes always alert. From a long line of chiefs, his reputation as a powerful war leader had been established early in his life. His wife, Auraria, was Andres's half sister.

Victorio's voice was deep like Lazaro's and he reminded Andres in many ways of his father. "What brings you to my village?" he asked.

"I want to see how your people are doing and if you feel the agent is being fair with you."

They sat on the ground, legs crossed, and Victorio spoke of the agent. "I do not trust John-Shaw. We don't have enough beef."

"What happens to the shipments?"

Victorio shrugged. "Who knows?"

"Do you think the Americans steal?"

"Yes, but I don't know how. I just know we don't get as much meat as we should."

"What does Lazaro say?"

"He says there is still plenty of game and we should tend to our crops." Victorio's eyes glinted blackly. "I tell him there is plenty of game in Mexico—right on all of those haciendas!"

"You won't raid here in New Mexico, will you?"

"No, I abide by your father's wishes."

Andres scribbled in his note book with a pencil as he continued with questions. Finally, he ended the conversation and looked around for Lizah. Actually, he'd tried to spot her several times during his discussion with Victorio. Now he got a glimpse of her by the horse corral. She turned as he called out her name. "Andres Murphy," she replied pleasantly. *"Hello,* as the White Eyes say."

They strolled away from the village, stopping near a rocky cave and sitting in the shade of a thickly foliaged pine.

"I've thought of you continually," he said quietly, looking into her light brown eyes.

"Why?" she replied.

The simplicity of the question stopped him momentarily. After a moment he managed, "Because you are, well, I just think of you."

"In what way?"

"Uh, as a . . . special person."

She just nodded her head slightly, continuing to return his gaze. *She knows she's special, why do I have to talk like such an idiot?* He could tell her he was gathering material for his book. . . . No, that wouldn't interest her. How could one who couldn't read be remotely interested in anything as alien as a book. And besides, she probably wouldn't believe him. Finally, he blurted, "I just *wanted* to see you the way a man wants to see a beautiful woman."

A smile touched her lips. "You think *I'm* a beautiful woman?"

"Yes."

"Why?"

She asks such disconcerting questions! He blinked. "Because you are, that's all."

"There must be some reason."

She was playing with him, pure and simple. "Reason? You, uh, you have beautiful eyes, nice teeth. . . . " *He was a writer, why the hell couldn't he find words?* Satin brown skin—never! "You have long, lovely hands."

"They are the hands of a warrior; they know how to kill."

That's the approach! "Yes, that's what I meant. You are a beautiful warrior with lovely, skillful hands that know what to do with an enemy."

She flexed the fingers of her right hand. "A warrior's hand is hard, not lovely." She smiled suddenly. "But you do not come to see me because of my hands, Andres Murphy."

He shrugged, smiling back. "No, I just feel warm and good when I'm with you."

She nodded. "Enjuh."

He wanted to take her hand and hold it, but he knew he couldn't.

The conversation switched to raiding. "Are you good with a rifle?" she asked.

"Yes. Or at least I *was.*"

"In your war?"

"Yes."

"Then you would still be good with some practice. Can you fight with a knife?"

"No."

She got to her feet suddenly. "Come, I will show you how to shoot with a bow."

The idea pleased him. "Okay. That's another White Eye word. It means, yes, or enjuh, sort of."

He had looked at bows and arrows before while visiting Lazaro, but didn't know much about them. She showed him a bow, explaining, "The wood of the wild mulberry is always used for good bows. You get a piece that is straight and has no knots, then work it into shape while it's still green. Then you hang it up in the wickiup to dry for about six days. . . .

"Then we make the bowstring out of sinew from the back of the deer. I like to make mine from the muscle on the back of the deer's hind legs. You peel off several long strips and let them dry. Then you wet the ends and splice them together to make one long string. You must judge from your bow how long to make the string, and you have to give it more length to allow for twisting. Making the string wet again, you double it over and put a stick through the end to twist it tight. You have to chew off any bumpy places on the string. Then you put it on your bow and let it dry. Later you tie it tighter. You may have to get someone to help you hold it when you finish."

She pulled the bowstring back, exhibiting her strength.

"An old man will check your bow to see if you did it right. He might also make arrows for you. If he's your relative, he'll make them for nothing. If not, you should pay him—maybe with a buckskin. In Apache, the arrow is called *k'aa'ist'aaní*. When arrows were first made, they wobbled in flight. Now the best arrows are made from reeds that grow in the river bottoms and they have feathers to make them go straight—three feathers, evenly spaced—from the red-tailed hawk, the turkey, dove, or the flicker. Many arrows have foreshafts of hardwood that is cut green and straightened by fire. Tips of flint or other kinds of sharpened stone are fastened to the shaft with pitch. Sometimes the tip is just the sharpened point of the arrow.

"A strong shooter at fairly close range can put an arrow right through a deer or a man, and nearly through a man standing sideways. Often the arrows are dyed different colors to show who owns them."

"Is it true that you often poison the tips?" Andres asked.

"Yes," Lizah replied. "For both hunting and war. The most common poison is made from the deer's spleen. This is ground up and dried, then mixed in with the ground stalk or roots of nettles and something with a burning taste, like chili. Then it's put in a little sack made from the deer's big intestine. You spit in this, tie it up so the rotten air can't get out, and hang it up for about four days until it's a good and spoiled liquid. You paint this on the arrowheads and it will kill anything. When it dries, all you have to do is spit on it again to make a good poison paste."

Andres was fascinated. "I've heard that you use snake poisons also."

Lizah frowned. "No, that would be bad. Snakes are bad luck."

She handed him a piece of cloth to wrap around his left wrist. "It'll keep the string from cutting your skin." She showed him how to hold the bow. "If you have a long shot, you hold the bow crossways. For a shorter shot you hold it vertical."

She showed him how to position it, putting her arms around him.

He could feel her breasts against his back. It was exciting, the first time they'd touched. He had trouble keeping his mind on what she was saying.

A tree some twenty yards away was the target. She put an arrow dead center into its trunk, but he had to shoot several times before he came close, then he hit it.

She nodded. "Enjuh."

But he knew better.

When the shooting session was over, they walked back to her wickiup. "I must leave now," he said. "But I want to see you again very soon."

Again her response was the cool, "Why?"

He decided to be more direct. "Because I have a feeling for you."

"What kind of a feeling?"

He put his hand over his heart. "Like a man has for a woman."

She looked into his eyes again, studying them. "If you mean *bil nzhą́ą́*—love—it isn't possible for me."

"Why not?"

She looked away. "I'm a warrior. It's the way it is."

"You are still a woman."

"But not a real woman. I'm more like a man. I must live my life in this manner."

He touched her hand, but she withdrew it. "Do you like me?" he asked.

"Yes, but only as Lazaro's son. Otherwise you are part Nakai-ye and part White Eye."

"I'm one-half Chihenne."

Her eyes hardened. "It doesn't matter. There can be nothing more for me."

23

Carlota spoke clearly in English to the banker. "I would like to deposit fifteen thousand dollars at your highest interest rate."

Richard Barnett, president of the two-year-old Silver City Bank, smiled over his short gray beard, unable to contain his delight. After all, this was a very large sum of money in this day and age. A very large sum. "I believe we can please you, Mrs. Murphy."

She had already told him that the money would be moved from the Santa Fe bank and that she wished to open the account with two thousand in cash. "I'll need ready access to the funds," she said. "I plan on going into business."

"May I ask what type of business, Mrs. Murphy?"

"To start with, I'm going to build a hotel."

"I see. There are excellent building materials available—fine clay for bricks, and plenty of lumber. How large will your hotel be?"

"I have plans for fourteen guest rooms, a dining room, and a bar. Not too large."

"With the growth of the town, it should be a good size. Do you have a builder yet?"

"No, Mr. Barnett, but I'll welcome your suggestions."

"There are a couple of very reputable men who can do that type of construction. I'll introduce you whenever you're ready."

"I would appreciate it, sir."

"What brings you to Silver City, other than your investment plans, may I ask?"

"My son is here—Andres Murphy, the newspaper editor and lawyer."

Richard Barnett nodded his head, his eyes shining. "Then you are General Murphy's wife, right?"

"That is correct."

"I've heard many good things about the general."

"Yes, he's up in the Dakotas now."

"And your son seems a fine young man. A bit liberal, but upstanding."

"Thank you. Now I would like to open my account, please."

* * *

Carlota had taken the largest room in The Exchange, a wood frame hotel with good food. The room faced Spring Street from the second story. She stood observing the midmorning traffic in the street—there were two buckboards moving along leisurely, one behind a pair of scraggly looking horses, the other behind a team of grays that had been well groomed. Both were driven by men in ranching clothes. Four women, one wearing a wide-brimmed hat and the other three in bonnets, were walking on the board sidewalk. Two boys played with a hoop, assisted by a jumping, barking black dog; and a couple of men—miners, by their clothing—were heading into the hotel, probably for a morning drink at the bar. The sun was shining brightly in a sky as clear as pale blue spring water, and the hills in the near distance added majesty. Not much different from any other place, she guessed, but she liked this little town.

Of course, the main reason she was moving here was Andres. She simply had to be near him. But she was also excited about going into business. A zestful new town like this could offer excellent opportunities for a person with ambition, brains, and capital. And there was always that gold out there somewhere in the place called Giant's Claw . . . the gold Lazaro owed her. . . .

She sipped from her lukewarm coffee. Silver City's growth had slowed from its silver rush days, but new people were still flocking in. There were over seven hundred citizens of Mexican blood and half that number of Anglos. Why, there might even be as many as two thousand people living in the town in another few years! She looked at the clock on the mantel over the fireplace. It was time to go down to the dining room to meet David Barton.

David Barton was a mountain man who had once been a school-teacher. He was stocky, about forty, wore a bushy blond beard and long hair, and had a zest for the local mountains. He'd been a hunter and a miner, and was now working a gold claim up near Pinos Altos, where he lived with his Mexican wife and four children.

"I understand you really know these hills well," Carlota said. The dining room was deserted except for them, probably because it was too late for breakfast and too early for lunch.

"I been around here since the end of the war," Barton replied. "When I first came to these parts, I moved in with an old mountain man up on Bear Creek. He had a cabin and a couple of claims he was workin' when he could. He was pretty much a drunk, but he'd been around these parts a long time. When he could get around, he showed me places no white man's ever seen. Most people who know anything about these hills navigate north and south; he showed how to go catty-corner. Yes, ma'am, I know 'em pretty well."

Carlota smiled. "Have you ever seen a high place with tall rock spires that the Apache call 'Giant's Claw' in Spanish?"

Barton frowned. "Hmmmm. That's a new one on me. You have any idea where it is?"

She wasn't about to let these people know her story with Lazaro, at least not from her. "No, but I've been told it was about a day to a day-and-a-half's ride west of Santa Rita."

The mountain man frowned. "Nope, don't know anything about it."

She had toyed with offering him a reasonable reward if he could find the place for her, but then he might notice the gold and that would be the end of that. She paid him ten dollars. "I might be opening a mining exploration company," she said as he stood to go. "Would you be interested in serving as an advisor at times?"

He grinned. "Yes, ma'am."

"I'll be in touch with you."

Carlota smiled when the general store's clerk finished waiting on a customer and greeted her. "I've been told that a man named Natalio sometimes works here doing odd jobs. He's part Mexican and part Apache."

"Yes, he's working in the back right now," the lady said. "What do you want him for?"

"I may have a little part-time work for him, if it won't interfere with what he does for you."

"I'll call him."

Natalio was the same half-breed who had taken Andres to meet Lazaro earlier. He was somewhat stooped for his age, but a most pleasant man with a ready smile. Probably from his Mexican side, Carlota thought. They went to a corner where some ginghams and other dry goods were on display. She spoke directly in Spanish. "I am the mother of Andres Murphy, the son of Lazaro. I am willing to pay well for certain information, if you can help me."

He nodded his head pleasantly. "I would be honored, Señora Murphy."

"Have you spent much time with Lazaro's people?"

"Yes, much of my childhood was with them."

"Did you ever hear of a high place called Giant's Claw?"

His eyes grew suddenly wary. "Why do you wish to know, Señora Murphy?"

"I have my reasons." He knew something! She withdrew a five dollar bill, probably more than he earned in two weeks at the store. Handing it to him, she added, "I was there once and found it most beautiful. I would like to go back sometime."

Natalio handed the bill back to her. "I don't know where it is, Señora. Only Lazaro and a few of his closest advisors know. The chief considers it a sacred place."

She smiled. "Keep the money, Natalio. But don't tell anyone I asked about the sacred place. No one, do you understand?"

"Yes," he replied quietly, sticking the money in his pocket.

"There is much more money for you if you can find out where the place is located. Maybe two hundred dollars." She knew what a huge sum that would be to the man, more than he'd ever touched in his life.

His eyes widened momentarily. "I will think about it, Señora."

"Don't think too long, or I'll have someone else find it."

She went outside and climbed into the buggy.

It was rented from the livery stable in Silver City. She liked doing her own driving, and she liked the pair of bays that the owner usually gave her. They were good-looking horses, both mares, and she enjoyed it when people turned to stare. Just as soon as things were going well and her hotel was built, she intended to buy some good horses. Rafe had asked her to hold off, stating that he didn't want her getting too involved in Silver City. But then, he always wanted her to live near his assignment. In this case, with him in Dakota country, that would have been some godforsaken place in Wyoming, or possibly Denver. Denver wasn't too bad, but the opportunities simply weren't as broad as in Silver City. No, she'd told Rafe that she had to be near her son, one way or the other. When her husband was finished with the army, then they'd have something worthwhile. She had some other real estate ideas, but right now the hotel would take most of her energy . . . that and finding Giant's Claw.

The sunshine made the open buggy most pleasant at seven thousand feet, she thought as she swung the team around in the street and headed out of town. In fact, she should explore the possibility of buying some land up here in Pinos Altos. If the place still had growth potential—

What was that?

A very tall Indian was standing in the middle of the road holding up his hand for her to stop. *What idiotic thing was he doing?* She reached for her handbag, where she kept the .36 pistol. No Indian would dare do anything right here at the edge of town; it would be suicide.

She should just urge the horses forward and run right over him— but she couldn't do that. She guided them to the right, to go around him, but he also moved. He was the tallest Indian she'd ever seen, almost as tall as. . . . He was wearing a high-crowned black Stetson and what looked like an Apache charm around his neck, over the plaid shirt. Reining the horses in, she was about to scold him when he spoke in an unmistakable voice—the voice she'd never forgotten. "Hello, Carlota."

She stared. It was *him!*

"I saw you go in the store," Lazaro said quietly. "And I waited. I've waited over thirty summers to see you again."

She blinked, unable to move, continuing to stare into his dark eyes. His hair was partially gray, and there were more lines in his face, but he looked almost as he had all those years ago.

"I've often dreamed of seeing you," he continued. "And when our son came to me, my love for you flooded back over me like the water from a mountain waterfall."

No, this couldn't be! This savage couldn't be standing in the middle of a civilized street speaking words of love to her. No! It was impossible!

Lazaro went on, "You are still a beautiful woman. I knew you would be. I always knew."

She found her tongue. *"Stop it, you wretch! Don't you dare speak to me like that! I'll have you arrested and shot!"*

His expression was gentle. "Our son is a good young warrior."

She jerked back on the reins, causing the left horse to start and try to rear. *"Get out of my way, you rapist!"* she shouted, slapping the reins on the horses' rumps.

Lazaro stepped easily aside, nodding his large head. "I'll see you soon, Carlota."

Carlota drove wildly down the mountain road toward Silver City, the horses enjoying their head in a mad gallop. She was staring ahead, caught up in a daze. The sun was too bright and too hot, and all she could see was the image of a tall Apache in a black hat. He had graying hair and eyes that bore into her. And he reminded her of a horrible time of her life, of terror, of being ripped from her loved ones, of worry to the point of sickness . . . of missing a handsome young husband beyond belief . . . of being made the wife of a beast . . . and discovering herself pregnant. The disgust, the revulsion of having to live like an animal. . . . But mostly, as Lazaro's eyes continued to bore into her, she felt the loathing.

And could there be a touch of fear?

Could he take her back again, tie her to a horse and take her to his village, throw her in one of those grotesque wickiups and once more make her his wife?

"No!" she screamed at the tall pines.

She shuddered. It was like yesterday, the smoke in the wickiups, the cold baths in the morning stream, the dislike in the eyes of the hateful Apache women. And always those repulsive, watching eyes of a huge man who wouldn't let her go. . . .

"No!"

She sobbed, brushing the tears with one hand. The buggy hit a bump and nearly rolled over. She shook her head, driving herself back to reality, and firmly drew in on the reins. In moments, the team was under control.

Lazaro had watched the buggy lurch off down the road and disappear around a turn. He, too, was dazed. Finally, after all these years, he'd just seen his Carlota. She was older, more—what could he call it— *ripe*, but then what else could she be? Still beautiful—not like the young girl he remembered, but the blazing anger made her sky-blue eyes sparkle in the same way. His Carlota. He inhaled as he stood staring at the turn where the buggy and her straight back had vanished.

He inhaled deeply, blew it out.

Carlota.

Andres had told him that she now lived in the new town.

He felt the excitement, even a strange weakness in his legs. After all this time, he knew nothing had changed. She was his woman. His love. Absolutely nothing was different, and it never would be.

How could he see her?

He could ask Andres. He could go to the new town. But she would only act like she did just now. No, it would take time, but he would find a way.

Maybe he could go to the new town and just see her sometimes. Yes, he'd find a way. . . .

24

After meeting Taza, the eldest son of Cochise, at Sulphur Springs, Arizona, Andres proceeded with the small party to the chief's *rancheria*. Located on top of a high butte, the powerful chief's camp provided a spectacular view of the surrounding valley to the Chiricahua Mountains to the east and as far as one could see to the north and south. The excellent defensive position of Cochise's camp also had the great Dragoon Mountains immediately to the west. Andres had met Taza before, and was surprised at the time that he had the same name as Lazaro's oldest son, his own half-brother who had been murdered over gold.

He found Cochise lying down, facing east, as if to watch for any enemies who might threaten his village. The chief was suffering intensely and was obviously very weak. He was being attended by a medicine man wearing a hat adorned by many charms, and by his wife, Gabriela. Andres's tall half sister, while still quite attractive at thirty-one, showed the stress of ministering to her husband for an extended period and looked at least ten years older.

"If you are too tired, Chief, I can come back another time," Andres said.

"No, I must answer your questions now. Tomorrow I may not be able." He pointed to Taza. "Bring my favorite horse, my son."

Andres looked at him in shock; surely the chief wasn't about to go for a ride.

Shortly Taza was back with a saddled spotted pony. Asking the medicine man to help him, he placed the ailing Cochise aboard the horse. With much effort, the chief held himself erect, though he had to hang onto the pommel to stay there. "I wanted once more to be on my best pony," he explained.

Speaking slowly and taking rests to catch his breath, Cochise told Andres of his boyhood and his successes as a young warrior and war leader. After nearly forty minutes of this, he told Taza to help him down, and immediately fell asleep when he was returned to his blanket in front of the wickiup.

Later, over an evening fire, Andres spoke with Taza. "What will happen when he goes?"

"I'll become chief."

Andres wanted to ask if he'd earned the right, but knew somehow that he had. It was the Way—no son automatically claimed the leadership mantle without first proving himself.

"When will you return to Lazaro's reservation?"

"When the first cold breath comes to the air and our people need food."

"How do you feel about your father's alliances with Lazaro?"

"I am honored that such a great chief as your father will be my brother."

That was good enough, Andres thought.

Cochise died at ten o'clock the following morning.

Andres rode on to Tucson, where a headline in the *Daily Citizen* two days later proclaimed: "Apache Butcher Cheez Dead!" He read with disgust an account that painted the chief as one of the most brutal murderers in history, accusing him of butchering over a hundred women and children, raping and cutting off the heads of many of his victims. He thought of confronting the editor, but he knew it wouldn't do any good. He'd heard about the "Tucson Ring" or "Indian Ring" and had quietly nosed around until he found a man willing to talk about it in a hotel saloon.

His informant was a former newspaper reporter turned miner, turned bartender. Short and beefy, with a blond handlebar mustache and hair that was plastered to his head, Win Thorp spoke freely as he handed Andres his second glass of beer. "The Ring is all powerful, Murphy. It's a shadow government here, made up of the so-called leading citizens of Arizona. They're mostly merchants who not only control the commercial enterprises of this territory, but its politics as well. The newspapers are in their pockets, so they keep the citizenry constantly inflamed and Indian-hating. The Apaches ain't got a friend in all of Arizona."

Andres sipped his beer. "What do the Ring members have to gain by all of this?" he asked.

"Simple. Indian war. It's good business. When there's recalcitrant Apaches to chase, the army has to send soldiers, who need to be fed. Members of the Ring supply the rations, as well as hay and grain for the horses. They also connive with Indian agents to furnish inferior rations for standard prices. They split the profits. You'd be amazed at the dirty tricks that go on at the weighing scale with beef."

"And no one challenges them?"

"Who's gonna do it?"

"What about the army?"

"The commanding generals get in so much trouble with the Ring that they seldom get involved."

Andres didn't tell him who his stepfather was. "Yes, I know there's a constant squabble over jurisdiction—who's going to run things."

"That's exactly what it is, and the governor usually gets his way . . . meaning the Ring wins."

Andres sipped his beer. It was worse than he thought. "What about the reservations? Have you ever seen them?"

"You mean San Carlos? Don't go out to that wasteland in the middle of the summer heat. The White Mountain, up by the Salt River where Camp Apache is? A better place, I guess. I only rode through there once, but I've *seen* San Carlos. I know one thing, I don't ever want to live there."

"What's the meaning of this shit?" James Spurrier asked loudly as he threw a copy of the Silver City *Guardian* onto the top of Andres's littered old desk. Spurrier was the sometimes blustery sheriff of new Grant County, of which Silver City was the county seat. Behind him, a handful of local merchants stared belligerently at Andres.

"The meaning of what?" Andres replied quietly. He knew exactly what they meant.

"This story about old Cheez dying, that's what I mean. You've got a hell of a nerve making that old bastard out to be a civilized human being!"

Andres remained in his chair as he slowly glanced down at yesterday's edition of the *Guardian* and then back up into the angry eyes of the sheriff. He spoke quietly. "Are you saying, sir, that an Apache is not a human being?"

A buzz of remarks from the others joined Spurrier's reply. "A savage who kills and burns isn't anyone who should have his death waved in front of good white folks and Mexicans as a sad passing, and you know damned well what I mean!"

"How would you have me write it?" Andres asked.

"You don't have to write *anything!*"

"It's my job to write the news, and the passing of a major Apache chief is certainly news. He was not only respected as a great leader by his people, but his death was major news in the Arizona papers."

Henderson, the grocer, thrust his jaw out belligerently. "I'll bet they didn't make him out to be no saint."

"I didn't canonize Cochise."

"Damn near it, Murphy. If not that, you sure as hell made him sound like a king—all that drivel about earning the right to succeed his father. Hell, you made it sound like a crown prince taking over the British throne!" Spurrier's eyes narrowed. "You know, Murphy, there's a rumor a-going 'round that the reason you write all these editorials about how bad the damned Apache are being treated is that you're a half-breed Apache."

Andres got slowly to his feet, looking directly into the sheriff's eyes. "And if I were?"

Spurrier edged forward, his jaw coming forward at the same level as Andres. "Then," he growled, "I guess we'd have to send you over to the reservation."

It was all Andres could do to hold his temper.

"Well, you can just cancel my ads in your damned paper!" Henderson snapped. "I won't do business with any Apache lover."

A chorus from the other merchants followed, all echoing the grocer's comments. Andres lost in just a few moments a good portion of his advertising. Still holding onto his anger, he shrugged. "If honest reporting forces you to take such action, there's nothing I can do about it."

"I knew it would come to this," Carlota said, shaking her head over her cup of coffee. They were eating dinner in the hotel dining room. "I knew your being the champion of the Apache would bring grief. Now what are you going to do to keep your newspaper afloat?"

"I still have some good legal fees coming in," Andres replied.

"But you'll also lose readers."

"I'm not worried about it." He grinned. "I've got a rich mother."

"But she isn't on a crusade, remember?"

Andres nodded his head. "Oh, yes, she is: making money. What's the latest on the hotel?"

"It should be finished by the first of August. That is, if the fixtures get in from Kansas City."

"The nicest little hotel west of the Rio Grande and east of California."

Carlota smiled. "Absolutely."

"Did you buy anything else while I was in Arizona?"

"Yes, a tract of land just outside of town to the east. Four hundred acres."

"I know—when the town expands, you'll make a big profit."

"Don't make fun, Andres. It'll be your money someday—that is, if you don't rile these Silver Citians up too much, and they throw us both out of town."

"Hear anything from the general?" Andres asked. He still called Rafe "Father" to his face, but referred to him as "the general" otherwise.

"Oh, yes, I almost forgot. There's a letter for you." Carlota pulled an envelope from her handbag. "It came today from Washington."

Andres quickly opened it. The precise, strong handwriting was familiar:

> Just a note to let you know that while I was here to report to General Sherman on conditions in Sioux country, I learned that another reservation move is afoot for the Apache at the Willows. In the near future, all of the Indians will be transferred, lock, stock, and barrel, to the San Carlos reservation. I just heard about this today and must leave early in the morning to return to my command. I know this will be a bad blow to Lazaro and Victorio in particular. And I detest the decision—but I don't know what I can do about it as an active duty officer, other than write a few letters of protest. The civilians in the Indian Agency and the Tucson Indian Ring seem to be holding all the cards.

Andres read it again, feeling the anger beginning to rise.

"What is it, darling?" his mother asked.

He quickly told her.

She knew better than to say anything about her own thoughts. But at least she wouldn't have to worry about running into Lazaro anymore. On the other hand, closing the Willows reservation would cut into her income—since she'd bought part interest in a grain company that was supplying hay and grain to the reservation. So the news had mixed values for her. One thing was certain: it would keep Andres away from that heathen Apache woman he was seeing so much of—

Andres slammed his fist down on the table. "The bastards can't get away with this!"

* * *

> ... and even this poor remnant of a once powerful tribe
> is fast wasting away before those blessings of civilization,
> "whisky and small pox."
>
> —*Ulysses S. Grant, Washington Territory, 1853*

"You know, I'm from Galena, Illinois, and the president used to wait on me when he worked in his father's store there," the older man said. "That was just before the war. Yup, he was just a lowly clerk."

Andres nodded. "That's interesting." He'd been waiting on the bench outside of the president's office for nearly an hour. Both Rafe and Richard Hartman had written to Grant, asking for an audience for Andres when he arrived in Washington. A note from the president's secretary had confirmed an appointment on this date. Richard Hartman was now a federal judge in Santa Fe, one of Grant's surprise appointments, considering that the lawyer and newspaperman was still such an unbending rebel.

Andres had met Ulysses S. Grant at a reception for general officers the night after the grand victory parade in Washington in 1865. Rafe had brought him along to the Willard where Sheridan had introduced him to the General-in-Chief in glowing terms. Grant had commented on his Medal of Honor. But that had been nine years earlier. Now, early in his second term as president of the United States, Grant was besieged by troubles—as Richard Hartman said—stemming from the fact that the general trusted too many people who either wanted to line their pockets or were just incompetent politicians. "He's never been a very successful civilian," Rafe had said. "He was a heroic lieutenant in the Mexican War, but after he resigned in '54, he was an abysmal failure—which is why he wound up clerking in his father's leather goods store in Illinois when the War of Secession broke out. Once he was established as a general, however, he was unstoppable. He had fine staff officers and knew how to use his commanders, and as much as I hate to admit it as a Confederate general, he was at times every bit as brilliant as Bobby Lee. But it seems he just can't realize what leeches these men in government are. He's just too damned good a man to be a politician."

Now his ridiculous Indian policy was belying such a statement.

The man next to Andres interrupted again with some inane statement. Andres nodded his head, but didn't reply. He didn't want to make small talk; he was still preparing his brief in his head. He wouldn't have too much time with the president and he wanted to get the most out of it. He looked down at the lapel of the new brown suit he'd bought for the meeting. The Medal of Honor was pinned straight. He'd thought long and hard about whether to wear it or not, and finally decided it might be advantageous. Besides, a lot of war veterans wore their medals on certain occasions. But he hadn't had his on since the day he took off his uniform for good.

He knew this trip to Washington was probably a waste of time and money, but he had to do *something*—wandering around New Mexico complaining and arguing was practically useless. Yet now he suddenly felt a little foolish. If his stepfather, a well-known general officer, couldn't convince Grant that the Apache policy was wrong, what could a former captain of volunteers do? He was sitting in the waiting room of the *White House*, expecting to see the *president of the United States*. Wasn't that pretty presumptuous? His knees suddenly felt a little weak. Looking around, he glanced at the others sitting on the benches and waiting. On the other hand, there couldn't be a single one of them with a mission as important as his. He inhaled deeply and blew it out. No, he had to try.

"Mr. Murphy?" the secretary asked.

He looked up, startled. "Yes?"

"The president will see you now."

The president's office was a large square room on the south end of the mansion. It was decorated with many of the accoutrements of a military man, including a red three-star general's flag standing in a corner. Several other flags of his former commands were in another corner. Ulysses S. Grant, looking much the same as Andres remembered him from the end of the war, sat casually at the huge oak conference table in the middle of the room. His short beard was somewhat grayer than at the end of the war, otherwise it was the same man who had come out of the west to save the Union for Lincoln. The former general was busy holding a wooden match to a fresh cigar. As Andres approached, he got quickly to his feet and stuck out his hand. "Well, Captain Murphy, it's nice to see you again. Your father, in his letter, reminded me that we met after the grand review." He glanced down at the Medal of Honor. "You got that up in the valley with Little Phil, didn't you?"

"Yes, sir."

"I understand you want to talk about the Apache problem."

"Yes, Mr. President. That's why I came all this way."

Grant, still reticent and unassuming, pointed to a chair at the table and dropped back into his own. "Sit down and tell me about it."

Andres blew out a deep breath and launched into the homelands problem. He spoke of Lazaro and Victorio and the People at length. When he finished, he pulled a sheet of paper from his inner coat pocket. "Sir, I've excerpted a thought from your first inaugural address, in which you promised to 'favor any course . . . which tends to improve the civilization and ultimate citizenship of the original occupants of this land.'"

"Yes, I recall."

"In the case of the Apache, it means recognizing their desires about where the reservations are designated. It also means adequate rations and honest Indian agents, among other things. And it specifically means not moving groups like the Chihenne to that hellhole of San Carlos in Arizona."

The president frowned and picked up a sheet of paper. "Murphy, this is a report of an Apache attack on a ranch some seventy miles west of El Paso last month. It states that everyone, including two women and four children, were killed and mutilated by Apaches. Their sign was all over the place. And this is due south of your Willows reservation—right in Lazaro's line of raiding into Mexico."

Andres frowned. He should have known that raid would be reported to Grant. "Sir," he said, shaking his head. "That was Bacho. He's an old renegade with a small band of cutthroats who has nothing to do with Lazaro's people. In fact, he's Lazaro's archenemy."

Grant puffed on his cigar and blew out blue smoke. "I can understand that, Murphy, but most people can't or don't want to. An Apache raid is an Apache raid. To most of the higher-ups in this Indian business, continued raiding means that wherever they're supposed to be living isn't the right place. They need to be placed under more central control."

Andres kept his anger under control. *That sonofabitch Bacho!* C'mon, he told himself, you're a lawyer, keep your wits and plead your case. You'll never get back here to do it again. He decided to be bold. "Mr. President, who's higher-up than you?"

Grant nodded his head and blew out another puff of smoke. "Good point, Murphy, but you have to understand that a president doesn't just give orders like a general. I've got a Board of Indian Commissioners to deal with. And also, your Apaches aren't the only Indians in the country. Right now we've got a whole mess of trouble with the Sioux and Cheyenne."

It was Andres's turn to nod his head. "I do understand, Mr. President, but have you ever heard of the Tucson Indian Ring?"

"Refresh my memory."

Andres did so, finishing with, "Those are the conniving people who are behind this move to San Carlos, the ones who will make all the money."

"I'll ask the people over in Indian Affairs to look into it."

He wasn't really going to do a damned thing! It was just as he'd thought: if Rafe couldn't convince Grant to do anything, what could a young half-Apache lawyer do? It was all so futile. He wanted to lash out and say, *The whole policy is a lie!* But he couldn't.

The president got to his feet. "I wish I could give you a better answer, but sometimes there are some pretty hard to understand trade-offs necessary in politics. I can only assure you of one thing—I still care for our Indians and I hope to see them treated as fairly as possible." He stuck out his hand for a farewell handshake.

Andres felt his face smart as he walked out of the room. He had seen the touch of resignation in Grant's face. The honest man who was supposed to care knew he couldn't provide what was being asked of him. And it apparently troubled him.

But it didn't make matters any better!

25

Andres watched the loaded wagons leave Lazaro's village. Jammed in them, with only the belongings they could carry, were the women, children, and old people of the Chihenne. The few horses they were allowed to keep were being led in the column. The barking dogs, seeming to enjoy a new game, cavorted around the sides trying to tease the children into playing. The businesslike and disinterested cavalrymen drove the teams and rode escort. And on a small hillock the captain commanding the move to San Carlos sat astride his dun-colored horse, watching quietly, saying nothing to the lieutenant beside him. It was a warm fall day, the sun shining alone in its clear realm, perhaps puzzled by the exodus below, obviously unaware that once more the People were being uprooted and moved like pawns on a mountainous chessboard.

Andres jotted his final notes in the little book and swung his horse around to ride away before he said or did something he would regret. Riding forward to the lead wagon, he spotted Benita and waved to her. He had wished her luck back at the village prior to loading. She had stoically accepted the move, just as she had calmly acknowledged the role of leadership among the women that Lazaro had thrust upon her. Old Man was long dead, therefore the nominal command had been passed to an elderly war leader named Ponce.

Tze-go-juni, not pleased with Lazaro's decision that she go with the column, rode in the wagon behind Benita. The medicine woman had fallen and broken her arm a month earlier and would be unable to keep up with any kind of a fast-moving war party. She had railed at Lazaro briefly, telling him he would be ineffective without her, but he was unwavering.

There were no Chihenne warriors in the column.

Nor were there any warriors in the column leaving the Warm Springs village, for all of Victorio's young men were away from the reservation, splintered into small groups in the Black Range, waiting to join Lazaro's party when it was time to wage war.

Andres shook his head angrily. Even Ulysses S. Grant had been too stupid to realize just how costly this relocation could be. And not only to the People, some of whom would surely not survive the trip to San Carlos and the ensuing stay there, but in the savage warfare that would result. He knew because he had sat in on the inner council when the chiefs and war leaders of the Willows Reservation had met to discuss the best course of action once the move to San Carlos was a reality. Lazaro had listened quietly as they spoke in anger and defiance. Finally Victorio raised his fist, barking, "My Warm Springs will *fight!*"

The leader of a group of Mescaleros who had fled their own reservation east of the Rio Grande concurred. Geronimo raised his rifle and snarled, "Death to the Nakai-ye and the White Eye!"

When the decision to fight was unanimous, Lazaro spoke. "I agree with my brothers. We have tried to be farmers, we have abided by our promises to the White Eyes. In return they have only cheated us and refused to honor our needs and wishes. I, personally, have been almost murdered and on many other occasions been a victim of their treachery. Much as I hate the Nakai-ye, it might be better for us to make peace with Sonora and raid into this country from strongholds in the Nakai-ye mountains. There are more rancheros here now, more settlers, and more livestock. The Chihenne will fight."

And that had been it.

Andres was certain that the Americans were in for the most devastating blow they had ever received from the People. And the majority would never know why. As he turned his horse to head back to Silver City, he felt a deep sense of depression. But it couldn't smother his anger.

Carlota had been unsuccessful in finding Giant's Claw, but her other endeavors had been productive. The hotel, where she maintained a pleasant three-room suite, had prospered since its opening; the two houses she had built had been sold for nice little profits, and the mining company which she had formed with David Barton to cover her search for the Apache gold was bringing in a handsome profit.

Two days after the Chihenne had begun the trek to San Carlos, Andres looked up from where he was setting the type for the next edition of the *Guardian* to see his mother entering the room. "Hello, darling," Carlota said brightly, "I have some good news. I talked that new butcher over on Main Street into running a weekly ad in the paper. He's new to this part of the country and doesn't have his back up about the Indians as much as some of the other merchants."

Andres nodded, picking up a proof of the editorial he had written the night before. Handing it to his mother, he said, "Maybe even he won't want to advertise after he reads this."

Carlota read quickly, frowning as she went.

> Savages, cattle, or people? A few days ago the women, children, infirm, and elderly of the Apaches on the Willows Reservation were packed up in rude wagons and shipped off to a barren reservation in Arizona. As a result, the fighting men of these villages will wage war against all Americans in this area. It isn't the fault of Silver Citians, or even most New Mexicans, but the retaliation will fall on our heads. Open warfare spares few innocents. . . .

She read on, scowling more deeply as Andres's words accused the Americans in general of being guilty of the crime of apathy in the minimum, and open hatred in the ultimate. When she finished she looked up and scolded, "You know better than this. Some time ago the merchants made it clear to you how everyone feels when they quit advertising in your newspaper. Now they are simply not going to put up with your siding with the Apache. What do they care if the Apache are sent off to Arizona? Good riddance to them. Now they won't be here to steal and murder and all the other things Apaches do. The people of this town simply don't *care.* They'll dance in the streets when they read this."

Andres shook his head, replying angrily, "I should never have shown it to you. You'll never change. You're just as bad as the rest, actually worse!"

"I'm just trying to keep you from getting hurt."

"Don't worry about me!"

"What do you expect? I'm your mother. You know I can't stand the thought of what can happen to you."

"I don't care. It's justice that matters, and there isn't an iota of it in what's happening."

"*Justice?*" Carlotta blazed. "There is no justice in *life!* Was it justice when Lazaro stole me from my marriage? Was it?"

"Don't go back to that again. I've heard that tired old song too many times. It boils up in you like poison and you don't want to let it rest. I don't ever want to hear about it again."

"Don't talk to me like that, young man. I—"

At that moment loud noises from outside interrupted. The sound of men's shouts and laughter could be heard. Carlota hurried to the window. Outside Sheriff Spurrier and a deputy were dragging two bodies through the dust as they slowly walked their horses through the crowded street. The rapidly forming crowd was jeering and shouting obscenities. Andres stared out the window. It was hard to tell for sure, but long black hair streamed from the heads of the bodies. They looked like— He spun toward the outer office and rushed to the door. Running down the sidewalk, pushing his way through the spectators, he saw what he had known would be the ghastly truth. They were young Apaches, probably still in their teens.

Reaching a tall oak the two horsemen stopped and quickly threw the ropes over a limb that spread some twelve feet above the ground. Swinging their horses around, they slowly pulled back until each body hung upside down five feet off the dirt. Eager to get a close look at the dead faces, the shouting crowd pressed around the bodies, jostling each other like rude animals. Andres thought he recognized one of the Apache boys as a son of one of Victorio's war leaders. He turned away, thinking he might retch, barely hearing the sheriff announce, "They was snooping around old Charlie Hendrick's place outside of town, no doubt setting it up for their war party. Old Charlie and his boys shot 'em dead, and about that time me and Eddie, here, rode by. I wanted you citizens of Silver City to know that we ain't gonna let these thieving savages have their way in Grant County, nosiree! They're gonna hang right here until tomorrow night so's any of you who thinks Injuns is innocent and God-fearin' people can remember that they ain't nothing but thieves and killers."

"Hear, hear!" someone bellowed and the crowd started shouting again.

Andres looked once more at the dangling bodies and stumbled away. There was a ringing in his ears as he stopped and was unable to hold back his nausea. He was suddenly convulsed by dry retching. He shook his head. *Why, after years of war, should he react so violently to death? Hadn't he seen enough of it to be steeled?*

A miner, slightly drunk, stopped and laughed at him. "Whatsamatta, Mexican, can't you stand the sight of two *good* Injuns?"

Carlota hurried over to Andres and put her arm around his shoulders. "Are you all right, darling? Come over to the hotel and I'll fix you some sassafras tea."

He flung her arm away, wiped his mouth, and walked briskly away from the crowd. Moments later he stumbled into his office and went directly to his desk where he kept a bottle of bourbon in a bottom drawer. Opening it, he took a big swig, almost getting sick again as the raw whiskey hit his stomach. He stared at the bottle, seeing nothing but a blur and the upside-down heads of the two young Apaches with their hair hanging away from their dead faces.

Andres rode to the edge of the ledge and looked off toward the Twin Sisters. The view was serene, the stillness broken only by the breathing of his horse. He dismounted and reached into his pocket for the tobacco pouch. After slowly rolling a cigaret, he lit it with a wooden match, shook out the flame and took in a deep drag. The acrid taste was good, sharp. He went to a round rock the size of a bushel basket and sat on it. Drawing heavily on the cigaret again, he pulled the silver flask from his coat pocket, opened it, and swallowed a couple of ounces of bourbon. Capping the flask and replacing it in his coat, he stared off into the hills. The scene in Silver City flashed back over him, the two bodies hanging tellingly dead in utter humiliation, black hair falling partway to the ground. Desecrated, jeered at, ridiculed. As if they were nothing.

Another flashed before him: wagons full of the women, children, and old people being hauled away from the Willows . . . their expressions blank, their identities being diminished yet another time. Cattle being hauled away to yet another distant pasture.

He saw Ulysses S. Grant, the President of the mighty United States, sitting at the table in his office and telling him that he would try to work out the Apache problem. The man who professed to care for the American Indian. A lie!

It was all a giant, hopeless lie!

He recalled the story his father had told him about being misled by General West and provoked into nearly being murdered. The idea of such a great leader being maligned and cheapened by nobodies was infuriating. Nobodies, that's what most of the Americans were— coarse, uneducated, syphillated, dirty, drunken, goddamned *nobodies* who inflated themselves in their own meaningless lives by ridiculing and hating the People. Many of them had less spirituality than most of the People had in one finger. And the Mexicans were no better.

Well, he didn't have to keep on being a nobody.

Not one damned bit!

No more lie for him. Or it would consume him.

He had one alternative, a giant step.

From this moment on he would be an Apache.

* * *

Andres carefully unwrapped the oilskin pouch that held the revolver. He had put a light coat of oil on it after firing it the last time, nearly two years earlier. It was a 6-shot, .44 caliber Colt army issue. With its long barrel it was over thirteen inches in length and weighed nearly three pounds. He had been a dead shot with it during the war. He hefted it, aimed it at a picture on the wall. It felt good, like an old friend. Replacing it in its oilskin he next opened the wooden box that held the bullets. They were a new commercial type that weighed 125 grams with a charge of 14 grains. He had run into a good deal of them up in Santa Fe a couple of years earlier and had purchased five hundred rounds.

Sounded like a lot, but with practice and what he planned to do, it wasn't. Opening another oilskin, he pulled out the flask and bullet mold. An extra pouch of top grade black powder and a couple of hundred empty cartridges completed his small handgun arsenal.

He next unwrapped the carbine, a Spencer seven-shot repeater that had been called at the end of the war "by all odds the best shooting weapon ever issued to mounted men." Of course, newer models were probably much improved, Andres thought to himself as he examined the oily caliber .52 carbine, but he was familiar with this model and wouldn't trade it for anything. He remembered the day when he was promoted to captain with vivid clarity—he had led his troop into a sharp engagement with a rebel cavalry unit and it had taken him less than a minute to kill or wound four enemy soldiers. It, too, was hefty, weighing over nine pounds loaded. But at thirty-nine inches it was short enough for any horseman to use effectively. He had less than fifty rounds of ammunition for the Spencer, so he'd have to buy more at the hardware store before leaving.

Next he took the binoculars from their leather case and dusted them off. They could prove extremely valuable.

An hour later he made a deal for the burro with a Mexican farmer outside of town. He was named "Orejas" or "Ears" for obvious reasons, and was a hardy little animal only two years old. He would make a nice gift for Benita later on. He took the animal into town and put him up at the same livery stable where he kept his horse.

After buying what he needed at the hardware store he went to a dry goods store and purchased two yards of bright red fabric. His final stop was at his mother's suite in the hotel. Just the day before she had been notified that some adjoining mining claims in which she had invested apparently contained a rich quantity of silver.

He found her reading and sipping tea. He knew what he had to tell her would create a scene so he didn't make small talk. "Mother," he said quietly, "I've made a decision that will displease you considerably."

Carlota put down the book and looked at him quietly, waiting.

"I've had enough of the perfidy against the Apache," he said softly, measuring his words. "It seems that no matter what the People do to get along with the edicts of the white man, it isn't enough. And it's only going to get worse. The ridicule of those two boys' bodies the other day is the final nail. I'm unable to accept any more. I—"

"No!" Carlota's exclamation pierced the quiet of the room. Her eyes were wide, unblinking, as she stared at him in alarm, knowing all too well what he was going to say.

He slowly nodded his head. "I'm finished with this way of life, Mother. Finished. There's nothing more I can do to help the People as I am, so I'm going to—"

"Oh, God, don't say it!"

His voice was even, dispassionate, just as he'd rehearsed it. "I'm no longer going to be a member of the white man's world. I leave in one hour for the Black Range, where I will join Lazaro and Victorio. From this day on I will be an Apache."

"But you are *not* an Apache. I made you in my image. I taught you the finer things in life, the literature, the *quality*." Tears broke loose and streamed down her cheeks as she came to him and touched his cheek imploringly. "Oh, dear God, don't do this terrible thing, darling. Don't."

"I must, Mother."

"They'll kill you, I know it."

Andres's voice was gentle as he put his arm around her. "They can't kill me, Mother, I'll be one of them."

She turned her face into his chest and sobbed. "You'll be killed being one of them. Don't do it, darling, *don't!*"

He held her for over a minute as more sobs racked her. He knew what his decision meant to her; he'd heard her hatred for the People all of his life. He knew she felt that she was losing him forever to her unforgivable enemy. He spoke gently. "We'll see each other now and then, Mother. Nothing has changed my love for you." He kissed her cheek, tasting her salty tears.

She looked up, brimming, whispering, "Please change your mind."

His tone hardened. "I can't."

* * *

Back in his office, Andres undressed, hanging the suit in the wardrobe by his bed. He would never again have need for a suit of clothes, he thought, as he dressed in the rougher clothes that would match his new life. As a final touch, he reached for the bright red head cloth that he had fashioned from the bolt of cloth he'd purchased at the dry goods store. Slowly he fastened it around his forehead. He would henceforth be known as *Cabeza Colorado*—Red Head—in the Apache world. It would be his fighting name.

Looking around, he regarded the law books that had meant so much to him. His next farewell was to the old printing press that held equal meaning. Like many a newspaperman before him, the ink had gotten in his blood. The tightness in his throat was momentary, the decision had been made. These objects were a meaningful part of his past now, from this moment merely memories. He would continue to chronicle the life of his People and possibly write their big story someday, but at this time only fighting for the People mattered. He went back to his desk where the box that held his notes for the big book sat wrapped in brown paper. It was addressed to his mother with a short letter asking her to keep them in a safe place until such time as he might come to claim them.

He then reached inside the bottom drawer and pulled out the whiskey bottle. Holding it up, he saw that it held no more than one good swig. Appropriate. He drained it, then regarded the empty bottle for a moment before throwing it against the nearby wall. Heading for the door, he drew in a deep breath. From this moment he was a Chihenne.

Lazaro was watching the training of a handful of young warriors in his mountain camp in the Black Range when he was told that his son had arrived. Pleased, he got quickly to his feet to watch Andres approach. There seemed to be something different about the younger man. Ah, it was the red headband he was wearing. No, it was more—something special in the way he walked, in the way he carried himself.

How he loved that boy! He was far more of a man than Taza had ever been, and, of course, he was the son of his beloved Carlota. He had gone to Silver City twice since seeing her in Pinos Altos, but had been unable to catch sight of her. He knew this feeling he had for her was no more than an old man's obsession, at this stage of his life, but he didn't care. He had relived her period with him a thousand times in these intervening years, and would never quit doing so. The memory was still as bright and fresh as ever. She had been in his heart for forty of his sixty-seven summers if one counted from the first day he ever saw her at Santa Rita. "Welcome," he said warmly to Andres. "Why do you come?"

Andres beamed. "I am now an Apache," he announced proudly in the tongue of the People. He pointed first to his headband and then to the revolver strapped to his waist. "I have come to fight the enemies of the People."

The war leader, Gordo, who was standing beside Lazaro, shook his head. "You are a White Eye and a Nakai-ye too."

"No, I *was* a White Eye and I've never been a Nakai-ye. Now I am Andres, son of Lazaro. Red Head to those who don't know me, for I shall always wear a headband like this."

Lazaro quietly asked, "Why do you do this?"

"Because I'm ashamed to be a White Eye any longer," Andres replied and then explained how he had reached his decision.

"Is this for a short time?"

"Forever," Andres replied fervently.

"Do you think you can always live the Way? It's often hard."

"I will live as any warrior, my father."

"What makes you think you can fight like an Apache warrior?" Gordo asked. "Our boys train for years."

"I was both a warrior and a war leader in the big White Eye war for four years. I can learn your ways and remember theirs."

Gordo was unconvinced. "I doubt it."

"I will speak to my other leaders," Lazaro said, nodding his head. "It's necessary for them to approve. In the meantime you are welcome in my wickiup."

"As you wish, Father. I want to join in the war as soon as possible, so I would like to start training immediately."

Lazaro nodded his large head again. "We will talk about it at tonight's fire."

Victorio's band was camped about half a mile away. He had ninety-eight of his warriors with him on the grassy bank by the tiny stream. Andres arrived on foot late in the afternoon and asked to see the chief.

Victorio was watching a bow and arrow contest, but broke away to meet his visitor. Andres quickly told him of his plan to become an Apache warrior, to which Victorio grunted approval. "Enjuh! Your father has told me you were a good war leader in the big White Eyes' war. Perhaps there are things you can tell us about the way that they fight that we don't know."

"Perhaps."

"You tell your father that I said you can fight with me any time."

"Gordo thinks I must learn the Apache way."

Victorio shrugged. "You will learn quickly." He eyed the army Colt. "Are you a good shot?"

"Yes, and I will practice. I have much ammunition."

Victorio nodded his head. "Enjuh! Welcome, my son."

Andres found Lizah at the corral putting a new wooden shoe on her favorite pony. He quickly told her of his big decision.

She continued to work on the shoe, saying nothing for several moments. Finally she said, "You are not an Apache."

"I'm the son of Lazaro."

"But that doesn't make you an Apache. You were raised by a Nakai-ye as a White Eye, so you can never really be an Apache."

He felt his anger rise. She should *welcome* him, be pleased that he had given up so much to dedicate his life to the Way and to their war.

"I suppose you think you're doing us a big favor," she added, looking up into his eyes. "Don't. Take off that red cloth on your head and go back to the White Eyes where you belong. We don't need you."

He scowled, but kept his voice even. "Why do you say that? I thought you, of all people, would welcome me."

"Because you don't come to us to be pure Apache in spirit. You come because you want me. But I will not carry this burden on my head." She walked away, but stopped a few paces from him and turned. "Go back to the White Eyes, Andres. This is no good."

Andres sat on a small knoll outside of the camp during the hour Lazaro and his subordinate leaders met around a small campfire. He'd watched the slender one-quarter arc of a moon pick its way up into the inky sky, thinking that he was little more than such a sliver to the People. Since the days of Silsoose they had been following their Way, and for millennia before that when they worked their way down from the Bering land bridge. He was merely a fragment in their history. What if they turned him down? Surely they knew of his attraction to Lizah. Would many of them think, as she did, that was his motive? *Was it?* He had thought of her in his decision process. Was she, deep down, part of the reason? No, he'd purposely pushed her from his mind the night he'd decided.

What would he do if the Chihenne turned him down—go join Victorio? Of course he would.

A figure appeared. "Come, Andres Cabeza Colorado," Gordo said. "Your father wishes to speak to you at the fire."

Andres followed the war leader to the ring of Chihenne leaders whose faces were highlighted by the dull glow of the flames. Lazaro pointed to a place on his left. "Be seated, Andres Cabeza Colorado."

Andres dropped to the cross-legged position, saying nothing.

Lazaro spoke immediately. "The leaders of the Chihenne have decided that your intention to be an Apache warrior is pure, and thus find you acceptable as the son of Lazaro to be a member of the People. But your red headband is not enough. You must soak it in your own blood before you are a Chihenne." He handed Andres a sharp-bladed knife and nodded toward his wrist.

Andres nodded his head in agreement, taking the knife and slashing the back of his hand. Instantly blood began to spurt. With his other hand he quickly untied the headband and wrapped it around the wound.

"Enjuh! Enjuh!" the leaders around the fire exclaimed as they nodded approval.

Andres refastened the bandana around his forehead and then held his bloody hand high. "I am proud to be Apache!" he said loudly. "I will kill many enemies for you."

The response was equally loud. *"Enjuh!"*

The white-haired lady nodded her head as the train slowed for the stop at Orogrande. She glanced out the window to her left where the few low-lying hills seemed to stare back at her like a big, baleful bloodhound basking in the warm afternoon sun. Orogrande was truly nothing more than a water and mail stop, since there were only three buildings there.

"You see," she explained, turning back to the reporter, "Victorio was the hard war chief, and he was younger than Lazaro. Furthermore Lazaro had injured a leg and was unable to lead a raid the way a chief should. So he accepted a support role during the following months of war. In the midst of this new campaign, Victorio proved his resourcefulness by twice leading his fighting force on the Sierra Blanca Mescalero reservation east of the Rio Grande for food. This was, of course, during the winter.

"But while he was there the second time he discovered that a grand jury in Silver City had indicted himself, Lazaro, and all of his followers for horse stealing and murder. Furious at that and at the Mescalero Indian agent for cheating on rations, Victorio led his war party, now bolstered by many Mescalero warriors, back into the mountains to begin a ferocious campaign."

The lady's blue eyes looked troubled as she paused and thought back before continuing. "Andres quickly picked up the role of an Apache warrior, learning the little skills that a youth masters in training. His use of the language improved dramatically, but acceptance among the war leaders would take time. Several of them shared a natural resentment toward him because he was Lazaro's half-breed son and also because he was a natural leader and a threat to them. He was now completely obsessed with Lizah, but she continued to keep him at arm's length.

"As Victorio and company created havoc throughout southern New Mexico, eastern Arizona, and into southwest Texas, more than a thousand American cavalry, reinforced by groups of irregulars, townsmen, and ranchers, and several companies of Indian scouts, were hunting the hostile Apaches. Even a contingent of Texas Rangers was in the chase. . . .

"By the way, I forgot to mention that the army had enlisted many friendly Apache men several years earlier to track and fight hostile bands. If you recall, Bacho had been one of them back when General West tried to have Lazaro murdered at Bayard during the Civil War. At this time a few companies of Navajo scouts were also brought into the hunt. Victorio was, however, audacious, seeming to take great pleasure in ambushing military groups and taking their horses and equipment. Since horses often had to be eaten, and ammunition was always in short supply, it was the best resupply system available to the Apaches.

"And since Victorio also swept below the border to raid, Mexican cavalry was vainly trying to aid the American effort. But Victorio's friend and ally, Juh, kept them off balance with other raids. In May of Eighteen-eighty approximately ninety people were killed by Victorio's warriors, and in the same month the weary American cavalry had to rest its spent horses and halt the pursuit to refit. Never before had the American army been so helplessly stymied by such an outnumbered force of irregulars with no supply base."

The tall reporter shook his head. "Victorio sure made them look foolish, didn't he?"

The white-haired lady sighed, fussing with the blue feathers in her hat. "Yes, but he couldn't continue to do this for long, not against two armies."

She smiled and reached for her knitting as the train jerked away from its stop in barren Orogrande.

≫ **26** ≪

*It is useless to negotiate with Apaches. They will observe no
treaties, agreements, or truces. There is no alternative but vigorous
war, until they are completely exterminated.*
                                        —Major General H. W. Halleck
                                        Commander, Army of the Pacific

The victory celebration had been going on since sunset in Victorio's
hideout in the Mexican hills southwest of Van Horn, Texas. The
drums had sounded incessantly and all of the available tiswin had
been consumed. The dancing of the warriors around the huge fire
ceased when Lazaro rose to his full height. Immediately conversation
stopped. "I have reason to be more than proud tonight of my son,
Andres Red Head," he announced in a ceremonial tone. "Today, when
the attack was made on the supply train and the hidden soldiers came
out shooting, his attack on his horse won the fight." He pointed with
his nose to a warrior. "Eduardo, there, told me about it. Many soldiers
came streaming out of the wagons, firing fast at our warriors. Almost
at once Andres Red Head rode in shouting louder than five young
novices and shooting his revolver. He killed four of them on his first
pass, and three more when he returned."

"Enjuh!" the celebrators shouted.

Lazaro went on, "I now make him a war leader of my Chihenne."

Victorio sprang to his feet. "Red Head is as much a warrior as any
of us!"

As the chief dropped back into his cross-legged position, Andres
looked around the fire and realized he had to say something. Getting
slowly to his feet he settled his gaze on his father. "I've seen much
of war, but never have I known better fighters than my brothers, the
Apache. I'm proud to be one of your new leaders, although I am
unworthy of the honor." His gaze shifted across the fire, lingering on
the brown eyes of Lizah.

She nodded her head slightly and he thought he saw a touch of a
smile cross her lips. That was almost as important as the honor he'd
just been accorded. He felt full of himself, even more so than he had
when General Sheridan pinned the Medal of Honor on his chest.

*   *   *

"You are pleased with yourself," Lizah said as they walked through the moonlight a half-hour later.

"Yes," Andres replied. "I guess being a successful Apache is so important to me that I can't help it. Accomplishments have been easy for me all my life. This accomplishment hasn't been. There has been resentment, doubt." He stopped and looked into the dark shadows that were her eyes. "You were the first to express it."

"Yes, because you have a Nakai-ye mother."

"There are others of mixed blood who haven't been rejected. Look at my half sisters who were all married to chiefs."

"They're women, not the son of a chief who wants to follow his father as nantan."

Andres frowned, shook his head. "I have no such plan. All I want to do is fight for the People and enjoy the rest of my father's years."

Her response was soft. "Is that all you want?"

He looked into her shadows again. Was this encouragement? Was she—

"Do you still want me?"

She was always so *direct.* "Yes," he replied quietly. "I want you to be my wife more than anything."

"But I'm a warrior and many think I'm a shaman."

"I don't care. You're also a beautiful and desirable woman."

"But I'm also like a man."

He smiled. "Not any part I've ever seen." Taking her hand he added, "I've loved you since the moment I first saw you."

She drew his fingers to her cheek and kissed them. "I think I've wanted you since the same moment, Andres. I was so pleased tonight when Lazaro and Victorio both recognized your fighting and proclaimed you war leader. So that does it."

Could she really mean this? "Does what?"

"Makes me your woman."

He put his arms around her, brushed her lips with his. "Will you be my wife?"

She smiled. "Do you know how to court an Apache woman?"

"What I don't know I'll find out."

"I'm no young girl, you know. But I've never been night crawling."

"Night crawling?"

"It's our term for making love before or outside of marriage."

He remembered the story of the chief passing through and how she had spurned all men since that time. "I would have bet on the fact," he replied, realizing the words were awkward. In spite of all her Power and strength the beautiful woman in his arms was looking at him with warm, open eyes, giving herself to him. He felt so full of love he could burst! Again he touched her lips with his, ever so gently, letting them linger. She responded, holding him tightly and kissing him warmly. He felt her breasts pushing against his chest and became immediately aroused. But it was more than that, the rich love erupting within him made him want to kiss her eyes, her nose, her hands. He wanted to hold her tightly and never let her go. It was like nothing he'd ever experienced with any girl or woman before. "I love you, I love you," he said fervently.

Their kiss was long, warm, and when they broke it she said, "We are now half-married."

He nodded, it was the term for an engagement. "Yes, now when do we get fully married?"

She paused before replying. "We are at war, but Victorio told me there won't be another raid until three days from now. I will marry you in two days." She smiled. "And since I have no family, you can just give the usual gifts to *me*."

Because they were in a temporary camp Lizah had no wickiup for Andres to tie the traditional gift horse near. He had acquired the animal just that afternoon after the sharp battle with the American army supply train near Van Horn. A medium-sized bay, he was about three years old and showed a goodly share of thoroughbred blood. He had belonged to the lieutenant he had shot during the battle, probably a gift from a well-off family back East somewhere. Or maybe he had just had him shipped in from some racing farm in Texas. It didn't make any difference, the bay was his courtship gift to Lizah.

The horse pulled back on the halter as Andres tied him to the bush closest to where Lizah lay sleeping. Afraid the animal would whinny and awaken his beloved, Andres softly patted his nose and stepped away. He stared down at Lizah's figure a few feet away. She was quiet in her blanket, not snoring like the other three women near her. He wanted to touch her, to sing out to the entire world that she was his woman. Lazaro had told him how he had been mesmerized by Carlota that long ago day near Santa Rita when she was fifteen. It hadn't happened exactly that way with Lizah, but he couldn't remember a minute when he was near her that he didn't want her. His woman.

* * *

"Do you think you can go to the town and find out what the Nakai-ye army is planning?" Victorio asked from where he sat on a rock cleaning his carbine.

Andres glanced at Lazaro, then at Lizah. "Yes, my chief," he replied, "I just need to get some Nakai-ye clothes. I can do that on my way." This would be an excellent opportunity to utilize his capability to assume other identities. Once already, in a close battle with United States cavalry, he had given them a bogus order that had helped swing the fight in favor of the People.

"Can you leave today?" Victorio asked.

"Yes, I'll leave at once."

It was October 11, 1880, and they were camped in the Candelarias, a small range of hills about fifty miles south of El Paso. With American forces pursuing them from the north—having permission to cross into Mexico—it was imperative to know what faced them from the south. Counting Mescaleros and a number of renegade Comanches, as well as the women and children who were not on the reservation, their band now numbered close to three hundred, not exactly a number a chief could hide in a barranca. Twenty minutes later he touched Lizah's hand. "I should return in two days."

She nodded, smiling briefly, once again more warrior than wife. But suddenly her light brown eyes softened, a worried look creeping into them. "Be very careful," she said. "I feel much danger in this entire move that Victorio is making. He should take us to the safety of the Sierra Madre, but he listens to the Mescaleros who are more comfortable closer to their own territory. I feel danger south of us, so be vigilant."

He kissed her hand before swinging into the saddle. "I'll be careful."

Andres reached the town of Carrizal, some thirty-five miles south of the Candelarias, early that evening. He had removed his headband and was wearing the sombrero he had acquired about five miles out of town, on the way down the El Paso–Chihuahua City road. It had belonged to a slightly inebriated vaquero, who had been friendly enough until Andres tied him to a scrub tree. He'd also let the Mexican keep his horse, since he had no use for it. The sombrero was essential to his role because his hair was now shoulder length and he needed to tie it up and conceal it. He was posing as an ex-soldier from El Paso del Norte who wanted to join in the hunt for the notorious Victorio.

Carrizal was a sun-baked scattering of single-story light gray adobe buildings sprinkled around a plaza that looked like it just happened, rather than being planned. It was on a tributary of the Rio Carmel. Andres could hear a guitar playing somewhere as he rode into the plaza. After engaging a small boy with a big grin to watch his horse, he entered a cantina, sidled up next to a soldier at the bar, and ordered a glass of tequila. He sipped quietly for several minutes before asking the soldier, "Where's the army around here?" in his best border Spanish.

The soldier, a corporal, replied, "All gone with Colonel Terrazas three days ago."

"What do you mean?"

"Terrazas came through with about three hundred soldiers and civilians and everyone here joined him. I was sick or I'd have gone. Now I'm in charge of the local garrison. Me and three privates." He laughed. "They ought to make me an officer."

Andres had read something in an old newspaper about Governor Terrazas of Chihuahua, a very rich man. "Do you mean the governor is in command?"

"No, his brother, Joaquin. Skinny, mean bastard. Been chasing and killing those murdering Indians for years. He'll find that damned Victorio and hang his scalp in the governor's mansion in Chihuahua City. You can bet on it."

Andres told him he was a scout and wanted to join Terrazas's command. "You know where he's headed?" he asked.

"One of his sergeants told me they had come all the way from Casas Grande and the Sierra Madres, and that the colonel thinks old Victorio might be holed up over in the Sierra de los Pinos mountains close to the Texas border. That's about seventy miles east of here."

Andres bought him a drink and they traded small talk for a few minutes before he said, "Well, I suppose if I'm going to find Terrazas I'd better get going."

The corporal grinned. "What's your hurry? He'll be out there tomorrow and a week from tomorrow. I know a place close by with some pretty *chiquitas* who are pretty lonely with all the men gone."

"No thanks, my friend," Andres replied. "It's cooler riding at night." He drained his drink and departed. His horse needed a meal and some rest, as did he. About six hours should suffice. He had spotted a livery stable on the way into town. He could probably just curl up in the straw beside his horse.

* * *

Andres arrived at Victorio's camp site in the Candelarias at just after sunup to find the place deserted. He looked around, but most of the sign had been wiped clean. Finally, on a rock close to where he and Lizah had slept, he found a small piece of red cloth from the bolt he used to make his bandanas. It was held down by a stone and below it, in white war paint, an arrow pointed east. Lizah! But again, why east? Had the Mescaleros once more talked Victorio into going into the barren desert with its small ranges of hills? Or had the chief received word that Terrazas was coming from the west? East could also mean Texas. The corporal in Carrizal had also told him that American forces of unknown size would soon come down from El Paso. Maybe they had arrived at or near the Candelarias, forcing Victorio to move. If the chief could double back into Texas on a night move, he could confuse everyone. It was about seventy-five miles to the Quitman Mountains across the Rio Grande and United States border, a two day march with the women and children.

Yes, that would be a brilliant move. He could then hole up in the Quitmans for a few days, then move up north through the Guadalupes into the Sacramentos, the home range of the Mescaleros. He would try to find their trail. But tracking was one of his short suits, something that took all those years of training that was required of Apache boys to learn the art.

However, Lizah had given him a good introduction.

He found some sign and followed it, but soon it split and then split again, finally fading in the sand. As usual, Victorio had divided his group into several smaller parts to avoid detection. He was still the wiliest leader in the field. Damn, Andres thought, what a general the chief would have made in the war! He'd sure have given Jeb Stuart, Wheeler, Nathan Bedford Forrest, Merritt, Custer, and the rest, a run for it.

Now Andres had to make a choice. He decided to go straight to the Quitmans and hope the People would be in the same camp site they had used previously. It was too bad that no one was literate, so that a written message could have been left for him. It was a good thing he'd packed everything in his saddlebags before going to Carrizal.

He should give his horse another break, then move right on. The information about Terrazas would be vital to the chief, giving him another good reason to remain north of the border. Victorio's problem was that his party had almost no ammunition, so unless some kind of a raid was made against a military unit or a town where they could find a well-stocked hardware store, they couldn't afford any kind of a major clash with an armed enemy.

The Quitman mountain hideout showed no sign of recent occupancy by anyone, let alone a party as large as Victorio's. Andres spent part of the next day riding through the hills, checking the other place he thought the chief might use if he had come to the Quitmans. He didn't bother with the south end of the hills because Fort Quitman with its pony soldiers was nearby, and he didn't think Victorio would be *that* bold. No, the chief must have headed southeast into Mexico, possibly toward the Sierra de los Pinos or the other smaller mountains that formed a chain running to the south—an isolated eruption on the flat face of the unforgiving desert. He spent another day searching southward through this range, growing more concerned as he went.

Where could they be?

Finally, near dusk, he rode into a canyon and found sign—a toy medicine cord that some child had probably dropped. Anxiously looking around, he spotted a touch of red! It was another piece of his red cloth sticking out from under a jagged rock. Beside it was another war paint arrow pointing southeast. Lizah had left another message.

He hurried on, pushing his horse. Some twelve miles later he encountered a small group of lakes. At the largest, Laguna, he found tracks of a number of unshod horses that had cut into and dried in the mud on its bank. The People. Someone had carelessly left sign. And it led to another small range of hills with the peak of Cerro Lagrimas sticking up in the distance. Probably the Hill of Tears, he told himself. A Mescalero who had been a captive and was raised in this part of Mexico had recently given him a thorough orientation and had helped him draw a crude but accurate map.

He was about to camp for the night when he saw the glow of a small fire. Riding into the arroyo he saw three men and their horses. Quickly he announced himself in Spanish. "Hello!"

One, wearing a dirty Mexican Army uniform with sergeant's rank on it, leveled a revolver at him. "Who are you?" he asked abruptly in an Apache accent.

"A newspaper reporter from El Paso del Norte," Andres replied quickly. "I'm down here looking for Victorio."

"Ha!" the sergeant snorted to the two other men. "He's looking for Victorio. Who isn't?"

"May I join you?" Andres asked. In the flickering firelight he was surprised to see that the sergeant's heavily lined features were definitely Apache. His long gray hair was held in a single braid down his back. He was thickset and quite old looking.

The sergeant eyed him warily for a moment, then shrugged. "Do you have money?"

"A little," Andres replied, dismounting and leading his horse to a small sapling and tying the reins to it.

"Bring your cup and you can have some coffee," the sergeant grunted, then said something in a language Andres thought was that of the Tarahumares Indians to the other two men. Turning back to Andres he said, "I am Sergeant Bacho, chief scout for Colonel Joaquin Terrazas." He introduced the two other scouts, who were squatting by the fire.

Could this be the terrible Bacho, the renegade and scout who had been Lazaro's enemy since their childhood? Bacho? In the Mexican army? But what was so strange about that—hadn't he been told that Bacho had been an American army scout when he had tried to murder Lazaro all those years ago with the West column? Why not the Mexican army? He'd find out later. "Why do you say everyone is looking for old Victorio?" Andres asked casually.

"Ha! For three thousand pesos, my Apache *grandson* is looking for him, and he has only three months of age!" He laughed aloud at his own joke.

"What do you mean, three thousand?"

"The reward, Mexican, don't you know about the reward?"

Three thousand! Andres hid his surprise. That huge amount of money would bring out every piece of scum in the West.

Bacho added, "That's for his scalp. But if I find him, I'll cut off his ears to go with his hair. Just like in the Mexican bull ring."

The Tarahumares laughed, so Andres knew they spoke Spanish. "Aren't you Apache?" Andres asked quietly.

"Yes, Chihenne," the older man replied.

"I thought I heard somewhere that Apaches never scalp."

"Ha!" Bacho laughed. "This one does—for money."

"Who's offering the reward?"

"The Chihuahua government."

Andres nodded his head. "Interesting. Does anyone know where Victorio is?"

Bacho shook his head. "That's none of your business. You may be a spy, or just a reward hunter like everyone else."

Andres found a smile in the irony. "I assure you that I'm the last newspaperman in the world who would want that reward."

"There are many liars in this world."

"Is Colonel Terrazas anywhere near these parts? I'd like to interview him for my newspaper."

Bacho shrugged, spreading his palms. "Half his command here, half there. Maybe within one, two hours. Not far away. I go to him when light comes."

Andres moved out to the south at dawn to search through the chain of hills, the Sierra Comenos, the Magueys, and the Puerto Frios, a search that would take him at least all day. He had to hurry, had to find Victorio. Now even more. This Joaquin Terrazas was apparently an unrelenting leader who knew what he was doing. God, Lizah, tell me where you are! And tell Victorio where this formidable enemy is, that's your gift. Use it, woman!

He had toyed with killing Bacho and the other two scouts. There might even have been some kindred justice in avenging the Wolf's attempt on his father's life. But that would have been no more than plain murder itself. The news about the reward was particularly unsettling. Three thousand pesos was such a huge sum that every man-hunter imaginable would be in the chase. And a lot of them would be in Terrazas's command. Terrazas. The Mexican colonel was the heart, the spur, of this whole campaign.

At a little after three in the afternoon he stood on a small precipice on the west edge of the Comenos, searching the chaparral to the south and west with his binoculars. It was a hot day and the shimmering sands were emitting wavy lines of heat, distorting the images he picked up. To the northwest he noticed an elongated blur with three peaks, probably Tres Castillos—Three Castles. Scanning back southward he suddenly noticed a telltale spot of dust that could be created only by large numbers of something moving northwestward.

A herd of cattle?

Not likely at this time of year.

Terrazas?

His breath quickened. He stared hard through the glasses, but couldn't define anything. He should—

"Hello, Andres."

He whirled to see Lazaro standing a few yards away. Two of the chief's warriors were at his side, as was Lizah. She hurried to Andres and touched his hand. "I did my best to tell you where we were heading," she said warmly. "Did you find my messages?"

He was so glad to see her! "I found two," he replied. Turning back to his father he asked, "Where's Victorio?"

Lazaro pointed with his nose to the west. "Out there somewhere with the main body. Those Mescaleros led him astray and now he's trying to circle back toward the Sierra Madres. He left me as a rear guard, but without ammunition we'll all die. Therefore, I raided a hacienda and filled our saddlebags with bullets." He pointed back to his horse, which was now surrounded by another fifteen warriors.

"Do you know about Terrazas and his large army?"

"Only that there are many Nakai-ye pursuing us."

Andres told them everything he had learned, causing Lazaro to scowl. Handing the chief the binoculars, he pointed to the dust sign he had spotted. "Could that be Victorio?"

Lazaro nodded his head. "Yes. This was to be our first meeting place, but otherwise it was to be the place of three hills."

"Tres Castillos."

Lazaro nodded again, handing the glasses to Lizah. Moments later she exclaimed, "I see two clouds of dust!"

Taking the binoculars, Andres quickly picked up another puff of what looked like dust east of the low-lying land mass of Tres Castillos. Two columns perhaps? "It could be Terrazas following them," he told his father.

Lazaro turned, snapping, "Arnoldo!"

Immediately a lithe warrior of about eighteen with bright black eyes and an eager expression ran up from the horses. "Arnoldo has the fastest pony," Lazaro explained. "And he is a natural tracker." He told the warrior to go straight toward Tres Castillos to scout both dust signs, then return and meet them at the next hill. "There." He pointed to a peak three miles to the north.

Andres looked at his crude map. The hill was called Cerro Tosisi-hua. He pulled out his watch. With as much riding as he had to do, Arnoldo would have to hurry to get it done in daylight.

Andres touched Lizah's cheek and she turned to smile at him. Tired as they were, neither of them had been able to fall asleep as the chilly October night dragged on. It had been so pleasant to be reunited with her after even a few days' separation, their first since the marriage day. He loved her so very much. Suddenly she sat up in her blanket. "I should be with my chief, not here with Lazaro. I feel a terrible danger for him and the People, and I'm not there to warn him."

"Is it your Power telling you?" he asked.

"I just feel it."

"Arnoldo should certainly have returned by now."

"That may be part of it." She shuddered, shaking her head. "I should have stayed with Victorio."

Andres nodded in agreement. It didn't look good. Their small party had pitched a hasty camp at the foot of Cerro Tosisihua as planned, and Arnoldo would have easily been able to locate them. Something *was* wrong. "I'm going to talk to Lazaro," he said, climbing out of his blanket.

His father was sitting alone, staring into the embers of the tiny fire. Seating himself beside him, Andres could feel the torment going through the chief's mind: *If* he hadn't gone off to raid for ammunition he'd be with Victorio now. *If* he hadn't sent Arnoldo, but had taken his party to the dust clouds . . . other ifs. Andres spoke quietly, trying to ease the burden. "Maybe everything is all right and Arnoldo is just spending the night with Victorio—or perhaps his horse went lame. There could be many reasons why he isn't back."

"No," Lazaro replied quietly. "There is serious trouble. I know it."

"You couldn't chase dust clouds."

"No. Now I'm forced to wait here." Lazaro turned from the fire. "I'm glad you are with me, my son."

Andres nodded, feeling the warmth of the simple words. All at once he remembered Bacho and told of encountering him farther north.

Lazaro shook his head. "I believe he is the worst Chihenne I've ever known. I should have made sure I killed him years ago."

It was almost ten o'clock the next morning before Arnoldo returned, his horse spent, a nine-year-old Apache boy riding behind him on the pony. He told them the terrible truth: "Victorio and his party reached Tres Castillos just ahead of the Nakai-ye soldiers, just in time to find some shelter behind rocks on the southern hill. It was before I got there, so I had to wait until morning, hoping to reach Victorio. But I couldn't because the Nakai-ye attacked. The boy told me what happened. He is Mata, son of Gallo. I found him wandering in the desert after the battle. It's terrible. Many of the People are dead, including women and children. The rest are captured." He paused, his voice choking. "Victorio is dead."

Lizah's hand flew to her mouth to stifle a cry of anguish.

Lazaro groaned, a look of pain crossing his face. He beckoned to the boy. "Come here, Mata. Tell me what happened."

The boy's face was grave and his voice caught in a periodic hiccup as he stood in front of the tall chief and began to speak in a hushed voice. "I, I hid in the rocks this morning when the Nakai-ye came. I was afraid."

"That's all right, my boy," Lazaro said gently. "Go on."

All of the warriors crowded round, straining to get every word. The only other sound was that of the soft whinny of a hobbled pony. Mata continued, "The Nakai-ye started shooting at, at us yesterday afternoon as the sun went behind the hill. Victorio gave the order to build a fort of rocks and we all, including my mother and me, helped. There was some shooting during the night, but our warriors had only a few bullets—"

Lazaro groaned.

"At dawn the Nakai-ye attacked with many soldiers, but we had nothing for the guns and soon they, they were on us and it was bloody. My hiding place was close to Victorio, so I saw what happened to him. With Nakai-ye all around him, he took his knife and stabbed himself in the top of his stomach. Soon the soldiers shot him several times too, and then they cut off his, his hair. I got sick, but they didn't see me. All around they cut off the hair of the dead and wounded, including the mothers and children. . . . "

Scalping had to be the most hideous, repulsive act ever devised, Andres thought angrily as he listened. He held Lizah's hand tightly as she tried to contain a groan.

Mata hiccuped again and continued, "Many more of the women and children were taken prisoner, but I stayed hidden until I could slip away. Then I ran as hard as I could until I fell in the sand and saw Arnoldo on his pony."

"You're sure Victorio is dead?" Lazaro asked.

"Yes, chief, I saw it."

Everyone was shocked, trading glances of pain, disbelieving. How could he be dead? Three of the warriors whose wives and children had been in the group at Tres Castillos plied the boy with questions, but he blankly told them he didn't know if they had been killed. Lizah fingered her rifle, saying softly, "If I had been there, my Power could have saved them."

"And if I had stayed at his rear guard, I may have saved them," Lazaro added.

"No, Father," Andres said. "Don't take the blame. What good would you and your warriors have been with just a few bullets? Now you're alive to fight."

Mata spoke up. "There are others who were not there, two smaller war parties. Maybe twenty-five or thirty warriors each."

Lazaro's eyes narrowed. Nodding his head slowly, then more vigorously, he spoke in a low voice. "Yes, I will fight. I'll fight like no one the White Eyes and Nakai-ye have ever known. They'll all pay."

Several warriors responded strongly, throwing their fists in the air. "Yes, chief, we kill!" "When?" "Can we go *now*?"

Lazaro crossed his arms, staring off toward Tres Castillos. "They'll take the captives to different places, dividing them up like horses. But at least they'll live. We can't attack such a big body. No, we will fight our own way." He pointed to one warrior after another. "Find the others. You, Mano Azul, ride north to your people at the Mescalero reservation. You, Delgado, go to Ojo Caliente and the Black Range to round up our wounded. Arnoldo, when your pony is rested, go to the Sierra Madre. . . . "

Once more posing as a Mexican journalist, Andres had heard that Colonel Terrazas would be coming up the El Paso–Chihuahua City road to Carrizal exactly ten days after the massacre of Victorio and his band. Lazaro's eyes had gleamed at the news. The trap was carefully laid at a point where the low hills came in close to the road, affording good cover. Minus the couriers the chief had dispatched to recruit additional warriors, the band was made up of the same warriors as it had been the day of Victorio's death.

Five days earlier, long enough to determine that no more Nakai-ye were observing the Tres Castillos area, Lazaro had led them into the massacre site. It had been grisly. The seventy-seven scalped and otherwise mutilated bodies were already beginning to decompose. The odor was terrible, the horror of so much death unacceptable. The warrior named Arturo found the body of his wife with most of the hair skinned off the top of her head and her face bashed in. He had lost control of the respected Apache self-restraint and had wailed openly. The other warriors' wives and children were missing, meaning they were probably prisoners. Victorio's body wasn't found, causing them to wonder if it had been further mutilated or carried away by Terrazas's soldiers.

Now this trap. If Terrazas was truly going to be in this party, Andres thought, God forbid what will happen to him.

Several boulders sat firmly emplaced on the edge of the ridge where the bank came closest to the highway. Behind them, the warriors watched quietly as a small contingent of soldiers approached from the south. Andres glanced over at Lizah across the dusty road and nodded his head. She gave him a return nod, then turned back to the chore at hand. He knew she was still grieving heavily, but didn't show it outwardly. She had told him that Victorio had been like a father to her.

Lazaro was in the center, next to him, his face grim, the white war paint on his cheeks a harsh contrast against his dark, sunburnt skin. Andres felt a surge of pride as he studied his father. In spite of the weight of losing his good friend, Victorio, and many of his warriors, Lazaro had seemed to cast away his years in the past few days. He ignored his limp and seemed indefatigable. The fire of a man on a mission lit his eye and his energy seemed to touch everyone in the party.

Lazaro made a slight signal as the Mexicans drew near.

Andres counted them. Only nine. He trained his binoculars on the leader, feeling the tension rise. It wasn't an officer, so the information about Terrazas was probably wrong. No, it was . . . *Bacho!* He put the glasses aside and trained his carbine on the renegade. But only for a moment. Moving quickly to Lazaro's side, he told him who was leading the enemy party and handed him the glasses.

Lazaro stared through the binoculars, his eyes narrowing, his mouth set tightly. *Bacho!* It had all come down to this with his longtime enemy. He flashed back over the years to his boyhood, seeing the taunting expression on his competitor's young face. It seemed they had always been antagonists, and he wondered when that word changed to enemies. He remembered when they had the knife fight and he had to cast the troublemaker away from the tribe. . . . and when he had left Bacho for dead after knifing him at Bayard. Now this, the traitor in a *Nakai-ye* uniform! Like almost everything else in the bad man's life, Bacho seemed to try harder than anyone else to be evil. This changed the ambush plan. He had to take care of Bacho personally.

It had been set in the stars from childhood.

He spoke quietly. "Pass the word. No one fires at the leader, Bacho. The others can be killed, but Bacho is my chore." Seeing Andres's look of concern, he added, "This meeting with my old enemy rises above simple vengeance."

"What are you going to do?" Andres asked.

"Kill him."

Lazaro trained his sights on the oncoming man in the sergeant's uniform. He should just shoot him and let the others kill the rest of his soldiers. This was war and a leader should always remain cold, never allowing his feelings to interfere with the mission. But this was Bacho. . . .

The enemy group was drawing closer, their conversation trickling up to the war party. Closer, closer. . . . When the Nakai-ye were within fifty yards, Lazaro eased his large frame around the boulder and down the bank toward the road. Holding up his Sharps carbine, he stepped into the middle of the highway. At that instant, fifteen rifles exploded and continued to fire. A black horse reared, throwing its rider. Another horse turned as the soldier riding it, trying desperately to escape the wrath of the furious gunfire, was slammed out of the saddle. In another few moments all eight soldiers in Bacho's party were either on the ground or slumping over in death.

Bacho had reached for his rifle the moment he noticed Lazaro standing in the road, but when the fusillade of shots began he had jerked around, looking up at the nearby boulders. Turning back to Lazaro as his horse shied, he started to bring the weapon up, but Lazaro calmly shot him twice in the chest.

Instantly the warriors swarmed down the banks to make sure every one of the soldiers was dead. Reaching the slumping Bacho, Arturo, the warrior who had found his slain wife at Tres Castillos, let out a roar of anger. "Victorio's saddle!" he shouted. "He must have killed Victorio! Bacho killed Victorio and has his saddle!" As Lazaro reached the dying renegade, Bacho looked up at him with hate, trying to speak, but emitting nothing other than a gasp as he fell from his horse.

Arturo pounced on him, jerking a thong from his neck. "Victorio's medicine cord!" he shouted. Whipping out his knife, he yanked Bacho's head back and slashed him across the throat. All of his suppressed pain exploded as he slashed and slashed, blood spurting everywhere, until the renegade's head was severed. Another warrior, then another, and finally a third joined Arturo with flashing blades. Andres watched grimly, standing beside the impassive Lazaro, as pieces of Bacho's body were hacked off: fingers, hands, a whole foot. Blood was everywhere, smearing the knife wielders. When Arturo cut off the penis and scrotum with two swift slices, it looked like a scarlet flood. Arturo held the genitals aloft and let out another roar of rage. Turning, he flung them into a nearby rock. Within a few more minutes, the largest intact body part was a shoulder. In a final gesture of revenge, Arturo tore the heart from its chest cavity, bit into it, and threw it high in the air.

Andres looked up to see Lizah watching impassively. It was the most sanguineous, most savage event he had ever witnessed. For a moment he thought of his mother and her eternal use of the word "savage" when she spoke of the People. But Carlota had never seen seventy-seven bodies as mutilated as those at Tres Castillos. Nor had she ever seen a mate's head without its scalp, its face smashed in death.

In the same amount of time, the other warriors had scalped the eight soldiers who completed the Mexican party. Each bloody scalp was stuffed into the mouth of its owner, a ghastly message to those who would find the remains.

"Enough!" Lazaro finally commanded. "Get their horses, guns, and ammunition. We must go."

As he mounted his pony, Lazaro heaved a deep sigh. In the Way of the People, one had to wander in the Happy Place forever with whatever parts of his body that were present at the time of death. Which meant that Bacho wouldn't even be a person. He didn't personally like what he had just witnessed, but he could no more restrain his warriors from venting their violent anger than he could stop the sun from rising—particularly the terribly bereaved Arturo.

Now his course was truly clear. He would lead his warriors across this country like no other chief before him, not even Victorio. He would kill Nakai-ye wherever he found them, and Blue Coats as well. Not just White Eyes, but the black-faced ones who also came in the Blue Coats. His party would remain small, and he would move fast, stealing fresh mounts, ammunition, and food as he went, sparing nothing.

Watching as the Nakai-ye army horses were rounded up, he felt his Power flow through his body as it hadn't done in many summers. He couldn't remember ever feeling stronger.

27

"I must get some more pencils," Andres said half aloud as he wrote the date in his journal with the stub he had been carefully preserving for over a week.

> Nov. 20, 1880. As we wait to attack a Mexican pack train north of Casas Grandes, I must comment on what an Albuquerque newspaper has described as "Lazaro's Raid." I doubt that any American Indian chief of my father's age, which by his account is sixty-seven summers, has ever performed such an amazing feat of arms over such a large area with such a small number of warriors. And on horseback, often at night, sometimes over seventy miles in one day. Just to ride a hard twenty miles and rest is an accomplishment few men his age can perform. To ride that far, be firmly in command, and able to fight at the head of his warriors—that is a miracle! In these few weeks since the Bacho incident he has led us north to the Sacramentos in New Mexico, up to Ojo Caliente country, savaged the river valley, then down through the Black Range to Willows Country and Santa Rita, thence west into Arizona, and finally back over the border and into Mexico. We have fought fourteen skirmishes with troops, mostly the Negroes who *can* fight, and we have won all but two that were draws. We have killed at least forty Americans and probably an equal number of Mexicans so far. We have also captured over two hundred horses and mules while eluding over a thousand troops and several hundred civilians. And part of this time, Lazaro had as little as fifteen warriors and never more than forty. I am proud to be the son of such an extraordinary leader. But I feel this campaign is nearing its end. . . .

The pack train they had ambushed three hours earlier had been smaller than they had anticipated. Still, its booty was a valuable addition to the war party's meager supplies. Safely hidden in one of Lazaro's old camp sites at the edge of the Sierra Madres, the thirty-two warriors were perched around a fire waiting for the division of the train's contents. It was quite cold, but everyone's spirits were high in expectation.

Finally Lazaro gave a signal and Arnoldo led the first mule to the edge of the group. The pack was already loosened so it took only moments to open it and spread out its contents. It contained mostly clothes, shirts and pants, and several pairs of boots. Only the shirts were usable, and were quickly divvied up. Next came exactly what was most needed: a pack of ammunition, which was immediately passed out to eager hands. The next mule's load was more of the same. The warriors lined up and filed past as Arnoldo and another young warrior handed out an equal number of bullets to each one. They would swap later to get the right calibers. The next pack was silver ore, useless. As was the next one. But the following load was highly valuable—thirty rifles, which were quickly handed out. Even though every man had a repeating carbine, he could pass a rifle on to a relative or barter with it. Another load was of cooking utensils and more clothes that the People didn't wear. The final packs contained gold ore.

Andres examined the ore, guessing that there could be a small fortune in the cowhide packs. He immediately thought of his mother and her long fixation on the gold in Giant's Claw. As Lazaro told Arnoldo to leave the gold alone, Andres leaned close to him and said, "We can buy a lot of ammunition and other valuable things with this metal."

Lazaro frowned at him, scolding, "You know the yellow rock is sacred, the tears of Ussen."

"Yes, Father, but this gold has already been disturbed and removed from Mother Earth. It isn't quite the same."

Lazaro shook his head. "Never will I permit any use of it."

Lizah tugged at his sleeve. "Don't argue with your father. It's the Way."

Andres nodded his head. "It was stupid of me to question you, Father."

Later Lazaro told Lizah and his son he wanted to talk to them alone. They walked quietly in the brisk moonlight to a clear space away from the camp where Lazaro sat on a large rock and sighed tiredly. "My son, I've reached an important decision. Winter is here and our warriors need to be with their families. I should also be with my wife and the rest of the Chihenne. Now, as much as ever, they need a chief. And I'm tired. I've avenged Victorio and proven that the People can fight as no other. As you know, the White Eyes have offered amnesty if we come in voluntarily. Tomorrow I will tell the warriors that it's time to go to San Carlos."

Andres pursed his lips. He wasn't about to become a reservation Indian. He'd given up his life with Americans to be an Apache warrior and going to San Carlos wasn't part of it. In fact San Carlos had been a major factor in his changeover. He hated to hear his father's next words. "I expect you and Lizah to come with me."

Andres drew in a deep breath and blew it out. Since first meeting his father, he had never failed to obey him. Quietly he said, "I can't come in with you."

"Why not?"

"I swore to fight, not sit on my blanket."

"There is much you can do for the People. You can teach them to write what you call the letters, the marks of the words. If the People are to live with the White Eyes in the future, they must learn to read and write with more than symbols. You're a shaman who can see ahead, Lizah. Tell him."

She nodded her head slowly in agreement. "Yes, my husband, the chief is right. You know I'd stay out with you and fight forever, but we have been away a long time, and there is much you can do."

Andres looked from one to the other, trying to read the dark shadows that were their eyes. He knew they were unwavering. And he had known this was coming. Finally he said, "Very well, Father, but I won't promise how long I'll stay."

To describe the San Carlos reservation as bleak would be a grotesque understatement. The People referred to it as absolutely the worst place stolen from them in their entire country. No one had ever lived there with any permanence. About the only vegetation was some form of cacti. The insects were terrible, hatching by the millions in the pools alongside the channel of the sluggish river that provided brackish, nearly unpotable water. Clouds of mosquitoes came from the same water except in the cold weather. Gila monsters, centipedes, tarantulas, and the hated rattlesnakes abounded on the reservation. In the summer the temperature could reach 120 degrees and in the winter the place could get as cold as a January mountain peak.

At least parts of most of the Apache clans were living there: the

Nednhi, the White Mountain—also known as the Coyoteros—and the other Chiricahua, the Lipan, Bedonkohe, Yavapais and the Chokonen. The Jicarilla, the Tontos and, of course, the Mescaleros had their own reservations. The Warm Springs lived with Lazaro's Chihenne not far from the Indian agent's headquarters. Many of the men of both clans had not been with Victorio's main body at Tres Castillos and had therefore escaped the massacre.

To Andres, San Carlos was an abomination, a vivid example of the mockery of American government, of the utter disdain in which the life of the Apache was held. He hated the place but he had promised his father that he would try to live among the People and bring knowledge to them in this deplorable environment.

The complete boredom was broken for Andres by his dictionary. Enlisting the aid of Lizah, Tze-go-juni, and Lazaro, as well as young Mata, who had a gift for words, he labored daily at putting the sounds into written form. Just producing a workable alphabet was difficult. In the middle of December Lizah had told him she was pregnant and his spirits had lifted. The news also made him think of his mother. She would be glad to know that she was going to be a grandmother, and with Christmas approaching, he decided to take Lizah to meet her.

"I don't think it's wise," Lizah said when he told her of the plan. "Riding into Silver City could be very dangerous."

"We can be careful," Andres argued. "Arrive at night. I'm getting good at playing roles. I'll be a Mexican miner coming to visit my cousin."

Lizah shook her head. "I still don't think it's wise."

Carlota removed her hat and placed it on the table. The Christmas Eve reception at the mayor's house had been most pleasant. Silver City's elite, which was a far cry below Washington or even Santa Fe society, she reminded herself, had been there in force. Going to the corner of the parlor where she had placed a small Christmas tree, she considered lighting the candles. But she decided against it. Seemed too much trouble, too much effort for just one person. Besides, a lit tree would only nourish the hollow feeling, the holiday loneliness. How many Christmases had she been alone? Too many, far too many. Rafe was back in Washington again for a conference. How could any general, let alone Sherman, hold a conference over the Christmas holidays?

And Andres. . . . How many Christmases had they been apart over the years? Actually not many. He was the one she really missed. God, how she longed for that boy. The damned fool, giving up everything for some stupid ideal. She went to the stove and added some wood. Might as well have some coffee, maybe add a little brandy since it *was* Christmas Eve. She had read where the Orientals, she couldn't remember which ones, went over their accounts and paid off all their bills on New Year's Day. She could do it on Christmas Day. Except that she didn't have any outstanding bills other than the usual ones for the hotel, and her manager could take care of those. Did she owe anyone a favor? No, she repaid everything in one manner or another as soon as possible.

The livery stable that she had opened six months earlier was doing well, as was her horse farm. The blooded stud that she'd gone to Texas to buy in July would put some more quality in the twelve good brood mares that were the core of her small herd. She hoped to have the best line of quarter horses in southwestern New Mexico in another three or four years. All she had to do was win a few of the bigger races and buyers would come from all over.

Yes, her horses. She would go out there early in the morning and pet the pregnant mares, that'd be a good way to start Christmas.

She should go to Mass as well. The church, St. Vincent de Paul's, on West Market, was having a special high mass at noon. It would be something to do. In fact she had a new dress that had just arrived from St. Louis that would be perfect. Going to mass was something she seldom did. It was such a hollow gesture, a farce in reality, since she'd lost her faith so long ago. At least most of her faith.

She thought again of Rafe and how she'd been apart from him for so many years. The stubborn fool still wouldn't consider retiring from the army. There were so many opportunities for a man of his capabilities in this booming country. Look at what she had done, and she was a lowly woman!

Ha! She was making more money than most of the male entrepreneurs. Now, if she could only find that Apache gold she'd be the richest woman in New Mexico. She'd—

The *tap tap* on the door interrupted her thoughts.

"Yes?" she said, going to it. Who would be calling this late on Christmas Eve?

"It's me, Mother," Andres said from the other side.

Her heart jumped. Her son on Christmas Eve! She quickly unbolted the door, ready to crush him in her arms. But her big smile froze as she saw them standing there in the dim light of the hallway. Andres with hair to his shoulders and a red bandana. A heathen necklace around his neck. Behind him wearing some kind of a fur coat was an *Apache woman!*

"Merry Christmas, Mother," Andres said warmly, stepping inside and holding out his arms.

She went into them woodenly, kissing his cheek, her eyes still on the woman.

Andres hugged her tightly for a moment before releasing her. "This is my wife, Lizah," he said brightly.

His wife?

The woman nodded her head, smiling as she said, "Hello" in English.

"We've brought Christmas presents," Andres said pleasantly. "If you'll pour some warm coffee for us, we have much to tell you. We've been waiting down at the livery stable, the *Murphy* livery stable. Is that yours too?"

"Yes," she managed, unable to take her eyes off the woman. Her son had married a savage. Of his own free will he had married a damned Apache! She couldn't, simply could *not* have this woman in her apartment.

Andres tossed his heavy coat on a chair and helped Lizah out of hers. Handing his mother a small newspaper-wrapped package, he said, "Lizah made this for you."

"Merry Christmas," Lizah said. "I don't speak much English."

"That's all right," Andres said. "We can speak Spanish. Lizah's a linguist."

Carlota tore her eyes off the woman and turned to her son, murmuring, "I didn't know they had a Christmas."

"She made it for you and your Christmas, Mother. But first we want to give you *our* present." Andres motioned to a chair. "Sit down, relax, Mother."

She sat stiffly on the edge of the rocking chair.

Andres smiled at Lizah. "Tell her, darling."

Lizah inhaled and let her deep breath out slowly, saying in excellent Spanish, "Andres and I will present you with a grandchild in seven months, Mrs. Murphy."

No, this was all wrong! Her son had thrown away everything she'd given him to play this stupid game and now he was bringing her this savage to tell him she was his wife and that they were going to produce an Apache grandchild! "No," she said, staring from one to the other. "This is not true. None of this is true."

Andres's smile faded. "What do you mean? Of course it's true. We've ridden all the way from San Carlos in the cold to tell you."

"No, no!" Carlota dropped her face into her hands, letting out a sob.

"Mother—"

"No!" She dropped her hands, blazing at Lizah, "Get out! Do you hear? Get out of my house, you, you Apache savage!"

Lizah blinked, looking into Carlota's hate for several moments before shifting to Andres in askance. Carlota watched as she drew herself up and quietly turned to walk erectly out of the apartment.

"*What are you doing?*" Andres shouted.

"How dare you?" Carlota shot back. "How dare you make a woman like that your wife and bring her to me with your unborn child as calmly as if you just married the president's daughter?"

Andres's eyes narrowed as he ground out, "She's more than some damned president's daughter, but you're never going to have a chance to find out why!" He grabbed the coats and stomped out of the apartment.

Carlota stood stunned, staring at the empty doorway. How could he do this to her? How could he? Suddenly she wanted to run after him and call him back. But she couldn't. And all at once the tears burst from her eyes and streamed down her cheeks.

The contents of the package spilled from her hand—a beautiful turquoise necklace. She leaned down to pick it up. There was a small card that read, "Merry Christmas, Mother."

28

June 28, 1881

Andres paced, smoking another cigaret from the dozen his father had given him. Since he seldom smoked, mostly only at important councils when it was customary, he wasn't used to the acrid taste of tobacco. He had been quite surprised on his first visit to the People to find that a so-called peace pipe wasn't smoked, as he'd read that Indians of all persuasions did at ceremonies and councils. He blew out another puff and stared in the direction of the birthing post. It was over a hundred paces away and hidden from his view. Lizah would never scream, so he didn't know anything about what was happening. "Many things can go wrong, you know," he said for the third time.

And for the third time Lazaro, who was cleaning his carbine, tried to ease his son's concern by replying, "Tze-go-juni has birthed hundreds of babies and Benita has brought many into life. Your Lizah is in good hands, my son."

In making the decision to cease being an American, Andres now relied on Apache custom in almost everything. But, with the life of his beautiful wife and their unborn child at stake, doubt was assailing him. He had even considered taking her to Tucson where he could once more use one of his false identities and have an American physician deliver the baby in a place free of germs. But Lizah wouldn't hear of it, actually getting quite angry at him for even suggesting it.

"How would it look to the People," she had scolded, "for a shaman to do such a stupid thing? We have the knowledge and the Power right here. How many thousands of our Chihenne have been born healthy in the Way?"

He didn't mention a doctor again. Blowing out another puff of the tobacco smoke, he said, "I've decided to name him Taza, Taza Murphy."

Lazaro nodded his head, allowing a quick smile. "Enjuh."

"He'll be another son for you."

"Enjuh, I like that."

Neither of them mentioned the fact that the child might be a girl. Both Tze-go-juni and Lizah had declared it would be a boy, and they should know. Several more minutes passed as Andres continued to fret. Apache men and women did not scream or cry out in pain, but a newborn child had no such knowledge or training. Surely something was wrong. He should ignore everyone and just run over there and find out—

"Waaaahh!"

Andres jerked around to stare in the direction of the birthing post. He turned to go but his father caught his arm, saying "No, the women don't want you there."

Twenty minutes later Benita brought a red-faced little boy to them, a tiny boy whose next protest was a vigorous, high-pitched Apache war cry.

In spite of having a new son, time continued to drag for Andres during the following year. Finally his restlessness and feeling of futility led to a new plan for war. "If we do this for the rest of our lives," Andres said earnestly to the twenty-one young men who sat listening to him by his wickiup, "we'll be nothing, dead waste, a disgrace to the People. Learning to farm and raise cattle is one thing, but not *here!*"

"But Lazaro wants us to remain on the reservation and be peaceful," a short warrior of twenty-five named Delgadito said.

"No one respects our chief more than I," Andres replied. "He has to think of the women and children, the older men and the infirm. I say we should bolt just as Geronimo and his Bedonkohes have done. Lazaro can stay here and lead our people in the quiet Way, and we will fight. If we're ever to get out of San Carlos, we have to force the White Eyes to make the change. Besides, we need to hone our fighting skills again."

"But if we go out, they'll cut the rations to our families," Domingo, a warrior of twenty-two, said. He had already fathered three children. "They warned us."

Arnoldo, the scout who had brought in the boy Mata from Tres Castillos, spoke up, raising his fist. "I go with Red Head!"

A chorus of agreements followed from the others.

"Where will we go?" Domingo asked.

"Back into New Mexico. We'll make our camp in Giant's Claw. You may have heard my father speak of it in telling about Silsoose. We'll raid along the big river and when we are tired of killing White Eyes, we'll go south and kill Nakai-ye. Our war will end only when we get justice!"

This time many fists jammed the air as "Enjuh! Enjuh!" erupted from the warriors. At the responses, Lizah, wearing Taza's tsach with the twelve-month-old boy on her back, walked up to the rear of the men and nodded slightly to Andres. "I go with my husband," she announced as the buzz of excitement settled down.

"When do we leave, Red Head?" Domingo asked.

"Tomorrow night when the darkness comes," Andres replied.

It was shortly after midmorning the next day when three members of the tribal police found Andres currying his favorite horse at the corral. "You are under arrest," their leader said. "Come with us, Red Head."

Andres had nothing but disdain for the so-called men who were on the tribal police force. He regarded them as two notches lower than the Apache scouts who worked for the army. These particular policemen were Chiricahua, all the more reason to be scornful of them. If their proud dead chief, Cochise, could see them he'd roll over in his grave, as the saying went. "Why am I being arrested?" he asked.

"For planning a revolt," the policeman replied nastily.

Andres eyed his Colt revolver hanging over a nearby post, but he knew he'd never get to it fast enough. He also knew he could never outfight the three policemen. They were Apache and better at hand-to-hand combat than he was. "What makes you think I'm planning a revolt?" he asked, remaining cool, letting the lawyer part of him take over.

"One of your Chihenne warriors told us."

"Which one?"

The leader was one of those small people who like to exert authority when given a little power. He scowled, grabbed Andres's elbow. "It doesn't matter. Come with us!"

Andres shook off his grip. "Keep your hands off me. May I go to my wickiup to tell my wife?"

The policeman glowered at him. "No tricks."

"No tricks. You can keep your rifles on me every moment."

Striding through the Chihenne village with the shorter tribal policemen trying to keep up, Andres went directly to his wickiup on the far slope. Lizah was outside in the shade of a lonely tree, sewing a buckskin shirt for little Taza. She looked up at his footsteps, taking in the policeman and the situation in a glance. "They are taking you to the guardhouse," she said flatly.

"Yes," Andres replied in English. "The charge is planning a revolt. Someone in our group may have turned me in for planning the breakout. Find out who. Be sure Lazaro knows exactly what has happened."

"I'll tell him when he returns."

He touched her cheek gently and smiled into her eyes. "I love you."

She nodded, keeping her remarkable reserve in front of the policemen. To the leader she said coldly, "If anything happens to my husband, you will be in the Happy Place with no head."

Agent J. C. Tiffany, a paunchy bald man with a short beard, spoke from outside the bars of Andres's cell. "You wouldn't listen, would you, Murphy? I told you to keep your mouth shut and go on back to New Mexico where you belong. But you have to play the martyr, don't you?"

Andres didn't answer, just eyed the agent coolly.

"Let me tell you what's in store for you, half-breed. You're going to be tried by tribal court and they're going to send you to Alcatraz for a long time. Then we'll see how high and mighty you are."

"Your kangaroo court hasn't got the authority to send me to an army prison, Tiffany."

"General Willcox has."

"What do you mean?"

"The general has already set a precedent by sending three former troublemakers there. You'll be easy—you're a traitor."

Andres disliked the agent intensely. Tiffany had his hands in all of the graft that went on in the issue of rations. He knew the man was totally crooked, working hand in hand with the Tucson Ring. He had documented everything he had discovered, and that was one of the reasons for the charge. Tiffany knew he had been recording information at each weekly ration issue. Andres laughed. "Have you been drinking too much of that cheap whiskey you're selling on the sly?"

Tiffany looked like he was going to explode, but found his aplomb. "You know, Murphy, there's an old saying about your kind of half-breed. You're part Mexican, part Apache, and all son-of-a-bitch."

Andres laughed outright.

The agent went on, "Tell you what, Murphy. You stop this stupid Apache role you're playing and go on back to New Mexico, and I'll drop the whole affair."

Andres moved close to the bars, looking around as if he didn't want anyone to hear what he was going to say. He wiggled his forefinger and Tiffany moved closer. After a short pause, Andres said loudly enough for all of the policemen within shouting distance to hear, "Kiss my arse, you bastard!"

The so-called trial wasn't even worth being called a travesty of justice. The court was composed of chiefs of each representative clan on the huge reservation, sitting in closed session. Andres was surprised; since most of these clans had never gotten along before coming to the controlled existence of San Carlos, they could hardly be expected to live in harmony at this time. Nor could they be expected to agree, even on a tribal court. But this time they were in full accord on one point: Andres was guilty of inciting a revolt. There would be no dissent because Lazaro could not serve on the court, since he was both father and chief to the accused.

When Agent J. C. Tiffany brought the charges before the court, Andres sat at a table off to the right of the witness box. Espinay, chief of the Tontos, was the spokesman or so-called president of the court. Andres guessed that he was most certainly under direct orders to find the defendant guilty, and there was little doubt that all of the other members had been in one way or another induced to go along. An army captain from General Willcox's headquarters was also in attendance, obviously to give credence to the tribal court.

There were no witnesses.

Andres broke into the discussion. "Because I am a lawyer, I am representing myself in defense against these charges."

Chief Espinay scowled at him. "Be quiet, prisoner."

"But I have a right under American law—"

"This is Apache law!" Espinay's deep voice boomed.

Andres turned his attention to the army officer. "What about that, Captain? Isn't this United States territory?"

The officer shrugged. "I'm only an observer."

"I want your commanding general to know of this farce. I'm being deprived of due process of the law." He wanted to mention his relationship to Rafe and warn them that he had important connections, but he'd heard that Willcox was jealous of his stepfather, so that would be useless.

The captain merely looked away.

Espinay glanced at each member of the court, who in turn nodded his head. Turning to Andres, the chief said in Apache and then in heavily accented Spanish, "Red Head, you are guilty of revolting and planning a new breakout. You make the young men think of war instead of farming as they should. You will spend five years at the White Eye prison in the water by Cal-i-fornia."

Alcatraz! Andres blinked. Impossible. These somehow bribed leaders couldn't send him to a military prison. As the captain got to his feet to leave, Andres snapped, "Tell Willcox that I appeal this miscarriage of justice!"

"Quiet!" barked Espinay.

Tiffany signaled to the nearest tribal policeman. "Take the prisoner to the guardhouse at once."

The policeman grabbed Andres's arms and pulled him toward the door. Turning, he shouted, "I'll take this to the Supreme Court. You're finished here, Tiffany. Mark my words!" He wanted to say more, tell the bastard that he'd get word to the newspapers, that they had just bought more trouble than they would ever know. But he curbed his temper and said nothing more as he was jerked from the room.

Carlota stared at the letter. It was crudely written in Spanish. She looked up as Natalio shifted from one foot to the other in the hallway of the hotel and said, "Chief Lazaro had me write it. I don't write good."

She scanned the page.

> Dear Carlota,
> Our son, Andres is in tribe jail. Apache court say he guilty make revolt. He go to place in Calyforn call Alkatras. Prison for 5 yeers.

It was signed with a mark, Lazaro's, Natalio told her. "The chief wants you to know how sad this makes him and asks if you can use White Eye friends and husband to help get the son out."

The page blurred back at her. *Impossible!* "What's this all about?" she asked.

Natalio told her rapidly what had taken place, also that Andres had refused to write to her for help.

She knew he would get into serious trouble! She told him it would happen, something would, she knew it! Five years in prison? "When does he go to California?" she asked.

"He left two days ago."

"Is he all right, I mean healthy?"

"Yes, and angry."

She had to know something else that had been on her mind for some time. "His child, is it a boy or girl?"

"A boy. His name is Taza Murphy. One year old now. Chief Lazaro told me to tell you."

She couldn't help but feel a small thrill. A grandson. She'd felt so sorry about her actions that Christmas, but there was nothing she could do about it. A baby boy, probably riding around on his mother's back in a tsach. She thought back to another bright-eyed little boy staring out at the world when he was a year old, watching with those curious eyes, learning words, waiting to have his chance to get out of prison and dash around. She sighed. Now he was going to a real prison called Alcatraz.

She gave Natalio five dollars and thanked him.

Alcatraz!

As soon as he departed, she went to her mahogany desk and wrote to Rafe at his headquarters in the Department of the Platte, asking him to intercede. The second letter was to Richard Hartman in Santa Fe. The former Confederate general and judge was now governor of the territory of New Mexico. She asked that he also use his influence to have Andres freed. The third letter was to the governor of Arizona.

Fifteen days later she had a reply from Hartman. He stated that he had no authority to intercede in the San Carlos justice system. He apologized, ending with, "I am sure that Andres will be out on parole or pardon in the near future."

But she knew Hartman was just easing her pain.

After twenty-one days she began to worry about why she hadn't received a reply from her husband. On the twenty-second day she found out. She was eating her light lunch of soup and a chicken sandwich at shortly after noon when a loud knock on her apartment door interrupted her thinking. Opening it she was greeted by a tall figure in a duster coat and a broad smile. "Hello, darling," Rafael Murphy said, bowing low. "Mind if an old acquaintance comes in and spends a few nights?"

She flew into his arms, holding him tight, kissing him. "Oh, Rafe, why didn't you tell me you were coming? I'd have—"

His kiss drowned her words. It wasn't one of greeting, but one from a long-absent lover whose fires were about to become fully unstoked. His lips moved to her neck, her throat, the swell of her breasts. Finally he murmured, "I adore you, lady."

She pulled back, shaking her head. "You really blow in, don't you?"

He chuckled. "Yup. I'm back to command the Department of Arizona again, or I should say the Department of the Border, since it still encompasses New Mexico. Seems the Apache are acting up again."

Oh, it was so good to have him back! She stroked his cheek. "Where will you be stationed? Not here, right? That would be too much to ask."

"I think I'll make my headquarters at Camp Apache, soon to be Fort Apache. That's north of San Carlos. I'll have a nice house built for us."

Her smile faded. She couldn't leave all of her business interests here in Silver City to go traipsing off to some crude little house on an *Apache* reservation. But she didn't want to talk about it now, and spoil the arousal of this reunion.

As soon as they finished making love, Carlota said, "What have you done about Andres?"

Rafe turned from where he was looking out the window. "Nothing, dear. His trial had nothing to do with my command. For me to meddle with General Willcox's affairs would have been improper. Orlando Bolivar Willcox and I had a disagreement way back in the Mexican War, and he has never forgotten it. It also troubled him that, while he ranked me as a brigadier, I went on to higher command ahead of him. That and the fact that he's a West Pointer and I'm not. Maybe he still resents the fact that I'm part Mexican as well."

"Then that's the reason Andres was railroaded!"

"Maybe not. I'll find out when I get to San Carlos. There may be more to it."

"Can't you just contact the prison authorities and have him paroled?"

He shook his head. "No, my dear. Alcatraz is out of my jurisdiction."

Tears came to her eyes as she snapped, "Well, you can't just let him rot there for five years!"

He took her hand, saying gently, "Don't worry, darling, I'll have him out of there long before that. It's just that I have to follow the rules."

She sighed, wiping the tears from her eyes. "We have a grandson, you know." She had written him about Andres and Lizah coming that time, but hadn't told him about how she rejected them. "Will you see him and write to me about him?"

"Why don't you come with me and see him yourself?"

"I can't, Rafe. There is so much to be done here."

"Nonsense. You have a manager for every business here. You can come and live at Fort Apache with me. I'll be in the field part of the time until I get these renegades under control, but it's pretty there and we'll enjoy the time we have together."

"I'd die of boredom, dear."

He looked deep into her eyes. "You're still my wife. We should be together. Our marriage has been little more than a shadow for twenty years now."

"It's your fault as much as mine. You know I've been busy. You're the one who had to stay in the army and bounce around the damned country like a wild goose."

"The army is my career, you know that."

"Look at the money I've made for us."

He sighed. "We've been over this many times. I believe in what I'm doing, and I'll never be content just making money. I don't need it. I need to do what is best for the army and now the Apache. And I need you."

"Maybe I'll come and visit you some time after you're settled."

He frowned. "That's not good enough, Carlota."

"What do you mean?"

"I didn't want to bring this up until I'd been here for a couple of days, but I guess now's as good a time as any . . . I want you with me as my wife, and I won't accept anything less."

Her temper flared. "What do you mean *you* won't accept anything less? Are you suddenly ordering me around like your *soldiers?*"

His voice remained calm. "I'm just saying that I've put up with your whims long enough. I understood your special love for Andres and I humored you when he was growing up, and after the war was over when you still wanted to be with him. I've even humored you in your more recent desire to stay here in Silver City trying to become the richest woman in New Mexico. But I've had enough. I'll soon be sixty years old, and it's time you shared my life and my bed on a permanent basis, not through the mail."

Carlota shook her head. "I'll not be ordered around, Rafe Murphy. I don't care how many stars you wear on your damned shoulders!"

He caught her arm, gripping it as he looked into her angry blue eyes. "Will you come with me when I leave?"

"No, I absolutely will not."

"Very well, then I'll move along today."

"I don't care if you leave this instant."

He looked at her for several moments, his eyes sad, saying nothing. Finally he said softly, "I love you, Carlota," and quietly reached for his clothes.

29

MAJOR-GENERAL MURPHY RETURNS, blared the Tucson *Citizen.* The front page story described the newly arrived commander as:

> Tall, ramrod straight, and broad-shouldered. He is the epitome of a military officer. His face is stern, his dark eyes alert under black brows. His full burnsides are nearly white. He appears humble, gentle, retiring from the least bit of notoriety. A captain who has served under him for several years said, "No soldier ever surpasses the general in energy, endurance, and indifference to exposure. He uses neither liquor nor tobacco, and no soldier has ever heard a profane or obscene word from his lips. So adverse to ostentation is he that he dresses casually, almost never in uniform. He even rides a mule on many occasions. No low ranking soldier or savage Indian is denied access to him." With the Apache again on the warpath, the Department of Arizona is indeed fortunate to have such a general replacing the incompetent Willcox.

At fifty-nine Rafe was everything the *Citizen* described, but he hated to see such a description in the paper. He tossed it on his desk and turned to Captain Bourke, his aide. "Most of this is nonsense. Good thing the Apaches don't read the papers, they'd fall over in awe and the war would be over in a minute."

The captain laughed. "I'm afraid it won't be as easy as that, sir." He handed over a report. "According to Tiffany, there are about two hundred hostiles on the warpath. A lot of them are of the usual lot—Geronimo, Juh, Chino, but there's a large party of Chiricahua out there under Naiche, Cochise's younger son."

"What's the condition of the Indians on the reservation?"

"Deplorable, sir."

"I want to talk to Chief Lazaro, and after that Agent Tiffany. Please send word to Lazaro that I'll come to his village at midmorning tomorrow. And notify the agent that I'll see him late in the afternoon."

"Why have so many of the People bolted?" Rafe asked.

Lazaro spoke solemnly as they walked through the sunlight. "The bad rations, another White Eye lie. Just a shoulder of a small cow each week for twenty people. A cup of flour for each adult to last a week, small amounts of other things. Not nearly enough."

The chief's comments coincided with other reports he'd received. They talked on about conditions in general until Rafe asked, "What happened to Andres?"

"He was planning to break out. When Tif-fany heard, he sent him to the tribal court. Tif-fany was afraid of Andres, afraid he would tell about his cheating in his White Eye writing. He paid one of my warriors to inform. The man has been banished from my village."

Rafe nodded his head. "Were you planning on taking your people out with Andres?"

"No, Mur-fee, Andres was going against my wishes. I have too many people who are not healthy enough to live down in Mexico now. Besides, I gave my word to stay in after the long raid."

"Was Andres given a fair trial?"

"No, Tif-fany gave the tribal court extra rations for their people and whiskey for themselves."

Rafe drew in a deep breath and blew it out. "But he is guilty."

"Yes, he and his wife would have taken over thirty of my fiercest warriors out. Sometimes he wants to do nothing but fight."

"I'm sorry to hear that. Still, I'll try to get him back here soon."

The conversation moved on to other things and finally, as they returned to the center of the village, Rafe said, "Very soon, my friend, the rations will be increased. I know the People don't like daily roll calls, but it's necessary to order the right amount of rations. In return, I ask that you use your strong power to keep those who are still on the reservation from breaking out."

Lazaro nodded. "I will, Mur-fee. What about those who are out?"

"You can send word that I wish to talk with them, that I want peace."

"Enjuh."

"And, Lazaro."

"Yes?"

"Carlota told me Andres and Lizah have a child. May I see him, please?"

Lazaro's eyes lit up. "Of course. I will send for the woman at once. He is a strong boy, Mur-fee. And . . . Carlota, is she still beautiful, Mur-fee?"

Rafe smiled. "Yes, and still as headstrong as ever."

Lazaro just nodded his head.

At three-thirty that afternoon Rafe was standing in Agent Tiffany's office at the San Carlos headquarters. Looking out the window, he said quietly, "Tell me about Andres Murphy, Mr. Tiffany."

The agent shrugged his thickset body from behind his desk. "There isn't much to tell, General. The tribal court tried him and found him guilty of inciting revolt. He was sentenced to five years in Alcatraz. I know he is your stepson and I thought of notifying you, but decided against it."

Rafe turned from the window. "Why?"

"Since he apparently lost his sanity when he became an Apache and went on the warpath, I thought he would be an embarrassment to you."

Rafe spoke softly. "I believe I'm the one who determines who is an embarrassment to me, sir."

Tiffany shrugged again. "It was an Indian affair, General."

"Not quite, Mr. Tiffany. I have talked to several people and they state that you brought the charges at the trial."

The agent drew in a deep breath and blew it out. "One of the Chihenne whom he was enticing to revolt came to me with the story. He swore it was the truth, but refused to testify."

"Was he a paid informant?"

Tiffany hedged. "I, uh, rewarded him."

"It has been said that you offered Andres Murphy freedom if he would return to New Mexico. Why?"

"Because he is a troublemaker. I don't care if he is your stepson, General. He is no longer a white man, or even a good Mexican. He's a goddamned, festering, war-making Apache killer."

Rafe tugged at his side whiskers. "Could any of this have been about your misconduct of affairs here at the reservation?"

"Sir, are you accusing me of—"

"I am not accusing you of anything at this point, Mr. Tiffany. That will be up to the grand jury that will soon investigate you. And to the Secretary of the Interior, to whom my report of investigation, when finished, will be forwarded."

Tiffany's face grew livid. "I'm a civilian in a civilian capacity here,

General. You have no right to either investigate me, or to report on me. You may leave my office, sir!"

Rafe eyed the agent coolly and slowly nodded his head. Finally he said, "People like you, sir, are the worst excrement on this earth. The worst renegade Indian is a saint compared to someone who cheats at the expense of other human beings."

Alcatraz was a small, bleak, rock island located in San Francisco Bay slightly over one mile from the mainland. Consisting of only twelve acres, the island was discovered by the Spaniards in 1769 when it was literally covered by birds. It was named Isla de Alcatraces, Island of Pelicans. Shortly after it became a United States possession in 1851 it was fortified. Later prison facilities were erected, and at the present, Alcatraz was a military prison housing mostly recalcitrant Indians.

There were generally about forty American Indians from different tribes among the military prisoners, and most of them were there for crimes committed on their reservations. There were four Cheyenne, seven Navajo, three Osage, six Sioux, three Shawnees, four Chickasaws, three Hopi, four Crows, three Pawnees, and a scattering from other tribes. Almost all of the inmates were incarcerated for normal crimes and were from tribes that were at peace with the United States.

Four of the five Apaches from the various clans were there not for normal crimes, but for committing acts of war against the United States. Andres was their leader.

He had a small cell to himself. It was barren, with a narrow bunk, a wash stand and a small table for reading and writing. A straight-backed chair, a straw mattress, a slop jar for elimination, a water jug, and a shelved box for his few clothes were the other items in the cell. It was painted a light gray and had one high window with bars opposite the barred wooden door.

He opened the letter from Rafe and read it eagerly. It was his first information about his family:

> December 2, 1883
>
> My dear son,
>   Firstly, I have just spoken with your wife, Lizah, and also had an invigorating conversation with little Taza. I didn't understand most of what he said, but I'm not as smart as he is. They are both fine, as is Lazaro and his family. The improved ration system on the reservation makes life there more bearable.

Agent Tiffany was castigated by a grand jury and accused of gross malfeasance. If you get to read newspapers, you know that Secretary the Interior Schurz has swung a big axe that severed not only the agent but the Commissioner of Indian Affairs and the Inspector General of the Indian Bureau. The new agent at San Carlos is named Wilcox—not the general, as you can see by the spelling. He seems honest enough. We'll see.

Several bands of Apache are still raiding down in Mexico and I am using my Apache scouts to try and locate them. There is no reason to fight anymore.

I have submitted your case to the Justice Department, recommending your immediate release, but you know how slowly such wheels turn.

I hope life is not too difficult for you there, knowing that any prison must surely be insufferable for anyone such as you.

I remain your Obedient Servant and Stepfather,
Rafael

Andres was surprised at the news. Seldom had the military commander in Apache country been able to effect much change over the representatives of the Indian Agency. He was glad for the People that the rations were better, but in a way he was sorry Tiffany was gone. Because he had already decided to kill the bastard when he got out of prison.

Just before he led a new breakout, which he positively would do.

If, when he got back, there were any warriors left with enough will to fight.

These months in prison had brought him to the realization that his father was just too old to fight anymore. Like a star flashing across the firmament with a bright but fading tail, Lazaro had had his final flash on his big raid. Now he was content to sit on his blanket.

Well, his son wasn't done fighting!

His eyes went back to Rafe's words: *There is no reason to fight anymore.* "That's the thinking of one who is not Apache," he said aloud. "We must *always* fight."

" 'Morning, Cochise," the guard said from the cell door window. "You smoked your peace pipe yet today?" He guffawed.

Jones, the guard, personified Andres's growing dislike for most Americans. Like the scum that had invaded the territories, he was another example of the refuse of the human race. He always jeeringly referred to Andres as Cochise. But he was a valuable asset because he kept Andres's anger burning.

His reply was quiet. "Have you learned to read yet today, Jones?"

"I can read, you goddamned savage," the guard blustered.

"What—cat, dog, cow? Who signs your Xs for you?"

"You want me to come in there and give you some of my billy club?"

"I wish you'd try. I'll make you eat it, you stupid arse."

"I'm reporting this to the warden, you know."

"Good. Now, go away and quit bothering me." The warden knew about his appeal and his connections, so he was safe from beatings. He knew the appeal might take years, but General Hartman back in Santa Fe had promised to lend his support toward a full parole. And now Rafe was working on it. God, how he wanted to get home to Lizah and little Taza.

He turned to the other letter, the one that had just arrived from Silver City. It was from his mother. It expressed concern over his incarceration, then rambled about her business interests in Silver City. Finally it got to the point: " . . . As Christmas approaches, my son, I can't help but remember how terribly rude I was to you and your wife when you came to me that other Christmas. Please accept my sincere apology. I love you so very much. . . . "

He reread the letter and slowly tore it into pieces.

"Bless me, Father, for I have sinned." Carlota uttered the onetime familiar words in the confessional at St. Vincent de Paul's church. It had been so long since she had gone through the ritual that she wasn't even sure it was the right way to initiate a confession. "It has been many years since my last confession," she added softly.

She heard the priest cough slightly behind the window. "The Lord be in your heart and on your lips," he replied, "that you may duly confess all your sins. In the name of the Father, the Son, and the Holy Ghost."

"I confess to Almighty God and to you, Father. I don't know where to begin, what to say."

"Just try to recall your mortal sins, my daughter."

"I haven't committed any mortal sins, unless turning my only son away because he married an Apache is one."

The priest's voice was gentle. "Would you turn him away again?"

Her tone was fervent. "*Never*, Father."

"Please continue."

The words tumbled from her lips. "I've been vain, longed for a man not my husband, not attended church, not received the sacraments, greedy . . . I've hated mercilessly. . . . " She went on, recounting more venial sins. Finally she came to a halt.

"Let's go back to the longing for a man not your husband."

"He was a man I was once very much in love with. It was during the war. . . . " When she finished the brief explanation about Agustin, the priest asked, "Would you want this man again?"

"No, Father."

"Are you ready to attend mass regularly?"

"I, I honestly don't know, Father. I'm so lonely."

"Then let the Lord fill your heart."

"I'll try, Father."

The priest asked her a few more questions, then said, "Here is your penance. Say fifty Our Fathers and one hundred Hail Marys. May Almighty God have mercy on you, forgive your sins, and bring you to eternal life. Amen."

Carlota walked down West Market, pulling her fur coat collar tightly around her throat. This New Year's morning was clear and quite cold. The streets were mostly empty because many people were still home sleeping off their hangovers and other late night revelries. She could have driven up to the church, but she had decided the walk would do her good. Besides, she would have had to get the man at the stable up early to hitch up the buggy.

She felt good, cleansed, after the confession and the early mass. She had been so threatened by going to the confessional, but it hadn't been too bad. She had felt so empty. Rafe had not come home for the holidays. In fact, he hadn't written to her but twice since going to Arizona, and both of those letters had been mostly insistent requests for her to join him. Most importantly, she hadn't heard anything from Andres. And after three letters. Perhaps they didn't let him receive mail, that was probably it.

But deep down she knew it wasn't.

Her son had simply not forgiven her.

That was it.

Oh, how she ached to know how badly they were treating him. She'd asked Rafe, but his curt response had merely stated that Andres was all right. Could she have lost him for good? Her eyes brimmed at the thought as she stopped to let a horse and buggy make a turn past her.

She had thought she would be fulfilled after returning to her religion, but somehow, something was missing. Nothing had really changed in her life. She hadn't even felt a deep emotional reaction from confession or receiving the sacraments. No, she was still hollow. Fifty-eight years old, healthy, a handsome woman with plenty of money and successful businesses, and she had nothing to warm her, no one with whom she could really share anything.

She knew Rafe meant what he said, but she simply couldn't leave her businesses to live in Apache country. No, she needed a new goal, something to which she could dedicate herself, something that would take up her time and energy, stimulate her.

But only the picture of a little black-eyed boy in a tsach came to mind, the grandson she might never see.

As she reached the hotel, the loneliness returned.

30

San Carlos
February 21, 1885

Andres stepped down from the buckboard at headquarters and looked around. He had been in prison for two and a half years, at least two more than would have been necessary had he behaved. But he couldn't stop fighting the prison system. Rafe had done his part by convincing the commanding general of the Division of the Pacific to recommend parole. But on precisely the day that decision was made, he had hit the prison guard, Jones, with his cell chair. When the second recommendation came through eight months later, he had just tried to escape. It was only through the patient perseverance of Rafe that he had been paroled this early.

The United States marshal who had escorted him from Alcatraz unlocked the handcuffs and said, "Well, you're home, Murphy, if you call this dreary looking place home. But then I guess Injuns can live anywhere. I can't say you've been very much fun."

Andres just ignored him as he pulled his valise from the bed of the small wagon. Same old barren San Carlos, he thought. Cold now, bleak—

"Andres!"

He turned to see Lizah running toward him. His heart jumped. Opening his arms, he held her tightly, kissed her mouth, her cheek, her neck, murmuring the words of missing her and of love.

"Welcome home, my son," Lazaro said as he walked up with his grandson.

Andres quickly embraced him, then knelt to hold out his arms for the boy he hadn't seen in far too long. "Come, my son. Come let me hold you."

Taza held back momentarily, a look of mixed curiosity and bashfulness on his face. After a moment he said in English, "Welcome home, Father," and ran into his father's arms.

Lizah beamed. "He learns English easily."

Andres smiled, taking them both in his arms.

Later, as they rode side by side toward the Chihenne village, Andres asked, "How is everything?"

Lazaro shrugged. "There has been more food since Mur-fee came, but the People don't like the constant head counts. Mur-fee says it's the only way to keep the agent from cheating."

Andres knew the winter had been cold because for the last year he had received rudimentary letters from Lizah. She was improving rapidly in her writing. He also knew that Geronimo and Naiche had broken out again. Another Chiricahua chief named Chihuahua was with them in Mexico. He made small talk with his father about what the People were doing.

"Many are looking forward to the planting time," Lazaro said. "Farming is not so bad for some of them, and others have a few cattle."

"Are they happy?"

"When the stomach has food, what is happiness? The Way is not the same, but we survive."

"There must be more than mere survival."

"What are you going to do?" Lazaro asked abruptly.

Andres blew out a deep breath. He had wanted to wait a day or two before telling his father about his plans. He had told Lizah in a letter that he was going to Mexico as soon as he returned. And she had agreed to join him. "I'm going to Mexico with Lizah and anyone who wants to join me."

Lazaro stared impassively ahead as they rode down a bank to cross a small frozen stream. "I won't try to stop you."

Major General Raphael Murphy glanced up at the twelve-year-old boy standing before his desk. He spoke gently in Spanish. "I'm told you have a letter for me."

"Yes, Nantan," the boy replied, staring stiffly ahead. "Red Head made me promise to deliver it personally."

"You've done a good job, my boy. What's your name?"

"Alchise."

Rafe turned to his aide, Captain Bourke, who was standing by his desk. "John, why don't you give Alchise a piece of that candy we have."

Bourke smiled and reached for the box. "Yes, sir."

The boy shyly tasted the piece of hard Christmas candy, then put it in his mouth while Rafe opened the letter from Andres. It read:

Dear Father,

Your invitation to dinner was waiting when I returned from California two days ago. I would very much have enjoyed spending a pleasant evening with you, but it would have been a deception. By the time you receive this I will be gone with my wife and son, as well as several warriors, to Mexico to join Geronimo and the others in the holy war. Only by fighting and showing the American leaders that we must protest their giving away our lands as well as stealing our spirit will we ever have a chance of returning to the Way of the People. Spirit is all, Father. Without it, the People may as well lie down and die. I thank you profusely for all you have done for me, including this latest effort in getting me freed from prison. But now I must fight and be your enemy.

Your obedient servant,
Andres

Rafe sighed in disappointment. It all seemed so illogical. He thought back many years to the Alameda, the parklike atmosphere in Mexico City. A beautiful young woman, a small boy playing. Sunlight sprinkling through the leafy trees, people strolling nonchalantly, relieved that a war was over. How he'd fallen in love with that young woman, and grown to love the little boy, had become his father and helped raise him. A beautiful, gifted child.

And now the beautiful young woman was no longer his. She was caught up in her money-making, and still nurturing a hatred so strong that she had alienated the human being she had most loved.

And that human being, his fine adopted son, was himself now a receptacle for hate, stating that he was the enemy of a man who had always loved him.

Such an unbelievable fable, except that it was all too true.

Juh had died of a supposed heart attack two years earlier, leaving command of the fighting bands to Geronimo, Naiche, and Chihuahua. Another strong war leader was Jolsanny, as was Nana, a Warm Springs. The warriors were all Chiricahua, Chihenne, and Warm Springs. Besides Lizah, who had brought Taza along, eleven other warriors had broken out with Andres, including Arnoldo, Domingo, and Delgadito. Nine other women and eleven children completed the band.

While there was a main base camp in the Bavispe Mountains northeast of Oputo in the state of Sonora, the body of hostiles, as the White Eyes referred to any Apaches who were off the reservation without permission, was splintered, as usual, into smaller groups that could hit and run in any direction. There were no arms problems, but ammunition was always scarce. Ten weeks after joining the war party, Andres listened around an evening fire as Geronimo outlined a plan to attack a large hacienda near Janos. "This place has always been too strong for us, so all we do is steal some cattle from its ranges. But I have heard that the soldiers who stay there have been sent away. There will be many guns and much ammunition for us." His wide mouth broke into a grimace that was the closest he ever came to a smile. "Also Nakai-ye whiskey and many good horses."

Grunts of approval filled the air around the campfire.

Geronimo went on in his deep, rich voice, "We will attack at daylight while the Nakai-ye are still asleep. There are dogs there, but we will be inside the buildings before the people can act on the barking." The old medicine man went on, going into more specific points of the raid.

When he finished, all of the other leaders were in agreement with the plan. Andres was most excited about it because it would be a raid in force, with most of the warriors fighting together for a change. Besides, he needed a good new horse and he knew that these wealthy Mexicans always had some. Lizah, too, welcomed the change.

Lieutenant General Philip Sheridan had been Commander in Chief of the United States Army since early 1884 when General Sherman retired. Now the man who had said back in 1868 that "the only good Indian was a dead one" was visiting the Arizona command. Rafe met him at Fort Bowie in the southeastern corner of the state when he got off his special train late in the afternoon the day after Geronimo made his plan. At fifty-four, he was still an energetic "banty rooster," full of himself and impatient with the hostile situation.

"The thing is, Murphy," he said over a glass of whiskey after dinner that evening in the commanding officer's quarters. "You've got to realize how this Apache situation is gobbled up by the public. All over this country the press dwells on the fact that a handful of goddamned ragtag Indians are making a fool out of the United States Army."

"But, sir," Rafe replied patiently, "these ragtag Indians you speak of are perhaps the most accomplished guerrilla fighters in the history of warfare."

"But how many of them are there, General? Less than a hundred warriors?"

Rafe nodded. "That's right, and that's also one of the reasons we can't just go out there and annihilate them. They hit and run and fade into the very ground. Then they hit and run some more. They never attack unless they have a big numerical advantage, and they can live off this barren land like insects. When their horses are worn out, they just steal new ones. Plus they're never concentrated."

Little Phil scowled, drawing in on his cigar. "What about these Indian scouts of yours. I've heard they send information ahead to their friends and relatives of the hostiles. Also I've heard that they often shoot things up themselves."

"They aren't perfect," Rafe replied, "but for the most part they're trustworthy. And they are positively the only means of finding these hostile bands. They track, think, even *exist* like the enemy. Their endurance is far beyond our white and black soldiers."

"Being able to go into Mexico should give you room for many options."

Rafe shook his head. "Actually, it merely means that pursuit is open. But it also adds to the vastness of the area in which the hostiles can hide. I could send thousands of soldiers down there and never find them."

Sheridan sipped his whiskey. "You get them back on the reservation, and I have a plan that'll keep them under control. We get them the hell out of this part of the country. That way they don't bolt anymore because they won't have horses or any place familiar to go. We ship them off to Florida, wives, children, old people, the whole kit and caboodle."

"Where in Florida?"

"St. Augustine. There's an old fort by the name of Marion there. They could be incarcerated there for a time and get used to the fact that we mean business."

It was Rafe's turn to frown. "I don't think you understand their powerful feeling about their homelands. That's been part of the problem here. How long would they have to stay in Florida?"

Sheridan shrugged. "Oh, two years."

"Huh." Rafe looked skeptical. "I think it'll be a hard idea to sell to them. And I personally don't like it."

"They don't have many choices."

* * *

Andres looked down from the ridge at the sprawling collection of buildings that was as large as some small Mexican towns. Contained by a wall that wandered around as if it had been added when its contents had finished growing—which it had—the hacienda was still in its nightly slumber. Two lights blinked back at them, like tiny stars in a fortress. The rest of the buildings were dark but beginning to pick up a touch of the gray light that was commencing in the east.

He slipped down from his pony, as did Lizah. A thirteen-year-old boy took the reins. They would go the final few hundred yards on foot. He looked over to his left where Naiche had his Chiricahuas and back to his right where Geronimo led the Warm Springs. Like the rest of his Chihenne, he had painted his face with the red of his People and the white of war. With a meaningful glance at his own warriors, he nodded his head and trotted down the slope.

His job was to silence any guards who might be on duty. His eleven warriors had ropes and knew exactly what to do once inside the enclosure. Spreading out and approaching the wall from three sides, Arnoldo was the first to climb on the shoulders of two other warriors so he could spring to the top of the barrier. Dropping to the ground inside, he fastened a rope so the others could climb over. Andres was the second one inside. He glanced around, breathing quietly, feeling the danger, the excitement, waiting for the first dog to bark, for the unknown.

It was eerily silent.

The others dropped quietly to the ground nearby, Lizah third. Quickly they spread out in the darkest shadows, darting to the nearest buildings.

Andres spotted a horse corral and guessed that was where the blooded animals would be. At that moment a white shape got to his feet and shook himself. Hopefully an Arabian, Andres thought. Still no dogs. Strange. There was one guard. He was dozing under his sombrero on a ledge near the top of the wall where it made a bend. Andres nodded in his direction and in moments Arnoldo had silenced him with a knife to the throat.

At least Andres was quite sure there was only one guard. As far as he knew this hacienda hadn't been attacked by the People in many years, meaning its security would be lax.

Knife in hand, he ran to the corner of what he thought was some kind of an outbuilding that connected to the huge main house. Just as he reached it he was startled by a loud *grrrr!* Whirling around, he met the leap of a large dark dog with the tip of his blade. Rolling with the animal, he silenced it quickly. Now they really had to hurry. Domingo and Delgadito darted to the main gate with two other warriors and quickly removed its huge bar.

Instantly Geronimo and Naiche led their warriors inside to spread out and surround the buildings.

Followed by Lizah and several of his Chihenne, Andres led the way to the back entry of the main house. That was the moment the first dog barked. Another picked up the alarm instantly, barking shrilly. A third, with a deep voice, came bounding around a corner. In moments the occupants would be awake! One of the warriors killed the third dog. A man in underwear stepped out of the door facing them and Delgadito rammed a knife into him.

The sky to the east was rapidly lightening, developing a bare tinge of pink. They'd have to hurry!

The first shot rang out near the bunkhouse where the vaqueros lived. That would be from Geronimo's party. Another followed around by the front of the main house, and then the shots began to overlap. Andres bounded into what looked a huge kitchen, waving his long-barreled Colt revolver to cover anyone who might be there. A fat man in underwear aiming a shotgun burst from a side door, and was greeted by two quick .44 rounds that slammed him back against the wall where he slumped to the floor, a trickle of blood coming from the side of his mouth as his eyes glazed in death. Like cast members of a play who had been through dozens of rehearsals, the nimble warriors poured through the lower floor of the huge house, killing three more members of the household staff. Many shots filled the outside air.

Andres dashed into the great hall where burning drapes created dancing shapes against the high-ceilinged walls. The room grew brighter as he reached the bottom of the steps and started to climb them. The blast of a pistol flashed in his face from near the top of the steps, and he heard a small moan from the warrior behind him. He jumped sideways as the pistol fired again. The man holding it was wearing pajamas and had a full head of tousled white hair. He looked somehow familiar. Andres stared.

It was Agustin de Gante!

The bastard who had so wronged his mother! The bastard who had turned her out like a piece of garbage with her half-breed child, the same bastard who had tried to seduce her in Washington—

From twenty feet he glared into those arrogant black eyes, held them.

"*I am Andres Murphy, you son-of-a-bitch!*" he shouted, and shot the general dead in the heart.

31

> *We were reckless of our lives, because we felt that every man's hand was against us. If we returned to the reservation we would be put in prison and killed; if we stayed in Mexico they would continue to send soldiers to fight us. So we gave no quarter to anyone and asked no favors.*
>
> —Geronimo

March 25, 1886

"Sir, this dispatch may be of some interest to you," Captain Bourke said, handing Rafe a sheet of paper. "It's about that those Tombstone Rangers, from the commander of Fort Bowie."

Rafe took the sheet of paper. The Tombstone Rangers were like the Globe Rangers, the Silver City Rangers, and other groups of vigilantes who did more shouting and drinking of stimulants than fighting. This particular group was more commonly known as the "Tombstone Toughs," and a more motley crew of drunken ne'er-do-wells had never before taken to the field as a quasi-military unit. The dispatch read: "The Tombstone Rangers, led by their saloon-owning commander, started for San Carlos two days ago to solve the renegade Apache problem. These rum-soaked bummers, staggering along the trail, found nothing but one Indian, a decrepit old man having a mescal bake. They fired at him, but fortunately missed. He fled north and they fled south. That ended the massacre."

The aide grinned as Rafe handed the dispatch back to him. "I guess they ran out of whiskey and expired of thirst."

Rafe chuckled. It was possibly the only light moment he would have for a few days. A few weeks earlier one of his troops of Apache scouts had located Geronimo's camp and had attacked it early one morning. The band escaped, but in its hasty departure, it had been forced to leave behind its horses and a large amount of ammunition. This had apparently been the reason that Geronimo had sought out Lieutenant Maus, who was in command of the scouts, and stated that he would meet with Mur-fee only to discuss the possibility of coming back to the reservation.

And this was the appointed day. Since Victorio, American troops chasing renegade Apaches had been able to cross the border freely into Mexico, so that was no problem. A pack train had preceded his small party to the Apache camp at Cañon de los Embudos—Canyon of the Tricksters. The Indian site was in a lava bed atop a small conical hill surrounded by deep ravines. The army camp was five hundred yards away, separated by several steep gulches. Now bathed in the brilliant spring sunlight, the lava bed was defensively unassailable. The Apaches weren't about to fall for any tricks.

Rafe felt a certain excitement. Could this really be it, the end of Apache warfare after all these years? Did the hostiles really intend to stop it, or was this just another of Geronimo's ploys?

At shortly after twelve noon Geronimo led several other Apaches into the Murphy camp, which had been pitched under some tall cottonwood and sycamore trees. Rafe came out of his tent to meet them and was pleased to see that one of Geronimo's party wore a red bandana around his forehead. Perhaps he would listen to reason if the others didn't. There were Naiche and Chihuahua, plus some Rafe didn't recognize. Probably war leaders. Another was his daughter-in-law, Lizah, who nodded casually to him. Two dozen heavily armed warriors with stern expressions accompanied the leaders. They looked as if they were ready to fight at the first hint of any treachery.

Rafe greeted them and turned as his ace-in-the-hole appeared from the tent. Lazaro, erect and noble as ever, nodded his head in greeting and stood beside Rafe—who noticed a surprised look pass through their eyes, a reaction he had expected. They retired to a small grassy bowl some fifty yards from the camp and seated themselves around on rocks and on the ground.

As he sat on a flat rock, Andres glanced again at Lazaro. *Why had he let Rafe talk him into coming along?* This wasn't his business. This was war and the chief had elected to stay out of it. Now he was in it, openly on the other side. He didn't want to confront his father . . . or his stepfather, actually. That was what made this whole thing so convoluted. His father, who was a great Apache leader and had been one of the major factors in his own conversion to the Way, was sitting beside his respected stepfather to argue against the son who was at war with them. Convoluted? It was wholly implausible.

But it really didn't matter. He didn't like what Geronimo was going to do anyway. The powerful war leader intended to cut a deal with Rafe, a deal that would rob the remaining fighters of their struggle. And he didn't like that prospect at all.

Lazaro's gaze flitted from one face to another, settling briefly on Andres for a moment. He wondered how difficult it would be to convince him, or even the others for that matter. Mur-fee's orders from the Great White Father in Wash-in-ton might not be what they expected. The general had come to him a week earlier, asking that he go along to this meeting. He had thought deeply about doing so, simply because it might make him look like a lackey to the White Eyes. But in the end Mur-fee's arguments won out: the White Eyes simply had too much power and could not help but win in the long run. And he would lose a son, a daughter-in-law, and a fine grandson in any fight to the finish.

Yes, sadly, the end was inevitable.

There were times when war was only a stubborn refusal to accept common sense. It had taken him a long time to understand this fact, but now he knew the long struggle was over. Even Silsoose, the great ancient chief, would have had the wisdom to understand this.

His eyes went back to Geronimo as the shaman spoke, with Andres interpreting—

"I want to talk first of the causes which led me to leave the reservation. I was living quietly and contented, doing and thinking of no harm . . . and then I began to hear those stories that people were speaking bad of me . . . I heard I was to be arrested and be hanged, so I left . . . I was praying to the light and to the darkness, to God and to the sun, to let me live quietly there with my family . . . I think every day, how am I to talk to you? There is one God looking down on us all. God is listening to me. The sun, the darkness, the winds, are all listening to what we now say. . . . "

Rafe listened to Geronimo's long apologia patiently. The arrogance of the man was almost humorous. To hear him tell it, he was an innocent victim of a plot, not a renegade who had many times broken out and led depredations on innocent people. When he finished, Rafe said bluntly, "You don't speak the truth. You blame your killing and stealing on something that simply isn't true. There is no warrant for your arrest."

Geronimo kept insisting that someone was out to get him, and Rafe countered by telling him it was all bosh. He then stated that Geronimo had frightened other Apaches into following him on the last breakout, but the war leader denied that he had. The arguments wore on until late afternoon, when Lazaro finally spoke. His plea was eloquent, stressing the values of having families together and preserving the Way, and of the inevitability of change from the old life.

When he finished, Geronimo made some other statements, intimating that the hostiles would just return to reservation life as always.

"No," Rafe said firmly. "The Great White Father in Washington has told me to accept only unconditional surrender. You must come in and do exactly what we agree upon. I have been given certain latitude, however."

He waited for Andres to interpret, but his stepson looked him coolly in the eye. "What do you mean by unconditional surrender?"

"The People must do as we dictate. There is a place in Florida, an army post called Fort Marion where a number of Plains Indians have lived for a time. All of you must go there for a period of two years."

"Two years?" Andres asked.

"Yes, at the end of that period you will be returned to Arizona."

Andres's gaze was unwavering. "To our original homelands?"

"I can't promise that."

When the translation was completed and some discussion had taken place, Andres turned to Rafe and asked, "Will their families be with them at Fort Marion?"

"Yes, absolutely. Now please interpret what I've said."

As soon as his stepson had done so and a murmur had gone around the Apache leaders, Rafe said carefully, eyeing each one of them, "If you do not do this and you stay out, I'll keep after you and kill the last one if it takes fifty years."

Two days later, again at midday, the same leaders and their heavily armed escort came back to see Rafe. Chihuahua had already made his decision a day earlier. He spoke first. "I am anxious to behave, Nantan Mur-fee. I surrender myself and my people to you because I believe in you and you do not deceive us. You must be our God. You must be the one who makes the green pastures, who sends the rain, who commands the winds. Everything you do is right. I ask only that you let my family come with me to this Flor-i-da or wherever you send me."

Naiche, son of Cochise, was next to speak: "When I was free I gave orders, but now I surrender to you. Now I am glad. I will not have to hide behind rocks and mountains. I'll cross the open plain. I'll go wherever you wish and do as you say because I trust you."

Geronimo grunted, saying, "My heart is yours and what the others say, I say also. Whatever you tell me is true. I put my trust in your hands because you have never told us a lie."

In spite of himself, Rafe was moved. He knew what importance these leaders placed on this decision, how vital such trust was to the Apache. His eyes moved to Andres. "And you, my son, what is your decision?"

Andres returned his gaze, taking a moment before speaking, "I do not agree with the others." He flicked a glance at Lazaro, who was watching him intently. "I have already spent many moons in American prisons, and I feel our cause is just. My Chihenne don't want to rot in a Florida prison. I'll stay out."

Rafe glanced from him to Lizah, whose face was a mask of inscrutability, and back to the face he had loved for so long. He spoke quietly in Spanish so Lazaro could understand. "You know what I said I would do, even if it takes fifty years."

"I translated it for you. It's what I have to do, Father."

Lazaro looked sad, but shrugged and turned away.

Rafe nodded his head. "So be it."

The Apache wars were, for all intents and purposes, over.

Rafe stared at the telegraph his clerk had just handed him. From Lieutenant General Philip Sheridan it read:

> March 30, 1886. You are confidentially informed that your telegram of March 29 causes me great concern. The president cannot assent to the surrender of the hostiles on the terms of their imprisonment in the East for two years with the understanding of their return to the reservation. He instructs you to again enter into negotiations on the terms of their unconditional surrender, only sparing their lives. If these terms are not acceded to, the hostiles are to be destroyed as soon as possible.

Suddenly Rafe's cheeks got hot. At great difficulty he had finally brought about the capitulation of virtually the last body of hostiles. But most importantly, he had given his word. Why was Sheridan reneging—was it because President Cleveland had balked? Or was it Sheridan himself? It didn't matter, the rug had been ripped out from under him. He had given his word and now he couldn't fulfill his promise.

He snapped the pencil he had been holding.

Picking up another, he wrote hurriedly, "I had to act at once with my best judgment, offering them the very terms you suggested. To inform the Indians that these terms have been disapproved would make it impossible for me to further negotiate with them. Nor can I justify destroying them after breaking faith."

They were harsh words of disagreement to an Irishman of Sheridan's temperament, but they were warranted, Rafe thought as he called his clerk to get the telegraph dispatch off.

"General Murphy!" Captain Bourke said loudly, knocking on Rafe's door. "Something terrible has happened!"

Rafe turned up the lamp beside his bed and swung his legs out of bed. "The door's open, Bourke. C'mon in."

"It's the Apaches, sir," Bourke said as he hurried into the room. "That bastard Tribolet, the Swiss trader who has an army meat contract and runs a trading post that's mostly a place to receive stolen goods from the Apaches—you know who I mean. He has gotten whiskey to Geronimo and his cohorts and the bastard has bolted again!"

Rafe's usual calm was shattered. *"What?"*

"They were on their way into Fort Bowie as planned and stopped for the night near Tribolet's place. He sold them the liquor and they got drunk. Somewhere along the line, he told them the American authorities were just waiting to hang them when they arrived at Fort Bowie to turn themselves in."

"Why would he do such a stupid thing?"

Bourke shrugged. "Who knows? To make some quick money. Or maybe at the orders of the Tucson Ring to keep the hostiles from coming in and ending the war. You know how much continued military and reservation contracts mean to them."

Rafe shook his head. Years of work, centuries of strife. And some money-hungry rascal ruins it all. "How many does Geronimo have with him?"

"Chihuahua came in with his band at Fort Bowie. We think Geronimo has about twenty warriors, including Naiche, and about a dozen women and half a dozen children. I don't know if Andres was with him or not."

"Any idea where they went?"

"Back into Mexico, sir. No one knows for sure. You want me to arrest the trader?"

Rafe sighed. "No. Who would convict him—of *what?*"

A smile touched the captain's lips. "Maybe I should just arrange to have him shot."

"I wish it were that simple. All right, let's start thinking about what to do. I'll have to notify Sheridan right away."

Sheridan was furious at the news, telegraphing: "Your dispatch is highly disappointing. Obviously your scouts were in cahoots with Geronimo. Prepare to best protect people and business interests of Arizona and New Mexico. Advise at once the details of your plan to recapture the prisoners."

Angry as he was, Rafe patiently wired back, explaining that an offensive to find twenty hostiles would be next to impossible. At the end, he added the only words left, the sad words that his pride dictated:

> It may be, however, that I am much too wedded to my own views in this matter, and as I have spent many years of the hardest work of my life with the Indians, I respectfully request that I may now be relieved from this command.

The white-haired lady looked up from her knitting as the train neared the little town of Alamogordo. "What a name for a town," she chuckled. "Fat cottonwood."

"I know," the reporter replied. "I wrote a story about it when they christened it. What happened when General Murphy asked to be transferred?"

"Sheridan promptly obliged him, sending him to command the Department of the Platte. Brigadier General Nelson A. Miles was named to succeed him in Arizona. Miles was an experienced Indian fighter, but he lacked Murphy's thorough knowledge of the Apaches, his brilliance, and most of all, his integrity. Also, Miles was given to glorifying his exploits and was noted among his contemporaries for tooting his own horn. He accumulated five thousand troops, one-fourth of the entire army, and ran them ragged chasing twenty-some warriors in the mountains of Mexico.

"He never gave Geronimo, Naiche, and Andres a chance to change their minds and come in. He discharged nearly all of the Indian scouts and set up heliograph stations to flash messages from mountain top to mountain top. But his efforts were a total failure. One wag wrote that he would have been more successful had there been more of the enemy. In the meantime, the hostiles struck in Mexico and back into Arizona, practically at will."

"And in the end," the reporter said, "he reverted to Murphy's methods."

"Yes. After a time Miles sent a small party headed by another officer the Apaches trusted—Lieutenant Gatewood—into Mexico, and he was successful in talking Geronimo into coming in. Miles made several promises that he didn't intend to keep, and Geronimo and his party were soon on their way to Florida."

The reporter nodded. "But Andres didn't come with him."

The white-haired woman shook her head. "No, he stubbornly clung to his beliefs. With only two warriors, his wife and his small son, he stayed in Mexico and carried on his private little war."

32

"Andres, I must tell you what I feel," Lizah said earnestly a few days after Geronimo and his followers went with Gatewood to Fort Bowie. It was after the new moon had risen, but before midnight, and they were lying in their blankets after making love a little earlier. It was quite cool and still for a late August night. But the Sierra Madre could be like that.

"Of course," Andres replied.

"I think you have proven what you said you would do. You have shown that you are fully independent of all the others."

Andres waited for her to continue.

"Your father is very disappointed that you would not agree with Mur-fee, and I know he is troubled that he cannot see you and his grandson. Also, I had a dream last night that I haven't told you about. In it, the People were getting on a White Eye wagon that smokes. All had sad eyes. I saw Benita and Tze-go-juni with your father, and they were all looking around and saying, 'We can't leave without Andres, Lizah, and little Taza.' "

Andres rolled over, leaning on one elbow. "You actually dreamed this?"

"Yes, and it was so strong, so real."

"Where was this wagon going?"

"I don't know, but the People had all of their belongings with them."

"Hmmm." He knew about her Power when it came to the enemy, also about her other intuitive gifts. Perhaps something *was* happening back at San Carlos.

"I have done whatever you wished because I'm your wife. But now I want to be with the People. Our little boy needs to be with other children, and I'm tired of running. I want to end this, my husband."

He nodded his head. He had been so intent on not giving in that he had forgotten what a hardship this renegade life could be on his loved ones. And she was right about his father, right about little Taza—

"The others are ready to go back too."

He made his decision. "Very well, we'll start for the reservation tomorrow."

By riding at night and staying away from the main roads, Andres had led his little group to Fort Apache without incident. Arriving at shortly after reveille two days earlier, he had startled the Officer of the Day, who quickly placed all five of them in temporary arrest. Later the commanding officer, Lieutenant Colonel James Wade, asked Andres why he had come in.

"Because the fighting is over," Andres had replied quietly. "We wish to be with our loved ones."

"Hmmm." Wade stroked his clean-shaven chin. "You know General Miles has people looking for you in Mexico, don't you?"

"I assume as much."

"He'll be quite pleased that you have surrendered."

Andres looked the officer coolly in the eye. "I don't consider this a surrender, Colonel. I was a captain with Sheridan at Appomattox. *That* was a surrender. I have quit fighting and will join my people to live a peaceful life. I have ceased resisting the wrongs that have been perpetrated on my people."

Wade shrugged, saying wryly, "I don't really care what you call it, Murphy. General Miles will make sure every newspaper in the country says that you are the last hostile to surrender to him. Fortunately he's presently in Albuquerque."

Andres nodded. "If I give you my word that we will remain here on the reservation, will you let me go to my father's village?"

"Your word?"

Again Andres looked at him coolly. "As a former officer of the Union army."

The commander slowly nodded his head. "I'll accept that."

Lazaro had moved his village, along with the Warms Springs and most of the Chiricahua, to Fort Apache a year earlier. While not his beautiful Willows Country, the reservation north of San Carlos was more habitable. The White Mountain Apaches were there, and although the relationship between them and the newcomers was not the warmest, it was cordial. Now, on September 5, it was all about to change.

All members of the same groups that had moved up from San Carlos were summoned to the main post from their various villages with instructions to arrive for a full head count by two o'clock in the afternoon. Lazaro led his Chihenne inside the compound at one-forty-five. There, soldiers were quietly collecting all arms. When Andres asked why this abnormal procedure was taking place, he was told it was a special occasion and that the commanding officer had ordered it. Only about half of the men had weapons, but they groused about giving them up, even for a short while.

At two-forty, after much milling around, the waiting Apaches became hushed as Lieutenant Colonel Wade climbed on a platform with his Apache interpreter and announced with the suddenness of a thunderbolt: "In two days all of you will be removed from Fort Apache to Fort Marion in Florida. It is a place beside the big water where it is always warm. The Great White Father will take good care of you there. You women are to go home now and pack only what belongings your family can carry. The men will remain in barracks three and four until they return. Good luck!"

When the interpreter finished, the People looked at each other in shock. They knew that Chief Chihuahua and his band had gone to the place by the water in Flor-i-da several weeks earlier, and that Geronimo and Naiche with their people were leaving for the same place from Fort Bowie. But this was a total surprise. Andres looked at his father quizzically. "Have they told you anything about this?"

"No," Lazaro replied. "Not a word."

Andres wheeled to step in front of the departing Wade. "What about the horses and the crops, Colonel? You can't just jerk these people away from the only things they have left."

Wade scowled. "These orders came straight from Washington, Murphy. All I can do is follow them. Now don't cause any trouble or you'll be back in Alcatraz."

"They're inhuman."

"You gave me your word you wouldn't cause trouble."

"But you didn't tell me this insanity was coming."

"The orders just came in last night."

"Can't we delay long enough to challenge them?"

"You know better than that."

Andres just stared at him. There was nothing he could do.

On the morning of the seventh, the dusty hot trek to Holbrook began. Although there were many wagons, most of the People had to walk. A herd of cattle was driven along with the column for food, but even the thought of a possible feast did little to lift the veil of sadness that enveloped the marchers. The dogs barked and cavorted along on each side of the column, unaware of their fate. Though the move had been discussed at length since Wade's announcement, the general attitude was one of depressing puzzlement. Why everyone? Why Florida? Why take away their prized horses and other things? Why, why, why?

It was ninety miles to Holbrook, one of those little towns that had just happened and then validated itself when the railroad came through. The painful exodus from Fort Apache would take five days. On the fourth day it began to rain, and by the time they reached their destination the drenched and muddy Apaches were stumbling through a quagmire. The next morning the Atchison, Topeka & Santa Fe train pulled into a siding. It was composed of twelve cars with rude bunks, ten cars for the prisoners, one at each end for the 84 members of the military guard. Cans and slopjars would serve as receptacles for human waste in the long ride to the Atlantic Coast—with no privacy afforded.

While the warriors had often seen trains, the women, children, and older people had not. Some of the old women and men even prayed to the locomotive as it approached blowing its whistle, but many of the terrified children scurried to the brush or hid in their mothers' skirts. The soldiers caught the women and children and forced them onto the train, and the men reluctantly followed.

Andres had considered trying to force a revolt before departing from Fort Apache, but had decided against it. Now he was sorry. The cars were already very hot inside, with the windows and doors fastened shut. Two hours passed before the train pulled out at noon, and the heat became nearly unbearable.

Finally the train jerked to a start, causing wide-eyed looks of fear from many. Little Taza pressed his nose against a window, trying to spot his beloved black dog. "*Ndoicho!*" he shouted over and over, but the dogs, running in a pack alongside, gradually began to fall back. Pets and masters would never see each other again, and most of the animals would die. Finally Taza slipped down to the floor, staring, tears streaming down his cheeks.

Andres was torn with indecision. He should escape, do what he could from outside, but he hated the thought of being separated from Lizah and Taza. Terrible things could happen before this nightmarish journey was over, and he couldn't bear the thought of not being able to rejoin them some time later.

He decided to stay.

Children were the first to have to relieve themselves, followed by the older adults. It wasn't long before the closed cars with their stifling heat began to acquire a stench that would build to an almost unbearable level before they reached St. Louis. An officer would later write, "When I think of that trip, I still get seasick. No other human being except an Indian could bear it."

When the train stopped in St. Louis a reporter from the *Globe-Democrat* visited the captives and wrote this headline:

> Through to Florida, Four Hundred Murderous Redskins Taken to Safe Quarters. Noted Chiefs of Geronimo's School and Tribe. With Their Bucks and Squaws, a Frightful Picture of the Noble American!

Fortunately the captives were able to transfer to a clean Louisville & Nashville train, but it wouldn't be long before it, too, became nearly intolerable. Knowing his geography as they headed southeastward, Andres did what he could to ease at least some of the concern. "Pass the word," he would say periodically. "We are getting closer to Florida, now maybe one more day away . . . now a half a day. . . ."

After being delayed, the train eventually reached Jacksonville and the prisoners were loaded aboard a steamboat to cross the St. John's River. On the other side they were placed aboard another train for the oldest city in America, St. Augustine. Finally the tired, dejected, frightened prisoners walked into the site of their new captivity.

Christened Castillo de San Marcos, the Castle of St. Mark, Fort Marion was started by the Spaniards in 1672. It was built of massive *coquina* rock blocks, an authentic medieval fortress complete with a drawbridge and surrounded by a saltwater moat connected to the Atlantic Ocean, which stretched out like a mysterious plain of water to the east. The citadel had been used as a base for independent Americans prior to the Revolutionary War when a number of patriots were imprisoned there, and as a supply base during the Seminole war. It played an important role in the Civil War and served as a prison for Plains Indians in the late 1870s.

The smell of the salt air, its dampness and clinging warmth, were new to the People, although it merely stirred memories of wartime Washington for Andres. They were welcomed briefly by Chihuahua. The Chiricahua chief was a handsome man, prideful of his polite manners, who was later known as the "Apache Chesterfield." He and his followers had arrived at Fort Marion several months earlier following his capitulation to Rafe. He and his clan had left Mexico separately and had missed Geronimo's drunken bout on Tribolet's liquor.

He greeted Lazaro warmly, then said in a loud voice to the group as a whole, "This is not a bad place. They give us more food than at San Carlos, and the air is warm, but not as clean and clear as our beloved mountain air. Sometimes we get sick and cough. They want us to eat water animals, but they have been told of our belief that the spirits of bad Apaches rest in them and we don't eat them. We also told them we don't eat pig."

The families were assigned Sibley tents that had been erected and jammed close together on the small parade ground. "Prisoners of war," Andres muttered as he went into the tent. He couldn't get over the label that had been assigned to the People. How a small child who had never been off the reservation could be branded a "prisoner of war" was more than illegal; it was utterly preposterous.

He glanced around the tent. A West Pointer who later became a Confederate general had modeled it after an Indian tipi and had given it his name. Because of its resemblance to a huge bell, the Sibley tent was sometimes called a bell tent. It was eighteen feet in diameter and twelve feet high in its center. At its top was foot-wide circular opening for circulation and a stovepipe that was attached to the famous Sibley stove. Sibley couldn't possibly have known that he was designing a tent that was similar to a wickiup—a shelter that would be used to house the very people who had lived for centuries in a smaller model made from brush.

And a cell, Andres thought bitterly.

Fortunately, Lazaro's family was assigned to one tent. Andres's half sister, Auraria, had died at San Carlos, but Gabriela, the widow of Cochise, was included. She had never produced any children. Auraria's two orphaned children were also included, as was Tze-go-juni. The tent was plenty large enough for this number of tenants. No, not tenants—prisoners of war, Andres told himself.

He looked up at the nearby castle wall where a large black cat sat staring at him with unblinking yellow eyes.

Even a cat was free to come and go as he wished.

The first person to die from a strange coughing problem was an older woman named Ih-tedda. She was a member of Chihuahua's band and she passed away three weeks after the arrival of the large body from Fort Apache. Four days later a middle-aged man died with the same symptoms. Two more women, three men and four children died in December, but it was when Tzes-ton, the twenty-one-year-old wife of Arnoldo, passed away that the problem was brought home to Andres. She had become ill in January and died late in February. A vivacious young woman, she was the mother of a three-year-old boy, and had been sturdy and healthy all her life. Her husband was devastated. "Why?" he anguished to Tze-go-juni after the burial.

The old shaman had but one answer: "The White Eye curse."

Andres, who had seen consumption in the army during the war, went to the post surgeon. "The husband of the dead woman," he said, "is very distraught. She coughed a great deal. Did she die of consumption?"

The doctor, Henry Perkins, replied, "Yes, I believe so. There seems to be a tendency among your people toward tuberculosis. I would like to perform an autopsy on some of these victims, but you know how your people feel about mutilation."

Andres shook his head. "No, they don't want that."

"Was there much of this disease in Arizona?"

"No, although I heard that two of the children who were sent to the Carlisle Indian School in 1885 died of the coughing disease. Another came back to Fort Apache and died later."

"Yes," the doctor replied, "I've heard that there have been several deaths at that school."

"Is the disease highly contagious?"

"It can be in confined places where people are in close contact— such as in that train during the trip from Arizona. It's conceivable that the disease was brought from Carlisle and it spread during the train ride. The weather here might be conducive to it, in fact it probably is. But mainly it can spread when people are close together."

Andres felt his temper start to slip. "Like where a bunch of people are penned up like animals?"

The doctor shrugged. "It can happen."

Andres's eyes narrowed. "What are you going to do about it?"

"Render a report. I can't change anything, you know."

That afternoon Andres wrote a letter to Rafe, reporting the conversation. It was his first contact with his stepfather since the meeting in Mexico. He ended with "I'm no doctor, but I believe an epidemic could start here in the damp confines of this old excuse for a citadel."

It was shortly after he finished making notes in his journal that he heard Benita cough for the first time. It frightened him. If what he gathered about the disease was true, it may have entered his own Sibley.

No, he told himself, he was jumping at shadows. She probably just had a cold.

The next day two people died of the coughing ailment, and word came down from Pennsylvania that a nineteen-year-old son of a former war leader had succumbed.

On March 21, Benita, the pleasant woman who had been such a comforting mate to Lazaro, died in her fitful sleep. Andres grieved, but he hadn't known her nearly as long as the others in the family. He tried to console his father, knowing how much Lazaro silently mourned for the woman who had first been his slave and then his wife, but there was little he could say.

It seemed as if her death was just one more nail in the deadness that seemed to have been numbing him since the day he laid down his arms and walked into San Carlos.

33

Carlota spotted the article on the front page of the *Albuquerque Review* the moment she opened her copy. It was a reprint from a feature by a New York journalist who had visited Fort Marion. The lead line said, "St. Augustiners Cheated over Geronimo." She read eagerly:

> *St. Augustine, Florida.* "We feel cheated." This is a statement by a group of businessmen in this ancient city. They were told that Geronimo, "the world famous killer Apache Indian would be one of the first savages to arrive at historic Fort Marion." But instead, Geronimo and Naiche, another renegade chief, were sent to Fort Pickens, outside of Pensacola, with fifteen other insurgents. "Now Pensacola gets all of the curious tourist trade," groused the leader of the St. Augustine group. When asked if Old Geronimo was that big of a draw, the businessman—who refused to give his name—replied, "He's a gold mine."
>
> On a more serious note, Major General Raphael Murphy visited Fort Marion late last week with Herbert Welsh, the executive secretary of the Indian Rights Association of Philadelphia. General Murphy was not only unhappy with the crowded conditions, but incensed about the fact that nearly all of the Apache scouts who had faithfully served him in the Army were incarcerated there. He also listened to complaints that promises General Miles had made back in Arizona were not kept.
>
> General Murphy met at length with Chief Lazaro, an extremely tall Apache who has purportedly been the main factor in keeping peace among the various tribes over the years. His son, Red Head, who speaks perfect English, did the translation. It is rumored that this same Red Head was somehow a hero in the War of the Rebellion. There was also discussion about the deaths from consumption of several of the Apaches, and whether there was a possibility of an

epidemic. But apparently doctors still know very little about the dreaded disease.

Both the general and Mr. Welsh insist that the Indians must be moved to a better location. Both also state that their reports will go to Congress and expose the Administration's "utter contempt" for the well-being of the Indians.

She slowly reread the story, clenching and unclenching her right fist. *Consumption!* She knew that someday the primitive life of those savages would be the cause of something like that. They never practiced good medical sense, always relying on their hocus-pocus. She pictured a little black-eyed boy, coughing with tears in his eyes, choking. What if her grandson really did catch it? No, little boys didn't catch such a thing, surely. But what about Andres? He was right in the middle of it all. Red Head. What an uncouth name for her beautiful son. She had written three more letters since the removal of the Apaches to Florida, but had received no response from him. She had, however, received a letter from Rafe stating that conditions were adequate at Fort Marion, although far from desirable. His letter was cool, businesslike. He didn't even mention her coming to join him.

She read the article one more time.

Consumption—the terrible word glared out at her as if it were on fire, burning its way right out of the page and leaving a black, scorched hole.

She was in Albuquerque for a horse auction, planning on buying a couple more brood mares for her string. But the auction wasn't until later and she was enjoying a light lunch in the dining room of the Bernalillo House restaurant on the plaza in Old Town. Old Town was distinguished as such because with the arrival of the railroad in 1880, New Town, slightly to the east, had been born. That was where most of the rapid development that a railroad brings to a city was taking place. Carlota had tried to buy up some land in the New Town area several years earlier, but hadn't been successful.

She sipped her tea and toyed with the piece of chocolate cake. It was a shame that Andres wouldn't come to his senses. He'd—

"Excuse me, but aren't you Mrs. Murphy?"

She looked up to see a ramrod stiff figure with a short reddish gray beard. It was Richard Hartman. "Why, yes, General. How are you, sir?"

The former rebel officer swept his hat from his head and bowed with a flourish. "You look as lovely as ever, ma'am," he said with a warm smile. "I thought you were living in Silver City."

"I'm just here for the quarter horse auction. What brings you down from Santa Fe?"

"I have a couple of legal matters to attend to before I depart for Washington. I'm a territorial delegate to Congress now, you know."

"Yes, I think I read something about that. Are you the same thing as a congressman?"

He smiled. "Just about, except that a delegate can't vote."

"But you do have influence."

"Yes, some. But I haven't been there long enough to hold much sway."

She pointed to the article in the *Review*. "Have you read this?"

Hartman nodded his head. "Yes, and it's all true."

"My husband is quite upset about the whole thing."

"I would think so. Seems as if the administration doesn't know what it's doing. Have you heard from Andres?"

Carlota tried to keep the pain from showing. "No, he doesn't write."

"I still can't believe that a man with his great potential could do what he did." Hartman shrugged. "On the other hand, perhaps part of that potential of his was his propensity for right. And he is convinced that what he's doing is right."

She looked in his frank, greenish eyes and knew what he said was the truth. "Yes, I suppose we tend to judge too often by our own concepts," she murmured, surprised that she'd even said it. Did she mean it? Could she, in any way, accept the foolish thing that Andres had done—was doing?

"Yes, perhaps when our final tally takes place, the Andreses of the world will score highest." General Hartman smiled, replaced his hat and touched its brim. "Well, Mrs. Murphy, I must hurry on. I'm delighted that I saw you."

Carlota watched sadly as he briskly walked out of the room.

God, her life was so empty.

The advertisement in the *Mobile Daily Register* was the talk of the town.

The very popular Alabama State Artillery will give a grand excursion to Mount Vernon by the Mobile & Birmingham Railroad on Sunday, May 8. This will afford an

opportunity to see the famous Apaches, who have just been
taken to the Barracks. The known urbanity and hospitality
of the officers stationed there is a guarantee of a pleasant
day's pastime. The fare for the round trip is fixed at the low
rate of $1.00, children 50¢, and there will be a special coach
for colored people.

Andres looked up from where he was dozing under a tree with a
baleful gaze at the sightseeing group. He hated each and every one
of them. They came in different batches, at different times, to stare and
laugh at the People. Freaks, sideshow freaks, that was what his proud
people had been reduced to. Subhumans. No better than the goddamned freaks at carnivals. And Mount Vernon Barracks, thirty miles
north of Mobile, was the latest midway.

The People had arrived there April 28, finding a comfortable military post that was manned by the United States Second Artillery.
Consisting of some twenty-one hundred acres, the Barracks were just
over two hundred feet above sea level and was surrounded by a dense
pine forest. The buildings were in good shape, the water quite good,
but the rations were too skimpy. Fortunately, the People had earned
and saved some money from the sale of Apache artifacts at Fort
Marion, so they were able to buy some additional food in the local
area.

But it was still nothing other than one more place of incarceration.

A young man with a sketch pad dropped to the grass nearby and
prepared to draw him. Andres scowled, but the young man merely
tossed the derby he was wearing on the ground and started making
strokes with a piece of charcoal. Andres turned away.

"Please," the young man implored. "You sit. I pay you money."

Andres decided to play the game. He held out his hand. The artist
handed him a nickel. He shook his head, throwing it to the ground.
The artist picked up the nickel and handed him a quarter. Andres
shook his head again, keeping the two-bit piece and holding out his
other hand. The young man stared at him and fumbled in his pockets
for another quarter, which he held out. Andres accepted it, grunted,
and sat on the ground again.

The artist worked rapidly, making three sketches before he stood
up and said with a broad smile, "Me like. Thank you."

As he turned to go, Andres caught his arm and pointed to the
sketchbook.

"What?" the young man asked. "Oh, you want see. Okay." He

opened the book to the first sketch and held it out for Andres to look at it. "You like?"

Andres raised an eyebrow, cleared his throat, and said, "Actually, you made my head a little too large. You see, in drawing, as in perceiving the embodiment of one's philosophy and immortal soul, one must relate to every element involved and determine one's approach accordingly."

The young man stared at him with incredulous eyes as if he had just heard a message from beyond. After a moment he said, "You . . . speak English!"

Andres looked at him blankly for a moment before replying, "Adios, asshole," and walked away.

Lazaro pocketed the money for the arrow. He had grunted in English the phrase Lizah had taught him, "I carry this arrow in my quiver when I make big war."

And the fat White Eye with the big oodo chain on his belly had paid him four dollars for it.

Lazaro had weathered the moves from Fort Apache quite well, at least on the outside. Actually, his pride continued to suffer as the indignities slowly kept mounting. But it was the death of Benita that had most wounded him. Although the song in his heart had always been for Carlota, Benita had been his mate—his helpmate, sometimes his passion mate, the mother of his daughters, and his friend. He had been able to share his troubles with her, holding back only his longing for Carlota. But she had always known about that anyway. Only on a few occasions when she had totally lost her temper had she thrown Carlota up to him. The rest of the time she had been his rock.

He would miss her for the rest of his life.

Gabriela, his daughter who was Cochise's widow, cooked and performed the other tasks that an Apache woman did for a man, so he was still well cared for. But his life was hollow. The White Eyes planned everything, so there was little for a chief to do. His people still treated him with respect, but other than that, he was another curiosity for the visitors to stare at. And particularly since he was so tall.

He continued to study the signs, reading and writing, as Andres called them. But his heart wasn't in it. The rest of the time, he made the bows and arrows to sell to the White Eyes who came to stare. They were never of the quality a warrior would use for hunting or war, but they were good enough to sell to the ignorant visitors. And it gave him an income to spend on the food that was needed to supplement the rations.

He was also worried about Andres. His proud son seemed to have lost some of his spirit. And he felt partially to blame. Perhaps he should never have tried to talk him into honoring his father's word, perhaps Lazaro should never have come in from Mexico. It was all so hard to weigh. He'd had to think about the People. But were they really better off now?

The day before, the post commander had told them they would commence building cabins that would constitute their own village. At least that would be something to keep the men busy.

He sighed and went to get another arrow.

Lizah began to cough in early September. At first it was barely noticeable, maybe once every couple of hours. Within a couple of weeks it was more frequent. She began to lose weight and one day there was a trace of blood on her handkerchief. She didn't tell Andres about it. Nor did she tell him about the dream she had, the dream in which she saw Victorio beckon to her from a bright, hazy place. She talked to Tze-go-juni. "I have the chest disease, and I have no healing power for it."

Tze-go-juni had shrunk at least four inches and was bent over, twisted now in her advanced age. No one could even guess at how many summers she had lived, but everyone was certain it was well over a hundred. The oldest person in the clan had eighty-one summers, but couldn't remember when the shaman didn't *look* old. And Tze-go-juni wasn't telling. Her voice was raspy, not loud. "I caught a mouse yesterday and I will fix a powder for you. And I have some hoddentin I've been saving."

Lizah nodded her thanks. "I don't want Andres to know."

"He knows you cough."

"I try to hide it."

"You can't hide it in your sleep."

"Maybe it's the cold sickness."

The old shaman shook her painted, wrinkled face. "No, it's the *kah-kaa ná'ilgani*, the killer. You know that."

They were alone at the clothes washing area. Pain crossed Lizah's face. "I'm not afraid to die, but who will care for Andres and Taza? Andres is so troubled."

"Your husband is Child of the Water. He is deeply troubled about how he can save his people. But he'll survive all. Remember, he is the son of White Painted Woman. Ussen will find a way for him. Always remember that."

The tubercle bacillus in Lizah's lungs gradually began to consume her. She suffered from fever, night sweats, loss of appetite, and weight loss. In mid-November, the assistant post surgeon, Dr. Walter Reed, admitted her to the post hospital. Captain Reed, who perhaps knew the Apaches as well as any doctor in the country, had been stationed at Forts Lowell, Yuma, and Apache in Arizona prior to coming to Mount Vernon Barracks. He seemed to be a highly dedicated person, Andres thought when they first met. Shortly after the medical officer's arrival, he was able to convince Washington that the Indians' daily rations had to be increased. Now he was struggling with the unknowns of the consumptive diseases that afflicted the prisoners from the arid west.

Naturally Andres had dropped all animosity in dealing with the doctor, and Reed agreed to let him sit by Lizah's bedside as much as he wished.

"I can't promise anything," Reed said the day they admitted her. "We simply don't have a cure. We can only hope she's one of the few who have that special something in their bodies to fight it off."

"She's a very special woman to the People."

"So I've heard. Maybe her powers will work."

But Andres saw the doubt in his eye.

Eight nights later, as he was sitting by her bedside half-asleep, Andres heard her faint voice. "Andres . . . are you there?"

He took her hand. "Yes, my dove."

"I just saw White Painted Woman."

"That's nice," was all he could manage.

"She smiled at me." She coughed and he wiped the scarlet-streaked sputum from her lips.

Her voice sounded worse, more raspy than ever. "She beckoned to me."

"Did she say anything, my dove?"

"Her lips moved . . . I think she said, 'Come.' "

The words sliced into his heart. "It was just a dream," he said softly, trying to keep his fear from showing.

Lizah closed her eyes and was quiet for several moments. Opening them, she smiled faintly. "She wants me in the Happy Place, my husband. She wants me to be with her and to take away my pain."

"But she means in many years' time, not now."

"No, I think she means soon. It's all right, my husband, I'm ready. There is much I can do to assist her in the Happy Place."

She quickly drifted off to sleep, her hand in his, a gentle smile on her face.

Forty minutes later she was dead.

And so was part of Andres Murphy.

34

Carlota moved into the house shortly before its full completion in May of 1891. Of red brick, the two-story house was built by the noted contractor, William Laizure, at 879 Santa Rita Street. Carlota had worked closely with him in the planning, knowing quite clearly what she wanted. But she had also been open to the builder's architectural ideas. In the end, they had agreed on using a combination of styles such as ornamental brickwork, particularly in segmental arches over windows and door openings. Queen Anne windows were his trademark and she found no objection to their inclusion, nor to the shingled Mansard roof. The three-sided angled Mansarded front porch was her idea. The house had just three bedrooms, but the upstairs master was quite large with a sitting area and a ceramic fireplace. The lower floor had a large enough parlor to entertain fifty guests, while the dining room held a mahogany table that could seat sixteen if necessary. The library had glass-windowed bookcases on each side of a Mexican style rounded ceramic fireplace that was larger than the usual kiva type. All ceilings were eleven feet high, the hardwood floors being covered in places by thick Persian rugs that Carlota had had shipped in from Cairo.

She had invited eighty-three guests to the housewarming, and only two women who disliked her had failed to attend the gala event. Everyone on the hospital board, of which she was already a past president, had brought gifts, although she had specified in the invitation that there would be none. Rafe had not attended, but had sent a small ornately gilded oval mirror to hang in the vestibule. His congratulatory note from Chicago had been formally brief.

Now, a year later, in response to the urgent summons of the brass knocker, she opened the front door to find a man who looked faintly familiar standing on the porch. It was the half-breed Apache who had once worked at the store in Pinos Altos. He had a touch of gray in his dark hair and some harsh lines around his mouth. He was holding his hat, a high-crowned black Stetson with an eagle feather in its band. He spoke softly in Spanish. "Forgive me, Señora Murphy, but I am

Natalio, and I have come from San Carlos. You once offered me money to show you where Giant's Claw is located. I have a family now. I need it."

"Do you remember where it is?"

"I have not been there in a long time, but I can find it."

"You're sure?"

"How much will you pay me?"

"For everything, I will pay you three hundred dollars."

His tongue ran around his lips. "You once told me two hundred."

"I'll add one hundred if we find the gold. Why aren't you in Florida with the rest?"

Natalio's eyes hardened. "I'm part Mexican and was living at San Carlos when the People were put on the train. Besides, my wife is White Mountain, and they didn't have to go."

"All right, you go down to my livery stable and give the man this note and tell him to let you stay there, and to give you something to eat. We'll leave in the morning. Do you have a horse?"

"Yes. He's old, but he does good on hills."

She scribbled a short note and handed it to him. "Where will we start?"

"At Pinos Altos, Señora Murphy."

"Good. I'll have a pack mule loaded and we'll leave at seven in the morning."

Natalio donned his large hat as he nodded solemnly and turned to go. Carlota watched him go to the front gate where he had tied the old brown-and-white pony. As he mounted and rode away, she felt a surge of excitement. Finally! After all these years, she'd find her gold, her repayment for the terrible crime Lazaro had committed on her.

Her gold!

She'd never be able to sleep tonight, not a chance.

She glanced at the grandfather clock in the parlor. It was two in the afternoon; she'd best get busy putting the camping equipment together. After all, a lady didn't have to live like a savage to go prospecting.

At last, her gold!

She dressed like a man, wearing pants, a loose fitting, long-sleeved shirt and vest to partially hide her womanhood, and boots that reached almost to her knees. Atop her head, she wore a faded white Stetson with a flat crown. She had picked her favorite horse, a big black gelding she had named Major when he was born four years earlier. A Winchester carbine that she knew very well how to use rode in its scabbard. A pack mule carried the tent and small stove, along with part of the month's rations; a second horse bore the remainder.

They rode out of Silver City, heading for Pinos Altos at shortly after seven the next morning. It was cool and clear, the sun being more friendly than menacing on this early summer morning as it began to work its golden way up over the hills to the east. Reaching the crest, they picked their way around the town of Pinos Altos and headed west, following Bear Creek for a way.

"I watch Twin Sisters to keep my line," Natalio said from his lead position as he pointed back toward the two peaks to the northeast. "I spoke with an old Chihenne man just before they went to Florida, and he gave me this drawing."

Carlota glanced at the crude map, then looked around, remembering that day so long ago when Lazaro had taken her into the mountains to make her his wife. He had said something about the Twin Sisters, but she had been so upset she hadn't paid any attention. And when she had ridden out to search for the Claw, as she called it, she had tried to keep them in sight. Three times she had tried to find the place of gold in the past few years, riding once with the mountain man, David Barton, and twice by herself.

As they continued down Bear Creek, the temperature began to rise. The rich green vegetation and tall trees exhilarated her; it was incredibly lovely here at this point in the hills. At a turn in the creek Natalio stopped. Pointing to the middle of the shallow, rapidly flowing water he said solemnly, "I was told this is where Taza, son of Chief Lazaro and half brother of Andres Red Head, was murdered by White Eyes from Santa Rita."

Carlota stared at the water, her euphoria suddenly shattered.

A picture of a small boy guarding her flashed back from the haze of her captivity. A solemn little boy who gravely took his mission of keeping watch over her as the most serious challenge of his young life. She could see his bright black eyes watching . . . and later watching another little pair of bright eyes, those of Andres . . . her beautiful baby boy.

"How old was Taza when this happened?" she asked.

"I think about seventeen summers," her guide replied. "It is said he was punished for disturbing the oodo he found here. It is also said that Lazaro hung the killers of his son upside down from that tall tree over there."

Carlota followed his point and stared at the enormous pine.

A shaft of sunlight shone directly through the tall trees on the high opposite bank, landing right at the place in the water where Natalio had first pointed. Its reflection flashed into her eyes, bright, ripply. God! A spot in the clear running water of an isolated creek could evoke powerful recall, powerful connections . . . her son and his half brother were tied to this sandy, secluded bit of water bed like two young eagles, two young eagles—one dead, one now half-dead in some prison in Alabama. Tied together by the blood of the man she so hated.

They rode on, descending from the Continental Divide along Bear Creek until they reached a big arc called Horseshoe Bend. There, Natalio pointed north. "It is somewhere up there, maybe one day's ride, maybe more."

"Is there a trail?" Carlota asked.

"I must find it. We sleep here, I look."

"No, let's ride on together."

The half-breed shrugged, turned his horse and proceeded up the wash of a small stream. Without a trail, the going was rough and slow. Two hours later, as the sun began to settle behind a high set of hills to the west, Carlota felt her years and told Natalio that they could stop and spend the night in the clearing that greeted them. By the time the fire was going it was a welcome friend. She could feel the chill in the air, and remembered that they had been ascending for the last hour of the journey. They were probably well above six thousand feet, possibly close to seven thousand, she guessed.

They ate a simple meal of beef jerky and beans, along with some strong coffee. She was in her bedroll early, a small .32 pistol at her side. But, tired as she was, she couldn't get to sleep. After all these years, she was soon to find the payment of her debt. She had pictured that cave, the one where she'd found the nuggets, so often that it was burned into her memory.

The Claw. It was one of the few goals, one of the dreams that had held her interest in the last few years. Was it Cibola, the heart of the Seven Cities of Gold that Coronado and so many other explorers and adventurers had sought for so long? It was possible. After all, what Coronado had called Cibola in Zuni country had held no gold. Perhaps the Claw *was* it, and only *one* city. Natalio had told her the legend of Giant's Claw held that the ancient chief Silsoose had experienced an earthquake there, a tremor so powerful that the city and many of its people had been swallowed up in its massive wake.

If this were true, it was entirely possible that the place where they were headed was the place that men for centuries had sought. Wouldn't it be extraordinary that a woman, a woman unaccompanied by legions of soldiers, a woman with just a half-breed guide would be the discoverer of Cibola? She laughed to herself. Had she lost her mind?

Still, it was possible.

Natalio found the barely recognizable trail at shortly after noon the next day. It was guarded by large bushes as it led up the side of a steep wall. Carlota shielded her eyes as she stared upward. *Was this really it?*

"We tie horses here," Natalio said.

She nodded in agreement.

A few minutes later, gripping her carbine tightly, she began to follow her guide carefully up the old path. The climb was steep, tiring for her. Twice she paused to rest. Finally, Natalio stopped and turned. "Here is Giant's Claw," he announced with a broad grin.

Moments later she stepped over the brim of a huge oval bowl. Suddenly it came rushing back to her, the scene she'd relived so many times. Rugged rock walls of faded earth tones lined its sides. It was the huge rock spires, rising as high as a hundred feet, that first caught her attention. Scattered among them were the huge boulders that teamed with smaller rocks to create what some Brobdingnagian creature might have used for playthings. Like a monster called Giant, if one believed in the Apache Way.

As if the years had washed away and she was eighteen again, she was awed by the imposing pinnacles of rock. What had she thought they were? Yes, huge chess pieces. She could see Lazaro, feel the abhorrence, the fear. Also something special. Yes, she had felt some kind of power, and she sensed it now. There was something unique about this cathedral-like place, something . . . spiritual. No, that was ridiculous. Still . . .

They wandered around for a few minutes, watched solemnly by a pair of eagles nesting atop one of the spires. Naturally she had no idea that an ancient tribe had once called this place Eaglestone, nor would she have cared if she had. All she wanted to do was find the cave, the same cave that had given her the nuggets. "What was the name of the ancient chief?" she asked Natalio.

"Silsoose the Inquisitive One."

"And is it true that the people who lived here when he came worshipped gold?"

"Yes. And Ussen broke the ground and punished them."

Carlota shrugged. Ignorant myths and mysticism. She tried to remember where the cave was located. She told him the little bit she could recall about it being behind some kind of a large rock, and instructed him to go look by himself.

"But, Señora," he replied. "I don't want to leave you alone. There are strange spirits here."

She patted her carbine. "I'm fine."

As she watched him walk away she tried to put herself in the same position as the other time so long ago. Of course she hadn't been thinking clearly then, not after Lazaro had assaulted her. It seemed the cave was on the far side, the west. Picking a light brown rock on an outcrop of bushes as a beginning, she slowly began to work to her left. It seemed to her that some kind of a boulder had guarded the entrance to the cave, so she first looked behind each large rock. But she continued to find nothing even remotely resembling a cave entrance. Once she examined what looked like a type of collapse, but it seemed to be just an outcropping ledge that had fallen.

A minute later Natalio shrugged and said, "I find no cave, Señora."

She frowned. "It *has* to be here. Did you see any oodo?"

"No, Señora, nothing."

"Hmmm, I wonder if someone else could have found this place and picked it clean?"

Natalio just shrugged again.

"But who could have found it? Do you think the Apaches could have brought someone else here?"

"No. Impossible. Maybe Ussen broke the earth again."

An earthquake! That was possible, and it could easily make a cave fall in, get totally covered. Yes, if it happened once, it could happen again. She pursed her lips, nodding her head. Very possible. But why weren't there any signs of gold? If there had been so much in Silsoose's time, and plenty when she was here in '42, there should certainly be some left around, regardless of any shifting of the upper crust of earth. "Well, let's bring the horses up and make camp. We may have a long search ahead of us."

At the end of the second day it was obvious that the cave as she knew it was no longer in existence. Now it was time to dig. She drew a grid on a piece of paper, sketching in the steeper parts of the bowl and showing it to Natalio. "We'll start here," she said. "Wherever it looks like there could be any kind of a crevice we'll dig. You go to the left, I'll work to the right."

He looked troubled.

"What's wrong?"

"What if I hit oodo with the shovel or pick?"

"That'll make you rich and me happy."

"But I don't want to anger Ussen."

She scowled and spoke sharply. "Now, look here. I've had enough of this nonsense about oodo. You are part Mexican and you agreed to bring me here for *money*—which means you aren't all that religious yourself. If we find any substantial amount of gold, I'll pay you an extra one hundred dollars. That's a bonus of *two* hundred, more than you can make working at San Carlos or Fort Apache for *years*. Now get busy!"

Just after the three-quarter moon came up on the fifth night Carlota sat on a small boulder on the north end of the bowl. The evening was cool already, the stillness broken only by the occasional hooting of a watchful owl. The moonlight, pale and silvery, washed over the strange landscape, creating exaggerated inky shadows behind the rock formations that stood starkly against the starry sky. They had spent most of every day picking at the ground in various places around Giant's Claw, but had failed to unearth one single piece of gold. She couldn't believe it. It was as if a giant carpet sweeper had gone over the place, sucking up every shred of the metal. Or perhaps a giant magnet would be more apt. Or was gold nonmagnetized? She didn't know and didn't care. Her lode, the payment for the crime upon her young life, was simply gone.

But the feeling she'd first noticed when she arrived was still with her. It was euphoric, there was no question about it, surely a sense of power. She felt strong, with a warmness, a perception of well-being. Not as alone as she'd felt for so many years now. It didn't make sense, but she recalled that she had felt something similar all those years ago. But then she'd probably attributed the sensation to finding the gold nuggets.

It was all so vague.

She sighed, thinking of a story she'd read about a woman who went into an opium den in San Francisco's Chinatown. Was this place her opium den? It was such an incongruity—here she was finally in the Claw and her gold was gone. She had been somehow robbed, but instead of gnashing her teeth and wanting to break a pickaxe over a rock, she felt *comfortable*. She had to shake this false sense of well-being and get back to reality. And also get back to Silver City to her other affairs.

She stood, stretched and looked up at the nearest stone spire as the owl hooted softly again. What a bewitching place. She'd have to write to Rafe and tell him all about it. No, as soon as she could get her affairs in order, she'd just go to Chicago to be with him for a while. Yes, that would be nice. Break her loneliness. She'd bring him here someday soon, share this beauty and this feeling with him. He'd like that.

≫ **35** ≪

Men's evil manners live in brass;
Their virtues we write in water.
—William Shakespeare

Headquarters, Division of the Missouri
Chicago, Illinois
May 23, 1892

"Then, General Murphy, may I say that General Miles is incorrect in his statement that the Chiricahuas were all hostile in 1886, including the famous Apache scouts?" the senior reporter from the Washington *Star* asked.

Rafe frowned from behind his large oak desk. "He was absolutely wrong. Those scouts were the only reason we were ever able to get Chihuahua, Naiche, and Geronimo to come in."

"Miles denies this."

Rafe shrugged. "I don't want to get into a long-range argument with the general, but he operated against thirty-some hostile Apaches for over five months without killing or capturing a *single* one of them. It was only when he sent Lieutenant Gatewood with two trusted scouts that they were finally able to bring Geronimo and his group in. He also promised that they would be sent to join their families in Florida. Instead, that party was sent to Pensacola, while their families were sent to Fort Marion and then on to Mount Vernon Barracks in Alabama."

"But that isn't the only breach of faith, is it, General?"

Rafe shook his head. Back to the old sore spot. "No, it isn't. When I dealt with them and Chihuahua brought his people in, I promised them they would be sent back to their homelands after two years."

"And it has now been six years, right?" The reporter was a large man with a red nose, who had been on several major newspapers around the country in his long career. His column in the *Star* would be read by many people in the capital and reprinted in papers around the nation.

"Yes. And they trusted me."

"Who else knew about your two-year promise?"

Sheridan had been dead for four years, so it wouldn't matter to Little Phil. Rafe cleared his throat and plunged in. "General Sheridan knew and reneged. He gave me the power to deal in any logical manner with the hostile Apaches, then refused to back my hand."

"But wasn't he obeying orders from the White House?"

"I'm sure he was."

"Then the crime really rests on former President Cleveland's head."

"Responsibility always rests on the commander in chief."

"And what is your solution, General Murphy?"

"Get the Chiricahua, which is the name now applied to all of those in Alabama, although the group includes Warm Springs and Chihenne, back to Indian Territory."

"Do you mean Fort Sill in Oklahoma?"

"Yes, that's the best solution next to sending them to Mescalero in New Mexico—which is politically impossible at this time. I've been to Sill and the area is good for farming."

"Won't there be objections from the other Indian tribes in the area?"

Rafe sighed. "Nothing that can't be resolved."

The reporter had apparently done his homework. "Won't the people of New Mexico and Arizona object to even the Fort Sill move?"

"Probably, but they'd object to anything involving the Chiricahuas."

The reporter looked at him directly. "Why? Isn't Fort Sill seven hundred miles away from their homelands in Arizona?"

Rafe shook his handsome head, replying quietly, "You have to understand how much hatred there has been over a great many years. It'll still be there a hundred years from now."

"In your final estimate, General, are these Apaches the savages the world thinks they are?"

Rafe paused, looking away. A framed photograph on the wall displayed him and Lazaro shaking hands. Another was of him and Andres, both in uniform, at the end of the war. And yet another showed him with Lizah as he held the little boy, Taza. Finally he said, "I'm disappointed that you should ask such a question, sir. These Apaches are people. They have a culture, including a religion, that in many ways is superior to ours. Their way of life was simple, and it was warlike, but it was their only means of survival. They had pride that created endurance beyond our means. And they have suffered

360 « ROBERT SKIMIN

our many indecencies—such as this ridiculous incarceration—with silence and dignity. Does this make them savages?"

The reporter was scribbling furiously on his pad. "I guess it was the wrong question, sir," he replied. "Finally, about General Miles. The people of Tucson were going to give him a bejewelled ceremonial sword to commemorate his so-called defeat of the Chiricahua. But they didn't raise enough money to pay for it so the general paid for it himself. Does that incident reflect on his credibility?"

"I have no comment on that matter."

The reporter got to his feet. "Do the Apache know what a champion you are for them?"

Rafe spoke softly. "Does it matter?"

It was about ten minutes after the reporter's departure when the pain struck Rafe in the chest. It was like a sledgehammer had slammed into him, knocking out his breath. He gasped, clutching his chest, fighting to breathe. Staggering to the nearby sofa, he collapsed on it, gasping to breathe, struggling against the terrible pain. He thought immediately of Carlota, whispering, "No, not yet, please not yet."

He saw her walking in the Alameda in Mexico City, the most beautiful young woman he'd ever encountered. He was limping from his Chapultepec wound, walking with a cane. She had a handsome, black-eyed little boy with her. The sun was shining, and life on the Alameda moved by him as if he were the only one staring at that lovely creature. Was that music playing? Yes, soft strings, a Spanish guitar.

She smiled at him, that flashing, lovely smile of hers.

He wanted her instantly, wanted her to be his, all his.

It was all so bright, hazy now. He was in the mountains near a fire, talking to a very tall man, an Apache, a great chief. He was reaching out to the chief with accusing eyes, imploring, trying to tell him that it wasn't his fault. But the chief looked away. A younger man beside him, wearing a red headband, turned and his eyes were angry. He had the same eyes as the little boy on the Alameda.

The beautiful young woman was in a house now, yes, in Santa Fe. She was holding out a glass of wine to him, smiling, saying something.

"Carlota!"

His voice was raspy as the pain stabbed into him again, his cry a harsh whisper, "Carlota!"

* * *

It was a gray day at Arlington Cemetery, a muggy hot day that made one's clothes stick. The morning had begun with a drizzle, the gray clouds lessening their output until the rain stopped completely shortly before noon. But then, funeral days are supposed to be dark and dreary. Carlota was wearing the black silk dress that she had hurriedly purchased the day before, right after her arrival by train in Washington. There hadn't been time for much shopping, so she had been fortunate to find a suitable outfit just before the shops closed. The blouse had a high lacy collar of pearl gray topping a bodice of tiny ribbons of black satin. The skirt was fashionably full at the hips, and of course, long. Her black hat was wide brimmed, with one simple silk ribbon, the veil tied up. She didn't like wearing a veil over her eyes, regardless of the occasion.

She was seated in the center of a row of chairs that was reserved for immediate family. But since Rafe had no surviving relatives and Andres had not responded to her telegram or the invitation of the commander in chief, she was the only one in the row. Behind her, various dignitaries not involved as pallbearers were seated with their wives. The burial site was on the slope to the east of Arlington House as it looked into the now dark and rather swiftly moving Potomac. A small steamer was passing, black smoke puffing vigorously from its blue and purple stack, adding to the drabness of the day. For some inexplicable reason a foghorn sounded from upriver, even though one could see clearly for miles, past the tall spire of the Washington monument to the white dome of the Capitol in the distance.

Glancing back to Arlington House, she was awed by the massive white Doric columns that overwhelmed the sixty-foot-long front portico. There were eight of them, eight massive guardsmen overlooking the ceremony that was about to commence on the slope below. She had often looked at the former home of General Robert E. Lee during the war when she had lived in the capital, and had always been impressed by it. She had heard that it had been confiscated by the Federal government for a pittance of back taxes that had fallen in arrears because its owners were supposed to pay them in person. *General Lee or his wife coming to Washington in person to pay taxes during the war?*

She turned back to the gravesite. The east slope was reserved for the burial of dignitaries and she couldn't help but feel proud that her husband rated such accord. Born in Ohio, raised in Texas, a half-Mexican boy had risen to an unbelievable level of respect and accomplishment. Her eyes brimmed.

She had cheated him for so many years, refusing to join him, share his accomplishments and needs. But she couldn't think about that now. The army had to finish its rites of death for a fallen leader. And she had to bear up, be strong, not show her guilt.

The procession to the gravesite had been most striking. It had consisted, in order, of the colonel who was the escort commander, the band playing martial airs that brought back a flood of memories and a fresh batch of tears to her eyes, the escort that included the national colors, the firing squad, and the bugler; the honorary pallbearers included ex-President Rutherford B. Hayes from Ohio, Lieutenant General John A. Schofield, who had succeeded Sheridan as commander in chief after Little Phil's death, and a number of colonels and generals—a few of whom she had met many years earlier. They were followed by the horse-drawn caisson bearing Rafe's remains in a flag-covered casket, the actual pallbearers, an old sergeant proudly carrying Rafe's bright red general's flag with its two white stars, and finally the handsome caparisoned horse—riderless, with a pair of boots facing to the rear, the special honor afforded a cavalryman.

The dress uniforms were everywhere, a sweeping splash of dark blue sprinkled by gold brass, joining the other rich colors of accoutrements.

But the day was still gray, sadly gray, the color of grief.

Now the casket was being borne between the honorary pallbearers to the top of the grave in front of her. In spite of the drabness of the day, the stars and bars of the flag seemed to blink back at her. The band played the hymn "Rock of Ages," as she had requested, and then was silent. Next the pallbearers removed the flag from the casket and folded it, moving away when finished. The chaplain, a colonel, began the service. After some passages that she barely heard, he began a eulogy that glowingly reviewed Rafe's long and productive military career. "Perhaps," the chaplain said at the end, "no other American officer has done as much from the root of his heart for the American Indian as Rafael Murphy."

Finally, he said, "It was Milton who told us, 'Death is the golden key that opens the palace of eternity.' "

Immediately following his benediction, the cannon salute crashed from a few hundred yards away: thirteen volleys for a major general, fired in five-second intervals. As the sound of the last burst died away, the firing party raised its muskets and a staccato three volleys cracked into the sky.

The final touch was perhaps the most moving musical rendition ever known to man. The bugler raised his instrument to his lips and the clear notes of "Taps" filled the silent Arlington sky. The tears came again to Carlota's eyes and a cry tried to escape, but she caught it in her throat as the last bars drifted hauntingly away.

She stared stiffly at the casket as the folded flag was presented to her by General Schofield. She didn't even hear his words. The tears were gone, only the remorse and grief remained. She had failed this fine man whose remains lay in front of her, utterly failed him in her selfishness for most of the years of their long marriage.

That was as great a sin as she could imagine.

And now, now she was truly alone.

She had written the letter four weeks after her return to Silver City from Rafe's funeral. It had seemed rather brazen after all this time, but she was so lonely and her curiosity had finally won out. After all, the man had been her first love and actually her first husband. It had been a casual letter to him, asking about his health and family, about La Reina and its life. Nothing forward and nothing intended, she told herself. But deep down, she longed to see him.

Now she looked at the postmark on the envelope with the Mexican stamp: Janos, Mexico. Eagerly she tore it open and read its short message:

> Dear Señora Murphy,
> General Don Agustin de Gante was killed during an Apache raid several years ago. It is believed the savages were led by the hated Geronimo, but I saw Don Agustin killed by an Apache wearing a red head-band. And strangely, I heard this killer speak and curse in fluent Spanish as if he knew the don. You will be proud to know that the don fought bravely to the end.

The note was signed by one Raul Nieto, the overseer of the hacienda. Carlota stared at the words, remembering clearly a time back in Georgetown when Andres had been very angry at Agustin, had indeed challenged him to a duel. She'd seen the dark hate in Andres's eyes when he told the man who could have been his stepfather that someday he wouldn't let him back down.

But this?

She glanced back at the note. It had to have been Andres, and in spite of the shock of knowing, she felt a certain understanding. Hadn't she wanted to kill Agustin de Gante herself at one time? Her son had, in his eyes, merely righted an old wrong inflicted on his mother. Still, it made her terribly sad. Regardless of the things he had done, Agustin was still . . . what? A memory, a memory of a tall, handsome young man whom she had adored. A husband for a fleeting moment, a memory to sustain her in her captivity. A weak mother's boy who had broken her heart.

Regardless, he was one more void in her empty life.

The priest's name was Father Ignatius and he was originally from Mexico City. Now, after several years in small-town New Mexico parishes, he was the pastor of St. Vincent de Paul's. In his mid-fifties, he had a generous shock of white hair and a craggy face above his wiry frame. Carlota had tried confession again and had attended mass a few times since her return from Washington, but her gloom lingered. Finally she invited Father Ignatius to lunch at her home.

Over a light repast of Mexican food, she told him about her emptiness. He listened quietly as she described the guilt that continued to plague her. "I simply must find a means of cleansing myself," she said with brimming eyes as she reached the end of her story. "And I don't know if my religion is strong enough to do it."

"Sometimes," he said thoughtfully, "a return to the Church is difficult after an absence of many years. I, of course, believe that if you apply yourself assiduously you will find the faith and comfort that will fill your heart."

"I'm trying, but I'm unsure of myself."

"Do you know the cause of these alienations of your loved ones? Let's talk about your late husband—why wouldn't you live with him?"

"Because I wanted to be near my son."

"And you cut your son off because of your hatred for the Apaches?"

It was hard for her to say it. "Yes. You see he threw everything I had done for him away."

"How do you know that? Are you measuring on your scales or his? It may be that the very moral base you gave him provided the impetus to follow his spiritual and conscientious leanings. Have you ever considered that?"

"No," she replied tentatively. "I don't consider living as a savage a moral issue."

"Apparently it was a powerful issue to him."

"Well, it doesn't matter now. He won't even acknowledge my existence."

They talked some more and she told him about the sense of tranquility and power she had felt in Giant's Claw.

At length he said, "I think there may be some salvation for you in that place." He smiled ruefully. "The reason I'm not a bishop is that I'm sort of a nonconformist. I think your problem can be solved through prayer. If I didn't, I'd take off this collar in an instant. But you need to somehow conquer the basis for your problems. I think you must find a way to overcome your hate. Forgiveness, you know, can wash away the most terrible of guilts."

It took her a moment to reply. "I'm not sure I *can* forgive."

They were at the end of the meal and discussion. Father Ignatius glanced at the mantel clock. "I must be going." He smiled. "Give the Church a chance, Mrs. Murphy. But try whatever may work for you."

She left two days later for Giant's Claw. Using the map that she'd obtained from Natalio, she followed the landmarks and arrived there just as the huge red sun was reaching for the western horizon. She had considered bringing a stable hand along to help her set up the little camp, but had finally decided against it. She was in good health, strong, and besides, she didn't want anyone else to know about this private place. As far as her safety went, she was perfectly capable of fending for herself. Topping the crest as the path reached the rim of the bowl, she stopped and stared in wonder once more at the huge rock formations. They were bathed in a rich, reddish glow from the departing sun, their earth tones at different levels, ornate in their layers.

She stood for a few moments, soaking in the beauty, the awesomeness of the place, waiting for the feeling of power to overcome her. It wasn't quite as remarkable as before, but there was a sense of comfort in the quiet of the breathtaking place.

She made the fire first, while there was still light, then pitched the tent and unpacked the horses. After nibbling on some hardtack and drinking some coffee, she wandered around the area for a short time. It was clean and cool in the early evening, and she did feel relaxed. But she knew it was mostly due to being tired from the long ride. Back at the tent she knelt beside a small boulder and began to pray, but it wasn't fulfilling for her. She fell asleep in her blanket shortly after finishing.

* * *

Three days later, after awakening from an afternoon nap, she walked toward a large column of rock that had a small outcrop near its peak. She had spotted two eagles there the day she arrived and guessed they might have a nest on it. It was a few feet from the base of this pillar that she saw something shiny in the grass. It was a charm of some sort on a dried, broken old thong of leather. Looking at it closely she thought it looked vaguely familiar. She'd seen something like it somewhere in the past.

She rubbed it on her pants and looked at it closely. It was shiny, some kind of stone, with a purplish caste like amethyst. Spear shaped. She *knew* she'd seen it or something similar before. *Where?* Its memory seemed a long time ago, what could it be?

A face came to her, a bizarre face above an amulet.

Tze-go-juni! God, how could she ever forget? That quartz amulet of hers had hung on her bony chest most of the time, her favorite charm. Benita had told her it was from a tree that had been struck by lightning, or something like that. Or maybe not. But the witch had worn an amulet just like this, she was certain. She'd once fixed her attention on it when the shaman was close to her, thinking that was just where she'd like to plant her knife. The old hag!

Staring at the amulet, she suddenly had a feeling of strength.

Could this be a sign?

Could this piece of quartz actually have been Tze-go-juni's? Could she have somehow lost it while Lazaro hid his people here? Andres had mentioned the shaman when he first started going to visit the Apaches; had, in fact, said that she seemed as healthy as a bear. But that had been years earlier.

What kind of a sign could it be? What could it mean?

Or was it just something that had been lost by someone else?

If so, why did she suddenly have this special feeling?

Surely it meant something.

This place, the charm . . . *could her answer be in the Apaches?*

An hour later she was still tossing her conundrum around when she found herself at the place where she thought the cave had been. Something cast a reflection back at her from the grass. Leaning down, she saw what it was—*a gold nugget!* She picked it up, hardly able to control her excitement. It was nearly a half of an inch in diameter, not too large, but it was gold! She looked around. Could there be more? Could something have uprooted the gold that had been here all the time?

She'd known all along she'd find it!

She rolled it around in her hand, feeling its coolness. She should start digging again. Good thing she brought the pick and shovel along. Yes, she'd start right here!

Suddenly the feeling of power grew, giving her a sense of unbelievable strength. And just as quickly it left her. She looked at the little nugget. Its coolness had gone, and there was no reflection whatsoever from it. It was as if it wasn't gold anymore.

For some reason she reached into her pants pocket and felt the quartz amulet. Pulling it out, she was greeted by a purple reflection. Glancing back at the nugget, she saw that it was still dull, as if something had suddenly coated it with dirty water. And all at once the words she had heard so often flashed through her mind: *"Gold is the tears of Ussen. It is sacred, not ever to be disturbed in the ground."*

Slowly, without questioning why she was doing it, she moved a couple of paces away to where she had found the nugget and placed it in exactly the same place.

36

Carlota arrived in Mount Vernon nine days later. Checking in at the small but clean Alabama Hotel, she learned that she could get a hack out to the army post quite easily. She asked the driver, who prided himself in his knowledge of the Indians at the Barracks, to drive her by what was known as Apache Village. In a slightly singsong delivery he rattled off his spiel: "These Apaches built their own cabins according to how the Army told them to do it shortly after they were shipped here from Florida. Them there cabins have two rooms, each ten feet square, with earth floors. They ain't got much furniture, and they cook and sleep on the ground. The army gave 'em Sibley stoves for heat, but I've heard those places get mighty hot in our Alabama summer. And you gotta remember, they's prisoners of war." He chuckled. "But you know how savages are—they don't suffer like us humans."

Carlota gave him a sharp look, resenting his comment, but saying nothing. Now she was here to find help and to see her son—who was far from a "nonhuman."

As the driver stopped the buggy near the edge of the village, she saw a group of boys playing marbles. Somewhere in there she had a grandson. God, she wouldn't know him if he walked right up to her! He had probably just had his eleventh birthday, she calculated. Unbelievable. Had she been estranged from Andres for nearly eleven years? *Oh, Andres, where are you?*

He had to talk to her, just had to. There was so much to be said, to be repaired, to be shared—

"Old Geronimo's in there, you know," the driver said. "They finally brought him and some of those other hostiles up from Pensacola some time back. At least he's there when he ain't running around with some circus someplace. I hear he gets mighty drunk and raises a little hell once in a while." He chuckled. "And they's another couple of chiefs. One of 'em's Naeeche, and another's called Chewawa. But the big one is the most important, I hear tell. Biggest darned Indian I ever seen. Old man, too, about eighty. Name's *Lazaro*."

God, for some reason she knew he'd still be alive, but she hadn't given much thought to seeing him. She drew in a deep breath and exhaled it. This cast a different light on everything. As much as she wanted to find peace from the Apaches and see her son, she would have absolutely nothing to do with the wretched man who had ruined her early life.

Her first stop was at the headquarters of the post commander. The major saw her at once, coming out of his office to the anteroom to greet her. "I once served under General Murphy," he said, beaming. "Up in the Sioux wars. How may I help you, Ma'am?"

He showed her into his office and held a chair for her beside his desk. "I'm here to see my son," she explained. "He is also the general's stepson—Andres Murphy."

The major, a man in his early forties with a short blond beard, looked puzzled. "I had no idea such a person existed. You say he's here?"

"Yes, he's living as an Apache, perhaps named Red Head."

The major nodded his head. "Yes, there is a Red Head, son of Chief Lazaro. But I had no idea—"

"It's a long story. At any rate, Major, I'll be staying in town for a while, visiting from New Mexico, and I'd like to be able to come and go among the Apaches as freely as they'll permit."

"That should be no problem, Mrs. Murphy."

"Thank you. Oh, and do you know if there is an old medicine woman in the Chihenne or Warm Springs group called Tze-go-juni?"

The major peered at a roster, finally looking up and nodding his head. "Yes, here she is. Tze-go-juni, age unknown, assumed to be in her mid-nineties. She lives in a cabin close to that of Lazaro."

"Good. Now do you suppose it would be possible to have Andres, or Red Head, meet me some place outside of the village? We've been estranged for a number of years and I think it would be best to do it that way."

"Yes, I can have him meet you in our small officers' mess if you wish."

"That would be nice of you."

"By the way, I should tell you. Your son may be ill."

Trying not to show her sudden alarm, Carlota asked, "What do you mean, *may* be?"

"Whenever I've seen him, he seems to be in a trance. I'm told he has been that way since his wife died several years ago. Consumption, like so many others, you know."

His Apache wife dead? Lizah, that was her name. She couldn't help but feel sorry. "When can I see him?" she asked, the anticipation building.

"As soon as my adjutant can fetch him to the mess. I'll escort you there myself."

Fifteen minutes later Andres walked into the dining room. Carlota wasn't prepared for the gray-haired man with slightly sunken eyes who greeted her. "Hello, Mother," he said quietly.

"Andres!" she exclaimed, smiling as she got to her feet. She went to him holding her arms open, but he turned away. She collected herself, opening with the words she'd rehearsed over and over. "Darling, I've come to apologize for all the horrid things I did and said years ago."

"Why?" he asked listlessly.

"Because, if you'll forgive me, I'll have something left in my barren life. Oh, my darling, I've missed you so. I didn't even know you had lost your wife. I'm terribly sorry."

She saw the lines in his handsome face as he said, "Why should you be sorry? She was just an Apache savage, remember?" He turned away.

She caught his arm. "Don't, Andres, don't keep shutting me out. I know you must have gotten the telegraph about Rafe's death. I'm just a lonely woman who has no one left in the world except you and your son."

"Huh," he replied. "I didn't know you even remembered you had a grandson."

Her eyes were large, pleading. "I want to see him so badly."

Andres looked at her, absently, not even with dislike or the loathing she had half expected. After a couple of moments he said, "Why don't you just get back on a train to New Mexico? Go back to your money and possessions. You can go there, you know. *You* aren't a prisoner."

It was time to tell him. "I can't. I want to help."

"Help what?"

"I have Rafe's papers, the ones that relate to getting the People back to Indian Territory. I have all of his correspondence, even the last papers he was putting together to present his case to the government."

Again Andres's tone was spiritless. "It's a waste of time. Washington will keep us here forever."

"No, don't you see—he had *hope!* He wrote about Fort Sill in Oklahoma, where he visited. It isn't your Willows Country, but it's a step in the right direction. He thought if you could be relocated there, another move to New Mexico might be made at a later date."

Andres just shook his head.

"Rafe also wrote that he thought one man could best influence the people in Washington, one man who could be more believable than any other . . . you."

Again Andres said nothing.

"Darling, you're a good lawyer," she pleaded. "You can be eloquent and logical, and you are half-Apache. Who could be better suited?"

"It would be a waste of time."

"A waste of time?" she retorted. "What is this you're doing now? I've been told you are just sitting on your blanket like an old brave who has nothing left to do but brag about his youth. And you don't even do that!"

A touch of spark showed in his eyes. "How do you know what I do?"

"I heard." Her tone softened as she tried to take his hand. "Oh, Andres, my darling, let me help. Let me provide the money for you to go to Washington and win this case for your people."

After a long pause he said, "I'll think about it."

She smiled. "Good! Now, when can I see my grandson?"

"Where are you staying?"

"In town, at the Alabama Hotel."

"Come back here to the village in two days, in the afternoon. Then I'll let you know if you can see him."

She wanted to hug him, but held back. "That's fine, darling, just fine. I'll be here then. Oh, and I was hoping to see Tze-go-juni, as well."

"For what?"

"I need to find some peace and I thought, as a healer, she might have some answers for me."

Andres shook his head. "I don't think she'll talk to you."

"Tell her I'll pay her well."

Andres just shrugged.

She arrived at the Barracks by the same hack at shortly after one in the afternoon, two days later. Getting out at Apache Village, she told the driver to wait and walked down what appeared to be the main street. It was a hot day and most of the Apaches were inside their cabins. Of the ones who were outside, or watching from doorways, she wondered how many of the older ones might remember a spirited young bride of eighteen all those years ago. She wondered if Benita were still alive. She'd have to ask. Encountering a boy of about eight, she said, "Where may I find Red Head?" in Spanish.

He looked at her bashfully and pointed to a cabin. "There," he replied in English, and quickly turned and ran away.

She remembered seeing in one of Rafe's papers that there was a school at Mount Vernon Barracks that was conducted mostly in English. She started for the cabin the boy had pointed out, but Andres quickly stepped outside and walked toward her. At his side was a tall young boy. She could feel her breath quicken. He had to be her grandson! As they approached she could see that he was slender, but well formed. His black hair was long, his eyes soft brown, like his father's. His carriage was erect and she could see his pride. A beautiful boy. She thought back to Santa Fe, when Andres had been about the same age. Another beautiful boy. And now she had a new young son.

If only they would let her into their lives.

"This is Taza," Andres said, introducing them.

The boy nodded his head stiffly and extended his hand, saying in good English, "I'm pleased to meet you, Mrs. Murphy."

She wanted to keep holding his hand, but he pulled it back. "What grade are you in, in school, Taza?" she asked.

"We don't have grades," he replied stiffly, adding, "Ma'am."

"Now run along," his father said.

"But, can't he stay a while?" Carlota asked.

"No, he has things to do."

She nodded her head. She couldn't push anything. "He's a handsome boy, Andres. And well-mannered. I'm proud to be his grandmother."

His tone was guarded. "At this point you are only Mrs. Murphy."

"Who takes care of him—Benita?"

"No, she's dead like so many others, of consumption. My sister, Gabriela, cooks for us. But his grandfather is a strong influence in his life."

"Oh, how is Lazaro?" she asked, knowing the words sounded hollow.

"As fine as ever."

She switched the subject. "Did you speak to Tze-go-juni?"

"She'll see you tomorrow morning, but only because she needs money. She still dislikes you."

She thought back to that vivid time when she escaped, remembering clearly how she had rammed the stiletto into the shaman's stomach. "She has reason," she said quietly.

"I've decided to read the general's papers."

"Oh, good! I have them in the buggy."

His voice was flat. "But it doesn't mean I'm going to do anything."

She nodded her head. "Just read them and think about it."

"How long are you staying here?"

"As long as it takes to find peace and get you off your blanket."

"Don't count on anything. Let's go get the papers."

Lazaro had watched their meeting from the window in his cabin. He couldn't believe how unsettling it was to see Carlota after such a long time. The picture of a beautiful young woman with blue-black hair and eyes the color of the summer sky had lingered with him all this time. The last he'd seen her was in Pinos Altos. How beautiful she had been in her middle years. Now—she must have well over sixty summers— she was still beauteous. Her figure looked still good, and her hair looked mostly still black, at least what little he could see under her hat.

She was here, in his village, not on some White Eye street where he was the visitor. He had every right to walk right up to her and say, "Hello, my wife, how are you? I'm glad to see you, and I still love you."

But he couldn't do it. Andres had told him why she came, also adding that she was troubled and wanted healing from Tze-go-juni. Besides, he had this feeling deep down that she still did not want to see her Chihenne husband. He shrugged. If he had waited fifty summers for her, he could wait some more.

Besides, there was a problem. Andres had told him she was very rich, that she had many White Eye houses and many horses. And now he had practically nothing, not even one good horse, practically no Power. When he stole her from the Nakai-ye, he owned many horses, and his words were heeded wherever the People lived and fought. Now, while the People still came to him for advice and the settling of problems—and the White Eye nantan, the major, treated him with respect—he was just an old nantan with nothing of value to give this woman.

Nothing but his pride.

In fact, there was little left *but* his pride and memory. Of course he still had his family, and particularly his fine grandson. There had been strain between him and Andres back in Arizona, but it was long gone.

He hated being away from the Willows Country, but he'd resigned himself a long time ago to what must be. The Chihenne Way had been overcome by the White Eye Way, and only an Apache could understand how to manage it.

Carlota.

He would never stop loving her.

Andres studied the package of papers his mother had brought along to Alabama by the light of the kerosene lamp in his father's cabin that evening. He had given them a cursory examination after getting them in the afternoon, but now he looked at them carefully. People, letters, opinions, and the maze of bureaucratic incompetence and disinterest . . . it all added up to nothing tangible. He did have to hand it to his stepfather for trying though. Rafe had never given up, not until his dying day.

Maybe he should have gone up to Washington for the funeral.

But it was too much trouble. He simply didn't want any part of that world anymore. How could he have attended that kind of a ceremony in his limited wardrobe with his long hair and moccasins? How could he have honored the flag he once so loved and fought for? Should he have worn his Medal of Honor on his wrinkled coat? And acted out a lie? Pretended he didn't despise that blue uniform? Those generals? He wouldn't have trusted himself up there—he might have lost his head and assaulted one of those senior officers or politicians.

On the other hand, he really had owed it to Rafe to attend. The man had done so much for him, been his father all those years. And what did he get in return—the surly side of an ungrateful adopted son.

One persistency stuck out in Rafe's papers: his concern that his two-year promise about the Apache stay in Florida be honored. For a man of his integrity, the breaking of this promise by his superiors must have been a terrible blow. The move to Alabama hadn't been the answer. He had promised they could go back home after two years. And he had died, knowing the People would never understand.

Of all the things he owed Rafael Murphy, this stuck out as something he might rectify. He'd have to think about it.

He looked at a letter with a familiar name: Richard Hartman, *Delegate*. Richard Hartman, Honorable Representative of the Territory of New Mexico in the Congress of the United States! The rebel general had risen high. He thought back to when Hartman had taken him in, also like a son, and treated him so well. He remembered an early-morning duel, kind words, the newspaper work. . . .

The letter from Hartman to Rafe was interesting. He stated that it would be impossible at any time in the immediate future to return the Chiricahuas to New Mexico or Arizona, such was the lingering hatred against them. But he was willing to add his support for a move to Fort Sill. At least this was one member of the government who was specific. And he knew Hartman was a man of his word. It would bear thinking about also.

But he wasn't even sure it mattered. As long as everyone was a prisoner, who cared where they spent their lives? All he wanted to do was keep on gathering Apache lore for his book. He had some two thousand pages of notes compiled now, and one of these days he would start putting it all together. Then the world would know about this great crime!

His mother had used the derogatory term "sitting on his blanket," but she didn't understand. What was it Descartes said? *"Cogito, ergo sum*—I think, therefore, I am."

Carlota sat on the bench under the oak tree by the edge of Apache Village. Pulling the watch from her purse, she looked at it for the fourth time. The old shaman was keeping her waiting on purpose and there wasn't anything she could do about it. Forty minutes was just too long! she told herself impatiently. The old hag was impertinent for doing this when she was no more than a hundred yards away, absolutely impertinent! She ought to just get up and leave.

But then she'd just have to come back and go through the whole thing again. She hated it when all of her control was taken away. Just hated it! She blew out a deep breath and watched a handful of little Apache girls playing hopscotch several yards away. Their laughter was gay and carefree as they jumped through the outline in the dust. At least they were becoming Americanized, she said to herself.

At that moment she saw Tze-go-juni come out of the village street, moving slowly on a cane. As the medicine woman approached, Carlota saw that she was wearing long moccasins to the knees and black pants. Over the trousers she wore a blouse or shirt of some kind of black material. This was adorned with various symbols stitched in multicolored beads and topped off by a number of charms that she wore around her neck. On her head was a man's black derby, which was also decorated with various objects. A black-and-white eagle's feather stood tall at the back of the hat. As the ancient shaman drew close, Carlota could see that her face was painted with only a thin stripe of red on each cheek and some black around her eyes.

She moved stiffly, and upon reaching the bench said in excellent Spanish, "It will cost you five American dollars each time you see me, woman." Her tone was cold, her dark eyes nearly lost in wrinkles, shadow and paint. The old scar on her nose was hardly noticeable. A couple of black teeth could be seen when she spoke.

I'd pay her five *hundred*, Carlota said to herself, if only she could help me. She smiled, reaching into her purse and finding a bill. "That's fine," she replied, handing it over.

Tze-go-juni seated herself stiffly on the wooden bench. "What is it you want, woman?" she asked in a hoarse but surprisingly strong voice. She peered closely at Carlota's face.

"I need to find peace," Carlota replied quietly. The woman's face was etched in a thousand wrinkles, deep-set lines, cross-hatched lines, sagging flesh that made up her remarkable network of aging. Carlota remembered that she had thought the woman an old hag nearly fifty years ago!

The shaman studied her for a full minute before replying, "Why do you think I can help you? Except for being a vessel for your sacred son, you have always been my enemy."

Carlota had forgotten that the woman had regarded Andres as Child of the Water when he was born. She wondered what she thought now, with Andres being so withdrawn. Taking the quartz amulet from her purse, she said, "Because I have been to Giant's Claw, where I found this. Since I think it once belonged to you, I saw it as a sign that I should come to you for help." She handed it over to the shaman.

Tze-go-juni looked at it closely for a moment, then nodded her head vigorously. "It *is* mine, woman. I lost it one night in a violent storm while we were staying in Giant's Claw. Yes, it could be a sign. Why were you there?"

Carlota decided to tell the truth. "I was looking for gold sometime earlier, but this time I was looking for something that would give me peace."

The shaman frowned. "Did you take the oodo?"

"No, none."

"Why did you go *there* looking for peace?"

Carlota told her about her long-term emptiness and loneliness, the loss of her husband, the special feeling she had experienced in her earlier visits to the Claw.

Tze-go-juni studied her for several moments before saying, "Did you come to take your son back?"

Now it was Carlota's turn to weigh her answer. She nodded. "I'm a mother, wise one. What woman wouldn't want her son near?"

"Huh!" was the only comment from the medicine woman, who continued to watch her with piercing eyes.

"But," Carlota continued, "I know he'll always stay with the People, so I wish only for him to forgive me for treating him so badly." With full candor she related her rejection of Lizah and Andres on that Christmas in Silver City.

The medicine woman shook her head, frowning. "He should never have stooped to coming to you."

"Can you help me?" Carlota asked softly, trying to read those strange eyes.

The shaman pulled herself to her feet on the cane. "I don't know, woman. Not today. I must think on it and see if I want to. Come back tomorrow at the same time . . . and bring money."

As she hobbled away, Carlota thought about how well she spoke in Spanish. It was as if she had been fully educated in the language. Was the woman truly a witch with powers from the unknown?

Moments later Carlota spotted a tall boy and her pulse quickened. "Taza!" she called out.

The boy turned from where he was talking to some other boys and looked at her quietly.

"May I speak to you?" she asked loudly.

He said something to the boys, then turned and came to her. "Yes, Mrs. Murphy?" he said politely in English.

"Oh, please. You know I'm your grandmother. Don't be so formal."

His eyes were guarded, those soft brown eyes like his father's. She guessed that it had something to do with the heredity, of her blue eyes somehow muting the coal black eyes of . . . of Lazaro. She still had trouble saying his name in any kind of a normal way. But then she thought that Lizah's eyes had been less than black also.

"My father told me to call you Mrs. Murphy."

She smiled. "Then you should do as your father says. But I'll tell you what—in Spanish you are my *nieto* and I am your *abuela*. When we're alone, why don't you call me *Abby*? No one will know but us, if you wish."

She reached in her large purse and withdrew a small box wrapped in white paper that was bound by a red ribbon. "I have a present for you, my dear," she said, handing it to him.

He looked down at, not taking it.

"Please," she said. "It would make me very happy if you would accept it."

Slowly his hand went out to the box. After looking at it for a couple of moments he began to carefully open it. Inside was a silver-cased pocket watch on a silver chain. His eyes betrayed him momentarily as he looked at it, showing his pleasure. His expression went back to a mask as he said, "Thank you, Abby."

They walked together for several minutes as she told him about her horses and life in Silver City. "Someday I hope you can visit me there," she said. "You can ride with me up into the mountains. Are you a good rider?"

His face clouded. "I don't know how to ride. We have no horses."

She hadn't even thought of such a thing. An Apache boy without a pony! And he'd been too young when they left Arizona. "Perhaps if you ever get back to Indian Territory that'll change," she replied. "Now would you please tell your father I wish to speak to him if he has time."

"No, I haven't made a decision, Mother," Andres replied casually. "But I don't think I want to get involved. It all seems so useless."

"Did you read all of Rafe's papers?" Carlota asked.

"Yes, but what did he accomplish?"

"He was instrumental in getting you moved from Florida to here."

"From one prison to another."

"Haven't the consumption deaths decreased?"

The sadness crossed his face. "Some, but they might cease altogether if the People were back home."

She touched his hand. "Oh, Andres, I hate to see you just *stagnate*. You have so much talent. What about your writing?"

"I continue to work on it—the book I started back in Silver City."

"Can I help you get it published?"

He looked away. "No, it isn't ready."

"What do you do all day?"

"Mostly think."

"You were always so energetic."

He just shrugged.

"If you were to go to Washington, it would give you incentive
. . . a mission."

"Mother, please!"

"All right, all right. I just hate to see your fine mind in limbo. Can
I get you some books?"

"No. Did Tze-go-juni have any words of wisdom for you?"

"Not exactly. She's going to think about it. But I know one thing,
darling. If you can possibly forgive me for my terrible *faux pas* in
Silver City, part of my problem will be solved."

He looked at her solemnly for a moment before replying, "I'll also
think about that."

Carlota saw Tze-go-juni three times in the next week, but each time
the shaman was guarded in her words. Now, on a Sunday, the two
women sat on the same bench in the shade of the oak tree. Finally the
medicine woman said, "Tell me exactly what you want, woman."

Carlota thought a moment before replying, "I want peace in my
heart and the love of my family."

"What about all of your big houses and your horses?"

"They're unimportant to me." She wasn't sure she was *positive*
about that statement, but they were totally unmeaningful to her at
this time.

Tze-go-juni's dark eyes, now fully surrounded by shiny black paint,
were boring into hers. "Would you give them all up for the peace you
seek?"

"I don't know about *all* of them, but I think so."

"Would you live like the People—here in these White Eye
houses?"

"Perhaps, if I could cook and do things for Andres and Taza." She
knew the government would never permit her to do so, which made
it such an easy answer. But, oh God, yes, she'd like to take care of
them!

The shaman shifted what appeared to be a cud of sorts in her nearly
toothless mouth. "Do you think that would be true peace?"

"I don't know."

"True peace could only come if you *enjoyed* doing it, and wanted
to do nothing else for the rest of your life."

Carlota waited as the medicine woman looked away for at least a
minute, apparently lost in thought. Finally her dark eyes came back
as she said, "But you could never do that, woman, because you still
hate us."

"But—"

"I can see it in your eyes, feel it when you talk. You speak of change, but it's merely words. You are old and lonely. And you're afraid. That's one of the big differences between you and an Apache. The hate is something you can't control."

"Control?" Carlota suddenly said more harshly than she wanted to. "I was taken from the young man I dearly loved on my wedding day, *stolen*, and forced to live in a manner I loathed, forced to be wife to a man I equally loathed. And I survived being a *prisoner* by hating. You're a woman, you should understand that!"

Tze-go-juni's wrinkles contracted into a frown. "You aren't listening, woman. What you just said merely proves what I told you. The hate lingers because you can't *control* it. You are Nakai-ye and White Eye and your way is to control everything. The Apache learns to accept that which he can't control and make an alliance with it. This way it lives only in a harmonious manner, not having importance. This is how we manage our captivity here. This is how our great chief can live in disgraceful humility, how our brave warriors can accept such a worthless way of life. Your son seems different to you. That's because he has partially made an alliance with this White Eye imprisonment. But some of his other way of life carries over and, like you, he can't quite conquer his hate."

"But there are things he can *do* for you people."

The shaman sighed, looking away again. "You see, you don't listen to me. By continuing to hate, or continuing this wish to control, you give it a right to exist, give it continued life. You want your son to save the People, *you* want him to do so. *He* must want to do so. Only then can he fully live in alliance with his hatred and conquer it."

"But how, after all these years, can I overcome my feelings and make such an alliance—other than as I'm doing now?"

Tze-go-juni hauled herself slowly to her feet, leaning on the cane, looking tired. "It can't be done all at once. You must remove a piece and put a new piece in, letting it take its time to heal."

"But I'm old," Carlota said, reaching out, wanting to touch her. "I haven't got much time for it to heal."

The medicine woman shrugged. "You have the rest of your life. Do you want it to change?"

"Yes, but—"

"Then do as I say, woman. Otherwise you are doomed. I still dislike you, but you've honestly asked for my help. I'm telling you all of this because I am a healer and you've paid me. Now listen carefully—you must remove *all* of the pieces of hatred and make alliances with them. And that includes how you feel about our noble chief, Lazaro." She paused, sighed deeply. "Have you forgiven him?"

Carlota stared into her shaded eyes, feeling a stark nakedness. All pretense was gone. The woman's years had slipped away. She seemed to have some kind of an aura about her. Maybe it was the way the sunlight struck her. But it didn't matter, only the real truth mattered. "No, I can't," she whispered.

"I won't see you this way again, woman. I've told you all I can. Until the day you fully forgive Lazaro, you will be imprisoned by your wall of loneliness, and you will never find true peace."

Once more Carlota watched the woman limp away. She wanted to run after her and stop her. There had to be more!

She would never be able to forgive Lazaro.

Andres sat up in his blanket as Tze-go-juni spoke to him in her creaky voice. "Child of the Water, you must go."

He blinked, unable to understand. She seemed bathed in some kind of special light, perhaps the moon. But he couldn't see any moonlight coming into the cabin.

"You must go to the White Eye Father and convince him to move the People back home."

He found his voice. "But I may not be able to convince him. I tried it once before, and I failed."

Her brightly painted face broke into a wrinkled smile. "But this time you will have all of your Power and all of mine."

"Will that be enough?"

"More than enough. It came to me finally in a trance that this is why you have been given to us as Child of the Water. You are to save the People."

"But it will take more—"

"Do not argue. Go to Wash-in-ton, go as soon as possible."

He started to tell her how much more there was to it, but all at once she was gone!

He rubbed his eyes, saying, "Tze-go-juni?"

But it was dark and quiet in the cabin, except for the snores of his sleeping father. Then he realized it was just a dream. Or was it?

When Carlota came to the village the next afternoon, she noticed that no one was in the street, not even the children. There was a certain stillness that was abnormal. A passing soldier, a corporal, told her why. "You know that crazy old hag, that witch they say was a medicine woman?"

Carlota nodded, feeling sudden dread. "Tze-go-juni?"

"Something like that. Well, anyway, she died last night and these savages have been putting up the damnedest fuss you ever heard in your life. The wailing started about midnight. I know because I was on guard duty. Damnedest scary thing. Then, this morning when the sun come up, everything got still like this. I guess they's all inside worshipping some devil or something."

Carlota just stared at him. It was impossible. That woman could live forever. Besides she *had* to talk some more with the old shaman.

The corporal went on, "I hear tell she wants to be burned like they sometimes did back in Injun country, but I don't think the colonel's gonna go along with that nonsense. Good thing—the old hag might put a curse on all of us."

Carlota wanted to go into the village and ask questions, but she sensed that it would be the wrong thing to do. She also knew from her years with the Chihenne that they didn't burn their dead. Regardless, she'd come back tomorrow.

It seemed to Andres that everyone who was part of his life tapestry was dead. Benita first, then his beloved Lizah, Rafe, and now this strange old woman who had so much Power, who had always thought he was Child of the Water. Strolling outside the village as the sun came up, he thought of how she had always been a rock for his father, a rock of support with ready advice that was most often sound.

The descendant of the ancestral medicine man to the legendary Silsoose, Tze-go-juni had given limitless care to the People. Mysterious, bizarre, unique, threatening, caring—she had indeed been a remarkable person. He knew she had always loved his father, even since he was a boy. But she had never manifested that love, except in singular service to him.

And now she was gone.

He felt immensely sad.

Who would replace her in the service of his father?

Little was required of a leader of prisoners of war, but a chief of his stature needed a stable counselor. Someone dedicated who could provide wise advice when it was needed. Someone trustworthy.

Like himself.

But he had no Power.

No, that wasn't true—he did have Power, the Power of White Eye knowledge, of his calling as a lawyer and as a writer. But these Powers were of no value in the world of incarceration if he didn't use it. What had Rafe said—that he was the one man best suited to influence the people in Washington. And his mother's words echoed: "You can be eloquent and logical . . . *who could be better suited?*"

He had remembered the dream when he awakened; it had been brought sharply into focus when he was told that Tze-go-juni had died during the night. In his sadness, he remembered it again. And now it revisited him. " . . . *You are to save the People.*"

He looked up from where he sat cross-legged on the dirt floor of the cabin. Lazaro was quietly smoking the old Meerschaum pipe that Rafe had given him so long ago, smoking it and staring at nothing. Andres wondered how much, in his stoicism, his father suffered from the loss of those dear to him. He never complained, never shared any of the hurts, the affronts, that had plagued him in recent years. "Father?" he said quietly.

As if bringing his mind back from a distant land, Lazaro said absently, "Yes, my son?"

"I've been thinking about what my mother has suggested, thinking and reading General Murphy's papers. Perhaps I can be of some value if I go to Washington."

Lazaro slowly nodded his head and puffed on the pipe, saying nothing.

"I can perhaps convince someone in the White Father's government to send us back—if not to Willows Country—at least to some-place nearby." He had discussed the possibility of Fort Sill earlier with his father, and the idea had appealed to Lazaro. "Or I could fail like the others. The White Man's government is like the medicine of Tze-go-juni, very difficult to understand much of the time."

Lazaro nodded his head, waiting for his son to finish.

"But at least I can give it a try. I've been no good for a long time, unable to be of value to the People. It seems I've been asleep. But last night I had a dream, or at least I think it was a dream. In it, Tze-go-juni stood before me and told me to go to Washington. What do you think, my father?"

Lazaro spoke quietly. "Do what I can't do, my son. Deliver us back where we belong. I want, once more, to be where we can not only look up at the sun in the clear blue sky where the deer runs, but see the mountains."

37

Washington, D.C.
September 2, 1892

Initially Andres had considered staying in a hotel or a boarding house, but then General Richard Hartman laid down his ultimatum: "If the man who was your law mentor and your first publisher can't put a roof over your head, he will consider the rejection an insult and challenge you to a duel. Do you understand that, you disrespectful Yankee *captain?*"

That took care of that. As soon as he arrived in Washington, Andres moved into an upstairs bedroom in Hartman's large, two-story home on "H" Street, a red brick structure across from Lafayette Park and quite close to the old Dolley Madison house. He had been adamant that Carlota not accompany him to the capital, even though she was bankrolling him. "Go back to Silver City and let me work this out in my own way," he had insisted. She had argued, but he had made her return to New Mexico a condition—at least until he could get organized, which in his opinion would be sometime well into the future. He simply didn't want her sticking her nose into what he knew would be a difficult challenge.

He had decided not to cut his long, gray hair, although he did forego his headband. His mother had wanted to have some suits made for him by Mobile's best tailor, but he had nixed the idea immediately. "I'm going up there as a poor Indian, which I am, to plead our case. Supposing one of those congressmen got a close look at me in an expensive suit? No, a couple of cheap suits from the local store is all I want." He had thought about wearing moccasins, but had decided that would be going too far. After all, he was still a somewhat sophisticated man of letters and the law, and he didn't want to appear artificial in any way.

He felt a sense of value and urgency in what he was about to do; he had a mission for the first time in years and it excited him.

Even with Hartman's help, it took time to get appointments with the major people having an interest in the Indian situation. And to compound his problem, Andres was dealing with a lame duck administration right in the beginning of the election period. He spoke to Senator H. L. Dawes, chairman of the Committee on Indian Affairs, who had earlier introduced Senate Joint Resolution 42, which would grant authority for the removal of the Apache Indian prisoners from Alabama to Fort Sill. With President Benjamin Harrison's support, the resolution passed—pending an agreeable negotiation with the Kiowa, Comanche, and other Apache tribes for relocation on their lands.

But when Resolution 42 was laid before the House Committee on Indian Affairs, it ran into trouble. And it didn't take long for Andres to root out the cause: Major General Nelson Appleton Miles. Now commanding the Department of the Pacific—and having had overall responsibility for the massacre of some two hundred Sioux at Wounded Knee, South Dakota, in 1890—Miles had connections in the House of Representatives. Furthermore he had differed harshly with Rafe over the eventual disposition of the Chiricahuas. His opposition to the resolution was "immediate, insistent, and actively supported by the majority of the western press."

Senator George F. Hoar was another friendly politician who had examined the betrayal of the Apache scouts. Although Andres had never been overly friendly with any of the scouts because he considered them traitors, the outrage of their treatment after having honorably served the United States Army, mostly under Rafe, was yet another example of government perfidy. And like it or not, it was a wedge in the overall case. At the end of their discussion, Senator Hoar said, "Mr. Murphy, I was a great admirer of your stepfather, and I'm distressed at the way your people have been treated. I'll issue a statement to that effect to the press tomorrow."

The following day Andres read the senator's statement in the Washington *Star*. He recognized its slant toward political advantage, but it was nevertheless a relatively strong stand in favor of the move to Fort Sill, and it brought the issue forcibly before the public. It also brought Andres into the public eye: " . . . A champion from the Apaches themselves has arrived in Washington to plead their plight. The stepson of Major General Raphael Murphy and the son of a noted Apache leader, Chief Lazaro, he is a former war hero who served under Sheridan, and is an eloquent lawyer who has lived and fought with the Apache. . . . "

Andres decided to do a complete background study on the different men in power who might be of assistance, or who would at least not present problems if he could influence them to his way of thinking.

He learned that the Harrison cabinet was mostly a collection of Republicans who were either Ohio born or who had been general officers in the Civil War. This wasn't too alarming a discovery since President Benjamin Harrison himself was an Ohioan and had been a Union general during that war. Secretary of the Interior John Noble was no exception, although following the war he had become a full-fledged Missourian. Alledgedly incorruptible—a unique reputation to have in this so-called Gilded Age—Noble was sixty and more involved in railroad operations in the country than other matters. He listened quietly when Andres made his plea.

Finally, after asking several questions, mostly about the health of the People in Alabama, Secretary Noble said, "I'll do my best to get approval from the other tribes at Fort Sill, but I must warn you, Mr. Murphy, this is more of a congressional matter now than one that I can dictate."

The next cabinet member who could be of value was Stephen B. Elkins. Originally from Ohio, the West Virginia millionaire and active Harrison supporter had assumed the portfolio of Secretary of War late in the past year. As the civilian head of the United States Army, he could be a major roadblock. Richard Hartman set the meeting up for lunch at the Willard Hotel's dining room. By now Andres's delivery was polished, yet obviously earnest enough to retain its vital message. Elkins listened carefully, asked numerous questions, then said, "I see no objection to the move from the army side, even though General Miles has been quite vociferous in his objections to the move westward for your people, Mr. Murphy. Apparently there is plenty of room at Fort Sill, if the local tribes don't present objections. But I, too, think this matter has gone so far into political hands that it has to be resolved in Congress."

Andres told Richard Hartman about the meeting at dinner that night. They were in a popular restaurant in Georgetown. "Noble and Elkins are right," Hartman said over his steak. "This problem has become somewhat of a political hot potato. Now Mexico's in the act."

Andres raised an eyebrow. "*Mexico?*"

"Yes, Mexico."

"In what way?"

"Romero, their longtime minister, is visiting from Mexico City, where he is currently the secretary of the treasury. I've heard indirectly that he's against any move that would bring the Chiricahuas or Victorio's people back to the Southwest."

"Can you arrange a meeting with him?"

"Possibly. I don't know when he's going back to Mexico." .

Andres shook his head. "That's all our opponents need—an international objection to hang their hats on."

Hartman poured a French red wine from the bottle. "Yes, that would certainly endear your old friends to you."

"Tell me something about this Romero," Andres said.

Hartman pursed his lips. "Matías Romero is a survivor. He first came to Washington before the war as a young envoy from Benito Juárez. That was when Lincoln didn't recognize the Maximilian government."

"Yes, I remember. I attended a reception at the legation during the war and met him just before I joined Sheridan." He had a vague recollection of the man, but it was clouded by the face of the despised Agustin de Gante.

"Later he became a Mexican senator, and after a period as secretary of the treasury under Porfirio Díaz, spent the last ten years as minister to the United States. He even married a daughter off to the Mexican dictator, so he's a pretty strong man to buck."

Andres sipped his wine. "I want to try."

Even with Richard Hartman's help it was a week before Andres could see Matías Romero. The regular Mexican minister to the United States was back home, a fact that Andres didn't like. But he had to make the best of the situation. They met in the minister's office, with a male secretary present to take notes. Romero, whose head was as smooth as a large egg, had a luxurious gray mustache and short beard. His dark eyes were moody and masked from behind the large mahogany desk. "No, I'm sorry I don't remember meeting you or your mother at that reception," he said. "I do, of course, remember General de Gante. A fine gentleman. He was killed, you know, in a barbaric Apache raid a number of years ago."

"Yes, I believe I heard something to that effect," Andres replied quietly.

"General Hartman has told me of your mission here, and I must be quite direct, Mr. Murphy. The citizens of northern Mexico have been quite specific in their desire that the Chiricahua and their allies never be allowed to return to your states of Arizona, New Mexico, and Texas."

Andres listened as Romero went on, reciting atrocities and describing the fear of Mexican citizens in the north. He then summarized by saying, "His excellency, the president, would prefer that these Apaches—your people—not be moved anywhere close to the Mexican border."

"But, Excellency," Andres said quietly. "Several years have passed, and the leaders of my people have no more inclination to fight. Nor do the younger men. They merely want to go with their families to a healthier climate where they may be farmers and live quietly for the rest of their days." He summarized how life had been for the People in Florida and Alabama and explained how far Fort Sill was from the Mexican border.

Romero's expression was pleasant enough, but his tone was abrupt. "I'm afraid, sir, that the decision has been made. Our government can only express its desires on the matter and hope that your government respects the manner in which they have been stated and gives them due accord."

Andres knew any further words would be wasted. This Mexican diplomat could only be swayed by force, and that, of course, was out of the question. He rose to go and thanked Romero for his time. His tone was even as he looked into the man's cold eyes. "Good day, sir." It took all of his will power to keep from telling him how Agustin de Gante looked when he shot him.

Unable to bring Resolution 42 into play before the national election, Andres tried to influence members of congress who would remain in office to support the measure. In mid-December, before the holiday recess, he was called to appear before a hearing of the House Committee on Indian Affairs. Carlota, having received the news a day after it was announced, took the first train to Washington so she could be a spectator at the open hearing.

Chaired by Congressman Kent Anderson from Illinois, the inquiry opened on a Tuesday at ten o'clock in the morning in the House of Representatives main chamber. A large number of spectators were present, including many members from the special interest groups involved. The mood was anticipatory as the committee members took their seats at the table facing the gallery and the witness table. Andres wasn't scheduled to appear until midafternoon, following several other witnesses—including Major General Nelson A. Miles. The fifty-three-year old general, wearing his blue undress uniform with the Medal of Honor he had earned at Chancellorsville in the Civil War—

but had just been awarded earlier this year—was sworn in as the last witness before lunch.

Andres had read about the awarding of the Medal in the *Star*, and wondered how a general got a decoration *twenty-nine years* after the act. Obviously someone had dug out an old citation at the request of an important person . . . such as perhaps a certain major general who blew his own horn a lot. He listened closely as Congressman Anderson first asked questions that qualified the general as the commander who had brought the last Apaches in from the warpath in Mexico. He squirmed as Miles built up his own part in Geronimo's final surrender and downplayed Lieutenant Gatewood's actions in bringing in the stubborn old warrior. No mention was made of the fact that the last holdout, one Red Head and his warrior wife, had arrived at Fort Apache of their own volition.

About the Apache scouts, the general painted a vague picture of disloyalty to the army. Adding that they had provided arms and ammunition to the renegades, he stated that they had been planning a fresh outbreak when he sent them to Florida. He made no mention of the fact that two of them had led Gatewood to Geronimo, or for that matter that they had found Geronimo for Rafe in the first place.

Andres had to hold himself in check to keep from protesting. How could a man in the general's position be such an out-and-out, goddamned prevaricator? And suddenly he remembered that Miles and Rafe had had a running verbal feud about the final outcome of the Apaches in Arizona. Still, it was still incredible that he should testify so falsely.

Miles spoke of conditions after he assumed command in Arizona: "In July 1866, I found at Fort Apache over four hundred men, women, and children belonging to the Chiricahua and Warm Springs Indians, and a more turbulent, desperate, disreputable band of human beings I had never seen before, and hope never to see again. When I—"

"*That is untrue!*" Andres barked from his nearby seat.

Heads turned as the chairman automatically pounded his gavel from the center of the committee table. "Sir, you are out of order!" Anderson snapped.

"The general is lying through his teeth!" Andres replied.

"But you, sir, are not a part of this committee, which is the *only* authority authorized to question his statements. You will remain silent, sir."

"Aren't you looking for the truth?"

"One more word and I'll have you removed, sir!"

General Miles had turned at Andres's outburst and stared at him. Now he glowered from his chair at the witness table.

"Please proceed, General," the chairman said.

Miles collected himself. "As I was saying, those Indians were as disreputable a batch of so-called human beings as I've ever seen. When I visited their camp they were having their drunken orgies every night, and it was perfect pandemonium. One of the most prominent leaders was named Lazaro, who at one time had led one of the bloodiest raids ever made in that country. The young men were insolent and violent, and I was told a breakout was imminent when I sent them all to Florida."

Andres seethed, snapping the pencil in his hand. "It's all a lie!" he whispered harshly to his mother as other spectators stared at him. "Drunken orgies! He's lying to justify the other lies, the perfidy he visited on us." He turned to listen to the chairman.

"General Miles," Anderson said. "There has been criticism that the rights of these Apaches have been contravened. What's your opinion on that accusation, sir?"

Miles cleared his throat and replied, "When these heathen renegades surrendered to me, they did so unconditionally. Therefore they have no rights on that score. As defeated enemies of the United States, they should be incarcerated as long as they present a threat to the country they defiled. And that's forever, because they'll never change."

"Do you, General Miles, believe that these Apaches should be transferred to Fort Sill in Oklahoma Territory?" Anderson asked.

"Absolutely not. Those savages can't even get along with themselves, let alone the other tribes who are settled there. And who knows when they'll break out and wind up back on the warpath in their old homelands. No, sir. They should be kept under lock and key right where they are!"

A cheer went up from a delegation from Arizona that was sitting to the side of the gallery.

"Silence!" Anderson shouted, pounding his gavel. "I'll have no more of that!"

It was all Andres could take. He jumped up from his chair, shouting, "I object! As the representative of the Chiricahua and Warm Springs/ Chihenne Apaches, I refuse to let this bald-faced liar get away with such untruths! He is—"

"Marshal!" Kent Anderson thundered. *"Remove this man at once!"*

" . . . He is condemning a group of innocent people—"

Two marshals grabbed Andres by the arms and jerked him toward the door as he continued to protest Miles' statements.

"Mr. Murphy has come to apologize, Mr. Chairman," Richard Hartman said as he and Andres entered Kent Anderson's office.

The congressman, a florid man of about fifty, nodded, but his eyes narrowed as he looked at Andres. "If I didn't think a great deal of your friend here, the honorable delegate from New Mexico, I wouldn't even consider speaking to you, Mr. Murphy." He stuck out his hand. "But the old bastard has said so many good things about you that I couldn't get out of it. Besides, I've long admired your stepfather, as well."

Andres shook his hand and quietly said, "I apologize for the disruptions. I should have known better."

"Yes," Anderson said, still scowling. "Richard says you are really a good lawyer, one who should understand the system."

Andres nodded his head. "I'm afraid I let my emotions run away with my judgment, sir."

"He hasn't practiced law in many years, Kent," Hartman offered.

"I understand," the congressman said. "Well, we know that's no excuse. All right, Murphy, I'm going to overlook your outbursts this morning and let you testify after we reopen the hearings this afternoon. But I warn you right now, I'll brook no more theatrics or deviance from procedure. You get out of order one time, and I'll have you thrown out."

"I understand, sir," Andres said softly. "But I may not be able to totally curb my emotions."

The frown on Anderson's face faded to the suggestion of a smile. "I didn't order a miracle."

Shortly after the committee reconvened at two in the afternoon Andres was called to the witness table. Carlota watched his erect form approach the table as he held up his right hand and took the oath. His long, thick gray hair was drawn back tightly on his head and braided into a queue that hung down between his broad shoulders. His inexpensive black suit was set off only by a turquoise charm below his dark blue cravat. She had never been more proud of him.

The crowded chamber grew suddenly silent as the chairman shifted some papers and cleared his throat. "Be seated, please, Mr. Murphy." As Andres did so, the congressman said, "In order for those present to know more about you, sir, I would like to state that you are one-half Apache, the son of a chief, and that, as a captain of cavalry, you were awarded the Medal of Honor in the great War of Secession. Is that not correct?"

"That is correct, sir."

"You are also the stepson of the deceased General Rafael Murphy?"

"Yes, sir."

"And how long have you lived with the Warm Springs Apaches?"

"Actually I'm living with the Chihenne, sir. But they've been referred to as Warm Springs and Chiricahuas for some time. Nearly eighteen years."

"Would you tell us about it, please?"

Andres paused, getting back to his feet and turning to look briefly at Carlota. He took a deep breath and began quietly: "Some men have never known their fathers, let alone have had great pride in them. I've been extremely fortunate, for I've been the son of two great men— both honorable, magnificent warriors. One is a respected and remarkable Apache chief, the other was a caring officer who did his best to aid the people he helped defeat—if defeat is the proper word. Actually, through all the years of warfare with both the Mexican and American armies, the Apache were never defeated. Their warriors have been the finest soldiers to tread this continent, and some of their leaders would have equaled the greatest of American generals had they had similar opportunities."

Andres looked around to the gallery for a moment, raising his voice in the stillness, using his oratorical skill. "But the Way of the Apache was disrupted as they were overrun by the horde of settlers coming to the West—in no way a crime, merely the inevitable in a growing land. No longer could the Apaches hunt and raid their longtime enemies, the Mexicans. The eternal search for riches brought the white man and all of his power, all of his greed. The innocent settlers who came along to farm and build towns were caught up in the bloodshed as the Apaches fought to preserve their way of life. To the Apaches, it was war. To the settlers it was atrocity."

Andres walked around the table, speaking strongly, holding his audience. "Treaties were made and broken. Chiefs took their warriors on the warpath to avenge the perfidy."

He stopped there, reaching into his inside coat pocket and withdrawing a bright red headband. Deftly he placed it on his head, pulled himself up even more proudly, and looked around for full effect before continuing, "One day, feeling disgust, so immense that I could no longer abide it, I said I would no longer be a white man . . . and I joined my father and his people in war. I married a proud and wonderful woman warrior, who gave me a fine son. We were the last to come in from the warpath, and we did it of our own free will, not because a man of falsehoods such as General Miles defeated us."

The chamber was completely still.

"And to what?"

He paused again, his voice lowering. "To be shipped off to Florida like animals as prisoners of war. Those over four hundred desperate, disreputable human beings General Miles described, the like of which he hopes never to see again, *are* human beings . . . not beasts to be treated as they were. They *weren't* disreputable! I have never known a cleaner, more spiritual and moral segment of society in my life. Yes, they have a problem with spirits because they have no tolerance for alcohol, but they did not and *do* not, as Miles described, have nightly drunken orgies."

He frowned, the anger in his voice evident. "How could anyone classify women and children, as well as old people who hadn't fired a shot in anger in decades, as *prisoners of war?*"

Andres went on, describing conditions at St. Augustine and in Alabama. "Nearly one quarter of these people have died of consumption from being in a strange, wet climate . . . including my beloved wife. And yet no one in power in this country wants to let us go home. Now we are told we can't even go to Oklahoma Indian Territory because we're too dangerous, that we'll steal off to our homelands and start the wars all over. . . . "

He raised his arms wide. "With *what?* Our leaders and warriors are old now, the young men trained only in the ways of the white man. They read and write now, and many of them are even Christians. How long must my young son be called a prisoner of war?"

His voice choked as tears filled his eyes. "All we want is to return to our mountain fastness where we can live in peace, but since we can't do that, we ask that we be allowed to go to Fort Sill, where we can have a semblance of what we once knew . . . the opportunity to regain even a portion of our pride."

He brushed away the wetness and sat down.

Slowly a few hands began to clap, and soon the applause spread as spectators rose to their feet, including first, Anderson, and then the rest of the committee.

Carlota, her heart bursting, unnoticed tears streaming down her cheeks, was the first on her feet as she whispered a choked, "Bravo, my son. Oh, my God, bravo."

The white-haired lady reached for her bag as the train slowed for their final stop at Tularosa. The long ride had tired her, but she was excited about what was to come. Now she had to finish her story. "It took nearly two more years," she said, "before the People were moved to Fort Sill. The tribes already there, in sympathy for their plight, accepted them with a degree of warmth.

"And you know the rest. They became farmers and learned the range cattle business. Houses were built on the military reservation, grouped in small villages according to the chiefs. The remaining Chihenne, including you, until you went off to Carlisle to school, were in Lazaro's village. Even Geronimo, the old curmudgeon, became a good farmer and a cattleman."

She sighed, getting to her feet. "A number of the men were enlisted in the army as scouts, but their only duty was guarding the cattle herd as it grew. And still people died. Often they were children past infancy, sometimes returning Carlisle students, adults in the prime of life. The cause was baffling."

"Yes," the reporter said, taking her valise. "I remember Grandfather saying that it was because we were taken from our homelands. It made more sense than any other possibility."

"Yes. As the years passed, Geronimo became a sideshow freak. He died in 1909, unfortunately the most visible example of what the world thought the People were like. And eventually Miles, proving that self-promotion can pay off, became commanding general of the whole Army.

"And then, well, you know all about it, the government finally approved the move to the Mescalero reservation, a few miles up in the mountains from here. It was made earlier this year."

"Yes, Abby, except for one-fifth of the People who accepted their own land in Oklahoma, the exiles moved here after twenty-seven years of captivity. This big reservation has a lot of dense forest, but there's ample land for grazing.

Father, with approval from Grandfather, set up our village near most of the Chiricahuas at White Tail, some twenty-three miles from Mescalero. You can tell by its name that it's a place with plenty of deer. And it's really got clear air at eight thousand feet."

The woman smiled. "I can't wait to see it." As she reached the door, she glanced outside. Her heart jumped. Standing beside a buckboard, was a tall man with nearly white hair. He held his low-crowned black hat in his hands as he searched the doorways of the train. "There he is, Taza!" she exclaimed. "There's your father!"

He spotted her as she reached the first step, and ran to meet her. He was still erect, the lines deeper around his dark eyes and in his handsome face. "Hello, Mother," Andres said, taking her in his arms and holding her tightly. "I've missed you terribly. Did this educated son of mine treat you well?"

She clung to him for a moment before pushing back and smiling into his face. "Every minute."

They all tried to talk at once as they went to the buckboard. Carlota glanced at the team of finely bred horses standing in harness, the gift to Andres that she had sent over from Silver City as a welcome present. She had been ill and unable to make the trip to greet him when they arrived from Oklahoma. In fact, she hadn't seen him in two years, not since her visit to Fort Sill in 1911. They laughed and chatted gaily as he drove up the road toward Mescalero. Finally she asked, "When is the ceremony?"

"Tonight at sunset by the biggest fire ever seen in these parts," Andres replied. He put the reins in his left hand and leaned over to kiss her on the cheek. "How would you like to be my sweetheart tonight?"

She tossed her head. "I'd love it!"

EPILOGUE

The bonfire *was* huge. Built in the middle of the open space in front of the Chihenne village, it was surrounded by all of the People who had come from Fort Sill, as well as the chiefs and other important members of the Mescaleros. The drum beat was steady, increasing when the men danced, changing tempo when the Spirit Dancers performed their ritual. The night was warm for the altitude, a nearly full moon adding its glow to the blazing firelight. In the place of honor, surrounded by chiefs and noted war leaders, Lazaro sat sipping a cup of tiswin.

No whiskey or other White Eye spirits were permitted tonight.

For it was Lazaro's birthday party.

His 100th.

His heavy shock of hair was pure white, hanging below his shoulders. He still had several of his teeth and while he couldn't see well up close, his eyesight was still quite good. Even his hearing had survived his many years on earth. And he was still able to walk rather long distances, with a cane, slowly but erect. He was pleased that the People should so honor him, although he knew it was his grandson, Taza, who had organized it. The boy—actually he was a man of some thirty-three summers—had come down from Albuquerque, where he worked for the big newspaper. He was very proud of that young man. Would have made a fine warrior.

He just couldn't believe he'd reached one hundred summers. There were so many memories that seemed as if they had happened yesterday. His first father's funeral, his first novice raid, courting Nadzeela . . . the terror of the Santa Rita massacre . . . finding his Power . . . meeting his beautiful young Carlota, making her his bride, losing her . . . his struggles and victories as a chief . . . Benita and his children, his son, Taza . . . his glory back on the warpath . . . his other son, Andres, the one who had given him so much joy, and now managed the affairs of the Chihenne . . . the beauty of his Willows Country, the spires of his spiritual place, Giant's Claw. He refused to think of the sad things.

Ah, his Carlota. He'd seen her several times when she came to see Andres and Taza during the years at Fort Sill, but always she had looked at him with that same cold look. Or she had ignored him. That was the great sorrow of his life. He had heard she was here tonight, somewhere. She probably hadn't understood all of the good things the chiefs had said about him, honoring his long life, but it didn't matter. She'd enriched his life just by being. . . .

He slowly hauled himself to his feet and looked around solemnly, shaking out the long headdress of eagles' feathers that the People had given him tonight. The drums stopped as he held out his arms. Taking in a deep breath, he began his favorite old song in a voice that was surprisingly strong for one of so many years:

> O, ha le
> O, ha le
> Through the air
> I fly upon a cloud
> Toward the sky, far, far, far,
> O, ha le
> O, ha le
> There to find the holy place
> Oh, now the change comes o'er me!
> O, ha le
> O, ha le.

A loud murmur of appreciation, including a few war cries, swept over the crowd when he finished, and everyone stood in respect. Many clapped their hands in the White Eye way, others shouted, "Nantan! Nantan!"

He began to speak, telling them of Silsoose, then of how it was to be Apache when he was young. He told them of Cochise and Victorio, and of how good the Way had once been. Speaking slowly, he ended with, "Do not ever forget what it means to be Apache, for no better people have ever soared like the eagle or fought like the mountain lion."

Still on its feet, the crowd now erupted in cheers. He nodded slowly, looking around and blinked the wetness from his eyes. There was nothing more to say.

Shortly after he returned to his blanket a figure appeared before him. He blinked into the firelight, not sure—

"Lazaro, it's me, Carlota," he heard in Spanish.

He couldn't believe his ears. Was this a dream?

"May I sit by you for a few minutes?" she asked.

Even if it was a dream, it was most pleasant. "Enjuh," he replied, moving to the side and making room.

Andres was holding her hand as she lowered herself to the blanket. He moved away when she was settled. "Are you all right, Lazaro?" she asked quietly.

"Yes, I am fine," he replied, not believing she was actually touching his elbow. "You like the ceremony?" he asked.

"Yes, your People think you are a great man. It is a fine honor."

He didn't reply, just looked sideways at her. She was still a handsome woman. White hair like his. Her eyes looked dark, but they should still be the color of the sky. He'd thought a thousand times what he would say to her when this happened someday, and now there were no words. He was like a boy staring at his feet when he met his first pretty girl.

"Do you know why I've come, Lazaro?"

"To see Andres," he managed.

"Yes, but there is another reason, an important reason."

He didn't say anything while she hesitated.

"It's time for me to do something I should have done a long time ago," she said, looking him straight in the eye.

He thought he saw a silvery tear run down her cheek. "Yes?"

Her voice wavered, then grew strong again. "I forgive you for everything, Lazaro, and I want to be **y**our friend."

P.S.

This story is based on true Apache history and the concept that the People came from Asia across the Bering Land Bridge in the eleventh millennium and migrated slowly south. Lazaro is based upon the greatest of the Apache chiefs, Mangas Colorados.

Mangas, who was six-feet-six, was the first Apache leader to recognize the strength of political alliances. He married off daughters to chiefs in order to cement his treaties, one to Cochise. The respected Mangas was taken prisoner by General West precisely as Lazaro was, but he failed to escape and was murdered. Purportedly he was decapitated and his large head was shipped East for study.

Rafael Murphy is based on Major General George Crook, Civil War hero, and the best of the generals who fought Native Americans after the war. Crook was a compassionate man who understood and cared about them.

The imprisonment of the Chiricahua and the Warm Springs in Florida, Alabama, and Oklahoma is comparable to the incarceration of the Japanese Americans in World War II. Each grotesque infringement of rights is a terrible stain on our proud democracy.

The Apache Museum is located in the Crook House at Fort Apache, Arizona.

The massive research involved in this book was a great adventure.

—Robert Skimin